The End of the World Book

The End of the World Book

A Novel

Alistair McCartney

Terrace Books

A TRADE IMPRINT OF THE UNIVERSITY OF WISCONSIN PRESS

Terrace Books
A trade imprint of the University of Wisconsin Press
1930 Monroe Street, 3rd Floor
Madison, Wisconsin 53711-2059

www.wisc.edu/wisconsinpress/

3 Henrietta Street
London WC2E 8LU, England

Copyright © 2008

The Board of Regents of the University of Wisconsin System

1   3   5   4   2

Printed in the United States of America

Library of Congress Cataloging-in-Publication Data
McCartney, Alistair.
The end of the world book : a novel / Alistair McCartney.
        p.   cm.
ISBN 0-299-22630-1 (cloth : alk. paper)
1. World book encyclopedia—Fiction.
    2. Gay men—Fiction.   I. Title.
    PS3613.C3565E53   2008
    813′.6—dc22   2007039995

For

TIM MILLER,

who is essential.

I want the world and want it as is, want it again, want it eternally.

Friedrich Nietzsche

Although all the names in this encyclopedia are real, as are many of the events, this encyclopedia is a work of fiction, a product of the author's imagination. No reference to any person or event should be mistaken for the actual person or event.

Actually, this encyclopedia is a dream.

The End of the World Book

𝒜

A

According to the *World Book Encyclopedia,* Perth, Western Australia, the city in which I was born in 1971, and in which I spent the first twenty-two years of my life, is the world's most isolated city.

For me, this isolation, along with the deep tedium of childhood, was eased, if not erased, by the *World Book*'s sense of beauty and order.

Every time I opened one of the twenty gold-edged volumes I felt as if I were approaching infinity. Though of course, whenever I closed a volume and placed it back on the shelf with the others, I felt distinctly let down upon reentering the world.

When faced with existence, it seemed the only thing to do was to describe and categorize.

One afternoon, sitting in my bedroom, leafing through volume *A—Abel, Abelard, Aberdeen, aberration*—I lay on the floor, using the volume for a pillow.

Half awake, half asleep, I lay there, I don't know for how long, until my mother came in. It must have been dinnertime.

Yet somehow, to this day, even though I have been living in Los Angeles, California, for a third of my life, the last third, I cannot shake the feeling that my mother was unable to wake me, and that I am still lying there, my drool streaming onto the gold *A* on the book's spine.

ABERCROMBIE AND FITCH

Surely there is nothing more melancholy than the thought of a dead Abercrombie and Fitch model! Except perhaps the thought of one dead model and one living one, best friends since child-hood, the model still living plagued with guilt—he must be re-sponsible for the death of his friend—digging a grave, getting dirt all over the butt of his jeans.

Whenever I walk past one of the Abercrombie and Fitch clothing stores, in particular one of the outlets that have those shirtless boys standing at the store entrance, this is all I can think about.

I am not sure if this is the desired effect, but on those cold nights when there is a full moon glinting off the delicate ridges of the boys' six-packs and the deep rosy pink of their erect nipples, it's somehow as if those two boys are the only boys left in the world, or guardians of the underworld, or Sirens, there to lure you in, and, once you have been lured inside, you'll forget your home and your friends and yourself, until you eventually starve to death, just like in mythology.

ABYSS, THE

In my old age, I've grown a bit tired of the abyss. I feel like that part of my life is over and there is nothing more frivolous than the abyss. But every now and then, someone turns up, or some-thing occurs, to renew my interest, and my faith, in the abyss.

ABYSS, DIMENSIONS OF THE

Before I first went to the abyss I expected it to be all primeval chaos, bottomless, unfathomable, immeasurable. So I was pleas-antly surprised to discover that it was extremely architectural and very modern; it had been built according to strict dimensions. Everything trapped in its void was sleek and neat and orderly.

ABYSS, GETTING OUT OF THE

Sometimes when I am in the abyss and halfheartedly trying to get out, I tug on the edge, and a sort of underlayer appears, with a lacy trim, just like when I was a kid I'd tug on the hem of one of my mum's polyester skirts, to tell her something, and I'd catch a glimpse of the lacy edge of her 100 percent nylon slip.

ADELAIDE

For a long time now, Adelaide, the capital city of South Australia, has been known as the city of churches. The ratio of parishes to citizens is slightly alarming; everywhere you look you see a spire or a steeple grazing the sky.

In the 1970s this moniker was replaced by one of a more sinister nature. A spate of abductions, rapes, and murders of young boys led to Adelaide being dubbed the city of boy killers. Delicate corpses were found in champagne crates. Politicians were involved.

Yet for me, Adelaide is the city of my mother, the city in which she was born on New Year's Day, 1928.

Sometimes, my mother dreams that once again she is back in Adelaide, and the world has ended. She wanders through the city, whose ruins are still smoldering, hot to the touch.

She finds herself back at the house in which she grew up, but the house is gone; nothing remains except the long porch that wrapped around the house, and on which she spent many an evening, but which now wraps itself around nothing, as if nothing were a kind of gift.

AEROGRAMMES

When my father turned sixteen he joined the merchant navy. It was the perfect job to get him out of the little town of Motherwell,

Scotland, and a good way to see the world, or at least portions of it. He liked the waves and the hems of girls' dresses. He liked the ocean's ability to drown out everything.

In 1956, during a stint in the Pacific, my father, James McCartney, met a woman named Beth Wildy, who would eventually become his wife. She was gentle and had red hair.

He wrote love letters to her, while he was away at sea. He wrote in black ink, on pale blue aerogrammes. Measuring eight by four inches, these letters were scattered in odd places all over our house.

Today, the handwriting in these amorous documents is virtually indecipherable. The aerogrammes themselves are soft and deeply creased.

AIDS, PRE-

The so-called golden era of gay life is usually said to have occurred during the 1970s, that decade of unbridled sex, set to a soundtrack of disco music; the decade leading up to AIDS, or perhaps leading down to AIDS, like a long set of steps. It is an era we have designated in retrospect, and we must ask ourselves: were the men who were part of this era aware of all their gold?

The era is said to have ended with the first case of AIDS in 1981.

However, when I gaze into my disco-mirror ball, I see that we have been looking the wrong way. The golden era actually begins in 1981, and then, not confined to the space of a decade, stretches backward like a long gold streak, far away from us, far away from disco, all the way back to antiquity.

ALPHABET, THE

In first grade, when I was taught the alphabet, led carefully from letter to letter, each letter linked to a word and a picture, starting off with the classic example of *A is for Apple,* I was very excited to be entering language, officially, finally. Although a part of me felt unsure as to whether I truly wanted to cross over this threshold, inside, I wanted to turn around and flee.

Perhaps, without knowing it, I sensed what waited for me on the other side of the alphabet—death, which, if anything, is not in alphabetical order. This explains that simultaneous thrill and sinking feeling as I learned to form each letter on the page in cursive writing, in those exercise books whose lines decreased in width as I became more proficient.

To this day, every time I encounter the alphabet, within each letter I detect the promise of annihilation. I continue to be filled with an overwhelming urge to turn on my heels and run in the opposite direction, as far away as possible from language.

ANCESTORS

I know very little about my ancestors, those persons from whom I have descended, those organisms from which I have evolved. For all I know, I could come from a long line of executioners, or labyrinth makers. Records might indicate a startling number of mental defects and physical abnormalities. I have to invent my ancestors, just as everyone will have to when we all become clones.

Still, it's nice to know they are there, preceding me, sodomizing me, as it were. Whenever I start feeling too heavy, I remind myself that, like my ancestors, I am just a fact, a fact amongst facts. I suppose I must bear a passing resemblance to a number of my forebears, and in this sense, I'm not even myself, but a ghost— or a combination of ghosts—stretched tightly over bones.

ANESTHESIA

I preferred it when they called it twilight sleep. When the angels have to be operated on, the surgeons, who wear long white flowing robes, like angels, put toy space helmets on the angels' heads, to reduce their anxiety. The surgeons part the wings, and then inject in the soft spot at the base of the wings.

ANGELS

To be perfectly honest, I'm not that into angels. I think they're deeply overrated entities. Slabs of meat capable of flight. Though I like the fact that the term *angel* doesn't denote a nature, that is an identity, but rather denotes a function, just like the term *homosexual*. And, like you, I wouldn't mind fucking an angel, yanking on its wings, sucking on its wings, cumming on its wings. There is something obscene about wings. You see this in certain paintings, like Caravaggio's *Seven Acts of Mercy*, where two angels grapple with one another sideways in midair. One angel's wings are *much* bigger than the other angel's. His wings are like exposed genitalia. I've heard that wings are surprisingly gristly and that most angels, like most humans, hate themselves, can't stand the sight of their own wings. On Sundays, in their bedrooms, they take razors to their wings.

ANNA KARENINA

Anna Karenina, which is my favorite novel, is not a book of infidelity, nor is it a book detailing the lives of the Russian upper classes: it is a book of blushing. On average, a blush occurs on every third page.

I find myself skimming over the story the way one skims over descriptions of landscapes, just to get to the blushes. Everyone in Tolstoy's book is subject to blushing. No one can avoid it. Each character finds himself in a moment when whatever is glowing inside of him is revealed, against his will.

Interestingly enough, it is not Anna who blushes the most (456 blushes) but Levin (512 blushes). Anna is too busy radiating and burning. She is subject to an odd glow that goes way beyond blushing. But Levin blushes to the point of compulsion. Agricultural theory causes him to blush. The sight of newly polished boots makes him blush. The arrival of spring sends him into a heavy blush. Vronsky is the character who blushes the least (one insignificant blush).

For 200 pages before her death, Anna stops blushing. She attempts to blush yet fails miserably. Then right before she is decapitated by the rushing train, she regrets her decision and wishes to reverse it, but cannot. It is a physiological impossibility to reverse a blush. Longing terribly for more life, she enters into one long eternal blush.

APPLES

One day back in fifth grade, during recess at Christian Brothers College, the Catholic boys school I attended, I was playing handball with my friends when all of a sudden, a boy in twelfth grade—who, with his raggedy, dirty-blond hair bore a passing resemblance to the pop singer Leif Garrett—came up behind me, grabbed me by the neck, and proceeded to stuff a half-eaten apple down my throat. I felt like one of those geese that French peasant women wearing polka-dot headkerchiefs force-feed, so the geese can get all nice and fat and their enlarged livers can be used for pâté, which is a delicacy.

The boy continued shoving the apple into my mouth, until one of the priests came down and put a stop to things. By this time, the Leif Garrett look-alike or impostor had pushed me down onto the concrete. I remember that as the priest hovered over me, I got a look up his black gown. I saw that he was wearing long black socks that went up to just below his knees, and that his legs were very white, but covered in thick black hair. His shoes smelled of the pink cakes of disinfectant that lay at the bottom of the bathroom urinals. I was seized by a desire to suck on the heavy black hem of the priest's robe but held myself back.

Up on my feet, I remember that the skin of the half-eaten apple looked very red against the sky, which was gray and pigeony. The priest held the apple as evidence, while the older boy claimed that I had thrown the apple at him. I denied having done this, but I can no longer recall whether or not I was being truthful. Either way, I was left with a life-long attachment to red apples.

Just the other day, I was at our local Venice farmer's market, surrounded by the usual hordes of white mothers with their gaggles of white babies. Pausing at a stall selling only red apples, I picked one of them up, and was taken back, transported on a rickety horse-drawn cart of red apples, to that incident. I felt an intense longing to once again be held in that boy's grip. The apple in my hand almost seemed to glow, and somehow felt terribly heavy. When the stall owner asked me if I was interested in purchasing some apples, his comment dragged me out of my reverie, and I was transported back on a cart—this time the cart was wholly devoid of red apples—to the present.

ARISTOTLE

Often referred to as the father of thought, the Greek philosopher Aristotle was thinking approximately 2,300 years before the Holocaust; he said that all things, like the Holocaust, could be understood as unities of form and matter. On the morning after the Holocaust, in an attempt to understand and explain the Holocaust, he developed the four causes (material, efficient, formal, and final), and the three unities (plot, thought, and character), though, he added, *in the end, the head is nothing but a death camp for thought: we need another language to explain this, a language of ash and bits of bone.* Aristotle taught at a place called the Lyceum, where they all wore robes with vertical stripes. He lectured to his boy students whilst strolling around the corridors of the Lyceum, always walking behind his students; all of the corridors led directly to the Holocaust, and as soon as Aristotle and his students had reached the end of the corridors, the hems of their robes brushing against the end of thought, they would turn around and walk back.

ASBESTOS

If there's one thing I love, it's asbestos. For me, no other substance is full of such pathos. The word comes from a Greek adjective meaning *inextinguishable*—if only I had that quality—and the Greeks maybe liked asbestos even more than me, weaving it into a cloth in which they wrapped the bodies of the dead for the purpose of cremation.

The other morning I woke up dreaming of asbestos, that fireproof material. Specifically, I found myself dreaming of the little asbestos so-called state or public houses that were scattered throughout Willagee, the neighborhood I grew up in. Painted pink and blue, there was something almost dainty about these houses, like petits fours. In fact, these houses were so dainty, the inhabitants were often putting their fists through the thin walls in outbursts or fits or drunken rages. Sometimes the holes were big enough for me to peer through and catch glimpses of what was going on inside.

Half awake, yet still dreaming—the state I find myself in most of the time—my mind also wandered to memories of the gray corrugated asbestos fences that separated all the houses from one another. This particular kind of asbestos was very soft. There was talk that the poorest people in our neighborhood used it to make sundresses for the little girls and underpants for the little boys. In my reverie, I saw our asbestos fence—how much daydreaming did I do leaning up against that fence? The image of the fence was so real I could almost taste the asbestos.

However, as soon as I was fully awake, I slowly remembered that asbestos was a thing of the past. Years ago, ever since the advent of the terminal condition known as *asbestosis,* all the asbestos fences in my neighborhood had been razed and all the asbestos houses destroyed, replaced with structures built out of brick.

I took some small comfort in the fact that whereas the actual asbestos structures may be long gone, my memories remain: in regards to time they are incombustible, just as in antiquity, during the ritual of cremation, the fire would eat away at the forms of the dead, grinding their bodies down into a fine powder, yet the asbestos funeral cloth would miraculously withstand the intensity of the heat, the fire merely serving to clean the cloth.

ASSHOLE, THE
I am peering through a keyhole, into eternity.

ASTEROIDS
Experts say that one of these days we can expect another asteroid, very similar to the asteroid that killed all the dinosaurs millions of years ago: bits of dark, murky green brontosauruses, hairy but muscled legs of cavemen, and ridiculously large jaws flew everywhere. It was positively *dinos,* the Greek word for terrible. Now we can only learn about dinosaurs from their fossils, just as one day, if people in the future want to know anything about us, they will have to study our fossils, which will seem as monstrous as those belonging to dinosaurs. Perhaps people will no longer be interested in us, though, and our fossils will just sit there, gathering dust.

This asteroid that we can expect, any day now—in fact, we should brace ourselves for the asteroid—will probably be quite like the one that in 1917 crashed into Siberia and incinerated two thousand miles of good and lush Siberian forest. All the snow covering the ground in Siberia lifted up, very high, and then came back down. It—the asteroid—will most likely look all silvery and shiny, like those silver foil asteroids in cheesy black-and-white B movies, but it will be real.

Even if it is very small, like Eros, my favorite asteroid, which is one of the smallest, and perhaps that is why it is my favorite—at fifteen miles long and five miles wide, it is the runt of the litter, and I guess I take pity on it—it will still do great damage.

Eros was identified and computed in 1898, forty years before the beginning of the Holocaust, which itself can be seen as a kind of asteroid that crashed into Europe and the Enlightenment and Western culture and hollowed it all out, leaving a big crater. It—Eros—was discovered by a German astronomer by the name of G. Witt. Eros's last favorable approach—which is when asteroids come close enough to the earth to be seen, but not so close that they smash into and mangle us, which would be unfavorable—was in 1931, two years before the appointment of Adolf Hitler and the beginning of the erosion of Western civilization.

But perhaps our asteroid is yet to be discovered, and if you browse the color catalogue of asteroids, and flick through the 1,570 asteroids inside, you will not find our asteroid. This is no matter.

There is an asteroid out there with our name on it, just like our mothers wrote our names on the inside collars of our gray school shirts with non-erasable Magic Marker, to avoid confusion. This asteroid is special because it will destroy all boys, only boys. There will be no confusion. When it hits us we will fall in love with it. Its arrival is imminent.

AVON LADIES

I haven't seen an Avon lady in years. In fact, I'm pretty sure that, as a species, Avon ladies are now officially extinct. The last Avon lady was seen in 1994. When I was a kid, there were plenty of Avon ladies. Our Avon lady would trudge around our neighborhood, weighed down by all her cosmetics. Burdened by cosmetics. She would knock on our door, and my mother would invite her in. I'd watch silently as mum and the Avon lady, stooped over the cosmetics, talked in earnest, conspiratorially, about the cosmetics.

AWE

Awe is a state located somewhere between reason and death. It seems that I'm almost always in a state of awe over something. Ayatollahs, Aztecs, azaleas.

When I am in awe, I open my mouth very wide. Bits of the world rush in and get stuck in my teeth. Stars get trapped in my brain. I point at things. I leave my jaw ajar.

Pretty soon, this begins to take its toll. My finger becomes arthritic from all the pointing. My jaw begins to creak like the hinge on the door of a haunted house.

But still, it is very easy to live in awe. To locate yourself in awe is not difficult at all.

$\mathscr{B}$

BAGGY CLOTHES

Just as in the Victorian Era, to conceal their bodies, women wore bustles and layers of stiff crinolines, and this had something to do with repression, in our era, boys wear baggy jeans and extra-extra large hoodies; this also has something to do with repression. These boys are also hiding something.

Sometimes when boys wear baggy clothes, the shapelessness of the cloth and the way it hangs on them draws attention to their mortality, like a pirate's skull and crossbones on a mast. We become painfully aware that boys have skeletons, or rather, that they are nothing but skeletons.

At other times, the bagginess distracts us from their mortality. We are able to forget this truth and relate to boys as if they are immortal, as if they are nothing but flesh, as if they have no bones.

BALLANTYNE, JOAN

My Aunt Joan died in 1992. Although her death was mourned, deeply, it did not come as a surprise. Her health had never been good. My mother put it down to the fact that her elder sister had never liked milk, and, ever since she was a child, had refused to drink it.

My aunt had her own opinion on this matter. She traced it back to 1938. She and her husband, Bob, were newlyweds, living on a ranch in the far north of Western Australia. Bob was away on business, and her stomach had been upset for a few days. Thinking nothing of it, she had been taking baking soda and eating lightly.

On the night of the third day, however, my aunt was woken up by a streak of pain. She had no idea what was wrong, but she could tell it was serious. Doubled over in distress, she stumbled outside and told one of the ranch-hands she needed a doctor.

Covering her in his moleskin coat, he lifted her up onto his horse and secured her to it with a length of rope. Together they rode through the night to the nearest hospital, almost 100 miles away in the town of Broome.

My aunt told me that for most of the journey she was delirious. She knew they were heading to Broome, but she thought she was a Chinese boy, on his way to join the pearl divers there, who are known to hold their breath for up to an hour at a time. At one point she thought she was a piano fastened to the horse. Every now and then she was lifted out of her delirium by the bumps in the ground and the dank odor of the horse's dark red coat, before plunging back into it, even more deeply.

The next thing she knew, she was lying in a narrow bed in a pale pink room. A nurse was placing a thermometer beneath her tongue. There was a tube sunk into the vein of her right wrist. She asked the nurse what had happened and the nurse explained everything to her. My aunt's appendix had burst. The doctor had gotten to her just in time, removing the organ before it poisoned her blood. The nurse gave her a cup of broth to sip and opened the curtains a fraction, to let in a dash of sunlight.

Elated at this second chance, yet still feeling somewhat peaked, my aunt resolved then and there to dedicate the rest of her life to showing God how glad she was. She would show God her gladness in every way: through prayer; through plucking the feathers from chickens; through watering petunias and ironing perfect creases.

BALLANTYNE, ROBIN

On May 7, 1943, at approximately 3:34 a.m., my Aunt Joan gave birth to a baby girl in her and my uncle Bob's pale blue house in the Canberra suburb of Holder. They named my cousin Robin, after the songbird with the rust-red breast and the dark back, though we should remember that this songbird is not singing for us. This bird's so-called song is not a song at all, but a deterrent, a warning.

For the next forty-three years, Robin worked and slept and dreamed and occasionally loved.

Then, on December 12, 1986, at approximately 2:32 p.m., having grown tired of life's intricacy, Robin gassed herself in the garage of the pale blue house in the Canberra suburb of Holder. She lay down on the garage's concrete floor to receive forty-three years' worth of dreams; the fumes wrapped around her like a feather boa.

I hardly knew Robin. I remember she was lean and wiry and kind, and had curly graying hair. She liked tennis and was good at it. Perhaps, upon entering that space we cannot enter, she immediately changed into a bright white tennis outfit, with a little white tennis skirt with crisp pleats, and she is spending eternity playing tennis, leaping back and forth over the net.

Canberra, the city in which Robin lived and died, is the capital of Australia. Planned as a model city in 1911, its foundations were laid carefully according to a series of so-called song lines, bordered by three power points. It is designed in a series of discrete circles: the center of the city, the government zone, radiates out neatly into a civic center, business and commercial districts, an industrial sector, the university site, parks, and tidy residential areas built on both sides of the curving Molonglo River. Not one of the circles overlaps or spills over into the other.

The end result of this design is not so much one of beauty, but of order.

BANAL, THE

Although we don't have a name for the era in which we presently live, in the future, long after you and I are gone, and we are nothing but skeletons, God's cages, future generations will look back at our epoch and define it as the Epoch of the Banal.

Historians will say that this era began around the year 2003, with the election of a former bodybuilder and actor—star of such illustrious films as *Twins* and *Kindergarten Cop*—by the name of Arnold Schwarzenegger, to the position of Governor of California. In a footnote they will mention that this man also happened to be the son of a Nazi SS officer. They will add that this epoch's status was really secured in 2004 with the reelection of one George Bush Jr., a simple, wizened little man, sort of like the postindustrial equivalent of the village idiot, to the position of president of the United States. A footnote will mention that he was the son of a previous U.S. president of the same name and was in a sense a photocopy of that president.

But historians will agree that the real arbiter of power during this era was a pop singer by the name of Madonna, who cast a long shadow over this entire period, and ruled the charts for sixty-three years, her reign equaling that of Queen Victoria.

Experts will describe our era as one in which there was no hope of doing anything even vaguely original, an era in which the imagination and all the tattooed, baggy-clothed muses were placed under court injunction. Although these experts will acknowledge our many efforts to overcome this pervasive banality, they will also be firm in saying that all our efforts ultimately failed.

They will conclude that our lives were heroic yet futile, a combination that, in retrospect, will seem somewhat poignant.

BAREBACKING

In the early twenty-first century, having grown tired of the plague, profoundly bored with it, men once again took to fucking without rubbers in a practice that came to be known as barebacking. Some people thought these men had a death wish. In interviews, these men denied having any interest in death. They claimed they barebacked because the tip of a condom felt like the tip of an inquisitor's hat, as if an inquisition were taking place deep inside them.

BEACH, THE

In summer, on the weekends, Dad would take us to the abyss. We'd leave first thing, so as to get there before all the good spots were gone, and to make a day of it. We'd place our blue and white striped deck chairs right at the edge of the abyss. When we weren't frolicking in the abyss, we'd just sit and gaze into the abyss. Dad would bring his little transistor radio, and listen to the cricket, or tune in to an easy listening station, which made the abyss even more relaxing. Mum always made us bring our cardigans, because even though during the day at the abyss it was hot, often by the end of the day it would get quite chilly. We always brought a packed lunch and sodas in a plastic cooler, because the prices at the abyss's kiosk were simply outrageous, though Dad often treated us to ice cream. We'd try and lick our ice-cream cones as quickly as we could, but in the heat the ice cream inevitably melted and trickled down our fingers, over the edges, into the abyss.

BEAR, BRUNO THE

Recently, a wild brown bear appeared in the Bavarian Alps, the first wild brown bear to appear in Germany since 1835. The bear was sighted in that disconcertingly beautiful landscape we have come to associate with Adolf Hitler, the landscape he loved to paint, in a style that would come to be known as evil pastoral, a landscape more recently known for gay porn, the location of films such as *Bavarian Bareback,* a film in which boys who look like Hummel figurines come to life to have unsafe sex. At first, all of Bavaria welcomed the bear with open arms, but gradually Bavaria began to rethink its welcome. Bavarian authorities claimed the bear posed a danger to humans and had already raided a beehive and a rabbit hutch. No one knew how to interpret the appearance of the bear, which had made its way across the German Alps from Italy. Some said it was a good omen, a very good omen, others that it could only mean bad things. Unable to decide, hunters killed the bear. *The shooting has happened, the bear is dead,* said the Bavarian government's bear expert, who then went on to say that the bear had been transported to a facility where a top taxidermist was ready to take accurate measurements of the skin belonging to the dead animal.

BEARDS

God wore one. Socrates had one. Marx and Freud and Darwin all had them. Where would the history of ideas be without beards? Gay men wore them until AIDS came along and hair became disconcerting: homosexual, all too homosexual. We shaved off our beards; some took this as a sign that we were distancing ourselves from God. Though perhaps we were merely waiting to direct our prayers to a clean-cut God, a God that was yet to be invented. Let me remind you, Kafka never wore a beard. If you have to wear a beard, let it be one of those fake beards, which must be glued on.

BEATLES, THE

Unlike the rest of the world, I have never really liked the Beatles. In fact, during certain periods of my life, it would be accurate to say that I have hated them; and even when I was not actively despising the most popular and most well-loved band in the world, it is safe to say that I've always held a deep-seated grudge against them. Although I have of course heard their songs, I have never sat down and listened to one of their records.

Disturbingly, there have been times when people have told me, *You look like one of the Beatles.* Equally disturbing is the fact that I bear the same last name as the Beatle who I have always entertained particularly violent thoughts against, Sir Paul McCartney, whom, I must admit, I bear a slight resemblance to. Our last names are spelled in exactly the same way; hence we are linked by not only physical but also grammatical sameness. McCartney is not the most common name, and it stands to reason that, somewhere down the line, we are ever so distantly related.

This leads me to think that just as with every form of hatred, this hatred I have for the world's most loved band is simply another form of self-hatred. Yet perhaps not everything leads back to the self—perhaps nothing leads back to the self—and this form of hatred is entirely justified.

A few nights ago I dreamt about the Beatles. Given the complex set of feelings I harbor toward them, this should come as no surprise. I dream of them often. Usually, these dreams are of a violent, sadistic nature. They tend to involve knives and feature scenarios in which I slowly cut one or more members of the band to ribbons (all set to a soundtrack of one of the countless hideous Beatles albums!). In some of these dreams, I wear a badge, like a fan might wear. However, my badge doesn't bear the inscription *I love Paul,* but rather, *I want to destroy Paul.*

But in this particular dream I was holding one of their albums (I believe it was their ninth album, the self-titled but nicknamed *The White Album*) and seriously contemplating listening to it. This album had an inner sleeve, which was not merely the inner sleeve for the record itself, but the inner sleeve containing all the liner notes necessary to explain the secret of who I am. The inner sleeve of myself. I saw very clearly that it was quite possible I could learn to like the Beatles.

Now that I have some distance from the dream, I cannot help pondering that, if I could learn to enjoy the Beatles, I could learn to embrace anything, even this ragged thing I call *my self*.

BEAUTY

Throughout Western history, philosophers have spent a lot of time contemplating beauty. As they've done so, drool has slithered out of the corners of the philosophers' mouths. (One need only look closely at the surface of philosophy to see that it is drenched in saliva.) Pretty much what they have come up with is that every encounter with beauty begins very promisingly but inevitably ends in a musty atmosphere of disappointment and a failure to return one's e-mails and phone calls. As Plato said so fittingly, *Beauty is barbaric, beauty must be destroyed.*

BEDS

At some point between 1774 and 1793, the wooden posts of beds, which formerly had been covered with draperies and hangings, became visible. Naturally we were pleased with this development, giving us, as it were, a better vantage point, and making it much easier to watch men dream.

BODY, THE

The term *body* is far too inaccurate and general to faithfully describe such a peculiar and complex habitat. I prefer to think of my body as a smuggler and of myself as the smuggled, illegal substance. Or, that my body is the suitcase the smuggler is carrying, made from 100 percent crocodile leather, containing a secret compartment in which the self will never be discovered.

BODYBUILDERS

At my gym, which you are welcome to join, all of the bodybuilders are really depressed and clutch at razors, bleeding all over the floor of the gym. At various stages of their workout they stop and see that there is really no point, because whatever machine they're working on, and whichever part of the body they're developing that particular day, ultimately, every machine is an abyss machine, one that, with every movement and every repetition and every set, only makes the abyss wider and wider, so as to more easily accommodate them. The bodybuilders pause to take all of this in, before resuming their workout.

BONES

Bones are eerie, no? However, there's something undeniably elegant about them. They're like evening gowns compared to the rest of our bodies, which are clunky, and more like safari suits with big lapels and flared trousers. Yes, our bones are chic; they'll never go out of fashion, like a classic Coco Chanel suit. At the same time, there's something deeply sinister about our bones, just as there is something sinister embedded in the elegance of a Coco Chanel suit, by virtue of the fact of her Nazi collaboration. Our bones are Nazis. Even if you do not agree with this, you cannot deny that our bones are in collaboration with death. It's like they're waiting patiently for us, just like our mothers waited for us outside the school gate. Some days our bones are not so patient. My bones have been expecting me, but I am running late!

BOOKCASES

Sometimes when he opens me up, the musty odor that wafts out reminds me of the smell of an inky nineteenth-century novel that hasn't been read in a long time. I find myself thinking about the bookcase in our house, which was in my elder brother Andrew's room. It had sliding doors of frosted glass and two rows of shelves. The shelves were lined in a kind of paper with a floral pattern, but the corners of the paper were always curling up. Its sticky underside captured flies, whose elegant corpses rotted away.

I spent so many afternoons by myself sitting cross-legged on the floor in front of that bookcase. Inside, there were outdated biology, chemistry, and economics textbooks that had belonged to my brothers and sisters; sets of both the *Childcraft* and the *World Book* encyclopedias; a *Book of Wonders; Reader's Digest*s; Bibles whose pages were so thin, semi-transparent, edged with gold; and best of all, the novels my mother had won when she was a schoolgirl, like *Jane Eyre* and *Wuthering Heights,* with her name, Beth Wildy, written inside each cover on a sticker explaining the reason for the prize.

As I take in my strange odor, I feel like I'm once again in front of that bookcase, immersed in solitude and wonder, utterly absorbed.

BOREDOM

In the West, everyone is bored. Boredom is a condition. Boredom sets in very early, during childhood—some say it is established even earlier, in the womb, which makes sense, because those nine months prior to being born must be very, very boring—but it is perfected during adolescence. There is nothing more necessary than a teenage boy who is bored. Sometimes, as adults, when we become so bored by the excruciatingly mundane setup of the days—morning, afternoon, evening; waking, working, sleeping (to be human is an act of repetition)—that we feel like doing ourselves in, we try and remind ourselves that things aren't so bad. After all, we say to ourselves, we are not currently in Beirut being bombed by the Israelis. And at least we are not in Israel, about to meet a teenage suicide bomber, and to be blown up into little pieces. For a few hours we feel better about the tedious nature of our lives; but soon the boredom of our existence begins to sink in. We see the boredom with a kind of blinding clarity, and we realize that the boredom is so terrible we would prefer being bombed. Meeting a teenage suicide bomber would brighten up our lives considerably.

BOTTOMS

The so-called bottom, the passive partner in the practice of sodomy, is a kind of trapdoor through which the top dramatically falls. In sodomy a descent takes place. The term bottom, however, is inaccurate. In effect, any bottom worth his two cents must be profoundly bottomless; that is the only reason why a top would keep returning to his depths.

BOUGAINVILLEA

My cousin Karen had long hair with streaks of silver; it wrapped around her shoulders like a mink stole. She was the only member of our family who had been divorced. Together these two factors lent her an air of fatal glamour.

One day Karen stepped on the thorn of a bougainvillea, and the poison flowed directly into her bloodstream, turning septic. She fell into a coma that lasted three days. As she slept, her mother, my Aunt Millie, sat constantly by her side, brushing her hair, hoping the steel bristles of the brush might rouse her daughter. On emerging from the coma, Karen said that while she was under, she could feel that her hair was being brushed, incessantly, and she wanted to tell whoever was doing it to stop, but of course she could not.

Everyone told her that in the future she needed to be more careful; Karen said that she must have been distracted.

Being punctured by a bougainvillea, she shrugged, *was one of the conditions of being in a garden.*

BOYLE, ROBERT

Seventeenth-century Irish scientist Robert Boyle devoted his life to gas. He was both delighted and troubled by gases, the odd place they occupied between matter and nothingness, their nightgown softness. *Gases,* he wrote, *are a constant and terrible reminder of what I will eventually be.*

Though considered by others to be a scientist, Boyle

regarded himself as a hunter, often referring to gases as *wild spirits*. He spent most of the seventeenth century in pursuit of that wildness: hunting gases, placing the gases in glass cages, watching the gases as they paced, creating laws that the gases would not obey.

Boyle's hair

Robert Boyle, who formulated the scientific method for the field of chemistry, and who is often referred to as the founding father of modern chemistry, had beautiful, long curly hair, which went down to his shoulders, and beyond, directly influencing the style worn by members of today's hard-rock bands.

Boyle's Law

All day, gases float out of boys like ghosts.

boys, box

Currently, here in the United States, the supermarket box boy—in his baggy black pants that vainly strive to conceal the curves of his body; in his drab and shapeless jersey T-shirt with name tag, that, paradoxically, reveals the perfect symmetry of his rib cage; in the unselfconscious manner in which he pauses in the aisles of the frozen food section, lost in contemplation; in the graceful way he hunches over and maneuvers the silver shopping trolleys; and in the extreme grace with which he takes a pair of box cutters to a box containing 1,000 cans of dog food—is perceived to be the ideal of beauty.

When compared to the box boy, all other young men are seen as ugly, deformed, and so hideous that they are executed in states that permit capital punishment. Some boys who can't bear the fact that they are not box boys do the work for the state and take box cutters to themselves. In states that operate from a more liberal perspective, boys who are not box boys are incarcerated, potentially even rehabilitated.

BOYS, IMPALED

Once, on the front page of the newspaper, there was a photograph of a boy who, whilst climbing over a metal fence, slipped and found himself impaled on one of the fence's big spikes. This was years ago, when I was nine or ten; the boy appeared to be my own age. The sharp black tip of the spike had gone right through his face, which bore a look of astonishment and deep surprise. The caption claimed that he had been trying to get into the yard of a house that he believed to be haunted. It seemed the boy was rescued and survived. Once a week or so, I still think of this boy and wonder what became of him. Surely he went on to do great things.

BRAILLE

Can you believe Louis Braille was only fifteen when he invented braille, the alphabet of small raised dots that can be read with the tips of the fingers? Apparently he got the idea from a dot-dash code punched on cardboard that some captain used to send important messages to his soldiers at night.

I wonder what Homer would have thought of braille? It's said that Homer liked being blind. You can see his point—that it might have been far richer and more exciting being blind in antiquity than being able to see everything perfectly well in modernity.

Apparently Homer wandered around from village to village, telling stories, led about by a boy. At night, when Homer made love to his boy, who was probably around the same age as the young Louis Braille—you know what they were like in antiquity—tracing the tips of his fingers over his boy's acned face and shoulders, he must have gotten a glimpse of what it would be like to read *The Odyssey,* or any epic, for that matter, in braille.

BRUEGEL THE ELDER, PIETER

When we recall childhood, it would be nice if our memory of said childhood was as complicated and intricate as that painting by Pieter Bruegel the Elder titled *Children's Games,* in which we see hundreds of small children in a village playground, engaged in violent action, participating in an alarming array of games: it is the two boys in the foreground of the painting, spinning hula hoops, that most capture our attention—one of the boys has a swollen head, though he could also be wearing a mask—as well as the boy who is slightly behind them, just to the right, strung over a wooden bench, each limb held tight by another child. Each game is utterly unique, yet despite this variety, all the games share in common a decidedly menacing, in fact, deeply sadistic, undertone, a quality all childhood games tend to take on; in fact, many of the games Bruegel depicts have a positively inquisitorial look about them, as if a little trial is taking place, a miniature inquisition—some of the children are even wearing pointy hats, just like those worn by the heretics, or was it the inquisitors?— but as I was saying, our recollection of our own childhood is not nearly so intricate.

What we recall is sinister, just like in the painting, no doubt about it, sinister with a capital *S,* but it is there the similarity ends.

Our memory of childhood is much more blurry and indistinct, far more vague. It takes place in soft focus, as if Vaseline, normally reserved for penetration, had been placed over the screen of our memory, resulting in a paradoxical failure to penetrate childhood. Our childhood, or our recollection of it—one and the same thing—has more in common with the work of Pieter's son Jan Bruegel the Elder, a minor artist, who has gone down in history known as "Velvet Bruegel," due to the fact that he painted many people dressed in velvet. We remember our childhood—and the accompanying proceedings—as if it were all one long, violent length of velvet.

BURIED, BEING

I am already looking forward to being buried. How infinitely cozier death will be, all snug in our coffins. I expect that in death my libido will be just as strong, if not stronger than it is in life. Just as now, whenever I'm feeling a bit frisky, I'll reach over to you, though I will have to crack open the lid of my coffin — which hopefully won't be too heavy — and then tap on the side of your coffin.

Dare I say it, but I think that our passion for one another will deepen in the afterlife. The feeling in my heart for you, or the feeling where my heart used to be, will cause the sides of my coffin to quiver and shake like the hips of Elvis.

Every now and then I'll flirt with the choicest earthworms as they wriggle their way into my orifices, and with the cute corpses with particularly exquisite skeletal structure. I'll probably develop a huge crush on the first handsome grave robber who ravages my grave, though this grave robber will be emotionally unavailable, in the strictest sense of the word, and this crush won't go anywhere, anywhere.

BURIED ALIVE, BEING

When I was a kid I would often wake up in the morning while it was still dark and feel like I was buried alive; I could taste the soft, black dirt that was falling steadily into my mouth.

Each night my mother would tuck me tenderly into my grave, which was extremely well made, each corner tight. The bedside lamp gave off its bleak glow.

BUTCHER, THE

When I'd walk to the local shops with my mum, my favorite destination was the butcher's. I don't think I've ever been happier than when I was there at the butcher's with my mother. I don't remember much about the butcher himself, except for his apron, which had thick blue and white vertical stripes. His assistant, who was still a boy, wore an apron that was virtually identical but a number of sizes smaller.

Sometimes I'd dream, not so much of the butcher, but of

his apron, that I was hiding beneath its folds. At other times I'd dream of a butcher's apron that had not only stripes but also little pink and yellow flowers in the white spaces, just like the flowers on my mother's apron. These aprons were worn by someone who was both the butcher and my mother.

As my mother inspected the meat, I'd stand there and daydream that I was the butcher's assistant, working there beside him, and that at night he'd take me out in a red-meat dress to a ball whose proceeds were all going to charity. I imagined him sticking little bits of the reddest meat in my mouth. As my mum pondered her decision, I'd breathe in the strange, sweet smell of the antiseptic, which didn't quite cover up the real odor.

All the various kinds of meat were arranged in the butcher's glass display case, just like my mother's Hummel figurines and Royal Doulton figurines in the display case in our living room. Whereas the contents of the case at home were set out somewhat haphazardly, the butcher had a real flair for arrangement. The meat was arrayed extremely artfully, carefully classified and categorized. How orderly death could be!

BUTTER

During the Holocaust, whenever Gertrude Stein began to think about what was happening to the Jews, it frightened her terribly. She'd take long walks, but out in the air one could not deny that Europe had gone rancid. So she would return to her work, yet even then she'd catch glimpses of the Holocaust, waiting there for her behind her endless sentences: a void so great it could not be covered up by any amount of repetition, one so vast it threatened to swallow all her things. She would put down her pen and set her mind to more pressing matters, like where to find eggs, sugar, butter.

CAKES

As a boy, when I used to go with my mother to the Museum of Western Australia, my favorite part was the reconstructions of rooms from the days of the early settlers. There was a parlor of a wealthy family, which was all dark and velvety. There was a dentist's office, full of monstrous equipment. But the best room was the general store. It had glass jars of old-fashioned candies, and, best of all, a glass case containing little pink and green cakes supposedly made in the nineteenth century.

Every time we paused in front of this display, I'd ask my mother what she thought the cakes would taste like. She'd try to explain that the cakes were no longer edible, and that, if I opened the glass case and picked one of them up, before it had even reached my mouth it would crumble into a fine pile of dust.

I never listened, or more accurately, I refused to accept her argument. I believed the cakes would be delicious. And, in a way, I continue to refuse to accept this argument. Offer me any cake, and I will eat it, but in my heart I'll be wishing that I were eating one of those ancient cakes.

CALCULATORS, POCKET

Pocket calculators were invented in 1972. During the 1980s pocket calculators were the height of eroticism. They were also very helpful, enabling us, as it were, to calculate our own worth; it was disconcerting to see how easily our worth could be calculated. Most pocket calculators were solar operated; these would not work in certain places, for example, if we found ourselves in a coffin with a lid that had been nailed shut.

CATASTROPHES

There are three main kinds of catastrophes. There are those that happen so suddenly, and without warning, that they do not even give victims the time to be surprised. Victims find themselves in a space just prior to surprise.

Then these are those for which a welcome mat is laid out. Victims line up in an orderly fashion and wipe the soles of their shoes before entering quietly into the catastrophe.

And finally there are those catastrophes that are inevitable and will occur in the future at an unnamed date. These are my favorite kind. They give us something to look forward to. I heard on the news that California is the state best prepared for a catastrophe. This puts me at ease. Now all I can do is wait patiently on all fours for the catastrophe.

CEMETERIES

For the visitor to Los Angeles, a must-see—in fact, the only thing you need to see during your brief visit to this city—is the Rosedale Cemetery. Located at the corner of Venice Boulevard and Normandie, it is home to approximately 150,000 citizens. The best time to visit is on a Friday morning, at around 7:45 a.m., which is when twenty or so shirtless freshmen from the nearby University of Southern California complete their three-mile run, which ends, quite fittingly, I think, in the cemetery's shady, slightly higgledy-piggledy grounds. (The somewhat disorderly aspect of the cemetery reflects the somewhat disorderly aspect of the boys, of all boys.)

Whereas the cemetery has been here since 1916, most of the boys have been here—here, meaning the world—since around 1988, which creates a nice contrast.

Taking advantage of their well-deserved rest, these boys flop on the ground, exhausted (as distinct from dead). Many of them lean their shaved heads against the gray tombstones, as if the tombstones are pillows. Through a pair of binoculars, one can see the sweat trickling down the backs of their necks, some of it finding its way into the worn grooves of the inscriptions.

CENTURIES

A century is a period of 100 years. Most relationships do not last this long. This is depressing. Almost none of us last the length of a century. Before a century has happened, we become skulls. I want to write a book that takes a century to read, or a sentence that lasts 100 years. Humans hang on the century they find themselves in, like shirts hanging on wire coat hangers; our legs dangle off the edge of a century into nothing. I'm glad I'm not living at the beginning of the twentieth century, because the Holocaust would still have to happen. It's better to be able to relate to almost everything in retrospect. I've only had seven years of the twenty-first century and I already know I don't like it. Oh God, I don't want this century. This century has already passed its expiration date. Can I exchange it for another kind of century?

CHRISTIANITY

I loved the stories the nuns told us about the Christian martyrs of ancient Rome, who, refusing to renounce their faith, were torn to pieces by lions in front of a crowd of thousands gathered at the Roman Coliseum. In one of my Biblical picture books there was a drawing of these martyrs awaiting their fate. In the drawing, the Christians were all standing in a cage, their eyes lifted up toward heaven. The lions were lurking just outside, saliva dripping from their mouths. My eyes were always drawn to one martyr in particular: a teenager with tousled hair, his muscles peeping out from the holes in his rags. I also couldn't help looking at the centurion poised to open the cage and to release the martyrs into their fate, whose short tunic displayed his muscled thighs to good advantage.

CLOUDS

Strictly speaking, I don't know anything about them (what they're made of, etc.). It seems that all of science went in one ear and out the other, as they say. However, you should probably know that I do like them. A lot, actually. Especially those big, dark gray storm clouds, and, even more, those big inky black ones—those are really exciting.

In fact, I'd be quite happy if there were always storm clouds on the horizon, looking lovely and threatening, like a handsome man with a touch of danger about him. I wish life was like one of those stormy, cloud-tossed, cloud-infested paintings by the nineteenth-century English Romantic painter J. W. Turner, as distinct from Turner's actual life, which doesn't sound romantic at all—apparently he was a bit of a miser, and slovenly, and he spent most of his time alone because no one really liked him.

In the days after the two planes flew into the twin towers of the World Trade Center, I remember riding about on my bike, and, perhaps because no planes were flying either in or out of LAX, really noticing the clouds. As I recall, they seemed particularly impressive, not exactly stormy, more vast and white and fluffy, though, in retrospect, they probably were quite average, or perhaps even below average, and it was all a matter of perception and contrast between the clouds and the destruction.

Either way, like most people, I spent a lot of time thinking about what had happened, trying to imagine the unimaginable—what it was like for the passengers in those planes—and looking up at the sky, thinking about clouds.

COLDS

I've had some good colds in my life. Childhood was full of colds, abundant with colds, like one long cold we could not shake. If childhood were a substance, it would be thick and sinister, probably very similar to that cherry-flavored cough syrup we were forced to drink out of little plastic cups. If childhood were a space, it would be narrow and bright red, like a sore throat. The night before swimming races, I would stay up all night, with the window wide open, and my mouth wide open, willing myself to have a sore throat, so I wouldn't have to participate. And you know, it worked! I've stopped avoiding things I don't want to do, but I still see boys in Speedos standing on gray concrete diving blocks, shivering, before diving into a pool filled with dark pink cough syrup.

COMMAS

After he fellates you, always insert a comma.

COMMUNISM

I would say I've been a Communist ever since I was about nine or ten and saw a picture in the *World Book* of an Eastern Bloc gymnast. I remember he had very pale skin, like white chalk, and dark black hair, like a blackboard freshly cleaned and waiting for propaganda. He was up on the parallel bars, wearing one of those sexy leotards with the feet in them. He had a look of grim determination on his face, and of disdain (for capitalism?) that was quite appealing. I began to have recurring fantasies that I was growing up in a Communist regime, one that was highly oppressive and took boys away from their families almost immediately.

Although today I am still a fan of Communism, I have to say that Marx perhaps focused too much on the bourgeoisie and the proletariat. He overlooked the truly revolutionary class: the heartbroken, the romantically rejected—surely the most lumpen of the lumpen. I think he would have had more lasting success if he had taken unrequited love into account, formulating a systematic theory of heartbreak.

If he had, the Soviet Union and the entire Eastern Bloc would surely be with us today, their bureaucracies of heartache pining away.

Still, when we look at those images of Eastern Bloc gymnasts, we have to recognize that this was the highpoint of beauty in the twentieth century. Despite those images of Eastern Bloc supermarkets and department stores with their empty shelves and barren window displays, and of long lines of grandmothers in heavy coats and headscarves, *lipstickless,* holding string shopping bags, lining up for hours just to get a poor cut of meat, there was no shortage on beauty. Those Communist nations had a surfeit of it, what Marx called *a surplus of loveliness.* Yet no one paid enough attention to these gymnasts; they went unappreciated, going rancid like those butter mountains in the West. Everyone in the East was more interested in butter, and that's why so many of the gymnasts defected to the West, not for freedom, but to be adored. The beauty of Communist gymnasts has not been surpassed; in this sense, when people talk about the failure of Communism, they are wrong. These gymnasts are the praxis of Marx's theory, which, ultimately, succeeded.

CORDAY, CHARLOTTE

A week before she visited Marat, Charlotte Corday had her favorite sunbonnet heavily starched until it sat on her head like a big piece of coral. She wrote a long essay, "Speech to the French Who are Friends of Law and Peace." The text is a seventy-two-page justification for the act she is about to commit. In it she refers to the bloody leader of the Reign of Terror by several names, including *the red monster, the itching one, the author of disaster,* and, somewhat obscurely, *the enemy of cotton.*

After stabbing Marat through the lung, the aorta, and the left ventricle, Charlotte went into hiding at the Hotel de Providence where she composed a much shorter essay titled

"What It Was Like Killing the Inflamed One." In this text she reveals that she hid the knife in her sunbonnet, and that the knife had *a very dark wooden handle. During the act,* she observes, *I caught a brief glimpse of his heart.* She expresses concern that she may have contracted Marat's skin condition.

We also learn that upon leaving Marat soaking in the bathtub, Charlotte noticed a crystal sugar bowl on a table and rapidly ate fourteen sugar cubes in succession: *I looked in the kitchen cupboards so as to replace the sugar,* she writes, *but without success. Historical acts,* she concludes, *make one feel homesick. I already miss our little stone house in Normandy. I miss the sailors, the apples, the iron ore.*

While awaiting execution by guillotine, Charlotte had her portrait painted by a guard. Each morning he brought her cherries, at which she brightened considerably. Each evening, she washed his paintbrushes. While she sat, they talked; apparently she expressed concern and embarrassment about the mob seeing her bare neck. Charlotte's final request was for a large number of hairpins, so, when her head left her body, her sunbonnet would stay attached to her hair.

COTTAGE, THE ENCHANTED

I like to think that the house my boyfriend, Tim, and I live in is enchanted, just like the house in the 1945 black-and-white movie *The Enchanted Cottage,* starring Robert Young and Dorothy McGuire. I only saw this film once, when I was a kid, sick, on a day off from school; the most important moments of our lives occur on such days. Ever since then the images of the film have been pinned to my memory, like a row of butterflies and insects stuck to little silver pins.

In the film, Young's character is a man called Oliver who's been horribly scarred by the war, and McGuire's character Laura is a very plain and ugly woman; no one could ever love either of them, they're both lonely beyond lonely, but—and this is where the enchanted part comes in—somehow the cottage makes them appear beautiful, both to themselves and to one another. I enjoy imagining that, just like them, Tim and I are both hideously disfigured—so much so that no one would ever want us—but the bewitched quality of our house protects us from the reality of this. As far as I can remember, eventually the enchantment wears off. Laura and Oliver realize they are still horribly ugly and disfigured, but they remain together and become even happier, even begin to enjoy their disfigurement.

CRUCIFIXION, THE

As we gaze upon Raphael's *Procession to Calvary*, depicting Jesus Christ and assorted company on the way to his crucifixion, although we try and focus on the unbearable sorrow of said crucifixion, on the heaviness of the big brown wooden cross that is balanced on Jesus's shoulders—surely it must be giving him terrible splinters—although we feel for his mother, Mary, who, unimaginably grief-stricken, is at the back of the line, fainting, and although we experience the magnitude of that which awaits not only Jesus but, ultimately, all of us, we find that our eyes keep wandering away from Jesus, along the length of rope: one end is securely tied around Christ's waist, the other end is being gripped by a man right in front of Jesus, assigned the dreadful responsibility of dragging Jesus, making sure he arrives to his crucifixion on time. The man has shaggy, dirty-blond hair, and although we are not usually interested in blonds, we feel as if we can make an exception given the unusual circumstances (i.e., a crucifixion). He is wearing an extremely short, pale yellow dress, very similar to the minis worn by women in the 1960s, leading us to think that the '60s began a bit earlier, quite a bit earlier in fact; it seems the '60s began on the day of Christ's death. It is precisely the length of the man's dress that causes our eyes to gravitate toward him, showing off, as it does to good advantage, his wondrous, almost miraculous, smooth alabaster, tightly muscled thighs. The man's mouth is open wide in a kind of scream but also like the mouth of a blow-up doll. Although we make every effort to follow the length of rope back to Jesus, inevitably our gaze returns to this man. It is as if the rope is tied around our waist, and he is pulling us along by our eyes. The man has been given the task all men have historically been given: that of distraction. He is distracting us from the crucifixion. If we were present on that day, undoubtedly he would have distracted us from the actual crucifixion; we would have been trying to make eye contact with him while the cross was being raised; we would have been getting his cell phone number as the nails were hammered in. Afterwards, the rope would have come in handy. We would have taken the man back to our home, or better yet, a room in an inn. We would have tied the man up and had our way with him, to try and get over the crucifixion.

CRUCIFIXION OF GEORGE BUSH JR., THE

After President George Bush Jr. was crucified, and after he died and was promptly resurrected, interviewers asked him what he thought of the people who had crucified him. *Well*, he said, in a decidedly upbeat fashion, *I expect there to be dissent. That's what democracy is all about. In a free society, people should be allowed to express themselves freely, and crucify whomever they feel ought to be crucified.*

Ever since his crucifixion, it's virtually impossible to get a crucifix with Jesus on it. When I inquired at the Catholic gift shop downtown at Second and Broadway, the saleslady told me that they don't make them anymore. They only sold wooden crucifixes with George Bush on them, his smiling face and tortured body carved delicately out of gray stone.

CRUSADES, CHILDREN'S

In the year 1212, 30,000 boys and girls, all of them twelve and under, led by a French shepherd lad by the name of Stephen, put down their Game Boys and set off to free the Holy Land. Most of them died, either on the way there, when they were there, or on the way back. Later on, another group, this time of about 20,000 children, led by a German shepherd lad whose name was Nicholas, did the same thing and met the same fate. At home we had a book about the Crusades, complete with illustrations. It seemed that all the children had their hair cut into severe bobs and wore tunics that finished well above the knee, so it was hard to distinguish the boys from the girls. In most of the pictures there was always a big sun shining over them; the children looked thirsty. Little dark spots on their knees were meant to indicate scabs. Just a child myself, I was fascinated.

In retrospect, I think the attraction lay in the fact that these children left childhood and did not return. In this sense, these diminutive crusaders set out not only to free the Holy Land but also to free themselves from childhood, to stop being children. The idea that one could just get up and leave childhood and never return was, and continues to be, immensely appealing.

CRYSTAL

Whatever you want to say about men on crystal, they're exceedingly generous and offer such easy access that, even if they're wearing tight jeans, it seems like they're wearing those baggy white pantaloons with the elastic waists more commonly worn by Pierrots, those figures you see in French pantomime. And as these men wander through the dark, sticky mazes of sex clubs and down the hospital-like corridors of bathhouses, or as they sit in the ghostly light of their computer screens, utterly still, yet roaming chat rooms like Cathy in *Wuthering Heights* roamed the blasted moors, they tend to have a drawn, dazed look on their faces that is a little scary, but also a little lovely, just like the pale, spooky face of a Pierrot.

However, as the Bible says in Proverbs 9:5–7, *Although it may be easy to get into the ass of a man high on crystal, perpetually greased up as he is, it is extremely difficult to wend one's way into his heart; it would be far easier to get your dick through the tiny tip of a silver sewing needle.*

That said, it is understandable that braver men than I have tried to access such hearts! Men on crystal have a faraway look in their eyes that can be quite seductive; it is a bit like the startled look found in the eyes of trolls on key chains. Indeed, some crystal addicts have claimed that when they take crystal they see tiny zombies, who, with their wild, hot pink and fluorescent green hair, look very similar to trolls; apparently, these zombies scream tiny screams directly into the addicts' eardrums.

When men on crystal get barebacked by strangers, this faraway look in their eyes gets even further away. Their bodies become time machines in which they travel back far in time to the kingdom of sluts, a kingdom in which they are sovereign.

CURIE, MARIE

Most of us will spend our lives thinking about one or two things. In Marie Curie's case, it was radioactive substances and dresses. Apparently, in Paris, every day on the way to the laboratory, she used to pass by a dressmaker's. In the window was a dress. It had black stripes crossing diagonally, little black buttons like cough drops, and a frilly collar of geranium silk. Each morning she would pause for a moment in front of the window and admire the dress. Every evening, on the way back home from the laboratory, she would stop and do the same thing. She would inhale the dress like a flower that opens only at night.

It is the kind of dress, she wrote, *that makes you want to destroy all your old dresses, and be faithful only to that one dress.*

In 1898, Marie and her husband, Pierre, discovered (that is, isolated) two new elements that contained far more radioactivity than could be accounted for by the uranium itself. They named them, like one names one's children, *radium* and *polonium*.

At the time of the discovery, Marie was wearing an ankle-length black frock, black buckled shoes (somewhat scuffed), and a white apron.

Knowing that this discovery would bring in a little money, she immediately rushed from the laboratory down to the dress shop and asked them to hold the dress. She was so excited about the thought of finally owning that dress that she was still carrying the glass tube containing the radium in her left hand, which was shaking. She had also forgotten to take off her apron.

You can see a picture of Madame Curie wearing this dress in the *World Book,* volume *C,* page 950. In this photograph her expression is stern. The stripes on the dress have a vibrant quality to them, like the radiation given off by radioactive things. It is said that she wore this dress constantly, including when she received the Nobel Prize in 1903. She also wore the dress one month later, when she was hospitalized for a deep depression.

CYCLONES

I had been looking forward to the cyclone for weeks. The weather forecast predicted this one was going to be terrible and destroy everything. My first grade teacher, Ms. Van Der Linden, handed out crayons and big sheets of butcher's paper and asked us to represent the cyclone. I drew a highly naturalistic representation of my family going happily about their business throughout the duration of the cyclone. I managed to slip some of the broken bits of crayons into my pocket. Ms. Van Der Linden must have been distracted, either looking out the window, daydreaming, or hunched over her desk, absorbed in correcting.

Later, a class discussion was held on strategies for dealing with the cyclone. *Perhaps,* I posited, *our hips are so narrow that this will allow us to slip through the so-called eye of the cyclone.* On the afternoon of the cyclone, my mother was the last to arrive. Ms. Van Der Linden sat with me on a long wooden bench and held my hand while we waited for my mother, and for the cyclone. My mother and the cyclone arrived at approximately the same time. As we walked home, the cyclone was slowly getting underway; the wind was whipping up sand, which stung my bare legs. My mother and I held hands, chatting about our separate days, and walked directly into the cyclone.

CZECH GAY PORN

I am glad that Franz Kafka did not live to see the rise of Czech gay porn and so-called gay Euro porn. For surely he would have been utterly dismayed by the sight of such vigor, such glowing health, such strapping, cheerful boys, and such ceaseless gratification of desire.

I suspect that right away he would have perceived there was something sinister going on beneath the surface of all those ruddy, rosy cheeks, and that something evil was dwelling within all the pastoral settings of so many of the earliest films. Kafka would have immediately identified that although the first known example of Czech gay porn did not appear until 1991, with the release of the film *Farm Boys,* its foundations were already being laid back in 1938, with the annexation of Czechoslovakia by Nazis who shared a similarly robust, bucolic aesthetic. He would have drawn up a timeline, which eventually would have been printed in every schoolboy's standard history textbook, on which only two dates would have appeared: 1938, for the Holocaust; and 1991, for gay Euro porn. According to this timeline, nothing else of historical consequence would have occurred between those years.

However, perhaps Kafka would have saved Czech gay cinema from itself. Maybe, if he were still alive today, he would have taken it upon himself to invent a more sickly form of gay pornography, a more sober form—one in which endless pleasure takes place amidst endless rows of gray filing cabinets; in which the actors are much, much thinner, where the bones get in the way and clank against each other during the act of lovemaking, like medieval armor; in which the boys all turn their heads and repeatedly cough between kisses, hacking up phlegm of the most lurid colors; and in which lust is exposed for what it is, the most efficient and insidious form of bureaucracy.

Yes: where is Kafka when we need him to develop a gay pornography in which loneliness is never overcome but, on the contrary, far more heightened, to the point of being crippling, a pornography in which boys are promiscuous with their sadness and spend all their time searching for new forms of hunger, new kinds of yearning?

𝒟

DANCING

I used to go out dancing every night. Then I cut back to Saturday nights. Lately, I have been going out dancing less and less. Before I know it, I will no longer go dancing.

This doesn't really worry me, because I figure I can dance when I'm dead. When I am dead, I'll have far less to do. Therefore I'll have more time and energy to dance. The issue of whether or not I'm too old to go out dancing will no longer be an issue. I'll also weigh less and therefore be a better dancer.

All you need to dance is a bit of music, the wind tapping against your skeleton, your skeleton keeping time with the wind; all you need is your bones.

DANCING, BREAK

Break dancing began in 1974. Since then it has gone in and out of fashion, but in my head break dancing has never gone out of fashion; in my head there are always boys break dancing. These boys are wearing Adidas tracksuits with zippers that aren't working; the majority of them haven't eaten for days. They're laying down sheets of cardboard in the public spaces in my head, and break dancing so rigorously they break their own bones; you can hear the bones snap beneath the music coming from their ghetto blasters. The boys continue until they can no longer break dance, until they have to be carted away to be incinerated and subsequently replaced by other boys who have been waiting all their lives for this opportunity.

DANDIES

We think about Kafka the bureaucrat, filing away, and Kafka the ascetic, skinny yet illuminated, like a lamppost passing judgment over lovers, but what about Kafka the dandy?

In early photographs of the writer, taken when he was a young man, he is quite the fop. In his frilly shirts and his beautifully cut three-piece suits we see that his body was less painfully thin back then, sensuous actually: Kafka with curves.

In my favorite photo, young Franz stands against a metal fence that encloses a cemetery. His fine hands with their long, elegant fingers grip the railing. His chin is lowered coyly, his left leg raised girlishly, as if he is about to do a high-kick. Tombstones peep out from behind him. There is the hint of a smile on his lips, but there is also something terribly earnest in his expression: already, he knows the seriousness of the pose.

If one investigates his face closely, one can see that he is already dreaming of the day when he will become the dandy of bureaucracy.

DARKNESS, THE

The other day I found myself at a loose end, wandering the hallways of the progressive university where I teach. The halls there are very clean and blank and smell of antiseptic, like in a hospital. I'm always expecting nurses to appear from around the corner, in their starched white caps, but they never do. Universities, like hospitals, have always frightened me; they're similarly full of illness, and so much learning takes place at them, it's eerie.

I went back to my vacuum cleaner of an office, and, as it was still my lunch break, I started to think about death. I recalled that game we used to play when we were children, asking each other questions like, *If you had the choice between being burned alive or drowning, which would you choose?* Of course, we always chose drowning. As an adult I have continued to play this game, but only with myself. Sitting at my desk, I posed the question, *if I were going to be murdered, would I prefer to be shot or stabbed?* I sat there for minutes, but couldn't decide; the method of death seemed less important than the issue of whether the murderer would be handsome or not.

Admittedly, these were not very progressive thoughts.

Feeling proactive, I decided to make a list of the various ways in which someone can exit the world, starting with the nearest exit and ending with the furthest, a sort of to-do list.

I was about halfway through my list when there was a knock at the door. Instead of pretending I wasn't there, I answered the door. It turned out to be my associate Gleah. She offered me a spoonful of a so-called Choconut Spread, but I declined; as a general rule, I only have sweets in the evening.

I tried to hide the list from her, but I think she must have seen it, she must have noticed the way my eyes were all glazed like those of a porcelain Victorian doll, because she looked directly at me and said, *Cheer up, Alistair; although the darkness can exhaust you, and although you may easily become exhausted by the darkness, you can never exhaust it.*

DA VINCI, LEONARDO

I like all those sketches of Leonardo da Vinci's, of which there are almost 7,000. His male anatomical studies are amazing, especially the close-ups he did of their assholes, particularly that famous one, where he drew the man's asshole as if it were a kind of whirlpool, full of all sorts of crazy currents, and with bits of moss and rock-like formations around the edges. What a genius! He really had a knowledge of men far beyond his time.

I also like those sketches he did of naked men with wings attached to them, anticipating airplanes by hundreds of years. The notes that accompany these sketches are very interesting.

(Incidentally, they were written with his left hand. Although Leonardo was right handed, he wrote everything with his left, and backwards, then read his notes with a mirror, taking being an invert to extremes, and showing off a bit, in my opinion.) Predicting the jet trails left by actual airplanes, Leonardo writes that his male planes *leave long streaks of pink in the sky, a result of the heat from the men's anuses coming into contact with the cold atmosphere.*

With these latter sketches, everyone thinks Leonardo was trying to solve the problem of human flight, but in this they're mistaken. He was trying to solve the problem of what to do with a man when he gets too much to bear: send him up, into the air.

DEATH

Death wears mirrored sunglasses, exactly like the shades Erik Estrada wore in the popular, award-winning late '70s T.V. series *CHiPs,* which followed the adventures of two California Highway Patrol motorcycle officers. Erik Estrada is Death. You can see your own reflection in Death's shades, but you can't see Death's eyes. That's the Death part. Paradoxically, the sight of the young Erik Estrada's thighs, encased in his tight crème regulation pants, is the only thing in the world capable of keeping Death at bay.

Death carries a green hose. Death is moving slowly toward the front lawn. It is summer, early evening. All the children are playing outdoors. Death is wearing an orange jumpsuit brighter than a thousand cans of Sunkist soda. Death is watering the front lawn for our mother. Where is our mother?

Death only wears jackets with shoulder pads, which reached their height of popularity in the mid-'80s, that decade of death. Death is a matter of style. Death wears shoulder pads to conceal the fact that he has very narrow shoulders. Death should really consider working out; but working out must anger Death, working out being nothing but a defense against decay, atrophy, failure—all the good things about Death. Death despises everyone who lives but especially dislikes bodybuilders.

Back in the late twentieth century, specifically in the decades that have come to be known as the 1980s and the 1990s, it seemed that every other day, teenage boys, tired of the *sturm und drang* of adolescence and inspired by the death-positive lyrics of so-called death-metal bands, were taking their own lives in very violent ways, which, according to sociologists, was typical of young men: a gun in the mouth and a car over a cliff were the preferred modes of suicide.

We can see these young North American men who were infatuated with death as direct descendants of the young European men, who, in the late eighteenth century, read Johann Wolfgang von Goethe's novel *The Sorrows of Young Werther*, which ends with the lovesick hero with the supremely heavy heart taking his own life. Upon its publication in 1774, the book inspired two crazes on the Continent: one for wearing blue coats, just like the coat moody Werther wears; and one for suicide.

In this sense, although the first death-metal album did not technically appear on the horizon until 1985, with the release of *Seven Churches* by the band Possessed, this genre or subdivision of heavy metal was already slowly getting underway in 1772 when the then-twenty-three-year-old Goethe, in residency at the Court at Wetzlar and fresh from a failed love affair, began writing the book to ease his own heavy heart.

And indeed, listening to death metal, it's almost as if all those black, stormy clouds Goethe's doomed hero swoons over had somehow been plugged directly into an amplifier; it's as if Goethe's Romantic period had gone electric, just like Dylan went electric and inspired the wrath of the hippies, who had long hair like death-metal fans and were really just like death-metal heads, but without the interest in death.

I actually think Goethe would have seriously appreciated death metal, particularly during his Romantic period, but maybe even after he abandoned Romanticism for Classicism—there's a sonic purity and structural complexity to this music that would have appealed to him during his mature phase—though he probably would have listened to it on headphones, so as not to wake the rest of the house.

Today, death metal is not quite as popular a genre as it was in the last century, perhaps because in our century death is everywhere: everyone is besotted with death, which is no longer the province of teenage boys. Historians argue that death metal's popularity peaked in 1994. Similarly, not quite as many fans of death metal are taking their own lives—historians argue that this trend also peaked in 1994. Yet one can still attend concerts where thousands of teenage boys with long, stringy, greasy hair, with acne-embroidered faces and shoulders mouth the death-friendly lyrics, bang their heads in unison, and twist their fingers into the shape of horns, so every one of their clammy fists become little sweaty Fausts. The black T-shirts they wear over their often scrawny frames bear in glittery silver letters the names of the bands they most favor, good names like Morbid Angel, Carcass, Suffocation, and Entombed; however, in acknowledgment of the debt these boys and this music owe, all their T-shirts should bear the one name: Goethe. These boys are completely unaware; they have no idea how Romantic they are.

DEMOCRACY

I'm as big a fan of democracy as the next homosexual. It gives us the freedom to choose between wings and claws. Sometimes we choose wings, sometimes we choose claws.

But I can't help feeling that at some point, while no one was looking, the whole concept of democracy and freedom became very small, miniature, actually, like the Diorama of Colonial Officials wearing three corner hats and thigh-high white boots with buttons running up the side, burning tiny little copies of the *New York Weekly Journal* in an attempt to put down criticism, and pushing the fire about with their tiny canes, all of which could be seen in New York City in the 1950s as part of an exhibit on freedom of the press at Federal Hall National Memorial.

If someone caught me in a weak moment and, just as Alcibiades was asked to pick between wisdom and beauty, asked me to choose between democracy and sodomy, I might choose the latter. I might place my faith and trust in sodomy, and the less democratic, the better.

DEPRESSION

Ever since my mother told me that this heavy, black feeling hovering in my head is actually a ball gown, made out of yards and yards of deep black taffeta, not only do I no longer dread these depressions, I actually look forward to them. They are the highlight of my year: for I am not depressed; rather, I am going to a ball. The whole experience has taken on a sumptuous quality.

And sometimes, just to make depression a bit more interesting and a bit more fun, I like to think that there's an octopus in my brain, whose body, like that of any old octopus, is soft and pear-shaped, like a dark blue pear, and whose head, which is joined to the body by a really short neck, contains those eyes that are eerily similar to the eyes of higher creatures—that's us—and whose mouth is surrounded by eight writhing tentacles, the undersides of which are lined with candy-pink sucker disks.

Although, on the one hand, my octopus' appearance is horrible, I remind myself that this is just its *appearance.* From another perspective, my octopus is quite glamorous. (If only I had an ounce of my octopus' glamour. Then I would no longer be depressed!)

Frightening or appealing, this octopus also has an opening like a funnel beneath its head, just as men have openings that are like funnels. My octopus uses its funnel to force out water, causing its body to shoot backward through my brain, like a rocket, with real force. Then, in a desperate attempt to escape from its pursuer—I suppose the pursuer must be me—my octopus squirts out that nice inky fluid through its funnel—a concealing device, like language—forming an inky cloud in my brain, so whenever I go inside there, it's impossible to see.

DESCARTES, RÉNE

It is said that Descartes had a great fear of dogs. He turned toward philosophy to dispel this fear and to master it, but it only served to distract him: in his dreams, the presence of dogs was constant; their snarls haunted every corner of his philosophical system. And he was subject to a recurring dream in which he was wearing a studded dog collar with his name engraved on the metal disk hanging from the collar and *cogito ergo sum* written on the inside of the collar.

In 1649, when Queen Christina of Sweden invited Descartes to her court to teach philosophy, he accepted, unaware that she was exceedingly fond of dogs and did in fact own 173 of them. All over the palace he kept on slipping in pools of the beasts' saliva.

During his third month at court, the queen's favorite, a tiny red schnauzer named Heartfelt, somehow got hold of the only copy of *Principles of Philosophy*. Descartes took to bed. Terribly weak, he did not have the strength to shoo away dear little Heartfelt, who slept at his feet. The philosopher never recovered from the shock of this incident, dying three weeks later.

Today, if you visit the museum in Stockholm, you can view this copy of *Principles,* which was retrieved from the dog. The manuscript is turned to page 172. If you look closely, beyond the words, you can make out tiny teeth marks.

DESCENT

When you write something, you write it *down.* This implies that a descent has taken place, between the time of the event and your recording of the event.

Let this be a gentle descent.

DESIRE

Desire is an earwig, which has little pincers and destroys bouquets of flowers and may be found in decaying bark and other moist places and enters the ears of boys while they dream.

Or, alternately: desire is a scorpion, which is also active mainly at night and slips into the boots of cowboys while they sleep, so when the cowboys who are still yawning get up in the morning and put on their boots, it can sting and hopefully kill the cowboys.

Desire must be one of these two things.

I need to be desired by everything, animate and inanimate: old ladies with lavender blue hair, ironing boards with covers of little toadstools, Slobodan Milošević, rotting red apples, but not rotting green apples.

Unlike desire, the world doesn't mean much to me. I'm rarely there, and I hardly ever use it. I have the world gathering dust over in the corner, leaning up against desire.

DESKS

The thing I liked most about school was those little desks we sat at when we were children, the ones with the wooden lids. Those desks were radiant.

In the top right corner was a round, scooped-out space for an inkwell, though by the time we were children, inkwells were no longer in use and this space was already redundant. Next to that purely symbolic space, there was a long, shallow dip for a ruler, pens, pencils, pencil sharpeners, and, best of all, our beloved eraser, which left its soft gray snow wherever we made a mistake.

Although the lid of the desk was made out of wood, the rest of it was metal. In winter, our knees chattered like teeth against the cold metal undersides of our desks, sometimes so violently the desks themselves trembled.

Exercise books and textbooks were kept inside one's desk: the wooden lid opened up like that of a coffin.

At some point during the school year, every boy took out the silver device used for drawing circles known as a compass and carved his name into his desk's lid. This was painstaking work. Some boys would turn the compasses on themselves, pulling up the gray legs of their trousers or the gray sleeves of their shirts, and carving their own names or the names of other boys into their skin.

Each desk's surface was already overcrowded with the names of boys who had gotten there before us, though by the time I read those names, many of those boys were no longer boys at all, but men, old men who smelled of vegetables and wore heavy coats, or dead men who were residing either in heaven or hell—depending on the kind of life they had led—just as by now, surely the frames of those desks have been melted down, the lids chopped up for firewood.

DESTRUCTION

If you are looking for me and need to find me immediately, you can always find me in that space halfway between the world and its destruction, halfway between category and daydream.

DEVIL WORSHIPPERS

Devil worshippers become devil worshippers in an effort to evade the dreariness of life. They turn toward Satan to make life a little more glamorous and to give it a little more pizzazz. *S* stands not only for Satan, sodomy, and sacrifice but also for satin and sequins! Yet being alive cannot always be interesting. No matter how many black masses they hold, and no matter how many dark and ominous surprises occur during these ceremonies, like us, devil worshippers are still forced to return to the humdrum of the everyday. Even for devil worshippers there must be long stretches of life that are simply, and sublimely, mundane.

Dewey decimal system

When it rains heavily, as it has been doing of late, the homeless people in our neighborhood sleep beneath the eaves of our local library.

Diana, Princess

I met Princess Diana once. It was back in 1983, shortly after her marriage to Prince Charles. She and England's heir to the throne came to Fremantle, the town where I went to school, and we all lined up, and she walked along the line and said *hello, hello*. I remember she wore a navy blue dress with white polka dots. Although this was still early days, long before all the problems, there was something gloomy about her even then, a sense of doom that passed as regal. It was as if, lurking beneath her fluffy bouffant blonde hairdo, there was an abyss, and that is why she wore her hair like that, to conceal the abyss. (Perhaps that is why everyone wore their hair like that in the early '80s.)

Of course when Diana died in the car crash in Paris in 1997, I was crushed, and quite hysterical, to be honest, along with the rest of the Western world—it's not often in the so-called West that we get to experience something on the level of myth. I recalled meeting her, and I wished I had reached out and touched the hem of her dress.

Shortly after her death, I had a dream that she sent me a little calling card, inviting me to come and visit her, and in lovely lettering it said, *Hey you, don't come too soon to the dark, but if you do, I'll welcome you.*

Diana's wedding dress

It is said that there is an exact replica of the dress Princess Diana wore on her wedding day back in 1981. The only difference between the replica and the original is that whereas on the original there is a length of Queen Mary's lace sewn on the bodice, on the replica of the dress there is a copy of this lace.

Similarly, I recently heard that under the supervision of Queen Elizabeth II, a company is presently at work on a replica of Diana's death. The only difference will be that this time, the hair on her head will be a synthetic wig—virtually identical to her actual hair. Apart from that, this death will be exactly the same as her original death.

DIANA'S WEDDING DRESS, THEORIES OF

A group of scientists in Paris are currently examining a possible connection between Princess Diana's wedding dress, designed by the Emmanuels, and the AIDS virus. The link, which at this point in time still remains tentative, is that both the dress and the virus appeared in 1981, and the dress was itself a bit like a virus, a virus of ivory silk. The scientists are conducting tests in an attempt to prove that the Emmanuels and the wedding and the dress—in particular the puffy sleeves—somehow caused AIDS, which up until then had been latent, to bubble to the surface.

DICTATORSHIPS, FASCIST

In my fascist dictatorship, organized around dreams, everyone would be required to sleep long hours and to dream relentlessly. In the morning, the first thing citizens would be required to do would be to write their dreams down in state-issued dream journals—even if they'd forgotten their dreams they would have to check a little box that says FORGOTTEN. Once filled, these journals would be handed in, and, at the end of the year, if someone had forgotten their dreams 100 times or more, they would be asked to report to the State Department of Dream, and they'd be sent off to hard labor camps that were very far away, where they would be forced to dream every hour of the day. Every now and then, someone with a particularly poor dream record or someone known to hold unfavorable opinions on the practice of dreaming would be executed, as an example, and a reminder, that people must do everything they can to dream. In the central squares of all the cities there would be monolithic, heroic statues of ideal citizens immersed in dream.

DISASTERS

When we watch the national news, we are always secretly disappointed when nothing particularly devastating has happened. However, as soon as the reporters with their oddly reconstructed faces speak of carnage, or disaster, on a grand, previously unimaginable scale, our excitement rises steadily, like a death toll.

DISEASES

Although all diseases are interesting—that is to say, despite our intense fear of them, they arouse and hold our attention—and although we are fascinated by all of them, from the plague of Athens in 400 BC, when the Athenian warriors who died wore very short, pleated tunics, to the bubonic plague of the 1300s, when the men who died wore tunics with similarly short, pleated skirts, we find that our thoughts constantly return to the disease known as AIDS, which is not technically a disease but a syndrome. However, for argument's sake, let us call it a disease, for who really fears a syndrome?

Of course most contract AIDS as a result of an accident or a mistake, yet the fact that one can actively seek it out, the fact that one can contract it willingly, the fact that, if one wanted, one could go out and buy and partake of a quantity of HIV, and most importantly, the fact that it can be passed on through an act, not merely of passion, but of love, and that in the process of acquiring it, one can thoroughly enjoy one's self, somehow makes AIDS very interesting.

It's safe to say that if there were a contest, AIDS would probably win the prize for the most interesting disease.

DISEASES, CHILDHOOD

Surely the best thing about childhood was its diseases (those dreaded vaccinations and inoculations against diseases, such as tuberculosis and rubella, for which we lined up as if we were heading to the guillotine, were also highlights!).

First there was chicken pox, which was like being covered in polka dots, but polka dots that itched so badly they were painful, polka dots that, when you finally gave in and scratched them, bled all over the linoleum in the kitchen. I still have one little scar from this chicken pox experience, a pale little one beneath my right nipple, like a white silk button, a souvenir, as it were, from the disease; in this sense, all diseases were like taking vacations from childhood, which is why we so looked forward to them.

Then there was mumps, which began with an alarming lack of symmetry: first the right side of my face blew up, like those blowfish I often saw flopping helplessly on the jetty at Point Walter, those fish who we were taught to avoid because they were poisonous, but which Japanese business men considered a delicacy precisely for their poison. It took three days for the left side of my face to swell up; finally I was grotesque according to classical proportions. Mumps was far more painful than chicken pox: it was like having polka dots blister their way along the inside of your jaw.

And then there was German measles; compared to the former two, this was a relatively simple disease. This disease was ideal, utterly painless. Again, as with chicken pox, I was covered in polka dots, but these did not scab or feel like anything; they were simply there for a while. I was placed in quarantine, and I felt like I had become one of my mother's polka dot dresses, and this is exactly what I had always wanted to be.

DISFIGUREMENT

Up until 1981, or thereabouts, homosexuals in the West had been designated as the arbiters of beauty.

Then in 1981 our job description changed, and we became the arbiters of disfigurement.

DOG

I was the last of seven children. Sometimes my dad would get confused and call me by the name of one of my siblings. Sometimes he'd get even more confused and refer to me by one of our dogs' names, either Bandit, the first dog, or Cossack, the second dog, both beagles, a noble breed, both of whom would die from cancer.

There were times my father became so confused he forgot I was his son and thought I was his dog. This is understandable: after all, someone needed to continue the family dogs' good name; the dogs required an heir. Dad would bring me home bones with tasty bits of gristle on them. He'd take me out for brisk walks on a leash that was unimaginably long.

DOG BITES

Recently, after an exhausting yet ultimately rewarding day at my job as professor at an obscure, progressive university, I was walking home from the bus stop when I was bitten on the inside of my forearm by a big, pearl-gray dog. Luckily I was wearing one of my jackets made from synthetic material in a factory in China. Otherwise the hound's fangs would have broken the skin. Instead, they merely left puncture points.

Nevertheless, I found myself quite shaken by the incident. There was something primal about it, and I never use that word, because nothing primal ever happens to me. I hadn't been bitten by a dog since I was a kid, and I found my mind wandering back to all those other times, like the time I was bitten by Bandit over a dispute involving a bone brought home by my father, and then, after we put Bandit to sleep, the time I was bitten by Cossack over yet another dispute involving yet another bone, and some jealousy on my part, what Freud called the Canine Complex, which is when you want to fuck your father and kill your dogs.

And then of course there was that time when a circus pitched its tent in the park at the end of our street, and I went down to take a look. There was a little clown dog wearing a ruffle round its neck and a gold pointy hat on its head, tied to one of the stakes holding up the so-called big top. When I knelt down to pat the dog, it promptly sunk its teeth into my left thigh, tearing through my cherry-red corduroy pants. This was perhaps my favorite dog bite. One of the circus hands came over and took the pointy hat off the dog's tiny head, then placed it carefully on my own.

As I walked back home, slightly dazed, to tell my boyfriend, Tim, that I had been bitten by a dog, I realized that I couldn't really complain. I'd had some very good dog bites in my life, which suddenly seemed like a series of dog bites, separated by long periods of blank silence. I could almost feel time, like a dog, sinking its teeth into me. At thirty-six years of age I had thought that part of my life was over, but it seems that I still have it in me, it seems that there are some stray dogs out there wandering around that still want to bite me, that salivate when they see me.

DOG FOOD

Back in the 1970s there were often stories in the newspaper about old men who lived by themselves and were so poor they could only afford to eat dog food. I'd see these men at our local supermarket, loitering in the pet food aisles, their shopping baskets filled with cans of wet food. I knew they'd go home and eat a third of a can at each meal, sitting alone at their small kitchen tables. I worried that this was going to be my fate. It seemed a natural transition, to go from being a lonely boy to being a lonely old man, living on dog food, with nothing but a can opener to keep me company.

DOODLING

Once when I was a kid my mother noticed a pad I had been doodling on; the page was covered in little coffins with crosses on them. *That's funny,* she told me, *but your dad doodles exactly the same thing, little coffins of exactly the same dimensions as yours, mainly when he's on the phone, talking to his family in Scotland.* She laughed and said she considered this habit of his *a bit morbid.*

Now, whenever I call up Australia and get my father on the phone, while we talk about the weather, beneath the grain of his voice I can hear the familiar scratching sound of pen on paper, like chickens pecking furiously for feed in the dirt.

DRAG

After the end of the world there will be no more drag, as there will be no women left to imitate. Actually, there will be no such thing as imitation, which requires an object. Still, we will come up with ways to make things camp. Anyone who has read the Book of Revelations, which describes the apocalypse as if it were a Busby Berkeley routine, knows that the end of the world is far more camp than the beginning of the world. For starters, we will put some sequins on the primordial slime and wrap the ooze in a feather boa.

DRAPER'S, THE

I was lying in bed this morning, putting off getting out of bed, wondering whether I should just stay in bed, when I remembered the draper's. It was two doors down from the butcher's, next to the chemist's. Is there even still such a thing as a draper? To be honest, I don't remember much about it, except that they sold bolts of cloth and ribbons and women's dresses, highly synthetic dresses in violently floral patterns. I had been led to believe that these dresses had been skinned right off the backs of violent, highly synthetic animals (in this sense, the draper's was just a variation on the butcher's). And it was always somewhat dark in there, like twilight. I literally haven't thought of the draper's for twenty or so years. I must have been repressing it.

DREAM DROOL

Dream drool is what streams out of boys' mouths while they are dreaming. It is mostly clear. In Communist countries, where boys dream very little, dream drool is considered a delicacy. It is very expensive, like truffles or caviar. The most prized dream drool comes from Romanian and Albanian boys. In these countries, they have special farms where women in polka-dotted headscarves grab boys by their necks and force-feed them dreams.

But in the West, where boys dream regularly and freely, and where there is an excess of dream, dream drool is cheap and plentiful. Little children love it. Old ladies stand all night over boys and scoop up the drool with silver teaspoons, making sure they catch it before it falls onto the pillow. They sell the stuff at church fetes, in empty jam jars, along with those gold slabs of toffee in pleated cupcake holders.

DREAMS

If I am perfectly honest with myself, the only thing I really like is dreaming (and sex, which is, after all, just a variation on dream). More importantly, the only thing I'm really good at is dreaming (and sex).

Each morning the first thing I do is write my dreams down in spiral-bound notebooks. I like to do this while I can still hear the dreams gurgling out of me, reminding me that I'm nothing but a silver drain for dreams.

As I scribble away, I feel as if I am taking dictation from my unconscious. I feel like I am one of those brassy secretaries in an old movie from the forties or the fifties, wearing a black pencil skirt, working in some office, and my unconscious is my boss, who is intent on seducing me.

And indeed, when I look at all my dream journals from over the years, stacked neatly on top of each other on the shelves in my office, I get the feeling that there is something distinctly bureaucratic about this whole process. All my life I've had a horror of bureaucracy, and have done everything to avoid the bureaucratic, but maybe all the spaces I flee to—desire, imagination, dream—are themselves bureaucracies, full of manila folders and filing cabinets.

In this sense, my dream journals are nothing but yellowing, bureaucratic documents. Without knowing it, I have become just what my mother wished me to be, a low-level civil servant, one who must report, not to the state, but to dream, one who is working in the strange yet reliable, and somewhat monotonous, bureaucracy of the unconscious.

DREAMS, THE ANTECEDENT OF MY

It's clear to me that I inherited this predisposition to dream from my mother.

My mother was a ravenous dreamer. Let me put it another way: she had an appetite for dream.

She dreamt every night, all night, and in the morning remembered everything. Her dreams were as long and detailed as a nineteenth-century Russian novel; in fact, she dreamt often of Russia—always pre-revolutionary Russia—her nights populated with dancing bears and onion-domes, Fabergé eggs and Nijinsky's thighs, Anna Pavlova's tutu and doomed czars and czarinas. Her dream journals read like *Anna Karenina* or *War and Peace:* it was as if Tolstoy had taken a razor, excised all the exterior detail, and written his books according to the characters' interior worlds.

My father, on the other hand, claimed that he never dreamt, that he was too busy to dream, that he worked too hard to dream.

Not a particularly conscientious housekeeper, my mother was fastidious in her dream life; she kept detailed transcripts of her dreams in those ledgers accountants use, which at our local supermarket were cheaper than notebooks. She kept these hidden from my father, burying her dream ledgers in the garden, little dreamy graves, but she began to forget where she buried them, and one day when we are all gone some children will unearth them (who, on the other hand, will unearth this?).

My mother was mainly successful at concealing her dreams, but sometimes she was careless: she'd fail to wash all the dreams off her skin, and my father would smell them on her, like in those old movies where wives smell strange perfume on their husbands.

Some mornings she had dreamt so much that her dreams would be swirling around her ankles. She'd forget to mop up the dreams off the linoleum. My father would come into the kitchen and slip in one of her little dream pools. The dog would race in and gobble the dream up. The dog grew fat on my mother's dreams.

DREAMS, BAD

Technically speaking there is no such thing as a bad dream (and there is of course nothing nicer than hearing a really cute guy tell you last night's nightmare in detail).

In my mother's dream ledgers, good dreams went on the left side *(credit)*, bad dreams on the right *(debit)*. With a few notable exceptions, all her dreams ended up in the left column.

Any dream by definition is a good dream, a credit to your being, even if you wake from it, your nightgown dripping, screaming.

DREAMS, DEATH AND

I recently heard from a highly reliable source that when you die all you do is sleep, but you never dream. Every now and then you wake up, and feel sleepy, and yawn a bit, and miss the world, but only for a few minutes, until you fall back into your dreamless sleep.

With this in mind, I now try to be awake as little as possible. I try to sleep as long as I can and to dream as much as — or perhaps even more than — is humanly conceivable. All this in an effort to cram in as many dreams as I can.

DREAMS, DEATH OF

When we got out of the car and peered over the edge of the chasm, we saw all our dead dreams lying at the bottom, rotting away. And we saw other things: a skeleton of a boy, a mattress covered in tea stains and sex stains, and a discarded sofa upholstered in green fabric with a pattern of roses.

DREAMS, FUTURE OF

On those days when I am trying to avoid writing, or to avoid living, I like to go and stare at all my dream journals, stacked there quietly.

They strike me as a kind of stockpile, a supply of materials stored for future use. Yet what a curious stockpile it is, for ultimately there is no future for the dreamer, and no one will require the use of his materials. Unused, my dream journals have already gone rancid. A stench seems to emanate from them.

By the end of this century, all dreaming will have ceased; most people have ceased dreaming already. People may come across my journals, but they will not understand a word of them. They will see nothing but scratches, strange night scratches.

DREAMS, MY FATHER'S

Once a week my father did the rounds, like a garbage collector, collecting all our dreams, sifting through them, and then, like a garbage truck, carefully compacting them.

More than anything, I would like to meet my father in Motherwell, Scotland, and go with him to the pub that his brother Davy, who wears the toupee, owns, and then go with him to the little two-up two-down red brick house where he grew up, and sit down with him at the kitchen table, and share some whisky, and listen intently, as he tells me in complete detail every one of his dreams.

DREAMS, PREVIOUSLY DREAMT

Where do dreams go, after they've been dreamt? Perhaps they have nowhere to go, and, like plastic, they don't break down; they just accumulate silently in the body. Perhaps science, in the investigation of what causes cancer, needs to look toward dreams.

DREAMS, WAKING UP FROM

Last night I woke up from a dream. As I tried to go back to sleep, I found myself thinking about those Dracula moneyboxes that were popular in the late 1970s. When you placed a coin in them, Dracula would sit up very erectly from his miniature coffin and cackle and grasp the coin, before taking it back with him into his coffin. Like Dracula, I had popped out of my dream, to grasp at something. The memory of this toy, which I had forgotten, and the thought of my resemblance to it, somehow calmed me. I withdrew from the world, into the dream, back where I belong.

DREAMS, WET

How wonderful that brief period of life was, when, during early adolescence, we had sex in our dreams, sex that was so real—perhaps more real than the waking sex we would come to have—that our bodies spontaneously shuddered, emitting strange, milky fluid onto our flannel or cotton sheets. Life was never so thrilling than during that period; since then, if the truth be told, life has been somewhat of a disappointment.

A wet dream is the only accurate record of a dream. All those thousands of dreams I have written down in my so-called dream journals, in an attempt to recapture the essence of each dream, are not only somewhat tedious but also utterly inaccurate.

DRIVING

I'm thirty-six and have yet to acquire my driver's license. Living in Los Angeles, you might think this puts me at a disadvantage, but you would be wrong.

You haven't lived until you've taken the number 33 bus from Venice Beach, all the way down Venice Boulevard—the Champs Elysées of this city—to Union Station in downtown L.A. The ride is especially beautiful during the summer, early in the morning, when the glare is so great that I start to think I'm in heaven and it makes me feel sick. It seems as if I'm not alone in this feeling; men carefully pull the edge of their hoodies over their shaved heads, concealing their faces.

As we pass by the thousands upon thousands of wonderfully anonymous pastel apartment buildings and houses and motels, I think about the thousands of men hidden behind those stucco walls, lying on their beds, probably in white boxers, dreaming or daydreaming.

Due to my driving defect, not only am I granted the intense pleasure of taking the MTA buses in this city, I also get to ride about on my red bicycle. You may have seen me. I ride my bike very slowly and sit very upright as I ride, with a straight back, like Miss Gulch in *The Wizard of Oz,* though, as I recall, she rode her bicycle with a certain urgency.

I suspect I will get my driver's license very soon, but it is common knowledge that my mother never got her license. Maybe I will take after her; maybe I am genetically predisposed not to drive. Sometimes it is simply not possible to overcome heredity; I'll be fused to my bicycle forever.

In that case, I'll have to be content with dreaming. At night, my mum and I drive around in a red sports car, just like the one Princess Grace of Monaco died in. Taking turns at the wheel, we speed along an endless road that is comprised wholly of sharp corners, each corner sharper than the one before. We are excellent, if somewhat reckless, drivers. In this dream, although both of us are still without our licenses, a license is not required, for in dream there are no laws.

DUNCE'S CAPS

Some of my best memories of childhood involve standing in the corner of a classroom, between two blackboards, wearing a dunce's cap. These caps were made out of white construction paper, which was thick but relatively fragile. You had to be careful not to knock the conical tip of your hat against the plaster wall. The hat only stayed on your head because of the elastic, which bit into your chin, leaving a nice pink mark. The *D*, written on the side of the hat in Magic Marker, was thick, black, and glossy. Although it was clear what the *D* stood for, it could have stood for all sorts of good things, like *death, doom, danger, decay, decadence, destruction, dissolution, dissipation.* Over time the *D* faded until it was barely discernible. There was something very intimate about the relationship each wearer had with his hat. I would never advocate a return to childhood—the second time around we'd die, or at the very least go insane—but I really would strongly advocate that we bring dunce's caps back.

DVDs

What would we do without DVDs or DVD players? One thing's for certain: we would find ourselves at an extremely loose end, like teenage boys in the summer holidays, bored out of their skulls. Actually, without the technological support of DVDs, all humanity would go mad, everyone would slit their wrists on the count of three—DVD players were invented in 1996 to stop humanity from doing so. The only thing keeping civilization from descending into complete madness and obliterating itself entirely, the only way we are keeping it somewhat together, is because of a thin little DVD (probably of an old Luis Buñuel flick). If it were not for the consolation of DVDs, things would get particularly dicey at the end of the day as the sun begins to set and nighttime envelops us in its navy blue sludge. After five o'clock there would be nothing to look forward to but an evening of bones.

DYLAN, BOB

The other day, sick to death of speaking, and thoroughly dissatisfied with the limits of my tongue, I decided to cut it out. To get myself in the mood, I put on Bob Dylan's "Sad-Eyed Lady of the Lowlands"—which covers one whole side of Tim's vinyl copy of *Blonde on Blonde*—grabbed a knife, and began working away on the tough old thing. I felt determined yet slightly ludicrous, like one of those colonial explorers in a safari suit and a pith helmet, hacking his way through dense undergrowth.

Halfway through, I lost my nerve. Perhaps, I thought, a tongue would still come in handy, if only for French-kissing my boyfriend and maliciously gossiping.

So Tim wouldn't know I had attempted to cut off my tongue, I washed the blood off the knife and dried it with a tea towel. Then I applied some iodine and Kleenex tissues to my tongue, the poor red thing. Dylan hadn't even gotten to his harmonica solo yet, so I sat on the couch, waiting for the bleeding to stop, and listened to the rest of his lovely, interminable song.

E

EAKINS, THOMAS

Thomas Eakins strived for realism, particularly when painting men's asses; see *The Swimming Hole*. He sought to depict the male ass with scientific accuracy and painstaking detail, without losing feeling, by applying the paint like a dog applies its saliva. In his paintings the asses seem to be illuminated from within, violently, rising out of the dark glaze like voluptuous lampshades.

EAR, THE

The ear is a listening abyss.

EASTERN BLOC, THE

Every now and then, when life gets too difficult, I find myself wishing that there was still an Eastern Bloc, and that I lived in it. This way, I could go to stadiums whenever I wanted and watch mass demonstrations of men performing perfectly synchronized gymnastics. I could be an informer and spy on everyone I love, and therefore have a concrete ideological reason for betraying them. Inevitably, I would be suspected of counter-revolutionary tendencies; instead of dreading myself, I could dread and fear the secret police, while secretly admiring them in those nice black leather trench coats they tend to wear. I'd try to scurry by them as discreetly as possible, praying that they don't notice me, whilst simultaneously hoping that they will notice me and come for me in the middle of the night and drag me away in my flannel pajamas, not even giving me time to put on a coat. In the meantime, while I waited for the inevitable knock on my door—this fate would at least be clearer than the fate that currently awaits me— I could go down to the open air bookstall on the state farm where I'd live, and buy communist propaganda, lots of it. I could flirt with the man who sells it and ask him to point out the passages he felt were most ideologically uplifting, which would give me something to look forward to, particularly when the days were dreary, as these days tend to be, more and more lately.

ECONOMICS

In a plague economy, demand refers to the kind of boy that other boys want at any given price. Demand for a boy in fact increases as the price rises. Demand continues to increase until the supply has melted away, and, in effect, what we have on our hands is the total disappearance of boys.

EGYPT

In 1997 six terrorists disguised as policemen opened fire on a group of tourists who were visiting the Temple of Hatshepsut at Luxor. Afterwards, the terrorists slit open the bodies of some of their sixty-four victims and stuffed letters containing their demands into the bodies, as if the bodies were envelopes.

More than forty years earlier, my mother visited this site. She wrote to her fiancé, James McCartney, about the temple. Within a pale blue aerogramme, just like those he sent her, she described to him how grand the temple was, columns upon columns. She said that she tried to imagine what it was like when sphinxes and myrrh trees lined the walkways.

When the man who would become her husband, and my father, received this aerogramme, he read it slowly. He folded the letter and then placed it into the inside pocket of his tweed jacket.

Einstein, Albert

To be honest, I'm not that interested in Einstein and don't really understand any of his theories. Though, if I think a little bit longer, surely there are certain things about him that interest me. Like his hair. Within the history of ideas, he clearly had the best haircut. It was so unruly, giving him the look of someone who had just stuck his finger into an electric socket or who had just seen a ghost. He looked either very startled or very frightened.

Though perhaps he found his hair too unruly—everyone hates something about himself. Being such a genius, he probably rationalized it by acknowledging that he was simply ahead of his time, just as he was in every other sphere of life. More than likely, he was fully aware that his hair would have been far more manageable if only he had been born into the epoch of the Afro, the Mohawk, or the beehive.

I'm also interested in the fact that Einstein smoked a pipe, just because my father also smokes a pipe; when I was little and no one was around I would sneak into my parents' bedroom and suck on my father's pipe. Coincidentally, when Einstein was five, his father showed him a compass: Einstein was so weirded out by the compass needle, always pointing in the same direction, that he took the compass, put it in his mouth, and proceeded to suck on it. Later, he would claim that this was what got him interested in science. It seems everything begins with fathers and mouths.

At the academy, the great scientist would stand for hours in front of blackboards, doing his equations in green or blue chalk, but never white. Apparently, whenever he made a mistake, he didn't use blackboard erasers, which he believed posed an obstacle to his thought. He used the palms of his hands, to caress the problem, as it were.

Speaking of black, what about black holes? Like everyone else, I have a ghoulish fascination with them. Even more interesting is that although Albert came up with the whole ghoulish idea, he didn't really believe in black holes and didn't like to think about them too much. (Maybe he saw one once, and that explains his crazy hair.)

On a more historical note, Einstein left Europe in 1933. He escaped the Holocaust, which would turn Europe into one big black hole, and which would make black holes an everyday occurrence, as common as moth holes. Perhaps this explains Einstein's hair: he not only escaped but also anticipated the Holocaust, he saw it and was terribly frightened by what he saw. Upon his arrival in the United States, on his first day out and about in New York, he ate four hot dogs in a row (probably to repress the Holocaust).

None of this, however, is that interesting compared to what happened in 1905, long, but not that long, before the Holocaust, when Einstein's so-called three papers of 1905 appeared. There was actually a fourth, but everyone only refers to the three papers, because whereas each of the first three established a new branch of physics, the fourth only proved the atomic theory of matter; supposedly this is less important. Einstein, who at the time was only twenty-six years old, sent his work to the *Annalen der Physik,* tying around each of the papers a flat silk ribbon.

E-MAIL

Somehow, when I am, as they say, *doing e-mail,* I feel like Jane Austen, but without the irony. Although people go on and on about the so-called global aspect of e-mail and how amazing it is to be able to connect so easily with someone on the other side of the so-called world, I cannot shake the feeling that, through e-mail, life has become very small, as compressed and stifling as it was in Austen's day.

Once again, humans rarely leave the confines of their neighborhoods or even their homes, just as it was common in Austen's time for people to be born and to die in the same village, and to rarely leave the village, like Austen herself, who was born in Steventon, didn't get out much, and then died in Winchester, right near her birthplace.

On the other hand, maybe Austen would have loved e-mail and would have in many ways felt emancipated by it, lifted out of the dreariness of polite society. Perhaps she would have been on it all day, sending arch little e-mails and struggling to convey subtle witticisms through instant messages. Often she would have been forced to resort to the usual online symbols like ;) and :o to express exactly what she wished to say. Yet it would have been so good for the novels, which would have been filled with heroines puzzling and fretting over the true meaning of e-mails sent by gentlemen admirers.

ENCYCLOPEDIA, HISTORY OF THE

The first encyclopedia was created by Aristotle in 322 BC; it was an attempt to bring together all the ideas of the time, but he also made things up.

After that, in terms of encyclopedias, there was a long dry spell. In fact, there were none, that is, until the publication of the *End of the World Book* in 2008, and the announcement of a policy of continuous and simultaneous revision and destruction: *everything in the world is marked fragile; destroy with great care.*

Here at the *End of the World Book* we firmly believe that we must keep categorizing and that this is the only thing keeping the world, and us, from ending. We also believe, firmly, that each category destroys the thing it describes; with each category we move that little bit closer to the end.

ENIGMATIC, THE

Leonardo da Vinci had it easy. It must have been so much simpler making something enigmatic in the early sixteenth century. All he had to do to create an ambiguity that would stretch out across history was to paint *La Giaconda,* otherwise known as the *Mona Lisa:* a nice picture of a woman with a smile creasing her face.

In the twenty-first century, to make something puzzling and inexplicable is far more difficult. We no longer need to wonder what is going on behind someone's face. Plastic surgeons can cut open any face, peel it back, take a good look around, and sew it up.

If da Vinci were around today, he couldn't get away with a mere portrait of the wife of a Florentine merchant. He'd have to do a miniature reproduction of the *Mona Lisa,* measuring five inches by five inches, quite alarming in its accuracy. Then he'd need to place his tiny painting in an aquarium, and have it tortured by a tiny stingray, the painting steadfastly refusing to offer a confession. But even this would seem too obvious, too decipherable.

And maybe I'm being too hard on him. Maybe, as soon as he had finished painting the *Mona Lisa,* he looked at it and immediately began to worry that although it was sort of enigmatic, it wasn't nearly enigmatic enough. Perhaps he saw that compared to the heart of a boy, which extends into infinity, nothing is enigmatic.

ENLIGHTENMENT, THE

One morning in the eighteenth century, Denis Diderot, sick to death of working on his *Encyclopédie,* and totally bored with the task of categorizing, went out for a spot of hunting. *N is for nature G is for gun C is for crow.* The black bird landed a short distance from his feet. Sunlight poured through the perfect hole in the bird's glossy body, giving the philosopher the idea for the Enlightenment.

Everyone had finally gotten used to the Dark Ages and had even begun to enjoy them, so when the Enlightenment arrived, people began to notice the side effects almost immediately, the main one being terrible headaches.

In his own encyclopedia, Diderot deescribed the Enlightenment as *a sort of giant photocopier, but one whose lid is always open. The invention of aspirin,* he went on, *is the direct result of the Enlightenment and is the Enlightenment's greatest achievement.*

ENLIGHTENMENT, MEN OF THE

When we think about the men of the Enlightenment, we do not think about their faith in objective reason, in the natural goodness of men, and in the value of scientific knowledge; nor do we reflect upon their distrust of orthodoxy and intolerance, their hatred of tyranny and social institutions, or their love of skepticism, freedom, satire and wit.

Whenever our thoughts turn backwards, toward the Enlightenment, we think of Rousseau and his persecution complex. We think of Diderot and his obsession with stains, particularly the grass stains on the knees of his breeches, and his numerous failed attempts to create an entry for *stains* in his *Encylopédie*. Most of all, we think of Voltaire and his chamber pot, his recurring dream that a realistic likeness of his face was painted on the side of his chamber pot. We ponder the fact that all his life's work ultimately led to the incident toward the end of his life, during which he ate the contents of his own chamber pot.

ERASERS

When we were children we noticed that our erasers, which were pink and gray, were rounded at either end like the tops of tombstones. The best thing about childhood was the erasers. We erased everything. We'd crouch down behind our erasers, peer over the tops, and watch the priests soberly fucking.

ETERNITY

There are conflicting reports regarding eternity. Some say that it's full of fountains and peaches blue as bruises, and that there's a very, very long clothesline, on which hangs nothing but rows and rows of sober black satin waistcoats and pearl-gray silk trousers, dripping on into infinity. They claim that upon arriving in eternity, everyone is greeted by Emily Dickinson, and she shakes your hand, and her hand is just as you would expect—very cold, and very lovely, like ice blocks wrapped in a handkerchief to reduce a fever—but her forehead is not as prominent as it appears in photographs.

Others state quite the opposite. They maintain that eternity is nothing but a big factory, run on a forty-hour workweek. With a half-hour lunch break. You have to wear a hairnet. You have to earn your keep.

ETERNITY, LAWS OF

Within these conflicting reports, both schools of thought agree on one thing. Taking measurements of any sort is strictly forbidden in eternity. Anyone caught measuring anything is subject to the death penalty (they used to behead people, but now they use lethal injection, because they want to act humanely).

As a result, a large percentage of eternity's inhabitants find themselves becoming deeply nostalgic for instruments of measurement. They miss terribly those measuring tapes forward tailors used to measure their inner thighs when fitting their school trousers. More than anything, they yearn for those silver measuring cups that they filled with flour and sugar when they helped their mothers bake cakes on those endless rainy days.

To discourage this pining, the authorities organize routine bonfires at which wooden rulers (the kind the nuns rapped on your fingers) are burnt to cinders. Everyone is required to attend.

EXPERIMENTS

Whenever I feel a little bleak around the edges, I try and remind myself that I'm just an experiment, an event that can happen again, and that I'm mainly attracted to men who can happen again. This scientific attitude toward myself really helps, it really cheers me up, and although I still feel grim, I begin to feel almost elated, simultaneously heavy and light. It's as if there's a balloon seller in my head who follows me everywhere and wears a heavy gray coat, even in the summer. He sells only gray balloons in differing shades of gray—dove gray, lead-pencil gray, nerve-tissue gray—and whenever he sees how I'm feeling he gives me a balloon for free, and I feel considerably less bleak.

EXPOSURE

The end of the world will not be very pleasant, but it will be extremely straightforward. Just as we had been led to believe, it will be horrific, like the best horror movie you've ever seen, or the most *real* nightmare you've ever dreamt.

Yet you will be able to take comfort in the fact that it will also be very orderly. There will be no incongruity between how we expected it to happen and how it actually goes down. God will simply strip us of all our irony. Without it, at best, we will be very, very skinny; at worst, we will be like skeletons. Unable to bear the literal, we will die almost immediately from exposure to the world's day-glo elements, its harsh beauty.

EXTINCTION

Sometimes when I look in the mirror on the medicine cabinet in our bathroom, I am reminded of the time my mother took me to the Museum of Natural History. We saw a tiny fossil of a small, strange, winged creature. The pattern of its wings was so delicate. It was as if the ancient bird was hurtling toward us, flying through the slate-gray rock. As I looked, my face pressed up to the glass case, some joy in me snapped.

Thought took us to the brink of extinction, but on further reflection, we have decided to come back.

EYES, BLOODSHOT

I like boys with bloodshot eyes. The whites of their eyes are full of red popes' hats, magnificent, violent sunsets. It's like there's a murder going on in their eyes, a tiny murder, done with tiny knives. Boys with bloodshot eyes are royalty, whereas boys with clear eyes are their lowly subjects.

ℱ

FACE, THE

Some days, my face feels like a ski mask, like the black wool kind commonly worn by terrorists. I feel like my eyes are twinkling coldly through the narrow slits in my face. And just as a ski mask hides the true identity of the terrorist, my face seems to be hiding something about me, something that will give me away and that I cannot show to anyone.

On my better days, although my face still feels like a mask, a mask I can't take off, behind which lies something so real and revealing that I must conceal it from everyone, it somehow feels spangly and glittery, more like a mask worn by a Lucha Libre wrestler.

FATE

Fate is a machine. The early model was hand-operated and looked like a very large sausage grinder; you had to crank a handle to meet your fate. This was labor intensive. It left thin red scars all over the user, like the flat red satin ribbons found in the pages of Sunday school Bibles.

With the new, improved model, all you have to do is press a button and a solid sheet of glass comes at you like a guillotine. According to the manufacturer, it cuts you from behind one ear and on to the voice box, slicing through both jugular veins. It works like a dream.

FINGERFUCKING

Surely there is nothing more melancholy than the sublime act of fingerfucking. Any man who has ever fingerfucked or been fingerfucked knows this.

During that brief intermission, when one is between acts of fingerfucking, and one either sniffs one's fingers or inhales the odor rising from one's own asshole—depending on the role one is playing—although one takes in a smell that is sweet and cloistered, similar to the clean yet close odor of a nun's room in a convent, even if the man in question has been most thorough in cleaning himself, inevitably one detects lurking just beneath this sweet scent the faint odor of feces, reminding us that all men, including ourselves, inevitably decay.

This explains why, sometimes, the fingerfucker, right in the midst of fingerfucking a really hot man, receives the distinct sensation that he is fingerfucking a really hot skeleton. He is painfully reminded that every man is a cemetery, full of little tombstones; in fact, the tips of his fingers can almost make out the inscriptions on the headstones.

Arguably, one can speculate that this experience of mortality is more intense for the gentleman fingerfucking; whereas the gentleman being fingerfucked is immersed in his own pleasure and in his own odor, the fingerfucker has distance from the act.

For the fingerfucker, perhaps the only thing more melancholy than the sublime act of fingerfucking a man is the aftermath of fingering, when, in the morning, still in a dream state, he absentmindedly lifts his fingers to his nostrils, and the faint smell of lavender soap that lingers, that mystical trace—of course still with the unmistakable undertow of feces—causes a kind of temporal abyss to open up—in fact, one might say that time takes on the spatial depth and complexity of a man's asshole—and transports him back not only to the man from the previous night, but to every man he has ever fingered, and even further, to every historical instance of fingerfucking, and further yet, to every bar of soap that every man in the history of humanity has ever used, in a hopeful yet ultimately futile attempt to erase the stench of death.

FINGERPRINTS

Although it is nice to know that at the end of every one of my fingertips there is a tiny little maze that is wonderfully unique, it is not so pleasant to ponder the thought that a miniature, barbaric, merciless—admittedly well-built—Minotaur dwells at the heart of every one of these little mazes. I suppose this means that I must sacrifice seven Angeleno youths every year to keep each of my Minotaurs content. Ten fingers means ten mazes, hence ten Minotaurs who demand to be satisfied. That's seventy sacrificial youths a year. Uniqueness is something from which no one can escape.

FIRE

When I was really little there was this man whom I would sometimes see walking around our neighborhood. His face was all burnt up. It had been burnt so badly that he had lost his nose. He just sort of had a hole there. He always wore a heavy coat and a pork-pie hat, even in the summer. People said that he had been burnt in a house fire, and that he had been the one who had set the house on fire, with the intention of incinerating both himself and his house, but something had gone wrong and he had managed to escape the fire.

FLIES

There have been a lot of flies around our house lately, and I've noticed that they're moving very slowly. When one lands on my skin it takes forever to leave. These flies linger on surfaces such as windowpanes and lampshades for so long that it makes it very easy to kill them. I have no idea what their slowness means, either for them, or for me. Perhaps they are depressed. All I know is that it gives me a longer time to observe the so-called compound eyes of the fly, which, like our hearts, are made up of thousands of miniscule jewel-like parts called facets. And I get a better look at their glowing bodies, which are like miniature, green satin ball gowns.

FLIES, SUICIDAL

This morning I came across a fly holding between its two black front legs, which were as dainty as a baby's eyelashes, the tiniest razor blade I have ever seen. The fly kept reaching back and slashing at its wings, murmuring over and over again Kurt Cobain's words, *I hate myself and I want to die, I hate myself and I want to die.*

Things can't be all that bad, I said, patting the fly's glossy, emerald-green hunchback. Gently, I took the miniscule blade from the fly, in the process cutting one of the wavy lines in my fingertip. Although I could not be sure, I thought I detected a smile on the fly's face, if it even had such a thing.

FLOOD, THE GREAT

I think my favorite story in the Bible is the one about the Flood. It happens early on if I remember correctly, very early, in the first few pages, and to be honest I've always thought it a bit funny that God decides to destroy all flesh (even the creeping things!) so early on, but still, I suppose he had his reasons.

There are so many great parts in this story that it's hard to pinpoint why it's so good. I like everything about it, for example, the whole business with constructing the Ark—out of gopher wood, no less—and how specific God is in his instructions to Noah regarding the dimensions. God's highly specific. And I like how everyone thinks Noah's a crazy old fool, a very old fool—when the Flood finally comes he's six hundred years old—but then when the waters actually arrive, of course everyone wants to get in the Ark. But they obviously can't, because of the business with the pairs, only one pair of everything.

And when the waters rise and don't stop rising, of course it's exciting. I think that's what I like most about the story. It's extremely visual. You can really see everyone getting blotted out. Ever since I was a kid I've had a very clear picture of this.

I remember in first grade, when it rained heavily, the courtyard of my school, Our Lady Queen of Peace, would often flood. And on those days, when morning recess or afternoon recess or lunchtime came, we'd leave our desks in an orderly fashion and file into the hallway, where our raincoats and rain hats and galoshes were hanging on hooks spaced at regular intervals. We would put on our bright yellow rain gear as quickly as we could and run outside to play and splash in the rain, which filled me with deep delight.

As we played, I liked to imagine that the Ark was passing by, bobbing on the water, and that I could see the animals in the Ark, their faces pressed up against the windows. Our parish priest Father Lions had made it perfectly clear that when, once again, the rains refused to stop and the waters steadily rose until they covered the earth, our rain gear would be of no use to us. I could picture exactly the big buttons on my raincoat coming undone from the force of the rushing water, and my galoshes slipping off my feet. And long after I and everyone else had drowned, I could see all our yellow rain hats, floating brightly on the water's flat gray surface.

In the actual story, it's nice when the waters gradually recede. Even today when it stops raining, I can almost imagine how Noah must have felt, filled with unimaginable hope and unimaginable dread. How organized everything must have seemed, the world so quiet and empty, and everything in it divided neatly into pairs.

FLOOD, THE NEW ORLEANS

In 2005, two days after Hurricane Katrina hit the city of New Orleans and the levees broke, flooding the region, President Bush flew over the submerged city in Air Force One, which is like an Ark with wings. He saw all sorts of things, from a height of only 2,500 feet. He saw the people stranded on their rooftops waving at him, so he waved back. He saw people using their doors as if they were rafts, paddling down the wretched waters like Jim in *The Adventures of Huckleberry Finn*! He saw a very dark skinned black woman and an albino woman wading through the filthy waters lugging a big stolen television. Even the open-eyed corpses floating through the stinking waters on their backs seemed to smile and wave at him. And he waved back.

FLY SPRAY

Nothing is more nostalgic to me than the image of my mother with a can of fly spray in one hand, spraying the toxic gases in the air, clouds of it lingering, like the harshest perfume, and with a big blue or pink flyswatter in her other hand, batting the flies' bodies against the windows, making tiny bloody stains and leaving bits of their wings on the windows' lace curtains.

Sometimes I dream that in the middle of the night there is a knock at my door and a young man is standing there, wearing nothing but the soft metal odor of fly spray.

FOOTBALL, AMERICAN

One can never truly know a football player. Every time his self appears it is almost instantly obscured by his big shoulders and his huge butt. Ontologically speaking, he is erased by his voluptuous butt.

FORGOTTEN, BEING

The one thing we can all be certain of is that we will be forgotten. Somewhere, not far from here, these words are already being erased. Although this is a bit depressing, the futility of this effort, of any effort really, is also somehow freeing. If I had really wanted to be remembered, it would have been better to have never been born at all. My chances for posterity would have been much higher if I had arrived on this earth in the form of the bullet that the poet Paul Verlaine fired into his lover Arthur Rimbaud's thin wrist on July 10, 1873. What a lucky bullet, to spend a whole week inside Rimbaud! It would have been far more profitable to have been the tree whose branches eventually became the crutches Rimbaud required the use of after his leg was amputated, on May 13, 1891.

FRA ANGELICO

I'm a great admirer of all of the work of the painter Fra Angelico, who was a Dominican monk who covered the walls of the monastery he lived in during the 15th century with gay pornographic images, but I especially like *Young Man Kneeling at the Urinals Waiting for a Fat Businessman* and *Man Fingering Himself upon Entering a Precariously Slippery Shower.* Both works are primarily religious in nature. One cannot help but admire the painter's restraint with gold leaf. In the latter work, everything is bright blue and gray and bright red except for the man's asshole, which is gold. In the former work, there is a just a trace of gold leaf, pooled at the bottom of the urinal.

FRECKLES

When we remember childhood, we recall very little, just those varied precipitations of pigment in the skin known as freckles. Occasionally, certain scenes and moments come back to us, but they are so overlaid with freckles we can barely make out the scene. Freckles obscure memory.

FURNITURE

The reign of Louis XVI, a dull man, 1774–92, saw many major developments in styles of furniture; this was because of his wife,

Marie Antoinette, who had a thing for furniture, and who hired hundreds of cabinetmakers to build furniture expressly for her, new kinds of furniture with nice names like chocolate tables and fire screens (her moans could be heard beneath and above the sound of all the constant hammering).

This period of furniture ended somewhat abruptly in 1793 with a new period of furniture that would come to be known as the *Furniture of Terror.* One of the most popular pieces of furniture during this period was designed by a doctor by the name of Joseph-Ignace Guillotin. Marie requested that the posts and beam of her guillotine be constructed from one of her favorite timbers, either satinwood or rosewood.

G

GAINSBOROUGH, THOMAS

It is said that British portrait painter Thomas Gainsborough hated painting portraits and only did them to make money. He preferred painting landscapes. So, whenever he did a portrait, he spent most of his time on the grass and trees and clouds and rolling hills, etc., and then placed the sitter in last. The sitter was incidental, secondary, getting in the way of all the spaciousness.

Apparently, when he painted whoever that boy was who would come to be known as *Blue Boy,* from time to time he'd stroll up to the boy and whisper things in the boy's ear, like, *If I had my way, I'd take a pair of scissors to all my canvases and cut carefully around the human figures, and throw 'em away, so there'd just be landscape and negative space.* Then he'd spit into the boy's ear.

Yet when you gaze upon this painting, which hangs in Los Angeles's Huntington Library, there's something supremely confident in the boy's pose. From his calm demeanor we sense that he can see further than the eighteenth century, and that he is aware that long after his body and the blue silk and the big bows on his shoes have decomposed, long after even the small buttons on his jacket that threaten to burst with all his repressed feeling disintegrate, he and his image will live on; he and his image will be endlessly reproduced, endlessly multiplied into millions of kitsch and inexpensive reproductions placed in gold gilt frames, like the one in my parents' bedroom, above my mother's bedside dresser.

GAMES

When I was a kid there was a game I used to play: I would gaze hard at the face of one of my friends and try to imagine what it would be like to have his face and to be looking at the world from behind that face. I found this game remarkably easy to play, and I became very good at it.

I still enjoy playing this game today: it is still very easy for me to slip behind the faces of my friends and while away some time there, fall asleep there; but, perhaps due to my increased age, it's much harder to find my way back. Sometimes it can take me weeks to get back to my own face.

GANG INJUNCTIONS

Naturally, whenever I find myself reading about the gangs of cholos in the L.A. area currently placed under injunction—court orders that prohibit all members of a gang from doing certain things, such as gathering together in public places, riding bicycles, owning cell phones and pagers, or wearing a particular football team's jersey—my thoughts inevitably turn toward the Brontë sisters, who were sort of like a gang. After all, there were three of them: Charlotte, Emily, and Anne, not to forget Elizabeth, who died when she was only ten, and Maria, who died when she was twelve. In 1820 the Brontës were similarly placed under injunction when their clergyman father took them to live in Haworth, in the parsonage, which overlooked a graveyard and was surrounded by desolate, graffiti-covered moors.

Life at the parsonage was so isolated and dull that the girls had nothing to resort to but the splendid exuberance of their imaginations. Although they would have probably preferred to fuck up the parsonage and then fuck up the moors, they had to make do with writing down their violent stories in longhand in spiral-bound notebooks.

The Brontës were, in a sense, the Victorian equivalent of the cholo, Victorian gangsters, and although grammatically speaking it would be more correct to use the feminine form here and call them cholas, given the Brontës' iconoclastic relationship to grammar let us stick to the masculine form.

One of the most common and cruelest features of a gang injunction is manifested in the form of a curfew, forbidding the members of said gang to be out between the hours of 10 p.m. and 6 a.m. A boy I used to know placed in exactly this position once told me, *Damn foo, I feel like I'm a cholo trapped in the nineteenth century.*

I lost touch with that boy, just as I lose touch with almost everyone, but I see the Brontës, under the curfew of their century: one's century can be an injunction in itself. I see them playing parlor games and smoking chronic, drinking Coronas and doing needlepoint—the latter bearing heartwarming messages like *THE HEART'S VIOLENCE IS THE BEST FORM OF VIO-LENCE AND MY HEART IS THE MOST VIOLENT* rendered in exquisite Gothic lettering, the text surrounded by a border of hummingbirds with tiny clown faces and thorny, blood-dripping roses. All this activity while waiting impatiently for the sun to shine.

One of the thirty gangs currently placed under injunction in the L.A. area is the Colonia Chiques gang of Oxnard. I'm not sure what the Brontës would have been able to do about this, but I just bet if Lord Byron were around today—though, realistically, the set of conditions we exist in could never create a Lord Byron—upon hearing of the injunction placed on this gang, he would have set sail immediately, just like he did when he heard about Greece and their revolt against Turkey. Upon arriving at Oxnard harbor, which would have been foggy—here and there a cholo's bald head peeping out of the fog—he would have immediately joined in the rebellion of the gang against their injunction. Yet his poor health would surely not have been able to withstand the rigors of cholo life, and he would have died in Oxnard, just like he died at Missolonghi, on April 19, 1824.

GARDENING

Although I do not like gardening in the least, I like it when my boyfriend, Tim, is out there gardening.

Maybe I don't like gardening because my dad was a gardener. Actually, he worked as a fitter and turner at the BP oil refinery, but on the weekends, to make some extra money, he gardened for wealthy widows who lived in big glass mansions on the other side of the Swan River.

As my father imposed some order on the gardens, the widows watched him intently through the dense screens of their black lace veils. Afterwards, they'd pour him a whiskey, and then another. He would keep them company. Their veils stretched across the river, all the way back to our house.

After he was made redundant, gardening became his full-time occupation. Dad kept his gardening tools in the back of our white station wagon. Sometimes I'd dream that I was lying there in the back with him, my head resting on the big bag of fertilizer, and that he was blowing the smoke from his pipe into my mouth, while my thigh was getting cut on the sharp edge of his shovel.

As I was saying, although I have no interest in gardening, my boyfriend, Tim, loves it. Every now and then when he is gardening I go out and join him. While he is busy, I like to wander around, absentmindedly, just as I did when I was a boy in my parents' backyard; I like to look at things, like the spiders and their webs and the insects trapped in the webs. It's somehow consoling to know that there is a miniature world of betrayal out there that is even more intricate and delicate than our own.

Occasionally, my boyfriend even sparks my interest in gardening by saying something exciting like, *The lemon tree is being engulfed by the bougainvillea and the pink jasmine!*

This interest of mine is always short-lived. The only thing Tim can ever get me to do in the garden is watering, which is extremely boring, but if coerced I will do it. The one part about watering that I like is when our dog Frida comes and drinks directly from the hose. Her small pink tongue laps away. I've even had dreams where I am watering, and, just as in real life, Frida comes up to drink. But whereas in real life she'll drink for a minute at the most, in the dream she drinks interminably; it seems her thirst, like mine, cannot be quenched so easily. And sometimes I dream that Tim is gardening, that he's tangled in one of the fruit trees, and I have to stop what I am doing and come out and extricate him.

Dreams aside, in waking hours, Tim is always out there in the garden. I have to say, for the most part, I'm never exactly sure what it is he gets up to out there. I've grown suspicious; he claims that he is out there gardening, but I know what he is really doing: burying things he thinks he needs to keep from me. So, whenever he goes away, I dig up these holes, learn his secrets, and then put them back, exactly where I found them.

GARGOYLES

I've always had a thing for gargoyles, ever since I was a kid and first saw a picture of one, all ugly and hunched, crouched on the edge of the roof of some cathedral in Paris. I like their name, which comes from the French word *gargouille,* which means throat and indicates their function: to drain.

Wouldn't it be weird to get a blowjob from a gargoyle? Although in light of their monstrous appearance it would probably be quite off-putting, I bet they'd be really good at it, and therefore the experience would be both frightening and intensely pleasurable.

The thing that initially attracted me to gargoyles, and continues to appeal to me, is how silent and lonely they are.

I'm not such a loner anymore, but I spent a lot of childhood by myself, dreams rushing through me like rainwater. You could say I felt like a gargoyle, and I believed that my purpose in the world was similar to that of a gargoyle, to be a kind of ornate drain for those dreams.

Even today, when you're behind me and inside me, something about the sound and quality of your moans running through me reminds me of dreams and rain. I feel half-human, half-something weirder and scarier than human. And if I stop talking dirty for a minute, once again I begin to feel like a gargoyle, very quiet and solitary.

GAY LIBERATION

After living seventeen years of my life in the so-called closet—though I prefer to call it *the coffin*—and after finally coming out—though likewise, I prefer to think of this as a process of *unburying oneself*, of clawing one's way out of one's coffin—to finally go out to gay clubs and be amongst my own kind, and to encounter all manner of boys, boys I was not in the least bit attracted to and had to reject immediately, boys I was semi-attracted to, whom I chatted to for a while before inevitably rejecting them, and at times, to even encounter boys whom I was genuinely attracted to, slavishly attracted to, who, noticing my desperation, were swift to reject me, was, all in all, still profoundly liberating.

GAY MUSIC

Surely there is nothing more hideous and depressing than the bland, monotonous, supposedly uplifting house music that is played at gay clubs throughout the world.

Gay men, I beg you: stop listening to this music! There are other rhythms out there that are far more uplifting and far more monotonous. Dance to the sexy beat of my microwave. Dance to the seductively robotic sound of the homeless man at the end of my street sharpening his knife blade.

GAY PORNOGRAPHY

Gay pornography began with my father's discovery that exposure to sunlight turns some things dark.

GAY PORNOGRAPHY, FILMS OF

In his journal, my father wrote, *A good gay porn movie must have basic unity, simplicity, and make several clear points.*

The earliest gay porn films were made by the alchemists in the fourteenth century. The images of the men fucking are technically crude, sometimes upside down; the focus is soft and unsharp, but the images are still obscene and recognizable.

GAY PORNOGRAPHY, MY FATHER AND

While my father sleeps in the living room in his favorite chair, I watch porn on the VCR. When the family dogs were still alive, they also used to sleep on this chair, which is covered in a kind of tweedish fabric. The chair was reserved exclusively for the dogs and for my father. The only VCR in my parents' house is in the living room, hence the necessity of my watching porn tapes in the living room. Although my father is a heavy sleeper, I watch the porn with the volume turned down very low, so as not to disturb him or his sleep, which are two separate things.

It's almost like watching a silent movie accompanied by a soundtrack consisting not of cheesy piano, but my father's snores, which used to disturb me as a child, sounding like something coming from a creature that was not human. His snores no longer bother me, now that I have made peace with the fact that none of us is fully human.

My parents' gay porn collection consists mainly of early

eighties porn, made when AIDS was brand new and still confusing; there's not a condom in sight. As I watch these tapes, the men, most of whom are now dead, look strangely happy: it's as if they are smiling in retrospect; it's as if they know what is going to befall them, and they're happy that for the time being they are still alive. Or perhaps they are smiling a little spitefully, in the knowledge that their pleasure is being stored and recorded for future generations, unlike ours, which is already disappearing.

Sometimes while I am watching, my dad coughs a bit, because even though the dogs, like the porn stars, have been dead now for close to twenty years, the chair has somehow still managed to retain some of their hair.

GAY PORNOGRAPHY, PHOTOGRAPHS OF

In the history of gay pornography my favorite picture is of this one boy, kind of slumped in a trashcan in an alley, his legs open and splayed. His shaggy hair is very dark and his skin is milk-bottle white. In the picture he's wearing nothing but long white socks with two thick, vertical black stripes at the top—the sweet obscenity of knees—and a pair of black-and-white sneakers. The look on his face is one of absolute abandon. There are other photos in this spread, in which he eventually gets ravaged in the alley, but I like this picture of him by himself, oblivious yet expectant. The photo is dated 1980, the outermost tip or extremity of the so-called Golden Era. After the boy died, his parents donated the socks to the Museum of Boys. Experts carefully catalogued the socks before placing them in a glass case.

GAY PORNOGRAPHY, AND U.S. IMPERIALISM

Although many people currently believe that the United States of America is in a period of profound imperial decline, and that proof of this state of decadence can be found in the fact that nothing of any cultural interest whatsoever is presently coming out of the United States, the one exception in this case is gay pornography. In this area, the United States still excels, and produces far more effective and delightful pornography than, say, for example, Europe and its so-called Euro porn. Gay pornography is the one area in which the United States continues to display imperial might; one can present this as evidence that the United States is not in a state of decline, but on the contrary, becoming more powerful by the day.

GENOCIDE

Superstitious, they bury the wings separately.

But first, to begin proceedings, they leave official-looking letters in everyone's post boxes, instructing them to gather in a certain place at a certain time. *Don't bother bringing any belongings,* the letters state at the bottom. Then they cart away their victims in trucks, into the countryside, which is scenic. The people who aren't being taken away watch, curious, relieved, ecstatic.

Before killing their victims, they hack off the wings with machetes or meat cleavers. Sometimes three particularly strong men take hold of each wing and rip it straight off the victim's back. On the corpses you can see the gouged-out places where the wings were once attached. On some corpses, there are the buds of new wings, nobbly, gnarled things, which have been known to continue to grow after death for a day or two.

Some villages, in an attempt to rigorously eliminate every trace of wings, have taken up the practice of burning the wings. In the summer this causes a terrible stink, like burning rubber mixed with sugar. Eyewitnesses say you lose count of all the smoldering pyres lining the sides of the roads. And that nearby there are always bands of wild dogs with numbers painted on them, circling, waiting for the wings to cool down. Some of the dogs don't wait and burn their mouths and quietly howl. They eat only the flesh, leaving the wing-frames.

GERANIUMS

My favorite odor in the world is that of the geranium—not its flowers, but its green, ragged leaves. If God told me that he was planning to eliminate every odor from the world, bar one, and wanted my opinion as to which aroma he should keep, I would be able to reply immediately.

Tim has planted perhaps ten of these plants in our garden. Once a day I find myself rubbing one of the crinkly edged leaves between my thumb and forefinger and bringing my hand to my nostrils. The smell I inhale is dense and dank, yet sweet, somehow reminding me of the smell that at times wafts out of the insides of boys. Even more, the scent takes me directly back to childhood, to summer, playing at dusk as my mother watered her geraniums, the odor rising up to greet us.

The musty odor is probably what a memory itself would smell like, what it would be like if you found yourself trapped in the cool, green chambers of memory.

GHOSTS

The act or action of haunting requires the involvement of at least one human being but does not require the presence of a ghost. Unlike humans, who are forever frightening one another and spooking each other out, peering into each other's transparency, and passing fleetingly through each other's lightness, ghosts are basically indifferent to one another's presence—or more accurately, absence. Similarly, ghosts are not attracted to one another; real love can only occur between a human and a ghost.

Two other common misconceptions. First, ghosts are not white, but pale gray, the same shade as brain matter. Second, ghosts are not made from cotton sheets but from that very fine twill corduroy.

We try not to think of the day when we will die and, losing our last little scrap of opacity, become actual ghosts. Everywhere we go, we try to leave souvenirs of ourselves, reminders; but there is nothing more difficult for a human being (or a ghost, for that matter) than to leave its trace.

GLACIERS

I love all things glacial, anything derived from glaciers, anything extremely cold. Up until now my life has been dominated by the existence of glaciers, which have given my life its sole purpose and meaning, so, when I heard that they were disappearing . . .

GLOBAL WARMING

Upon hearing from an international team of geological surveyors that the Alps were melting, the Swiss government immediately organized an army of 10,000 boys dressed in skin-tight lederhosen. Group leaders marched the boys to the rim of the Alps, promptly ordering them to get down on all fours and to start drinking the ice-cold water.

GOD

Some say God was just a gleaner, collecting bit by bit. You'd always see him down at the garbage dump, finding treasure in goods discarded by others. He saw beauty in broken-down washing machines, in mattresses covered in semen and tea stains. Found buried pleasure in the waste of accumulation.

But others say he came from a relatively bourgeois background and started off with stamps; a prim little boy, he was a run-of-the-mill stamp collector. He moved on to baseball cards. From there, on to buttons (his mother worried he was a homosexual).

Then he began to collect anything and everything: suns and floppy sun-hats, hair ribbons and sex, dreams and silver drains, Holocausts and hubcaps, desire and desire, species, species, species. He was a regular at Christie's. He was a rabid collector, collecting rare things until he was foaming at the mouth with categories.

Until one day he legally had enough objects to constitute a world.

GODMOTHERS

My godmother, Mrs. Ida Pearson, lived two doors down from us. She was born in Sheffield, a city situated in the north of England, and she told me that everything was softer there—the accent, the grass, even the water—perhaps to compensate for the difficulty of life in the region.

Sheffield is known for its factories that make silverware, the kind you use only on special occasions. From the age of twelve, my godmother worked in one of these factories. At first she was on the production line that made forks. Then she moved over to the production line that dealt with knives. She said she came to understand how different forks were from knives.

One day when she was fourteen, as the workday was nearing its end, a knife flew into her left eye and blinded her. A doctor took out the ruined eye and replaced it with a glass eye, fashioned from thick glass, like the kind used to make fishbowls, and this eye was unblinking like that of a fish.

My godmother said she could see God much better through her glass eye. She told me that it was like having a window in her, and she was always standing at this window, looking at God, who was constantly lurking just outside the window, looking in at her.

She told me that afterwards she thought she would never marry, and that she would have to get used to living alone in a world with one God and one eye. *After all,* she said, *what man dreams of a one-eyed bride?*

But eventually she did marry a man by the name of John Pearson.

Mr. Pearson did not believe in God. He was profoundly deaf, and if I went over to the house when only he was there, he would not answer the door, as he could not hear their musical doorbell. Whenever I visited, Mrs. Pearson would give me fruit-cake from a gold tin that was very scratched; we'd drink tea out of dusty, dainty teacups. Mr. Pearson never joined us. He would sit by himself, either in their gloomy living room or out on the sunnier enclosed back porch. From the porch he'd watch as my godmother and I wandered aimlessly around in the backyard amongst the pear trees and the fruit flies.

GOETHE, JOHANN WOLFGANG VON

When Goethe heard they were building a concentration camp around his favorite oak tree, the tree he loved to rest against and think beneath, the tree he hoped would provide a little shade for future generations, he quickly wrote a four-volume work in response titled *On the Ruthlessness of Trees*. But as he worked, the sound of all the hammering got to him. So he went to the wood-shed and fetched an ax. Fully intending to cut the tree down, Goethe set out on foot, at night, silently promising that no one would ever think another thought beneath his tree's shade. But somewhere along the way he became distracted and paused, admiring the ease with which the ax trapped the moonlight.

GOSSIP

I thought I had stopped believing in God, probably when I turned fourteen. Yet twenty years later, I find myself having lengthy discussions with him, usually at night, when my boy-friend's away and I'm in bed by myself, just after turning off the bedside lamp.

When I speak to God the quality of my voice is quite particular: hushed yet deep. It's like I'm having phone-sex and trying to sound sexier than I actually am. It's my God-sex voice, a voice I use for no one else. His voice is a little hoarse. Nietzsche made a dramatic mistake: God is not dead, he is just laid low with a cold. Sometimes I think I can hear God sucking on cough lozenges, but very quietly.

All this makes me realize that one never really stops believing in God: it is not a question of belief; one simply stops talking to him.

It is very interesting, then, to pick up the thread of the conversation so many years later. How strange—yet how sweetly predictable! And despite the time that has passed, it feels surprisingly natural, quite convivial. I gossip and chat away with God, just like my mother gossiped with her sister Helen on our olive green telephone.

GRAFFITI

Lately I find that I have little interest in anything, except for graffiti. In Los Angeles, one of the most scenic sections of graffiti can be found along that stretch of the L.A. River that separates downtown from East L.A.

This panorama is best viewed when taking a northbound train from Union Station, preferably when undertaking a journey by oneself, just as I did recently. Graffiti lines the steep, gray concrete walls of the river for a good mile or two. The overall effect is so enthralling that you forget the river; the river becomes secondary (in the future, people will talk not of the L.A. River, but of *the L.A. graffiti;* they will refer to the river disparagingly, how it is an eyesore, ruining the sublime beauty of the graffiti, and they will form committees strategizing as to how to get rid of the river). In fact, as I rode the train and, with my face pressed up against the window, gazed upon the stream of graffiti, I found myself so enthralled that I left the faintest trace of snot on the glass. Just as with the river, I almost forgot myself, but not quite.

Even better than taking in this sight from the train is going for a walk along a section of the river, so you can get a closer look at the graffiti. It is best to take this walk alone, just as I did upon returning from my journey.

As I walked, I felt a bit like Wordsworth (Dorothy, not William) out for a stroll in the Lake District, though surely, I thought, the beauty of that region of England would pale when compared to the beauty of this region of graffiti, which up close was like a deep thicket of hot pink and fluorescent green brambles.

Continuing to walk, I found myself thinking decidedly pantheistic thoughts, feeling very strongly that this was all God: not only the graffiti, but the syringes and the discarded condoms and the empty Corona bottles, even my own awkward body was a part of it all, though perhaps a less important part.

As I paused to examine an especially artistic so-called tag, or signature, by one *Sorcerer,* who had a particularly nice cursive style, I felt an odd affinity with the graffiti. Sensing deeply my own mortality, I realized that to be human is to be, in essence, God's graffiti: something bright and impermanent and squiggly.

I couldn't help but notice all the tags that had been white-washed by the authorities. Big blocks of white paint covered many of the names, but the names beneath were still faintly visible; somehow, paradoxically, the names lingered on, even more exuberant, more defiant, more jubilant than before. We can only hope that when it is our time to be erased, they will similarly not be able to get rid of us so easily.

GRAY, THOMAS

Thomas Gray was an eighteenth-century poet who was very unproductive and wildly ambitionless and had curly hair. Gray precedes the Romantics and is considered to be a forerunner of Romanticism, primarily because he was always depressed and had a thing for cemeteries. He spent eight years working on the poem for which he is best remembered, "Elegy Written in a Country Churchyard"; every day he'd work on the poem in his room at Cambridge, and then every night he would go out cruising in the local graveyard. He liked his men like he liked his scenery, rugged, and enjoyed nothing better than being sodomized whilst licking a tombstone (*it was romantic only in a very partial and external sense,* he said). Often, after his trick had left, he would stay on in the cemetery, looking like a morbid rag doll there in the moonlight, and would begin to feel a little guilty about being a homosexual in the eighteenth century, but would remind himself, *I can fuck all I like amongst the tombstones / AIDS is over 200 years away.* Gray continued working on the "Elegy," crossing out lines and re-crossing, sodomizing the poem, until he was forced to publish it in 1751; otherwise someone else was going to print *a mutilated copy.* But he did write a handful of other poems, all of which are characterized by a fastidious sense of form, like little verbal corsets, attempting (but failing) to constrain something in his heart that was irrepressible. He lived an exceedingly quiet life, rooming at Peterhouse at Cambridge, though in 1757, in consequence of a homosexual disturbance, he moved from Peterhouse to Pembroke. His boyfriend, Henry Tuthill, had been involved in a homosexual scandal and had promptly drowned himself; it is said that Gray was so profoundly embarrassed by this state of affairs that whenever he visited Tuthill at the cemetery, he would blush, and the tombstone itself would blush; death began to seem positively gay. This affair left a permanent mark of melancholy upon Gray's life; as he wrote in my favorite fragment, *Sodomy is sentimental / But melancholy is pink and gray.* In his final years, he turned toward God and toward muffins drowned in Dionysian amounts of butter. He spent the rest of his days thinking about how to annihilate the hours, until 1771, when his time for annihilation came; eternity opened up, into which he minced his way.

GUILT

Regarding the present moment, we are all guilty, though no one seems even vaguely interested in the verdict or the outcome. I am possibly more guilty than anyone, so guilty that someone has bothered to do this highly realistic drawing of me standing next to a guillotine, my very own guillotine. Rendered in lead pencil, the drawing measures seven inches by seven inches. On my face there is a broad smile, and on the side of the guillotine it says *Alistair's guillotine.*

GUNS, MY BOYFRIEND'S

When my boyfriend, Tim, wishes to avoid doing something, he gets some oil and a soft rag and cleans his grandfather's 12-gauge shotguns. The guns are sleek and long, crafted from metal and dark brown cherry wood. An intricate diamond pattern has been delicately carved into the wood, a little to the left of the trigger. Eighty years old, they are very beautiful. There are two of them, just like there are two of us. I can only hope that when I am eighty years old, I will be as beautiful and as necessary as my boyfriend's grandfather's guns.

GUTENBERG, JOHANNES

In the first half of the fifteenth century, Johannes Gutenberg invented the so-called Gutenberg press, which made printing practical and almost easy for the first time, thus initiating the deluge of words and books we're presently drowning in (the next great flood will be purely textual).

To be perfectly honest, I've read about the method he developed, but I'm not technically minded and don't really understand it at all. It had something to do with moveable letters and led people to believe that everything was moveable. Yet if we have learned anything since then, over these almost 600 years of rearranging letters, it is that some things are so deathly still they do not carry within them even the possibility of movement.

However, there's a picture of Gutenberg and his press that I like a lot and that I think helps me understand. In the picture, the inventor is standing in front of the press, examining one of the proof sheets. But what interests me the most is the man who is working the press. The man has killer forearms, and it seems the press requires a fair amount of his strength, in fact, the entire weight of his muscular body. Actually, this guy is totally hot, wearing a white cotton shirt with the sleeves rolled up (to show off those forearms), tight, black velvety pants, and best of all, a kind of black pirate hat with gold trim. (In my opinion, he'd look really good wearing nothing but the hat.) Gutenberg himself looks a bit queeny, standing there in his white apron, with his hand on his hip. On closer inspection, it appears that although he is checking the proofs, he also has one eye on the boy, who is the kind of boy anyone would want to invent something for. From looking at this drawing, I think I begin to understand the Gutenberg press perfectly.

ℋ

HAIR, BODY

It has been well documented that with the appearance on the horizon of the AIDS epidemic, and with the subsequent disappearance of the species known as the *gay clone,* gay men, associating body hair with clones, and therefore with death, began to shave off their body hair, in a frenzy, and in an attempt to make themselves deathless.

Although this attempt to deceive our mortality proved to be as futile as Thetis's efforts to make Achilles immortal by dipping him in the River Styx, in the process, we became as smooth as the sculptures of Praxiteles, which were famed for their life-likeness.

Equally drastic changes occurred in the once wildly picturesque landscape of gay pornography. Whereas much of that vintage so-called pre-AIDS porn took place in nature, and the majority of its actors were very hairy—so much so that one feels as if one is observing a document filmed not in the distant decade known as the 1970s but during an even more distant epoch, for example, the Pleistocene era—early-AIDS and post-AIDS porn rejected nature and moved inside. The majority of this porn takes place in pastel bedrooms and crème living rooms; there are lots of glass coffee tables, and the men are as smooth, though not quite so transparent, as these coffee tables.

But, in the meantime, what happened to all that hair? It is not generally known that in the early 1980s, that period of economic savvy, enterprising entrepreneurs in polka-dot bow ties found a use for the hair. They began to collect the hair en masse and ship it off to warehouses in El Salvador. They went so far as to visit the morgues and shave the bodies of dead clones.

This hair was and continues to be used to stuff pillows and eiderdowns.

It is more than likely that you are sleeping on the hair of gay men, some of whom are still living, some of whom are long gone, but this probably has nothing to do with those nightmares you have been having.

HAIR, BODY, THE BEGINNING OF MY

Hairs first began to sprout on my legs at the end of 1983, the summer I turned twelve. I was, to put it mildly, disconcerted. I remember going into the kitchen to complain to my mother, who was peeling potatoes at the sink.

Intending to cheer me up, she took me to the bookcase in my brother's room and pulled out one of her old *Glamour* annuals, which contained interviews with various Hollywood movie stars from the 1940s and '50s.

She turned my attention to an interview with the actress Betty Grable. According to this interview, Betty Grable seriously loved hairy men, particularly men with hairy chests. *I haven't a clue why, but I'm just crazy about them,* she claimed. The actress actually went so far as to say that she was *slightly repulsed by men who didn't have body hair.* Before concluding the interview, she stated (with a wink!), *I wouldn't dream of dating a man who didn't have some hair on his chest.*

Upon learning of this, I immediately returned to the kitchen, took a pair of scissors out of the drawer, and went outside. Sitting on the back steps in the warm sun, I proceeded to cut the hairs off my legs, going directly against the desires, the orders, and the directives of Betty Grable.

HAIR, BODY, DREAMS ABOUT

Ever since this incident with the scissors, I've felt somewhat ambivalent about my body hair. But this is changing. For example, recently I had a dream where I met the pop singer Justin Timberlake out at a club. Actually, it wasn't Justin Timberlake per se, but a version of him, a kind of cover version of him. (Similarly, in dream, whenever we encounter ourselves, it is not our actual selves that we are encountering, but cover versions of ourselves. Unlike cover versions of songs, which are generally mediocre versions of the original, these cover versions of the self are far superior to the actual self.)

As I was saying, I met Mr. Timberlake, whom I am by no means a fan of—either in dream or out of dream—out at a club. He looked a bit different. His hair was darker, and I noticed he had a very hairy chest. Afterwards we drove home together, and I kept on looking at the hair creeping out from the neckline of his T-shirt, but I tried to ignore it. I told him that I loved the color of his car, and asked him what color it was. He replied *warm rabbit-fur brown.*

This dream was sort of like a Socratic dialogue (except with Justin Timberlake—actually, more like a Socratic dialogue with myself) in which I questioned myself about my own opinion, and then the dream took over and asked more questions, ultimately showing me how inadequate my opinion was, and helping me go beyond my opinion, i.e., if Justin Timberlake doesn't shave his chest, maybe I don't have to. Maybe Justin Timberlake and Betty Grable (and my mother) are all correct. Dreams are instructive.

HAIR, BODY, THE RETURN OF

And one must remember that in the grave our body hair will grow back quickly, so quickly that our corpses will be unable to shave it off, and if the state confiscated our electric razors and our disposable razors and our Nair hair removal, our hair would return and carpet our bodies like wildflowers in spring: we would all be a little more mortal; we would all be clones.

HAIR, DYED

My mother dyes her hair red. She began dyeing her hair red in 1943, when she was fifteen, and the Holocaust was already well underway. That year she also read Jean-Paul Sartre's *Nausea*. Suddenly, the business of dyeing her hair took on great meaning, especially the waiting for the dye to set, the anxiety over the outcome of the color. In 1945, when WWII ended, to celebrate, she dyed her hair a shade redder than she normally dyed it. She knew she was running a risk, but in the context of the end of the war, and sailors, such brightness could be overlooked.

After the Holocaust, my mother continued to dye her hair. Once a month, she bought hair dye from the local chemist's. Leaning over the basin in the bathroom, she would apply the dye with a soft brush and then occupy herself for an hour. While she waited, she'd make herself a cup of tea, watch a daytime soap opera, or read a big-print mystery. There was a science to it.

These days I am told she goes to the local hairdresser's, where a nice girl does her hair for her.

Heredity is the process, small and mysterious, by which living things inherit characteristics from their ancestors. My three sisters all dye their hair red: in my family this is the limit of resemblance.

HAIR, GRAY

Before too long, I may have to go get a blue rinse or a lavender rinse, like my godmother. Or I will also have to dye my hair red with such cunning that *no one can tell,* just as my mother does on a monthly basis. From that day on, passionately, I shall correct my identity.

HAIRCUTS

Interesting things happen when you get a haircut. When I was a kid, I remember more than one occasion when the barber cut my ear with his bright silver razor. Once, to distract me, he gave me a copy of *Playboy* and turned it to the centerfold, which I stared at while my ear continued to bleed steadily. Today, whenever I go to the barber's to get a so-called crew cut, I often think about Joan of Arc and everything that resulted from her crew cut—being burnt at the stake, etc.—and I worry that, just like hers, my crew cut could also have unforeseeable consequences. My barber gives me good advice and says things to me like, *Homie, no need to flinch from the blunt side of my blade.* Generally the aftermath of my haircut is less dramatic than that of Joan of Arc's, but there is always a deep depression that immediately follows a haircut.

HALLOWEEN

If you look closely at my body, you will see that it has been produced cheaply in a factory; it has an edge, and a bit of elastic at the back, like a long and scary mask.

HANGING ONESELF

We've all got necks and we've all thought about hanging ourselves, at one time or another. We've all gone to Home Depot and spent far too much time in the section where they sell lengths of rope. I gave up on the idea of hanging myself years ago, realizing that in my case it was just not practical: there was simply no length of rope in the world that was long enough for me. While one end would have to be tied around my neck, the other would have to be secured to the moon.

Still, the other night, out of curiosity, and for old time's sake, I hung a noose from the highest, sturdiest branch of the peach tree in our front yard. Although I quickly gathered that I would not require its use, and that a rope had failed me yet again, I left it hanging there, to save myself the bother of untying the knot. I wanted to keep my options open; *and after all,* I thought, *the rope could very well come in handy for someone else.*

HARDY, THOMAS

In the novels of Thomas Hardy, the effects of the second wave of the industrial revolution on rural England can be seen everywhere, particularly in the more efficient forms of sadness emerging in humans; there is an increasing speed to his characters' melancholy.

Yet the grayness of the English landscape is being constantly and exuberantly interrupted by the simple movement of young farmers taking off their breeches, bending over, and exposing the bright pink of their assholes, which pierces through the gloom, suffusing the landscape with a shade Hardy called *bonnet pink.*

HARDY BOYS, THE

As a boy, I enjoyed reading about the exploits of the Hardy Boys, particularly any story in which the swarthier of the brothers, dark-haired Frank, who was older by one year, was kidnapped, taken to a mansion, blindfolded, and bound to a chair that was usually placed in front of a grandfather clock.

I also enjoyed their *Detective Handbook,* in which I learned that asshole printing was the principal means of positive identification for boys, particularly boy criminals. In the chapter titled "No Two are Alike," I discovered that the asshole of every boy is unique, and that although many assholes are similar, none are identical. One Marcello Marpighi, an Italian professor of anatomy and pornography, stumbled upon this fact in 1686.

The chapter also explained that there were eight basic asshole patterns; I have retained a memory of all eight patterns to this day, my favorite ones still being the classic *plain whorl* and the denser, more intricate *accidental whorl.* Sometimes criminals, like the infamous John Dillinger, who was seduced by the

FBI in 1934, tried to erase their asshole prints by burning their assholes with acid. However, at the FBI there were thousands of gray filing cabinets containing the inked asshole print of every criminal ever arrested, and these records were classified according to both an alphabetical and numerical formula. On a more melancholy note, I learned that asshole printing was used not only to solve criminal cases, but also to identify boys who had died in airplane crashes and other disasters. *Once a boy is dead,* the chapter concluded, *the specificity of his asshole leaves the world.*

HATS

In many of the photographs taken of my mother as a young woman, she is wearing a hat. Often they're very big hats; I recall one photo where she's wearing a huge, black hat; its brim is upturned, threatening to fly away. As a child, for some reason I imagined that in this hat she looked like Mata Hari.

All these hats were lost to time except for one pillbox hat that was kept in the top cupboard of the closet in my parents' bedroom. It was covered with a sort of ruched material that must have been white once, but had gone gray; the hat had come to resemble pictures I had seen of the brain. When no one was around I would try on this hat and say to myself, *I am wearing my mother's brain.*

I'd often ask her what had happened to the rest of her hats, and she would tell me that she had no idea; a look would pass over her face like the crisp shadow cast by one of those hats' wide brims.

But then my mother's face would brighten. She'd tell me that it didn't matter; when she entered heaven all those hats would be waiting for her, in their boxes. Upon arriving in heaven, the first thing she planned to do was to take those hats out of their tissue paper and try them on, one by one.

HAUSFRAUS

We have visited so many gay men in their tasteful, sparsely decorated houses that we have lost count of both the houses and the
men inside these houses, in which, on first glance, not a trace of
dirt or dust is to be seen; nothing appears to be out of place.

On closer inspection, though, everything installed in such
houses, even if it appears to be clean, is actually residing at the
edge of decay, and everything, while it seems to be in order, in
reality teeters on the brink of the abyss and at the edge of the
higgledy-piggledy.

With these findings, we can safely say that gay men are the
neurotic Viennese hausfraus of the twenty-first century. Though,
in Freud's absence, I'm not sure what we can do about it.

HEAD LICE

One morning when I was in third grade, the health authorities
came to our school. They had us form neat lines on the handball
courts and carefully checked our skulls and the state of our spines,
writing down the results on yellow pads of paper they kept in
their clipboards. Although I was disappointed that I did not have
curvature of the spine, I was elated to learn that I had head lice
and was to be sent home immediately.

That week I spent in quarantine with my mother was the
happiest week of my life. Every day she would wash my hair,
which had been cropped close—like Joan of Arc's or one of those
French collaborators who slept with the Nazis—with tincture of
larkspur, a shampoo that stank of tar. Afterwards, she'd sit me
down at the kitchen table and run a comb with metal teeth
through my hair to brush out the dead lice. Their minute, wing-
less, almost transparent corpses fell quietly onto the sheet of
semi-opaque wax paper she had laid out.

Last night I dreamt that once again I was a child with head
lice. In the dream I could feel their tiny hooked feet clutching at

my scalp and their little beaks drawing my blood. Then, just as my mother appeared, bearing a silver comb and a roll of wax paper, I woke up. It took a few minutes for it to sink in that I was no longer a child, and that I had been cured of head lice; upon realizing this, I sank into a depression that stayed with me the rest of the day.

HEART, THE

I think it's interesting how much the heart can hold. Sort of like a vast handbag. Yes. My heart is like a bloody handbag with crude stitching, hanging from a red leather strap; the strap is attached from the vena cava to the right ventricle. My heart is like Anna Karenina's red handbag, which matches her plush red lips, the one she takes on the train after she's first met Vronsky, on that night journey where she's trying to suppress her delight, but she can't. Let us be more like Anna Karenina.

Just like her handbag, my heart contains all sorts of things: English novels, and paper knives, lots of paper knives. And like Anna, I have a tendency to surrender a bit too quickly to delirium. It seems the heart can hold so much—it amazes me just how much my heart can accommodate—but then suddenly it seems it's had enough, and then? Let us recall Anna Karenina.

HEART, HISTORY OF THE

The history of the heart begins around 1200 AD with the Aztecs, whose complex religious practices emphasized large-scale human sacrifice; this frequently involved ripping out the heart of their sacrificial victims with a big knife made out of volcanic glass, and holding up the heart to the sun, to get a better look at it in the light. I've been a big fan of the Aztecs ever since I was a kid and saw an etching of one such sacrifice. When confronted with the opacity of the heart, what they did seems very practical.

Shortly after, on May 30, 1431, Joan of Arc was burned at the stake by the despicable English; long after she was all ash, her heart refused to burn. Everyone who had come to watch her burn went home, but Joan's heart sat in the near dark, casting a low, squat shadow.

Afterwards, the heart went through a relatively quiet period, that is until the late nineteenth century and the arrival of the author Henry James, whose early novels were fairly simple but whose style became increasingly complicated in a concerted effort to reach his heart, which was red and hard and curved, its elegant lines somewhat resembling the red granite tomb housing the remains of Napoleon at the Hôtel Des Invalides.

In the twentieth century, nothing of great interest occurred to the heart until the birth of my father, and the appearance of his marvelously bleak heart. When he is not using it, he places it on the mantelpiece on a little stand, so everyone can admire it.

And then we must return to my heart. Unlike St. Joan's, my heart is highly flammable. Sometimes I experience this four-chambered organ as something Bach might play, blood pumping out with the melodies; sometimes it hangs there inside me like a red Chinese pear. But then there are those other times, when my heart feels like an impostor, just like the man who uttered, *Louis XVII, c'est moi,* claiming to be the true son of Louis XVI and Marie Antoinette, but who, after all, turned out to be nothing but a clockmaker. After he died his heart was placed behind glass in a royal necropolis; over two centuries, it came to resemble a small piece of driftwood. Now there is a problem: what to do with this false heart?

I need you to drop me off deep in a forest, so I can go searching for the monster that keeps watch over my real heart.

HEAVEN

Very little is known about heaven, except for the following: all wings must be taken off immediately upon entering heaven. Wings are detachable: they are inserted into the wearer's skin on bits of twisted wire, like the wire we used to attach those raffia flowers we made when we were kids. All along heaven's walls there are wing racks, just like coat racks, with hooks spaced apart at regular intervals.

The economy of heaven is built around disposable razors; all inhabitants must work at these disposable razor factories.

There is no carpeting in heaven. This puts an end to those little electric shocks we gave one another in our first year of school. It destroys the possibility of receiving carpet burn when engaging in sodomy on the living room floor. Heaven has a concrete floor. Heaven will be hard on the ankles.

HEGEL, GEORG WILHELM FRIEDRICH

In 1807 German philosopher Georg Wilhelm Friedrich Hegel published his first book, *The Phenomenology of Boys;* it quickly became a favorite of Continental boy scholars. In this book Hegel stated that the historical sequence of boys was crucial, and that various boys represented successive phases in the historical development of boys toward ever-greater stages of cuteness. Hegel taught at the universities of Jena, Heidelberg, and Berlin, though, as he noted, *it was at Heidelberg where I gained my deepest insights into the essential nature of boys, obviously because at Heidelberg the boys were by far the cutest.* Some of his other titles include *Boy (Logic), Boy?,* and *Boys Are Not and Never Will Be Systematic, Even If I Want Them To Be.* More than any other philosophy-lecher, Hegel established the philosophy of boys as a major field of study; no attempt as ambitious as Hegel's has been undertaken since.

HEIDELBERG MAN

Sometimes when I think about the Holocaust I feel that the only way it could have been avoided—and that perhaps it would have been all for the best—was if everything had stopped with the so-called Heidelberg Man, who lived in Europe when it was nothing but glaciers some 400,000 years ago, and of whom there is no record except for a segment of his lower jawbone, found in 1907, near Heidelberg, in glacial gravel.

HELL

Despite all our rather fancy Hieronymous Bosch–like visions of hell—this idea we have that hell will be one monstrously scenic panorama—apparently in hell there is really not much of a landscape to speak of. The surface is flat, like your mother's ironing board, except for a ledge that runs along the length of hell, narrow as a ribbon. There is little variety by way of postcards.

HELL, CHAINS OF

Apparently, when you arrive in hell, first of all they let you freshen up and unpack. You're allotted five coat hangers and one drawer. Once you are settled, the first activity, as it were, that you must participate in is the fitting of the chains that you are to be shackled in for eternity. The chains are not real chains but chains made out of crepe paper, in shades of pink and green, very much like the chains we made on rainy days, when we were children. Once you have been fitted, you are instructed to move extremely carefully, so as not to tear the chains.

HELL, CUISINE OF

There is plenty to eat in hell and after every meal they give out mothballs, those small white balls that fascinated us when we were children, which we found inside the pockets of coats and jackets in our parents' closet, and which closely resembled candy, but were merely deterrents to stop the moths' pale, fluttery bodies from feasting on sleeves and collars.

HELL, PSYCHOLOGY IN

I've got bad news for you! You assumed that when you died you'd finally escape psychology, but no: it seems the discipline of psychology continues on after death.

According to Carl Jung, who is now in hell, psychology in hell is just the same, but reversed. For example, while I am still alive, I am what you would call an introvert in both the technical and non-technical sense of the word. I am shy, somewhat unsociable, and my mental interests are less in people and events than they are in the exciting world of my own inner thoughts. In hell, it seems I will be an extrovert, hardly interested at all in my dreams, and mainly interested in parties and current events. Most likely I will be one of those extroverts I can't stand, outgoing to the point of being annoying. And although currently, while alive, I am also what you would call a narcissist, in hell, according to Jung, I will be far less caught up in myself and far more considerate of others. People who didn't like me on earth and thought I was self-obsessed will like me a lot more in hell.

HELL, PUNCTUATION IN

In hell, I am told, the rules of punctuation are very simple. In fact, there are only two forms of punctuation. I imagine this must come as quite a relief to hell's weary citizens, things already being hard enough.

When one ends a sentence in hell, instead of using a period, one makes a mark resembling the pointy tip of a devil's tail. And if one wishes to emphasize a particularly strong feeling at the end of a sentence, one draws a little pitchfork, standing upright, which basically serves the same function as an exclamation point.

It is interesting to note that pitchforks appear far more often than tails, hell being a place that brings out exceptional feeling.

When one seeks to express one's immortal suffering in hell, one conveys it through short, simple sentences.

There used to be a third form of punctuation, resembling one of the devil's horns turned upside down; this served as the equivalent of a comma. However, it was removed from hell's grammar just over a year ago. At first this resulted in a certain amount of misunderstanding, along with shortness of breath, but people have adapted their style, as people will do.

HELL, TEMPERATURE IN

Remember when you were a kid at the beach on a really hot day, and the sand was so hot, as was the bitumen in the parking lot, that you ran across both surfaces going *ouch ouch,* and in the process burned the smooth soles of your feet? This is what hell will be like. Hell will be deeply nostalgic. Your eternal damnation will be spent walking on tiptoe.

HIBISCUS

The flower I most associate with my mother is the hibiscus. In particular, the dusty pink hibiscus. There's a huge hibiscus bush near where I live, covered in hundreds of these flowers, their petals creased and pink like her skin. It's perpetually in flower. Naturally, whenever I walk or ride my bike past this hibiscus bush, I think of my mother. I think of hundreds of my mothers. All of them with dyed red hair. I imagine she has found a way out of this terrible and beautiful singularity and has been launched into immortality, unlike the hibiscus; whenever my boyfriend picks one of the flowers and puts it in a vase on the ledge above our kitchen sink, these flowers die quickly, always by the end of the day.

HIP-HOP

Once in a while I forget who I am and I think that I'm the white hip-hop bride of Jay-Z, which is funny, because although I love hip-hop's exuberance, and although like so many white males I gravitate toward this music in a concerted effort to forget my whiteness, I don't really like Jay-Z. Yet still, there are times when I am convinced I'm going to marry him, and am almost certain that he's bought me an Oscar de la Renta gown, all beaded and crème, like a heavier version of my mother's wedding dress, and I'm carrying this gown everywhere with me. But even though I'm about to marry the biggest hip-hop artist around, and despite the gown's exquisite beadwork, I'm still really insecure; in fact, I'm positive that before the big day Jay-Z's going to break up with me.

HISTORY

Hegel believed that history was tapering to a sharp point, like the tip of a witch's hat. Doodles of witches' hats can be found in the margins on every page of his lecture notes. *History is a witch!,* he was fond of saying to his students, *and you are history's bitch.*

HOLES, BLACK

At some point humans will no longer use the word *boy*. Instead, we'll refer to young men as *black holes*. I love black holes, those stars that can't bear being stars, like a boy who can't bear the weight of being a boy, and so collapses in on himself, sucking everyone and everything that is around him in, all objects. Surely everyone has known a boy like this, a boy from whom nothing, not even light, can escape. Surely everyone has gotten dangerously close to such a boy.

HOMOSEXUAL

I think I am mentioned somewhere in the Bible, if I remember correctly.

HOODIES

The most significant cultural product to come out of the West in the late twentieth century is what is commonly known as the hoodie, those sweatshirts with hoods that boys and young men wear. Eventually, the only thing our generation will be remembered for will be the hoodie, our most noteworthy cultural achievement, though, in a way, hoodies originated with monks in the Middle Ages, so in this sense we are not even original. Hoodies are illegal in public places in English cities, where video cameras are everywhere, because the wearing of a hoodie does not allow the cameras to see the boys' faces, and thus gets in the way of proper surveillance. The English authorities are acknowledging not only the resplendent nature of boys' faces but also the transcendent power of the hoodie, though a hoodie is really nothing more than a shadow, a shadow worn by a shadow, a shadow that can keep you warm, a shadow you can hang on a hook.

HULA HOOPS

Hegel claimed that he was inspired to become a philosopher when he was just a boy, playing with a hula hoop made out of birchwood, just like the hula hoops the Nazis used in their mass rallies in sports stadiums, where thirty thousand boys would hula-hoop as displays of Hitler's armed might; boys and spectators alike were hypnotized. *Something in the hula hoop suggested the movement of thought,* he wrote. Hegel also claimed that unlike his ex-boyfriend Immanuel Kant—or that *cunt Kant,* as he disparagingly referred to him, who liked to go out walking through the birch forests to get all his ideas—he did his best thinking whilst hula-hooping; in his later years this became a problem: he could not think without his hula hoop. Still, Hegel hula-hooped his way through systematic philosophy and met the deadline for his final book, titled *After My Death,* at five o'clock on the afternoon before the Holocaust.

HUMANS

I think I'm getting a little bit better at being human. I've become more used to that continuous, low droning sound, and to the idea of death, and until death, the fact of duration.

Now that I've finally worked out the system, it's quite easy, even relaxing. At times, life takes on a quality that is almost vaudevillian, structured as it is in a series of short, independent acts.

Though I shouldn't speak too soon: sometimes I get so over being human that I begin to search out other possibilities of what I might be—a dog's muzzle, or a boy's bicycle—and the alternatives look promising.

Hummel figurines

Surely there is nothing more revolting or disturbing than those so-called Hummel figurines, which are much loved by white supremacists and by women of my mother's generation. These German figurines first appeared on the horizon in 1935, two years after the Nazis' rise to power.

Standing four inches tall, these figurines are mainly of plump Bavarian children with chubby knees and fat, rosy cheeks; their swollen heads are usually out of proportion to the rest of their bodies. As a rule, the boy figurines are dressed in lederhosen and alpine hats; the girls wear traditional dirndls and kerchiefs. The children are generally depicted in states of idleness, lolling beneath the shade of a birch tree, or feeding geese, though occasionally they are represented in states of pain (see Hummel figurine number 7,641: boy with toothache).

The Hummel phenomenon was the result of an artistic collaboration between a nun fated to die of tuberculosis, Sister Maria Innocentia (formerly Berta Hummel), and a porcelain manufacturer by the name of Franz Goebel.

It is of interest that although Hummels were immediately popular, they were almost immediately banned by the Nazi Party, on the grounds that they did not adequately represent the "noble Aryan race." However, some historians of the Hummel suggest that the ban was for entirely different reasons, namely that Hitler was deeply unsettled by the uncanny proximity between his misshapen physiognomy and that of the Hummel. Far from being distortions of the German race, the figurines were suppressed for being far too accurate.

Of even greater interest is the fact that after WWII, when workers cleared out the ruins of the so-called bunker, the underground structure in which Hitler took his own life, thousands of tiny fragments of Hummel figurines were found amidst the debris. Despite concerted efforts, the figurines could not be reconstructed.

HUMMINGBIRDS

God, I love hummingbirds! I like how stressed out they are, and how they move their wings so quickly—sixty to seventy times a second—that they look as if they have no wings, like their wings have been amputated or hacked off. Their wings beat as fast as the eyelashes of anxious boys, as fast as we humans tend to think. And their intricate flight patterns are weirdly similar to our patterns of thought: they can fly not only forward, into the future, or hover there, in the present, but they are also the only bird that can fly backward, just as we humans are the only creatures so hopelessly committed to thinking backward—that is, to remembering. It seems like all hummingbirds can think about or care about is nectar, and if they couldn't get it, they'd kill themselves, slit their tiny violet throats. At night they must collapse into a state of honeyed torpor. Always on the go, on those rare occasions when you see a hummingbird pause on a branch, to take everything in, it really doesn't resemble itself.

HUNCHBACKS

The moon's been hanging so low in the sky lately that I keep hitting my head on it. I'm beginning to develop a stoop. Its *starkwhitebrightness* gives me a headache. I bet if you licked the moon, it would taste like aspirin. Soon we will live on nothing but aspirin. Soon we will all be hunchbacks.

HYDRA, THE

I have nine voices, all of them terrible, just like the dreaded Hydra and her nine heads. Whenever I encounter any one of my voices, they horrify me; I'm turned to stone, like those who gazed upon the Medusa. Whenever I cut off one of my voices, two more voices grow back in its place. To truly kill these voices I have to behead them, one by one, and burn the neck of each voice, but then there is the one voice that refuses to die; to do away with my immortal voice you'll need to bury it under a heavy stone.

$\mathcal{I}$

I

Naturally I resent every letter in the English alphabet, but there is no letter I resent more than the letter *I*. In fact, this so-called letter is not a letter at all. It is nothing but a mask, like a plain white mask one wears to the Carnival in Venice; and just as in porn director Kristen Bjorn's *Carnival in Venice,* what the *I* conceals is obscene, pornographic.

However, as much as I dislike the *I,* I am fully aware that it is essential: like a sea green mask worn by a surgeon in an operating theater, it protects not only the wearer, but also everyone around him. One needs this mask, one requires the services of this letter and cannot live in the world without it.

IDENTITY
Scalpel.

IDENTITY THEFT
Whereas everyone else in this country seems concerned about identity theft, I am, on the contrary, intrigued by it, vaguely titillated by it. I hold out hope that someone will come along and relieve me of the burden of my identity, so I will finally be able to do what I have always wanted to do: replace my identity with

another identity, or better yet, just leave it empty and continue happily with no identity. It seems, however, that my identity does not appeal to these identity thieves; they are not attracted to my identity, which is homely and is forced to wait all lonely in the wings like a wallflower at a country dance.

In the meantime, just as a teenager I practiced kissing in the mirror, I now commit identity theft against myself, nightly.

IMAGINATION
Leave the cage door open.

IMPOSSIBLE, THE
There are periods of life when nothing interests me, other than the impossible. Up until such times, I am interested in other things, but I subsequently lose interest, and the impossible becomes the only thing I am interested in.

INDEX LIBRORUM PROHIBITORUM
Begun in 1559, the Index Librorum Prohibitorum is an official list of books the Roman Catholic Church strictly forbids its members to read, considering these books to be antithetical to the Church's teachings. In the Vatican there is a library housing every one of these books, staffed by young priests. More than anything, I want my book to find its way onto a shelf of this library, a very high shelf, a shelf so high that whenever one of the young librarian priests has to retrieve my book, he will be forced to stand on a little ladder, and whoever is below will be able to look up his robe. I keep sending a copy to the Vatican. I even had my mother write a letter, the gist of which was *My son's book is evil,* signed not only by my mother, but also by our parish priest and the parish's choirboys, and I enclosed the letter inside the book. But the Index keeps on sending it back with a letter of their own saying that they don't think my book is antithetical enough. They aren't fully convinced that my book poses a real threat to the faithful and the devout.

INDUSTRIAL REVOLUTION, THE

My favorite epoch of sodomy occurred between 1760 and 1790, when men tended to crowd together, and there was a rapid expansion of sodomy, a speeding up *in the rate of sodomy itself.* This was the result of using both science and capital in solving the problems of sodomy. Sodomy was completely changed by steam. Observing the men who worked in the factories of Sheffield, Engels wrote that *soot and dirt cover their faces and hands like the grimmest form of glitter.* Young men subjected to serious social evils, wearing nothing but black silk top hats, sodomized one another against a backdrop of smokestacks. Even the machines blushed.

INFIDELITY

What we learn from the character of Oblonsky in *Anna Karenina* is that when you are on your way back home from adultery, first off all, turn down the volume on that cheerful pink glow.

And second, don't bring your boyfriend back that gift of a giant pear. The pear is bigger than Oblonsky's head. His wife, Dolly, having just learned of the infidelity, wants to smash in her husband's skull with the pear. The pear is not mentioned or seen again after page two, but it lingers, rots. We never find out what happens to the pear.

INFORMATION, THE AGE OF

We live in the age of information, an age in which we are all very informed, and in which dead bodies are highly prized, much more than living bodies, because you get far less information from a body when it's alive.

INHERITANCE

My mother has promised to leave me her travel diary from 1956, and some Hummel figurines, and her hot pink dressing gown, and her pale pink nightgown, and then some things that can neither be grasped nor displayed.

It is said that in 1856 my great-great grandfather on my mother's side somehow came into a piece of property in lower Manhattan. To claim the property, he had to sail from Scotland to Manhattan. Violently seasick, he was forced to disembark at the first port and had to forgo his claim.

When my father dies, I will inherit his pipe, and his olive green cardigan, and the love letters he wrote to my mother. I will inherit his gathering silence and the inky clouds in his brain.

INITIALS

Using the jagged edge of a torn-up can of Coca-Cola, I used to carve my initials into the pink and gray bark of the eucalyptus trees in our front yard. I watched as thick, golden sap oozed slowly out of the letters. Once in a while I imagined slitting my wrists with the Coke can, and my mother coming back from the shops, only to find me lying at the base of the tree in a pool of my own blood, my initials above me like the inscription on a headstone, the Coke can placed carefully nearby.

Inquisition, childhood and the Spanish

My favorite period of history is the Spanish Inquisition, particularly the most intensive times, when there were regular burnings, between the years 1480 and 1530. My interest in this period began when I was a kid; in my *Book of Wonders* there was a drawing of one of the Inquisition's all-night torture sessions. Needless to say, I spent some quality time with this picture.

In it, heretics were being stretched out on racks and suspended by hooks. It appeared that the torture was just getting going: one man's tongue was about to be removed from his mouth with pincers; the soles of another man's feet were ready to be prodded and tickled with a red-hot poker that had just been heated over a round pot of fire.

Whereas the smocks worn by the heretics had hems that covered their ankles—out of modesty, I suppose—the inquisitors' smocks barely reached their knees. I recall that one of the inquisitors had very muscular calves. Everyone had a big cross on the front of his smock, like the crosses on the hot-cross buns we ate during Lent. The inquisitors wore smart hoods that concealed their faces, while the heretics wore nice dunce's caps, so-called *corozas,* with bits of blood spattered on them, that exposed both their faces and their grimaces. The face of one of the heretics was shadowed, as if to suggest that he was blushing. The tips of the inquisitors' hoods were so high that they almost (but not quite) touched the torture chamber's smoky ceiling.

INQUISITION, GYMS OF THE SPANISH

As a child I also read up on the Inquisition so I could learn more about it. I discovered that during the Inquisition, especially during the long, difficult cases involving heretics with exceptionally tricky souls, the inquisitors would go and work out, on their breaks, to take their minds off the Inquisition and to release some of the stress of the Inquisition, though, predictably, and more often than not, at the gym, all they could think about was the Inquisition.

Still, the thought of the heretics' fate, or more specifically, the thought of their own relationship to the fate of the heretics, really motivated the inquisitors and pushed them on as they were doing their reps. Yet sometimes, whilst working out, an inquisitor would be so caught up in contemplating the depths of a particular heretic's heresy that the tip of his hood would get caught in the machine, not only posing a risk to the inquisitor, but, because it would take a while to untangle, also causing an inconvenience to the other gym members waiting to use the machine. (Historically, the Inquisition was in many ways a great inconvenience.)

Although historically the inquisitors were members of various gyms, there is one gym that appears throughout the history books, a certain 24-hour gym. Apparently, all the main inquisitors went to this gym, and you often saw them in the locker rooms, wearing nothing but their inquisitors' hoods, displaying their muscular, vascular bodies, discussing various issues pertaining to the latest Inquisition, like the kind of wood that would be best to use for a particular heretic's stake, and how long they thought a certain heretic might take to burn.

According to historians, the heretics themselves did not work out and were either skinny or fat. Between proceedings, it was quite boring; denied a valid gym membership, there was nothing for the heretics to do. Often the boredom became so unbearable that supposedly many heretics began to look forward to going to hell, which surely would not be so monotonous. At the very least, they could look forward to the next torture session.

Inquisition, my Spanish

Some mornings, my boyfriend cooks sausages for me. They make a nice sizzling sound on the hot plate, like the burning bodies of heretics whose souls must be saved.

Inquisition, our Spanish

I wish I had lived during the Spanish Inquisition! However, it is pretty good to be alive right now during the current Inquisition, which is very official, and in which we are all under scrutiny. The look of our Inquisition is basically the same as that of the former inquisition: a lot of hoods and smocks; its methods are very interesting and include attaching men's hands to electric cords so the men think they're about to be electrocuted, but the cord is not even plugged in. Our Inquisition is unplugged, just like those MTV Unplugged acoustic sessions, like the one Nirvana did shortly before Kurt Cobain shot himself, because, as he said in his suicide note, *Psychology has turned the self into an inquisition*. At this point in time, if one is to survive philosophically, one must be a heretic; one must commit philosophical heresy and practice heretical poetics. Historically, whenever there is an outbreak of bliss, an Inquisition appears on the horizon, almost immediately, to suppress the bliss.

INSANE ASYLUMS

When they finally come and take me away to the insane asylum, the walls of my padded cell will be the exact shade of hot pink and made from the very same synthetic material as my mother's padded pink dressing gown.

INSOMNIA

After tucking me in, my mother would go into the kitchen and put the knives to bed, but not before they knelt on the linoleum and said their prayers. Only then would she tuck them into the drawer lined with sticky shelf paper of a gay and floral design. She'd sing the knives some lullabies. But still they'd lie awake, tossing and turning. They had great difficulty sleeping.

In our house the knives were up all night.

INSPIRATION

Quick, before it evaporates!

INSURGENTS

Toward the end of the twentieth century, in an effort to be taken more seriously, homosexuals began to refer to their boyfriends as *partners,* since *boyfriend* seemed too juvenile and insubstantial a term to convey the gravity (and terror!) of a lifelong union. Although there are numerous definitions of the word *partner,* the one that sticks in my mind is *one of two persons who together own a business.* The idea of our love being reduced to a mere working arrangement makes me distinctly uncomfortable. With this in mind, I have decided that from now on I'll refer to my boyfriend as *my insurgent.* Although this is still not quite the right word, and although currently it has other connotations, I like it better, and I think if we all used it, we might be taken considerably more seriously.

INTERESTS, MY

The only machines I'm interested in are the ones that are yet to be invented; the only behavior I care for is the kind that will never be understood; the only feelings I want to feel are the sort that will last a thousand years.

INTERIORITY

Currently, we find ourselves subjected to the seemingly endless chatter of people nattering on their cell phones in public, letting us in on their most banal intimacies, and spilling secret after secret, but this is just a taste of things to come. Soon there will be no such thing as interiority. Everything humans used to do quietly inside themselves will be carried out in public. Our dreams will be dreamt in full view of one another; we will attend other people's dreams like they attended public hangings in the nineteenth century. In each of us, our unconscious will be lewdly on display, like a prostitute sitting in a shop-front window. Our thoughts and fears will be organized neatly for all to see, like those pieces of raw red meat in my butcher's display case. (Whereas our thoughts will be available for purchase, our unconscious will be rented out by the hour.) And our perversions that we once concealed at whatever cost will be set out for all to admire, like the porcelain figurines in my mother's glass cabinet. To get to the soul, humans will have to go very far away, so deep inside themselves that most will die of thirst or exposure long before arriving.

INTERNET, THE

I suspect that death will be exceedingly boring and a bit like being on the Internet, which is also, let's face it, rather boring. Well, it's interesting for a moment or two—and probably death will at first catch our interest—but then very quickly, it gets tedious beyond belief. Just like the Internet, death will not be a space per se; death will be more like *myspace.*

As one searches the Internet—and perhaps we will similarly *search* death—one fades away from life and drifts off into the ether and gets that glazed-out feeling until eventually one just sort of disappears. The longer one stays connected to the Internet— when we are dead we will similarly be *connected* to death—one feels as if one is already dead. In this sense, the Internet is a prelude to—and a kind of dress rehearsal for—death.

INTERNET, PLACES OF INTEREST ON THE

The Internet was discovered in the early 1990s, and one of the most popular *places* on the Internet is the so-called chat room, which is where people go to overcome their crippling loneliness and to meet other people, without ever having to face them or smell them.

Because of this popularity, and due to the severity of loneliness at this point in time, chat rooms can be difficult to get into, but once you are in them you feel as if you could spend the rest of eternity there. In this sense, chat rooms are like coffins, but ethereal coffins, coffins made out of Cool Whip, coffins that are light and airy. Actually, considering the communal nature of chat rooms, it would be more accurate to say that chat rooms are like spacious mass graves.

There are all sorts of chat rooms where people can go to meet people with common interests. If they want, they can even arrange to meet these people in person, face them and smell them. For example, gay men who are interested in getting infected with a virus known as HIV can go to so-called barebacking chat rooms, and suicidal Japanese youths who want to meet other suicidal youths, so they can commit suicide together, can go to group suicide chat rooms.

Although there are specific areas on the Internet that cater to the needs and interests of people with a healthy death wish, the entire Internet is sort of like a plug-in death wish. With its combination of Eros and Thanatos, Sigmund Freud would have probably felt very happy on the Internet; most likely he would have become addicted to it, just like us, and he would have formulated a complex theory, but ultimately would have been unable to cure his addiction.

INTERNET, PRIOR TO THE

Apparently the Internet runs on remarkably few wires. As we speak, birds are busily pecking away at the wires that keep the Internet up and running. Some of these birds are real and some of these birds are fake, just like in Alfred Hitchcock's *The Birds* (which reminds me: I should be more like Tippi Hedren).

Eventually, the birds will wear down all the wires, causing the Internet to break down, and then things will become grim and very lonely; life will quickly turn violent and bloody, just like when the birds arrive in Hitchcock's film. Whether we like it or not, we will have to go back to how it was prior to the Internet.

INVENTIONS

I find the whole notion of inventions somewhat disturbing and kind of creepy. Having a name is bad enough; the only thing that could possibly be worse would be to see one's name branded into a new machine that everyone touches. I can't think of anything more horrible than inventing something with a smooth, shiny surface, a machine that never ceases to work, a machine in which you must constantly observe your own reflection.

(Though perhaps just as bad is the fate of those inventors whose name is immediately forgotten, whose very memory is devoured by the terrible usefulness of their object. Please, I beg you: don't invent anything. If I catch you inventing anything, I will immediately destroy it; I will do everything I can to ensure that no one will ever know how to use it.)

I am interested, however, in the slow distortion of inventions, the way the bonnet was originally designed to look like a Greek helmet, yet its form gradually altered, over time losing all resemblance to the original. I am also drawn toward the blueprints of inventions never realized, especially ones where you can still observe traces of the inventor's tears. And inventions that have been gently vandalized or defaced with graffiti are, of course, splendid.

What interests me most is when inventions become obsolete almost immediately, the quicker the better, and said objects are placed out on the curbside, left to fall slowly into a graceful state of disrepair, left to rot in direct moonlight.

INVENTORIES

The world is made up of nothing but sorrow. (Except for this birdsong, sweet knives, just to the right of me.) The world is filled not only with objects, but *death objects*. And I have been assigned to take inventory.

IRA, THE

As I watched the news report in which Gerry Adams, leader of the Sinn Féin, announced that the Irish Republican Army was renouncing violence and decommissioning its weapons, I found myself growing deeply nostalgic, associating as I do the violent heyday of the IRA in the 1970s and early '80s with the violent heyday of my childhood, so much so that the memories blur and mingle, explode into one another.

When I recall childhood, I recall the hunger strikes I went on, just like Bobby Sands, except I wasted away on nothing but red meat and refined sugar. I recall the bombs that were detonated as I opened kitchen cupboard doors. And how Adams's bright red beard tickled me when I kissed him goodnight. Most of all, I remember my mother, how kindly and gentle her eyes looked through the little slits of her black wool ski mask. And how soft the wool of her green ski mask felt against my smooth face whenever she held me.

So, when Adams made his public statement, I felt deeply betrayed, as if he were announcing that he was decommissioning memory.

Unlike Adams, I will never renounce the bright violence of my childhood.

IRONY

Whenever anyone is not blushing in *Anna Karenina,* he or she is being ironic. In the men, irony mainly takes place beneath their mustaches, though sometimes their calves are ironic. For the women, irony is associated with childbirth, with household budgets, with evening. Every now and then irony and a blush will occur in the same sentence, but always in that order, for the blush dissipates, dissembles the irony. Irony cowers when faced with a blush.

No one excels more at irony than Anna herself, who is like Socrates in a ball gown. She is the only character who is able to blush ironically. She is the only one whose irony can withstand a blush. Her irony is so refined it is capable of destroying blushes. To distract herself from her pain, she has gowns made to order, sewn out of yards and yards of irony.

ISOLATION

Isolation is good. Any boy suspected of carrying the imagination will be forcibly detained and placed under the brightest quarantine, for a period of time.

J

JACKSON, MICHAEL

Although in regards to mishandling the boy with cancer, Michael Jackson was found innocent in a court of law, and upon leaving the courthouse made the statement, *I am innocent and I will always be king,* my twelve-inch-high Michael Jackson porcelain doll has just been found guilty in a court of dolls and will be executed tomorrow right before dawn.

JAMES, HENRY

Unfortunately, I don't really have anything to add to the discussion on Henry James, except that when I read his sentences for some reason I think of hooks, tiny hooks, like the hooks that can be found running down the backs of curtains. I imagine him composing his sentences out of these hooks, whose minute prongs are just the right shape and size to plunge into his characters' psyches; I see him at the end of each day, his fingers raw and bloody from working with such fiddly, tricky hooks.

As I peruse the work of James, I also recall one of my train journeys, during the course of which I had a conversation with a cholo by the name of Ricky, who had a tattoo of roses around his collarbone, and salmon pink bandages on his legs, but who never disclosed to me the reason for the bandages. Toward the end of the journey, which was long—the train had been somewhat delayed—as downtown Los Angeles loomed in the near distance, Ricky said to me in a manner that was distinctly Jamesian, *Downtown, you can get up to anything. You can find individuals of all persuasions and appearances;* as we parted I found myself wishing that our train had been delayed endlessly. (Of course a cholo into Henry James would be the ideal.)

And of course, upon opening one of James's novels, I think of the obvious: his loneliness, and his exceptional forehead, that marvelous cold marble church dome of a forehead. I envision him on those particularly desolate nights, at a loose end, lining all his books up in a row, from left to right—beginning with the least difficult and ending with the most difficult—trying not to think about boys, yet every now and then failing and wondering if his ideal could be waiting out there only for him, a young man, the intricacy of whose beauty would not match but exceed the intricacy of James's own melancholy. However, on the whole, I imagine James successfully avoiding the subject.

JERSEY

In 1958 my parents went on their honeymoon to the island of Jersey, which occupies an area of only forty-five square miles in the English Channel, and which is known for its buttery cows and its Nazis, who occupied the island between the years 1940 and 1945.

While my parents were there, they went on a tour of a dairy. Some of the cows were gray and dark fawn and almost black, while others were reddish brown, the same shade my mother dyed her hair. There were big silver canisters full of yellowish milk; as they walked, my mother saw her reflection everywhere: a bride, multiplied. When the workers weren't looking, my father scooped the cream from the top of one of the canisters.

I remember finding in a shoebox at home a postcard from their honeymoon, with a picture of some cows on the front. On the back, written in lead pencil, in my mother's hand, there was a note of a dream: *Dreamt that I lost my veil.*

Below this brief account of my mother's dream was the postcard's description of the cows: *Notice how the horns curve inward.*

JEWELERS

The task of erasing one's self is painstaking. There are many little sides or facets to self-destruction, and each facet must be polished and cut to exactly the right shape and size. If one wishes to destroy oneself, one must be a diamond cutter, like the kind they have in Belgium; one must have a steady hand and a jeweler's eye.

JOAN OF ARC

We need to burn Joan of Arc again. We need to give her another haircut, but this time, let's make it half an inch shorter. We need to make sure the flames rise higher, yapping suddenly at her ankles like small orange dogs climbing out of volcanoes, and we need to make the flames stylized, like those painted on the side of a cholo's lowrider. We need to rewind Joan of Arc. We need her to defeat the English four more times, and then we need to mark the spot where the stake stood in the marketplace at Rouen with a statue, but this time place it a little to the right. We need the Burgundians to sell her to the English for 17,000 francs (not 16,000 like last time), and we need to place peaches on the pyre. We need to condemn her and then just as before we need to turn away from the dreadful sight.

JOCKSTRAPS

It is not until one observes one's jockstrap hanging on the back of a chair that it sinks in that one is mortal, and that long after one is gone, one's jockstrap will remain, off-white, somehow skeletal. It is only then that one fully realizes the harsh and profound melancholy of the jockstrap.

JOURNEYS, SEA

My mum and dad tried living first in Motherwell and then in London, in a little basement flat. But my mother missed her sisters. In 1962, with their two young ones—Rory and Fiona—my parents took the slow sea journey from Portsmouth to Perth, Australia. It took four weeks and cost the family of four twenty pounds.

My mother tells me that to pass the time she knitted. She spent a lot of time washing the salt out of her curls. Sometimes she dreamt that her wool was getting tangled with the waves. And that the world was full of tiny portholes, just like the ones in their cabin, and if you wanted to escape the world all you had to do was smash the glass in those holes.

JUPITER

Like Jupiter, the heart has extreme gravity. You're so much heavier on the heart. It has some red spots on it, some unusually red, and you can never see the heart because it is covered in violent gases.

In this sense, Sappho, in her explorations and expeditions into the vastness of the heart, was the first astronaut. She faced many dangers, the chief one being the impossibility of escaping the heart. Of all her discoveries, the most significant was that love would never dream of inhabiting the heart, which is basically uninhabitable.

Notice that Sappho's helmet flattens her curls. Look at her staring out the window of the rocket, how pale and solemn her face is through the glass.

𝒦

KAFKA, FRANZ

When I think of Kafka, which is often, I never picture him writing. I prefer to think of him doing mundane things, like working in the moderately sized asbestos factory of which he was part owner for four years, his feet up on the desk, doing a quick sketch of an asbestos nightgown designed especially for his mother, telling the workers not to weep on his machines. This job supposedly ruined his lungs and probably led to his early demise from tuberculosis at the age of forty.

I also like to think about him in his last days at the sanatorium, his temperature rising in the late afternoon, and his cough, mournful and melodious, as if his lungs were an accordion playing the most unheard-of music. The kind of cough that lacerates the listener's heart.

Some of the thoughts I have of Kafka are decidedly impure. I blush easily (did Kafka blush?) so I don't want to go into detail, but let me just say that afterwards the pages of my copy of *Die Verwandlung* are all sticky.

Whenever I am asked the question *Who is your type?* my answer is always immediate: Franz Kafka. However, this position is untenable and everyone compares unfavorably because no man is quite sorrowful enough; no man's hips are narrow enough. No one can dance as soberly as Kafka. No one's love is as pitiless.

KAFKA, FRANZ, AFTER

Kafka of course died at the sanatorium in Kierling on June 3, 1924. Hence we live not in 2008 but in 84 AK—*After Kafka.* Yet there is nothing after Kafka: nothing of interest has occurred since his death; everything written since then should be destroyed; and the farther away we get from Kafka, the worse it all gets. However, adjust your calendars accordingly.

KAFKA, FRANZ, DREAMS OF

I've never been lucky enough to dream of Franz Kafka; naturally he makes a highly disdainful ghost, and he would never stoop so low as to enter someone else's dreams. He waits for you at the burnt-out edges of your dreams. But sometimes I do dream of a day laborer who has the face of Kafka and the build of Kafka; Kafka has returned, not as a writer but as a worker, and he builds houses and digs ditches with the same bleak genius, the same gloomy relentlessness.

KANT, IMMANUEL

No journey ever took eighteenth-century German philosopher Immanuel Kant farther than sixty miles from Konigsberg, the town in which he was born. It is said that nothing distressed him more than the idea of travel and that he had a deep horror of other places. Yet every now and then, he dreamt that he had gone far beyond this carefully marked radius. On waking, he would shudder at the very thought of what he referred to as *das Fortgehen,* the going away.

He did like to take long walks though, despite his bad knees, and maintained that all his ideas came to him while out walking: *der denkende Spaziergang,* the thinking walk.

Wandering through the town, he would observe the children as they played with their birchwood hula hoops: a remarkable act of concentration. On sunny days he would go out into the fields and watch the snow melt. As soon as he felt his thought taking flight, he would turn around, so he could go back to work, dutifully separating his thinking from his walking.

KEATS, JOHN

Just minutes ago, scientists in tight white lab coats announced what they now believe to be the first reported death from AIDS: on February 23, 1821, a young porn star who went by the name of John Keats (real name unknown) died of AIDS-related complications in a little room in Rome. Only twenty-five, John had been in the porn industry (or as he liked to refer to it, the honey factory) for six years. He was associated with a certain school of gay pornography known as English Romanticism. The movies that he made between the autumns of 1818 and 1819 have never been surpassed by any other porn star in a single year. The film that launched him to fame was the remarkable *Though I Was Gangbanged I Remain Unravished*. Keats became known for the sublime look of melancholy that hovered upon his face whilst he was being topped. He is perhaps best remembered for the film *I Place Beauty before Any Other Consideration*. Just two days before his untimely death he had completed filming what would be his last starring role, in the controversial barebacking extravaganza *Negative Capability*.

KNIVES

We love all knives: butter knives, miniature steak knives, birthday cake knives. Knives are so useful. We lust after those fishing knives from boyhood fishing expeditions. During the day these knives were used to gut fish, like they were silver Glomesh purses. At night, in the tent, they were pressed against the throat. We have kept these knives; their rusty, serrated edges retain the odor of the fish, like a memory. But we are *in love* with that knife with the mother-of-pearl handle our mother used to open—that is, to gut—airmail letters.

KNIVES, BOYS WITH

There are boys who keep knives concealed on their skinny bodies and then, like magicians, pull these knives, as if out of nowhere. Do not hold this against them.

KNIVES, DREAM LIFE OF

After conducting a number of highly intensive sessions with knives, Freud came to the conclusion that the dream life of knives was unrelenting but limited. It seems that knives dream constantly, but mainly of butter—and wrists, wrists, as far as the eye can see.

KNIVES, VARIETIES OF

There are so many different kinds of knives in the world, just as there are so many different kinds of boys. Most people are surprised to learn that there are in fact more varieties of knives than there are varieties of boys. Yet the uniqueness of each boy demands a certain kind of knife, in particular a distinct kind of blade.

KREMLIN, THE

Lately, during sex, at the extreme moment of pleasure, I've been seeing the Kremlin, specifically the view from Lenin's study. I believe it's the Cathedral of the Annunciation I'm seeing, though it could be the Cathedral of the Assumption. Sex can be as bewildering and complex as all the wildly varied, rather ornate architectural styles of the buildings contained within the Kremlin's walls. Sex is a matter of style. Sex is also very historical. Some of the Kremlin's buildings were built in the late 1400s, while others were built as late as the early 1800s; every man we've ever had sex with is enclosed within us. The Kremlin has been considered by many critics and tourists to be somewhat *over the top,* sort of like porno sex, reminding us that during sex it's good if there is at least one top. (The Kremlin is obviously a top.) There are extreme contrasts in sex, like the contrast between all the lavishness inside the Kremlin and the somewhat stark, threatening outside wall. Sex should be threatening. Sometimes, just like the Grand Palace of the Kremlin was almost burnt to the ground during Napoleon's invasion of Moscow in 1812, during sex we're almost completely destroyed, but in a good way. And sometimes after sex, we feel incredibly bright, just as after Stalin's death in 1953, all the gold domes of the buildings inside the Kremlin were regilded, to make them even more golden.

KRUEGER, FREDDY

After Kafka, I would say that my other type is Freddy Krueger.

Though most of you are already familiar with the former's scrawny, sorrowful sensuality, let me tell you a bit about the latter. Freddy Krueger is the leading man of the horror movie *Nightmare on Elm Street,* the first version of which, released in 1984, sixty years after Kafka's death, is arguably the greatest film ever made in the history of cinema. Ruggedly handsome, Freddy has a sort of burnt face, and wears a fetching, dirty sweater with red and green horizontal stripes. His trademark is, of course, his elegant gloves, equipped with their long metal claws for fingers.

Surely it is more than just coincidence that these two men, the daimonic writer and the demonic hero, share the same magical initials, F. K.

And on further reflection, the two have far more in common than just their initials. Both are thoroughly despondent, abject figures; both are at home nowhere but in dreams. Both men are utterly undeviating, their very names streaked with the brightest kind of violence.

Though whereas the violence of Freddy Krueger's soul is always projected outward, resulting in those long metal fingers tearing nubile teenage boys to shreds, Franz Kafka's violence turns gently and consistently inward.

Lake, Veronica

When I was a teenager I had long hair, and it seems most of my adolescence was spent at parties sitting on the floor with other boys, all of whom had long hair. You could almost reach into the past and drag us by the ends of our hair into the present. For years now I have been getting my hair buzzed short and cropped close to the skull, like a nun's or a collaborator's. I thought that my long hair was a thing of the past; as the years receded, baldness would be waiting patiently for me. But I must have been mistaken, or become confused, for once again I have found that my hair is heavy and long. I have a fringe hanging down over one eye, just as I wore it in high school. Once again I am in the kitchen with my mother, who, in her exasperation, is telling me that I look like Veronica Lake; she's warning me that the actress went blind in one eye, and that if I'm not careful, I will suffer the same fate.

LANDSCAPES

If I were able to return to childhood, the landscape that I would encounter would be primarily flat, like the top of my mother's ironing board, and wonderfully monotonous, the monotony interrupted here and there by slag heaps of corduroy, low hills of pencil shavings, and quarries filled with rotting baby teeth.

LASSOOS

Desiring to forget myself, I went for a walk down by the Pacific Ocean. I walked for a great distance and thought for an even greater distance, but still I could not shake the feeling that I was nothing but a stain.

Pausing for a moment at the edge of the ocean, I caught sight of what appeared to be a lasso. I found a stick and pulled the lasso out of the brown, foamy water. The lasso had been fashioned out of bright red rope and was covered with green bits of algae. When I arrived home, I left the lasso in the sun to dry.

That night, at a club, I met a man with a considerable number of tattoos.

The man gave me a brief yet satisfactory lap dance. As the man danced, I had the thought that I myself was a tattoo, which cheered me up. I noticed that he had a small, green tattoo of a lasso on the back of his left hand. How lovely it is, even if only for a few seconds, when the conditions of life meet the conditions of dream.

LAUGHTER

I like laughing, and I do it a lot. I like how it does strange things to the mouth, makes you want to pull out your sewing kit, get a needle and thread, and sew the damn thing up. Still, I am not wholly satisfied with my laugh. I listen to the crow's laugh and find it far superior; it's the most raw, the most violent form of laughter (though maybe if I really applied myself and put my mind to it, I could offer the world a laugh that is even more ragged, more coarse).

And while we're at it, I wouldn't mind replacing my heart with the heart of a crow, which weighs barely an ounce; I could live so lightly. Surely this weight would be preferable to the present weight.

LAVOISIER, ANTOINE-LAURENT

Although French chemist Antoine-Laurent Lavoisier did not discover oxygen, he did name it, in 1775. He also named his Pekingese dog after the life-giving gas, in 1783. Six years later, in 1789, he wrote *Elements of Chemistry*, laying the foundations of this science as we know it today. Then, in 1794, at the height of the French Revolution, the first modern chemist found himself sentenced to death by the revolutionary tribunal for not being modern enough.

What did Lavoisier think about as he walked up the five wooden steps to the guillotine? Did he think about oxidation, and how terrible it is to be human, with its promise of rusting and of certain decay? Far better to be an element. Did he try to calm himself by repeating his own law of conservation? *Matter can neither be created nor destroyed; when something disappears, it is still there.* Or did he think of nothing, perhaps just his little dog, as he took in big gulps of oxygen?

There is a sublime painting of Lavoisier and his wife, done by Jacques-Louis David. In it, Lavoisier sits at a table, writing with a quill. He is surrounded by the things he loves most: his wife and the glass instruments in which he conducted all his experiments.

Looking at this painting, one almost forgets the abrupt nature of Lavoisier's end. Instead, one's eyes linger on his legs, specifically his right leg, poking out from under the table. It is remarkably long and slender in its glossy black stocking. If he had been born in another place and time, he could have been a Rockette! And indeed, contemporary accounts state that as Lavoisier approached the guillotine, many people remarked on how shapely his legs looked in their pale gray breeches.

LEDERHOSEN

Back in the late eighties, I wore my lederhosen tight. I had just come out, and I had just begun working out, and I wanted to show off my muscles and my butt. Wearing something constricting somehow felt deeply liberating. There was even a brief period where I went around with one strap of my lederhosen buttoned and one unbuttoned, somewhat coquettishly. When I see photographs of this, I blush: my face turns as red as the apples that were appliquéd along the lederhosen's straps. Although I wouldn't dream of wearing tight lederhosen anymore, this continued well into the mid-nineties. Then, I got into hip-hop and began buying lederhosen three sizes too big for me, as was the fashion, wearing them nice and baggy, keeping it alpine gangsta. Now that we are in the twenty-first century, and what with me getting older, I'm not really sure how to wear my lederhosen.

LEGS, MY FATHER'S

There are black-and-white photos of my father when he was in the Merchant Navy, before he gave up the sea. He looks devilishly handsome, especially in his summer uniform; the white shorts display the dark hairs on his muscular legs to good advantage. As a boy I pored over these photos; I spent far too much time scrutinizing my father's legs.

LENZ, JAKOB MICHAEL REINHOLD

My favorite writer is the eighteenth-century German poet and madman Jakob Michael Reinhold Lenz, memorialized in the novella *Lenz,* written by the equally troubled Georg Büchner. Lenz penned odes to Immanuel Kant, hung out with Goethe, and wrote a comedy, *The Tutor,* a play that ends with the hero castrating himself. Lenz also had a habit of tearing his hair out in clumps; he would claim the ragged haircut was not his doing but had been done by *God's scissors.* In an effort to avoid the feelings that were constantly overwhelming him, Lenz would take little walks out in nature, what Goethe called *God Nature,* but even that was too much for his frail senses. In English, the sensation that nature instilled in him translates roughly into *being fisted by*

God. Although Lenz didn't die until 1792, at the age of 41, an obituary for him came out in 1780. For the last twelve years of his life he lived on posthumously.

LIBERACE

It is said that Liberace, in an attempt to come to terms with the Kaposi's sores that covered his body, thought of them as sequins. In the days leading up to his death from AIDS-related symptoms on February 4, 1987, he made numerous references to his sequins, often remarking that his sequins were hurting him. *Yes,* he said in his final interview, *I am disfigured by sequins. I am studded with the strangest, darkest sequins.*

LIBRARIANS

At my library the librarians are very strict and always extremely busy. They look inside every book and check the handwritten names of the boys who have taken that book out. Then they make a list, and they execute certain boys who have borrowed a particular book one time too many. My librarians wear thick, horn-rimmed spectacles and walk around, cutting out the tongues of any patron found talking. Once they're done with this, they get on all fours and start cataloguing lightning.

LIE DETECTOR TESTS

I had been experiencing a moderate yet persistent bout of depression when the invitation—or should I say order—to take the lie detector test, issued by the Los Angeles Department of the Imagination, arrived in the mail.

As I read the document I was so excited that when I closed the metal mailbox, I cut my hand on its corner and bled a little bit over the very official-looking, powder blue envelope. This was just the thing I needed to lift me out of my depression, I thought, even if it was just momentarily, like being lifted on a wave, only to fall again. After all, even the glamour of being forced to take a lie detector test would inevitably wear off. Still, as I walked back up the footpath, clutching the envelope, which, unless I was mistaken, was scented with gardenia—or was it frangipani?—wondering what outfit I should wear to my first lie detector test, wondering what it would feel like to tell the truth, wondering if I had ever in fact told the truth, I could not help but notice a definite spring in my step.

LIPSTICK

Our parish priest would refuse women Communion if they were wearing too much lipstick. He'd give long homilies, referring to the passage in Revelations that mentions the time when there will be only one stick of lipstick left in the world.

Sometimes, after Mass, he'd confiscate the lipstick. He kept the offending items in a metal box above the stove in his house, which was just behind the church. There were rumors that he'd redistributed the lipstick to the altar boys who came over on Tuesdays and Thursdays, who put aprons on over their robes, cleaned and cooked him kippers, and did the dishes. There was talk of altar boys trying out the different shades, coloring in the holy wafers with the shades that didn't suit their complexions, but these are just rumors.

LISTS

I found myself at a club the other night, standing at the edge of the dance floor, feeling supremely unfulfilled, sort of solitary and glittering like a disco ball, when a shirtless young man who happened to be wearing his jeans low, allowing me a glimpse of the sublime aspect of his abyss, came up to me and handed me a list.

At first I thought it was a Billboard chart list, but it turned out to be a list of my dreams. Not of the dreams I have already dreamt, but of all the dreams I am yet to dream, with the title of each dream, the subject of the dream, and the amount of time the dream will take.

LONELINESS

Whose bright idea was it to turn his loneliness into an art? To fine-tune one's loneliness until it is bleak loveliness? Whoever it was, we are indebted to you. This is the most important discovery in the history of loneliness.

LOSS, TOWER OF

The glass tower of loss has one hundred floors, all made out of glass. On each floor, to distract themselves from their loss, boys look up the skirts of the boys on the floor above, except for the boys working on the 100th floor, who have only the sky to look at and who must confront their loss.

LOVE

All tasks are strange and carry with them a certain kind of monotony, but surely this task is the strangest, the most monotonous.

M

MACRAMÉ

The most significant art form of the decade known as the 1970s was undoubtedly macramé, that coarse lacework produced by weaving cords into a pattern. However, some contest this and argue that, on the contrary, mime was the greatest cultural achievement of the decade: mime, that subtle art form in which people with white pancake makeup on their faces, with black markings on their lips and around their eyes, dressed in overalls and horizontally striped T-shirts, brilliantly expressed something, anything, by virtue of movement and facial expression alone, that is to say, mutely, as if their tongues had been cut out of their heads. Although I admire mime—if only I could have mimed this entire book, instead of having written it—I still believe macramé is the higher and purer art form.

In the late 1970s, at the height of macramé's popularity (though some argue that by this point, interest in macramé was already beginning to decline, rapidly, and it had become, in fact, a dead, decadent art), while other children made charming macramé potholders for their mothers, and macramé owls that would serve as tasteful wall hangings, for my mother, using off-white wool, I made a realistic macramé psyche.

MAD COW DISEASE

At the moment, the disease I am most interested in is mad cow disease, otherwise known as Creutzfeldt-Jakob Disease.

I've been a fan of this disease for a while, but I think my interest was really sparked that night I saw the news report about the French teenage boy who had contracted the disease. Although it had not yet been proved, it seemed he probably acquired it from eating hamburgers at McDonald's.

The report showed video footage of the boy prior to his becoming mad, looking bored and sullen, wearing a hoodie and jeans as baggy as cow udders. Although in these images he appeared to be attractive, since he had been infected, he had become devastatingly beautiful.

He lay in his hospital bed, with nothing but a white sheet to cover his skinny, naked body, which was elegantly elongated, like a boy in an El Greco painting. His skin was so pale, almost semi-transparent, like a bar of soap.

Inhabited by an odd glow, he looked directly into the camera. Unlike in the earlier footage, the boy was smiling, and he appeared to be calm, as serene as Christ in El Greco's painting of the Resurrection, though of course the smile and the sense of serenity probably meant nothing, considering that the disease makes the brain as soft as a kitchen sponge and forms holes in the brain.

His mother sat by his side, holding her son's constantly shaking hand. She told the reporter she was first alerted to the fact that something was wrong with her son when she noticed he was crying more than usual.

The report then cut to a paddock of cows, I believe they were of the Schleswig Holstein variety, with white patches on their black coats, like clouds, and horns slanting forward, but curving inward. It seemed these cows had just been tested, and one of the cows had turned out to be mad, so the authorities were going to have to destroy (as opposed to slaughter) the whole lot.

The cows were waiting around in the paddock, waiting to be destroyed, seemingly unaware of their fate, looking as bored as teenage boys, though perhaps they were aware of their fate and simply bored by it.

We were then taken back to a final image of the boy, who, by the look of things, had gone far beyond fate. There was no question of Resurrection. He mumbled something in French, which a voice-over translated as *Take me away from here, to a country where all the boys are mad.*

MAD COW DISEASE, LIVING IN A TIME OF

The French teenage boy with mad cow disease left a profound impression on me. Ever since seeing the report I have stopped eating beef, not out of fear of catching the disease, but on the contrary: I will only eat beef if the butcher can say with absolute certainty that the cut of meat he is selling to me is from a cow infected with mad cow disease. No butcher has been prepared to make such a claim.

MAGPIES

When I was a boy, most of spring was spent avoiding magpies. They lived in the branches of the eucalyptus trees scattered all over our neighborhood; whenever we walked beneath these trees, the mothers would swoop at us, in an effort to protect their newborn babies. Periodically, there were stories in the newspaper of children who had been blinded in one eye as a result of such incidents. Although I carried a rolled-up newspaper around with me, waving it over my head, it didn't deter the vicious birds from coming down, again and again, to thwack their black-and-white wings against my head, wings that were muscular, as if the birds worked out. At best, I got a bit of newsprint on the parts of them that were pure white. There were times I went about with a black umbrella, which worked better.

I knew that these birds wouldn't stop at the eye. They'd peck open your skull with their black beaks and drag out little bits of your brain and your dreams to line their nests, which opened at the side and had a domelike cover, like St. Peter's Basilica.

Although these encounters left me with a certain dread of magpies, not to mention a pronounced fear of spring, I don't hold a grudge against these birds. In fact, today, there are times when I'm out walking, and I find myself almost wishing to be swooped by a magpie. I recall particular instances of swooping and feel something approaching nostalgia.

I also feel somewhat of an affinity with these birds. Perhaps it's because of the delight they take in imitating the sounds of other birds. In the early twenty-first century we have been reduced to imitation; we might as well learn from the magpie and enjoy our mimicry.

Sometimes I just want to retire from the twenty-first century, with nothing but a magpie, keep it in a cage, reform it from its thievish ways, and teach it to speak a few simple syllables.

MAN

The term comes from a Latin word meaning *dark chamber.* A man is essentially a kind of box that light cannot enter except by uncovering the anus. Those men who have too much light in them are basically uninteresting. The device for holding the sensitive memories, like a strip of negatives, is at the other end of the man.

A man is one of the least important instruments of communication and expression. Actually, he is the least important.

"MASQUE OF THE RED DEATH, THE"

The 1985 gay porn movie *The Other Side of Aspen* plays out in a remarkably similar fashion to Edgar Allan Poe's short story "The Masque of the Red Death," which was first published in 1842. Just as the revelers in Poe's story, seeking to sequester themselves away from the red plague, which has been devastating the country for years, party on in Prince Prospero's heavily fortified abbey, the men in *The Other Side* seek solace from the ravages of the gay plague—the so-called hot pink plague, which has been devastating the country for close to four years, and is, in this sense, a new plague—by hiding away in a ski lodge and engaging in an endless orgy.

And just as in Poe's story, where a sinister masked figure arrives at the party, in this porn classic, a guest whom no one knows appears at the lodge—he's somehow gotten through the snow—his identity concealed behind a red wool ski mask. (In the future, all gay porn actors will wear ski masks. The face will be considered un-erotic.)

However, whereas the guests in Poe's story are horrified by this ghoulish masked stranger, who is Death himself, and attempt to turn him away—an attempt that of course in the end proves to be futile—the guests in *The Other Side,* perhaps knowing that there is no longer any point in hiding and that any attempt to do so would be ineffectual, welcome the masked stranger, who is Death himself, into the fray.

McCartney, Alistair

One Sunday at Mass, in the usual hubbub of leaving, a woman who was not my mother took my hand, under the impression that she was my mother and I was her son. I must have been six or seven. I became aware of her mistake almost immediately, and with my free hand I tugged at the hem of her dress, which had flowers on it and was made from a slippery material, like the dresses my mother wore. But this woman paid no attention, and I was too timid to say anything. It wasn't until she got to the door of our church that she realized her mistake. Blushing by the wooden collection box, she returned me to my mother and located her actual son. I remember my mum had a good laugh about the whole incident in the car on our way home.

But maybe I've got it all wrong. Maybe that woman, utterly oblivious, took me to her car, buckled me in, and drove me home. Perhaps on arriving home, she saw that she had taken the wrong boy, the wrong son, but, too embarrassed to admit it, kept me, and raised me as her own, while some other boy went home with my family. That is, I was not returned. I am only under the impression that this is who I am. On that Sunday in 1978 an exchange took place.

McCartney, Andrew

My brother Andrew was named after one of my father's brothers. Uncle Andrew died when he was just five years old. My mother told me some things about him, this ghost uncle, that she had learned by way of my grandmother, Margaret McCartney.

Apparently, Andrew loved Westerns and liked to wander around the streets of Motherwell, Scotland, in a big cowboy hat and with a little lasso. He would traipse around the town, the lasso wound about his tiny hands, the hat slipping down his skull.

Everybody in the town knew him; he talked to everyone. According to my grandmother, *he was such a bright little boy.* People said he had a glow about him. On his walks he lassoed everything he encountered: dogs, clouds, milk bottles, the church, women's under-things hanging on backyard clotheslines.

In the winter snow would collect on the wide brim of his hat. He would go home and hold the hat in front of the stove, watching the snow melt.

One day while Andrew was out on one of his walks, he found a bottle of soda waiting for him on a red brick wall. The bottle was full, not of soda, but of bleach, and apparently Andrew drank every drop.

McCartney, David

My grandfather on my father's side died of a heart attack in 1946 at the age of forty-six. The symmetry of his death unnerved certain members of the family; others somehow found it consoling. He was washing himself at the basin in the upstairs bathroom of his little house in Motherwell, Scotland. Did he have a chance to look up at the plaster statue of the Virgin Mary that stood on top of the medicine cabinet, surrounded by rolls of toilet paper? No one knows, but when enough time had passed, it became a running joke that he died looking up the skirt of a virgin.

When he died it was still early in the morning, that gray hour when milkmen place milk bottles on doorsteps. Was that the last sound the world had to offer David McCartney, the clink of glass against glass? In fact, it was the milkman who first heard the commotion of my grandfather's dying. The milkman knocked on the front door to see if everything was all right. No one else in the house had heard a thing. The children were still asleep, deep in dreams; my grandmother was in the kitchen making breakfast, where the teakettle was shrieking. And the plumbing always made such a racket.

Before he died, my grandfather made roads for a living. He went around with a team, all over Scotland and Ireland, laying the bitumen down to surface and waterproof the roads. He was in charge of painting the white lines down the center of each road. I am told that he liked his work. And why not? Roads are useful. They take you where you long to be. More importantly, they take you away from where you no longer wish to be. They make yearning possible. Roads get you places. Everybody needs roads.

McCartney, Frank

In 1955 my Uncle Frank, who worked as a detective for Scotland Yard, died of cancer. He was thirty-four years old. He went quickly. My mother never got to meet him, but she told me that he was supposed to have been very kind. Frank was (so she was told) a terribly kind and extremely gentle man.

At the time of his death, my uncle was working on a case involving the corpse of a young woman found floating facedown in the dirty green water of the river Clyde, the river on which Glasgow is situated, the river that empties out into the Firth of Clyde and from then on into the Atlantic. That's where she was heading.

According to Scotland Yard's records, the victim had long red hair and was wearing a white dress with red polka dots, cinched in at the waist with a wide red belt. A group of fishermen scooped her up in their net. This woman's name was Margaret O'Riley. Her case was never solved, though there was vague talk of her getting involved with *a bad lot*.

I have a photograph of my father and his elder brother, taken shortly before Frank's death. In the photograph my father wears a dark wool overcoat, a white shirt with a sharply starched collar, and a black silk tie. There is something suggestive in his crooked grin. His ears stick out boyishly; his dark eyes glitter and his black hair curls and shines. He looks like a boxer or a handsome young gangster.

Frank chose to be photographed wearing a camel trench coat with a boxy cut and the collar turned up. He has a broad face and bushy eyebrows; a ray of freckles spans the bridge of his nose. To conceal from the camera his thinning hair, Frank wears a jaunty porkpie hat. The felt brim of the hat has been curled and pressed so well that its shadow casts a deep incision into the white backdrop.

The manner of his dress leaves no doubt in your mind that he is a detective. He could not be anything but a detective. As if to make sure there will be no confusion, Frank holds a magnifying glass up, a joke shared by the brothers. The glass magnifies nothing but the empty white space between them.

My father and my uncle have the same lopsided grin. The right sides of their mouths veer drastically up. When Frank is dead, my father will smile and people will sigh and say how much young Jimmy looks like Frank; *the resemblance is quite eerie.*

Whereas my father's smile is unabashedly cocky, Frank's smile does in fact seem kind.

Gazing at the photograph, I imagine that my father is thinking about girls. Not one girl in particular, just girls, plural. At church, in the baker's, down at the pub, in the factory, on plush velvet seats in the darkened cinema.

Frank, on the other hand, is surely thinking of only one girl: Margaret O'Riley. Her swollen blue-yellow body. The bits of green seaweed they found tangled in her red hair.

I cannot help but detect a trace of weariness in my uncle's smile. He looks worn out. Is he tired from work? Or can he already feel the cells overmultiplying in his body, like sinister polka dots? Perhaps he feels nothing as he stands still for the photographer. Perhaps he waits for nothing but the miniature explosion from the camera and for the photographer to reappear from beneath his black cloth.

McCartney, Margaret

When I was eight, my grandmother came all the way from Scotland to visit us in Australia. I remember she wore the same yellow dress every day; it was very plain, not unlike the uniform worn by cashiers in supermarkets or hospital cafeterias. It buttoned up at the front, with large buttons made from the same material as the dress. Each morning she ate half a grapefruit, topped with white sugar.

My grandmother brought framed photographs of her late husband and of my Uncle Frank. She kept them on the table next to her bed and wiped the glass down every day with a rag dipped in vinegar. I recall my grandmother as a particularly silent, dour woman, but once, she told me of a dream she had about Frank, that she reached into his coffin and extracted his lovely green eyes and then kept them on a mantelpiece in a glass jar full of vinegar.

She didn't bring a photo of Andrew. They say that my grandmother never recovered from his death. There are only a handful of things that will not buckle beneath time: grief is one of them. Up until she died, if someone happened to mention Andrew's name, her face would fall like the rush of ice that begins an avalanche. It was as if her child had died just moments ago, and she was learning of his death for the first time. People would pass her their handkerchiefs: some monogrammed, some not. But she refused to be consoled. She would not accept them.

MEAT

Though the imagination is not *like* anything, if I had to compare it to *something,* it would be to one of those silver mincing machines you used to see at the butcher's. To my ears, the music this machine made was so much sweeter than any organ grinders.

On some days, images keep grinding out of my imagination, raw and pink, like minced meat. They leave their stains. This is one of those days.

MELANCHOLY

God recently took me on as a sort of consultant. In an effort to cut back on (human) expenses, one of our first joint decisions was to get rid of the mornings, effective today. Starting tomorrow there will only be afternoons and evenings. Dusk will be much longer.

At our first meeting the issue of melancholy also came up.

Shall I make the boys less melancholy, do you think? he asked. *So they don't even think about their wrists?*

It was toward the end of the meeting, and I was getting tired, and I found myself saying, *Oh, no, make them more melancholy.*

Upon my recommendation, God's started making boys with twice as much longing and even darker circles under the eyes.

MEMORY

Thank God Marcel Proust is not around today to see what's happened to memory, how bad we've all gotten at remembering, and
how good we all are at forgetting. Memory has become so tinny,
like those poor quality recordings we made on cheap tape cas-
settes on tape decks when we were children. I'm probably the
worst of the lot. If Proust only knew how poor my memory of
childhood really is, and how much I have to invent to cover up
this fact, and if he saw me watching VH1 classic alternative music
videos, ones from my childhood, which evoke powerful, murky
feelings in me that must be attached to actual memories, yet I've
forgotten the memory itself entirely, and only recall every lyric of
the song, he'd probably rise out of his grave and feel extreme disdain for me.

MEMORY, FIRST

I have no first memory.

MEMORY, MY SECOND ATTEMPT AT MY FIRST

I suspect it may involve a white wicker crib: I'm lying in it, surrounded by toys; my sisters and their girlfriends stand above me.
They're playing with me like I'm a baby doll, but I must be older,
four or five. In the crib with me there's a clock with a rabbit on its
face, the rabbit from *Alice in Wonderland,* who's perpetually running late. He's wearing a waistcoat and holding his own little
clock. But this seems far too convenient, too symbolic. If I am to
speak truthfully, I suspect I am still standing at the entrance to
the world, wondering whether or not I should enter, poised on
the threshold of memory.

MILK BOTTLES

This morning I was woken up just before dawn by a soft clinking
sound. Still half asleep, for a moment I believed I was once again
a child, being woken up by the noise of the tousle-headed,

acne-ridden, gently yawning milkman's boy who left bottles of milk on our doorstep five days a week. I only caught sight of this boy on a few occasions, on those mornings when I had to rise particularly early, but that handful of sightings was more than enough to furnish my dreams for many years. Throughout childhood and into early adolescence, I imagined the milkman's boy coming to my bedroom window, peeling back the fly-wire screen, and climbing into my bed; I thought of him there in the back of the van, by himself, sprawled out amongst the creamy glow of the milk bottles.

It took me a minute or so to realize that this could not be the case, that surely the milkman was dead by now, and surely his assistant had gone gray. I slowly remembered that milk bottles were a thing of the past, irretrievably lost, quaint antiques from the twentieth century. I had all but forgotten that lovely glassy sound of milk bottles gently knocking against one another, so used had I become to drinking milk from cardboard cartons decorated with the smiling faces of missing children, as if the children were somehow happy to be missing.

So where was that sound coming from? Was there a milkman and his boy doing deliveries in the depths of my heart? Was it the sound of my heart breaking? Or perhaps it was merely the sound of my heart adjusting to something?

MILLER, TIM

When I first saw you at that lecture in London in 1994, it was so eerie and momentous. I knew how Goethe must have felt, when, on his twelfth birthday, he was given that puppet theater, for which he wrote his first play, an event that utterly changed the path of his life and altered the course of who he would be.

At that moment, I sort of felt like I was fate's hand puppet. Despite being very aware that there were so many hot puppets, so many heartless puppets, so many puppets that were not for me, I had always sensed that there was one special puppet out there in the world who was dreaming only of me, whose wooden limbs and strings were itching to get all tangled with my wooden limbs and my strings. All my life, I had been waiting with the radical patience of a puppet, and, as soon as I saw you, I knew you were *the* puppet.

Of course, it wasn't that easy. The first year of our relationship, which had a rather turgid, romantic quality to it, was, how can I put it? Somewhat Wagnerian. But full of lots of good parts, like when we were walking past the Starbucks in the East Village in Manhattan, and you said, *It's sort of comforting to know that in one hundred years we'll all be skeletons.* I think I really fell in love with you then and there.

And of course there was that letter I wrote to you, in which I said that if you didn't break up with your boyfriend and invite me to Los Angeles, I'd come to you in the night like a specter, or like Satan in *Rosemary's Baby,* and I'd drug your boyfriend and kill your dog (or vice versa) and fuck you, so you'd give birth to something—what a charmer I was! So, I ended, you might as well invite me anyway, and you did, and the rest is, as they say, history.

I've known you now for how long, almost fourteen years? Inevitably, there are those moments when I really don't feel like I know you at all. Normally I rationalize this by reminding myself that there's nothing wrong with living with a handsome stranger; in fact, it's quite nice and has its advantages. But once in a while, I really do want to solve the riddle of who you are. There are times when I feel like you're the Sphinx (Greek, not Egyptian) and I'm a passerby, attempting to answer that riddle. Though I always stop myself before I get too caught up in this game, remembering that if I do solve it, you'll have to get really mad at me, just as the Sphinx did with Oedipus. We'll have a terrible fight, and then you'll have to destroy yourself (and besides, look what happened to Oedipus afterward!). Or, if I don't, you'll have to devour me; neither of these outcomes is particularly appealing.

Perhaps when I think of you I need to stop thinking in terms of riddles and metaphors altogether. For surely the word *boyfriend* is itself a metaphor, a figure of speech, describing one thing—you—in terms of another. I kind of like the idea that whoever I think you are, you'll always be thoroughly dissimilar.

What I do know for certain about you is that when you were in fourth grade, every day to school you wore a three-cornered brown felt hat in the style associated with the American revolutionaries. You keep that hat in a cupboard. The hat's dusty and slightly battered, as objects salvaged from childhood tend to be. I like the feel of it in my hands. I hold my breath and wait for some deeper secret to pour out of the hat, to fly out.

MINSK

My favorite place in the world is Minsk, capital of what was formerly known as the Belarusian Soviet Socialist Republic, but what is today known as the independent nation of Belarus. One day I hope to retire and buy a nice little prefabricated house in Minsk for me and my sweetheart, Tim. In its heyday, Minsk was renowned throughout the Eastern Bloc for the beauty of the young men who worked in its factories, in particular the boys who made Minsk's highly sought-after peat-digging machines. Since the dissolution of the USSR, just as the architecture of the city itself was subjected to severe damage during World War II, the architecture of the city's boys has been in an increasing state of disrepair. One can still see traces and remnants of their devastating beauty; nonetheless, they are no longer so much boys as they are the ruins of boys.

MIRRORS

When we go to dream, one of the first things we notice is that there are no mirrors. No mirrors on the ceiling, like in sleazy seventies bedrooms; no mirrors on medicine cabinets; not even a little mirror hidden in a handheld compact. We are not sure of the reason for this. Perhaps dream exists in a space prior to the invention of mirrors. Maybe someone (God?) has hidden all the mirrors. Or possibly all the mirrors in dreams have been shattered and put to other, more practical uses. Either way, there is no surface capable of reflection; we never see ourselves. This is a great relief. This is precisely the reason why, every night, we go back, again and again, to dream.

MOANS

The eeriest noises in the world are surely the moans that come out of cats' mouths when they're in heat. It sounds like the cats are attempting to speak, but whenever they do, their claws get in the way and they tear the heads off consonants, slit the throats of vowels. Basically, they fuck up the alphabet, massacre it.

I think what's particularly unearthly about their gurgling is that it sounds like something almost human, but not quite. Something that has tried to become human but has failed miserably in its attempt.

I first heard this noise when I was a kid, lying in bed one night. It was coming from the roses right beneath my window. I had no idea what the noise was, and I called my mum in. She told me it was cats; they were very unhappy, she said, and they were taking their unhappiness out on the roses.

But what about the moans that come out of our own mouths? They're equally eerie, similar to the moans that issue from ghosts—except whereas ours express deep bodily delight, theirs express a ragged sense of loss over no longer being in a body and a terrible longing to once again reside in a body, in all its complexity. (On further reflection, our moans are identical to those of a ghost.)

Some say our moans are the sound of words falling apart, of words having little black nervous breakdowns. Others say moans are the enemies of words, out to get words, and that words should always be on the lookout for moans. Either way, we can agree that these moans will be our undoing.

MODELING

When I was ten years old, I decided to become a model. If you wanted to be a model, it seemed the first thing you had to do was to walk around with a book on your head. It gave you good posture. Balancing volume *M* of the *World Book Encyclopedia* on my skull, I walked slowly up and down the brief length of our hallway, proceeding as carefully as possible, so the book wouldn't fall.

Once I had mastered one volume, I took to walking with two volumes stacked on my head: *A* and *M*. After that, I tried three. Gradually, I accumulated volume upon volume, until finally I was able to balance all twenty volumes of the *World Book* on my head, until my neck had sunk into my spine, which itself had melted down like snow, or ice cream, until I crawled on all fours with the poise and grace of our prehistoric ancestors.

MODERNITY

Modernity ended in 1953, when hearing aids became so small as to be almost invisible.

MODERNITY, POST-

Postmodernity began in 1978 when my father threw me off his shoulders into the Indian Ocean, screaming.

MONARCHS

Last year there was talk that monarch butterflies, known for their strong flight and long migrations, were about to become extinct; we would have to be content with observing these butterflies in glass cases. But this summer there were so many of them in our garden, nice big orange-brown ones, and even bigger yellow and black ones, that it almost seemed a bit excessive. Although I'm glad that they are still around, or back, somehow this overload of monarchs is as worrying as their absence. There is such a thing as too many wings, too much beauty, too much abundance. One can easily be overwhelmed by paradise.

MONOTONY

At least when we were at school, the deep boredom of the day was constantly interrupted by the brothers, who, depending on their moods, would get out their canes or their belts, and who, again depending on their moods, would then swat us on the backs of our thighs, on our knuckles, or, of course, on our behinds, for committing some minor infringement. Even better was when other boys had committed the crime. Brother Santa María, my fifth through seventh grade teacher, would line these boys up at the front of the classroom, and allow us to watch—in fact, make us watch—as he took his glossy brown belt, or, as he referred to it, *my friend,* to the boys. Now we are no longer at school, yet the days are still profoundly boring—if anything, the boredom of the days has increased exponentially. We have to be more inventive; we must come up with other ways to overcome this monotony.

MONTAIGNE, MICHEL DE

In 1571, exactly four hundred years before I was born, French writer and philosopher Michel de Montaigne, having grown weary of the horrors of the world, withdrew to the cool quiet of his castle to write his rambling, chatty essays. Apparently, whenever he grew tired of writing, he'd go outside and raise the drawbridge over the moat of his castle up and down, up and down, listening to the squeaky noise the mechanism made. Montaigne, who, with his shaved head, walrus mustache, and light goatee looked a bit like a sixteenth-century cholo, usually wrote wearing his white ruff collar, but sometimes, when it tickled the base of his earlobes to the point of distraction, he would take the collar off. Eventually, he always put the collar back on, knowing that one is confined to the style of one's century. Skeptical of rationality, and unconvinced of reason's ability to illuminate anything, Montaigne was subject to a recurring dream where he was wearing a collar sewn out of molten hot lava, and his essays were erupting out of him, one after the other, at times violently, at times mildly.

MOON, THE

There is a theory that millions of years ago a meteorite collided with the earth. A big chunk of the earth broke off and floated away, and that chunk gradually formed into what we now call the moon. Thus today, when we gaze at the moon and are moved by its pale strangeness, we are simply longing for reconciliation with what was once part of us. The implications of this theory are dazzling: nothing is further away than the self; nothing is colder or lovelier than the self.

MOTHERS

Just as they say a mother-to-be has a certain glow about her, it can be said that boys who have been recently diagnosed with HIV have a certain look about them that could also be construed as a glow. After all, both the boy and the expectant woman are in a state of apprehension. And both must be full to overflowing with a feeling that is strange and uncertain, though the boy is surely less certain and even more fearful of what is inside him. Both are giving birth to *something*. In another epoch, one even stranger and more twisted than our own—if such a thing is conceivable—people might even shower gifts upon these boys.

MOUTH, THE

Some days I feel like I'm nothing but a mouth, a giant, gaudily painted mouth, one hundred dogs' drooling mouths, and from each of my mouths issues forth a length of shining.

Perhaps in the future we need to consider eradicating the mouth.

MOVIES

Humans spend so much time at the movies. By the end of this century, humans will spend all their time at the movies. They will refuse to leave the cinema. They will be born and they will learn to talk and they will fall in love and they will eventually die, all within the air-conditioned confines of the cinema. At the movies, what's on the screen is of little to no significance. What's important is how dark it is. We can't really see one another and we are not permitted to talk with one another. What matters are the ushers in their red uniforms, with their flashlights, enforcing silence. The little red and black ticket stubs that litter the floor of the cinema are also essential. What is crucial is the accidental or intended rubbing of knees or pressing of thighs against the legs of handsome strangers. As we sit in the near dark, which gets us used to the grave—which will not be pitch-black, but will actually have a certain source of light, what is known as *corpselight*— we forget one another and we begin to forget ourselves. This is why we go to the cinema. The odor of teenage boys mingles with the odor of popcorn, creating a dense, stale, buttery stink.

MUSES

Lord Byron claimed his muses were boys with buzz cuts wearing baggy jeans. They'd come down on their skateboards and hit him over the head with their skateboards. He'd emerge from his daze in a fit of inspiration. A couple of centuries earlier, in 1598, after Irish rebels set fire to Edmund Spenser's lace collar, Spenser, depressed in mind and spirit, wrote a long poem called "The Cum of the Muses."

My muses don't live on Mount Helicon, but in Pomona, California. Before I write, I call them up on their cell phones. Sometimes they don't answer. You can always tell if my muses were just here; they leave long trails of their saliva. My muses are nice and violent. It's only when I fail to create that I learn what they are truly capable of. If ignored, the muses are quick to exact revenge. They behead everyone I love with machetes. One must always be alert; one must always be listening out for the muses.

MUSTACHE, HISTORY OF THE

If one examines and then ranks the history of the mustache, it is unarguable that Friedrich Nietzsche's, with its shaggy exuberance, takes first place. He purposely grew it to absurd proportions, so his lips, that red, fleshy part of his body that uttered the truth, would be permanently concealed. This philosopher's mustache has been hugely influential; take, for example, the bushy mustaches of the so-called gay clones of the 1970s (direct descendants of Nietzsche) that come in second. It was their mustaches that sealed their fate. Nietzsche's influence can also be seen in the walruslike mustache that tickles the upper lip of the cholo—or anyone lucky enough to kiss a cholo—and occupies third place.

It is the drastically different pencil-thin mustache that hovers subtly above the lips of young Mexican men that comes in fourth. This mustache was directly influenced by Franz Kafka, whose mustache falls into fifth place. In true style, Kafka lags behind those he inspired, those young men who wear this mustache so slight it almost fails to exist.

MUSTACHE, HITLER'S

Though one cannot condone such a mustache, and though one might wish such a mustache had never been seen on the face of this earth, one cannot undertake any serious study of the mustache without thoroughly examining this terrible, blunt, oblong example. Hitler's mustache haunts the history of the mustache.

MYSTERIES

Inside me there is a dead boy lying beneath the shrubbery, the rhododendrons, and there is a lot of tweed; tweed is a fetish.

There are boy maids wearing frilly little aprons and caps, and at night the boys change into tuxedos or evening gowns. Everyone is very dotty and very arch and very witty, and everyone is suspicious; adultery is the norm. Everyone is consuming excessive amounts of tea, and can everyone gather in the drawing room at eight. Before morning another boy corpse will turn up in me, then another in the evening, and no one will feel anything, just like in an Agatha Christie mystery.

MYSTERIES, BIG-PRINT

When my mother and I walked to the local shops and the local library, we'd hold hands, and on the way we'd talk about different things. Sometimes I'd look at the sunspots on the back of her hand, which were like polka dots, but less precise. Some of them were brown, like my slippers. Others were silver and matched the watering can.

The other mothers would stand outside next to their mailboxes, in their polyester floral dresses. As we passed by, they'd snicker and whisper.

Upon arriving at the library, mum and I would go to our separate sections. I would head for the *National Geographic*s, while she went to the shelves where they kept the big-print mysteries. We took our time in choosing our selections, because there were limits imposed upon our library memberships.

Upon leaving, each of us would hold one side of the string bag that was filled with books.

One afternoon, leafing through a *National Geographic*—I think it was an article on a European city, maybe Madrid—I saw a picture of a teenage junkie. He had dark curly hair, blue-black circles under his eyes, and blue track marks covering the inside of his pale arms, like birds seen from a great distance.

That night the boy crept into my dreams, as boys have a tendency to do. But I dreamt that my mother was the junkie, injecting mystery directly into her veins. She wore long-sleeved flannel nightgowns to cover up the track marks. In the dream, I was standing over her, holding a magnifying glass in my hand, just looking.

~ ⌒ ~

Today, my eyesight is beginning to fail me. Is this the way we begin to leave the world? Very slowly, gradually seeing less and less of it, until our eyes have had enough and finally it's time to leave altogether.

Soon, just like my mother, I suppose I too will have to read the big-print mysteries.

~ ⌒ ~

It's possible the experts are wrong about eternity. When I arrive there, I will find an exact reconstruction of my local library. And I will also find my mother, browsing the shelves of the big-print mysteries, resting beneath the shade provided by the shelves.

Eternity will be a space where either nothing is overdue or where everything is overdue. One would assume that its library card would allow for unlimited access, but maybe there are limits even in eternity.

Either way, I will spend most of my time there leafing through the *National Geographic*s, looking at the pictures with a different kind of longing. Every now and then, my mother and I will meet somewhere neutral, probably the reference area, and show each other what we plan to take out before returning to our separate sections.

NAME, A

A name is a word fastened to a body, but tentatively, like the labels on the pajamas and dressing gowns we wore when we were children, which gave the name of the manufacturer and conveyed other necessary information, such as the reminder that these garments were highly flammable.

NAME, MY

Like all other human beings, whenever I venture out into the world, I have to bring my name. This is very inconvenient. There are eight letters in my first name, but if you need my last name, this comes to seventeen letters, and if you must have my middle name, Duncan, this adds up to twenty-three letters. If for some reason you require my Holy Confirmation name, Sebastian, we're left with a grand total of thirty-two letters. This means that wherever I go, I have to drag along with me a minimum of eight letters.

Each letter of my name is made out of plywood and measures three feet by three feet, except for the first letter in each name: they measure six feet by six feet (so, even on those lucky occasions when I only need to bring along my initials, this is still a schlep). Each letter is painted bright yellow, like the lettering for McDonald's, and, in fact, the style of my lettering, especially the *M* for *McCartney*, often gets mistaken for a McDonald's sign.

When I'm getting on a bus, I carry on one letter at a time; by the time I've got all the letters on, the bus driver and the other passengers have usually grown very impatient with me, and often curse me (and my name). I'm always getting splinters in my fingers (the plywood), and generally by the time I arrive wherever it is I am expected, I'm worn out. I sense how Jesus must have felt, dragging his cross all the way to Golgotha. In fact, I carry the *t* in *Alistair* over my shoulder, just like a cross. Having a name is such an exhausting, lumbering business. I've become increasingly interested in spaces where names are not necessary, in places that look down on names. And I'm seriously considering taking some of the letters from my name *out back,* as they say, and then burying them in the garden.

NEGATIVE CAPABILITY

In the early twenty-first century, we are still in this era of AIDS, the era that directly followed the golden age, just as we are still in the epoch of Romanticism.

Technically speaking, any man who lets a handsome stranger take him without a rubber is a Romantic poet, in that he is following Keats's dictum and surrendering to beauty, placing beauty before any other consideration. In this sense, the bathhouses and sex clubs and chat rooms are full of poets, many of them wan and young and doomed!

And surely there is nothing more Romantic than sitting in a bland, dreary clinic, awaiting one's HIV test results, suspended in that state of mystery, doubt, and uncertainty Keats described as negative capability.

NERVOUS BREAKDOWNS

A nervous breakdown is when a boy polishes himself so rigorously you can see your face in him. It is a special occasion, one that calls for the good china and the best cutlery.

NIGHTGOWN, MY MOTHER'S

I remember that my mother's nightgown was pale pink, 75 percent cotton, and delicately edged in barbed wire; you'd get electrocuted if you touched the hem, and anyway, they'd shoot you if you even tried to escape from my mother.

NIGHTMARE ON ELM STREET

There are times when I feel like I'm Johnny Depp circa 1984 in the first *Nightmare on Elm Street,* when he was at the height of his beauty, specifically in that scene where he's lying on his bed, wearing sweats and a tiny midriff top from which spills the sensual trace of puppy fat, and listening to music on headphones, trying very hard to stay awake so as to avoid Freddy Krueger. I know that just like Depp's character Glen Lantz, one day I too will become a fountain of blood; I too must eventually fall asleep, and dream that dream from which it is impossible to leave, the dream to which we must all succumb.

NOISE

Writing is such a fragile business, far more sickly and nervous than the business of living, which by comparison seems positively robust. So, quiet birds! Otherwise I will be forced to cut out all your tongues; I will then be obliged to place them in a little pink-gray heap by the side of the road, as a warning. That will put an end to your boasting, your banal joy at the morning, your digging it in that, as humans, we do not have wings.

Dear neighbor, I can't bear the harsh sound of your broom, its coarse bristles, the effect of your sweeping combined with your interminable whistling. Whistling is a minor art, though not as lowly as writing! Cease at once, otherwise your tongue will be next! Besides, don't you know that all housework is futile? (Though aprons on boys are adorable.)

And to those birthday revelers three doors down: stop singing "Happy Birthday" immediately, or I will come over, knock politely, and, taking the knife normally reserved for cutting into birthday cakes, orally castrate every one of you, the birthday cake's pink frosting and the accumulation of wishes still staining the blade.

Finally, to my own tongue: yours will be the last to go. This will be just punishment for telling the wrong story, always the wrong story. We have to move into silence, and how can I do this while you're still drooling and approximating?

NOOSES

Ever since the Stonewall Rebellion in 1969 and the subsequent birth of Gay Liberation, gay men have been wearing their T-shirts as tight as hangmen's nooses.

NORTH KOREA

Just as I expected, all the sadness in my heart promptly disappeared when I gave up love and joined the nuclear program in North Korea.

NYQUIL

Whereas Arthur Rimbaud, Charles Baudelaire, and other French poets of the nineteenth century partook of the green intoxicating drink known as absinthe, we indulge in the green cold and flu formula known as Nyquil, which is maybe even more decadent, and like absinthe, leads to heavy sleep, and to an increase in dreams.

O

Objects

The most beautiful object I have ever seen is Kafka's first writing desk. He received it when he was nine years old. The desk is very plain: dark wood, four spindly legs. No drawers to conceal secrets or legal documents. I can see him sitting at that desk, trying to resist writing with every ounce of his puny body, trying to ward it off, but eventually, unable to resist, giving in. The desk was lost during that onslaught of objects known as the Holocaust. Unlike Kafka's sisters, all three of whom died in concentration camps—Elli (1941), Valli (1942), and Ottla (1943)—the desk reappeared some years later. Somehow, inexplicably, it survived the onslaught.

ODORS

Last winter, during the first heavy rain, as soon as the rain was over I went outside, eager to inhale the fresh vapors. I was, however, greeted by a terrible stench rising from the ground and lingering in the air.

I called the Los Angeles County Health Department and eventually got hold of a nice official with a sexy voice—I think he said his name was Franz—who explained that this rotten, sewer-like stench of death was the result of the rain flooding storm drains, which were filled with the rotting garbage, animal corpses, and human waste that had collected steadily and quietly over the summer. Spurred on by the rain, the detritus had quickly begun to decompose.

So Baruch Spinoza was right, I said. I told my Health Department official about the ideas of the seventeenth-century Dutch philosopher, who claimed that we are literally living in God, coughing and crying inside God.

But, I added, *this proves that we are not merely residing in any old part of God, but that we are living, for the most part quite happily, in the asshole of God, and this explains why leaving the world is so difficult, for we have to squeeze our way out through the tight sphincter of God.*

Franz seemed genuinely enthusiastic about this idea and promised to offer my explanation to other callers.

ODYSSEY, THE

In my *Odyssey,* nothing much happens, except for each morning, when men, still yawning, are fingerfucked by the rosy fingers of dawn.

OLD MEN, DIRTY

I'm profoundly ambitionless! Actually, I have one ambition: to become a lonely, dirty old man.

It's lucky that I have this ambition, because, whether I like it or not, one day, before I know it, I will wake up to find that there is a glass of water on my bedside table containing a pair of clunky false teeth. Just to check, I will swill my tongue around in my mouth, and sure enough, it will be empty (thank God for my tongue, otherwise my mouth would die of loneliness!). My upper gums will be hanging loosely, like drawing-room curtains.

I will then pick up the duvet and look down, only to discover that I am wearing nothing but an antique, red satin jockstrap. Perplexed, I will look up, and there will be a gold hook on the back of my bedroom door; no, there will be three gold hooks, and hanging on each hook will be an olive-green raincoat, three olive-green raincoats, the kind that only dirty old men wear, and all these raincoats will belong to me. It will be a lovely, gray, rainy day. It will be a time of discovery.

Oedipus

Once a week I find myself picking up volume *O* of the *World Book Encyclopedia* and turning to a reproduction of Ingres's sublime painting of Oedipus. Gazing upon this painting, my initial response is always one of sorrow; this is not so much because of the terrible fate of the *unfortunate king*—the whole business with killing the father and marrying the mother, not to mention the gouging out of his own eyes, and then the ultimate indignity of having a complex named after him—no, my sorrow is on account of the fact that Oedipus lived so long ago. With his head of dark, curly hair, and with his sensuously fleshy, almost overripe, yet smooth, supremely muscled body, the boy is just my type. (Both when he could still see and, even more so, once he became blind.)

Ingres depicts Oedipus in a face-off with the Sphinx, who, incidentally, with her lion's paws, woman's head, bird's wings, and serpent's tail is not at all my type physically, though I will be the first to admit she has a great personality. The two of them are participating in a kind of staring game, just like the one we used to play when we were children, but theirs has particularly high stakes. However, Oedipus is not making eye contact with the Sphinx: he is looking directly at her rather large breasts, which resemble fake ones, though this cannot be, as it will be a few years before silicone is invented and injected into mythology.

It appears that Oedipus is deep in the process of deciphering the Sphinx's riddle; he is on the verge of solving it. We are privy to the moment just prior to the solution of the riddle.

Oedipus is about to speak, continuing that chain of dreadful, though seemingly inevitable, events that constitutes his life.

Yet we can almost imagine that things might have turned out differently. Staring at this painting, we can conceive that Oedipus, bored with trying to guess, could have given up and gone home. If this were the case, we would still remember Oedipus, though for a divergent set of reasons. We would not associate him with tragedy, with incest, or with those useless, burnt-out eyes. (The incident of patricide might have been left undiscovered.) We would not affiliate him with fate at all. We would remember him only for the beauty of his calves, the muscularity of his thighs.

OEDIPUS COMPLEX

They say that Oedipus blinded himself with a brooch of his mother's. My mother had a so-called cameo brooch: on it there was a white silhouette of a Grecian lady's head set against a dark blue background. Its gold pin left tiny holes in her cardigans. So I wouldn't have to go through the whole drama Oedipus went through, I jumped ahead and stuck the gold pin of my mother's brooch into both of my eyes, eager to get on with the myth.

ORGAN-GRINDERS

The art of organ-grinding is fast disappearing, almost as quickly as we are.

There used to be an organ-grinder and his little monkey on every street corner, distracting us from our troubles. Now we have nothing to distract us and we must pay attention to each trouble, individually. They say that when the world ends, almost no one will be spared. God will destroy virtually all of his inventory. No one will be left except for one lone organ-grinder, cranking the handle of his hand organ; its tinny, jerky music will issue forth into the newly vacant air. Though, of course, no one will be there to listen. And no one will be there to give a little money to the organ-grinder's little monkey, in its red Chinese silk coat and its red fez with the black and gold tassel, whose withered little hand will be extended out, waiting patiently.

ORGASMS

In Ludwig Wittgenstein's *The Sad Investigations,* scribbled on pieces of paper whilst he was out cruising in the Wiener Prater park in Vienna, he writes of orgasms: *One sees things (primacy of skin, annulling of the world) like windmills, thousands of them, turning slowly in the wind.*

ORIGINALITY

When one man is fucking another man doggy-style, the dogs are the orange of orange rinds, the dogs are burning, the man who is fucking is guilty of copying (by virtue of the physical fact that *he is behind* the man being fucked). *Being is Fucked,* as Heidegger would say. The man who is getting fucked was there first. He is somehow more original, more infinite.

OUGHTS, THE

Apparently the name for this decade we are currently in is *the oughts,* as in *I have everything I need so I ought to be happy, but I am not.* Our decade will be remembered as one in which things began to happen so quickly that it was impossible to grasp anything. *Nothing of note occurred in this decade,* the history books will say, adding, *this decade is best forgotten.*

OXNARD, CALIFORNIA

Dear reader: when the self feels like a sickness—that is, when saying *I have a self* is the equivalent of saying *I have a cold, and a nasty one at that*—and if every time you say *I,* you feel as if you are committing a senseless yet mundane act of violence, and if, because of all this, you are seriously considering a major career change—instead of working in life, you are planning on taking up a new career in death, which you believe will ultimately be more fulfilling—hold off! Wait until fall, so I can show you the exuberance of the pumpkin fields that lie just north of Oxnard.

P

PARROTS, WILD

There are wild parrots here in Venice. Every day they fly over our house and laugh at us. I don't know what exactly it is they're laughing about, though I suspect it has something to do with how colorless we are, unlike the parrots, which have more color than they know what to do with.

Theirs is a form of laughter so jagged it seems capable of lopping the branches off trees, cutting down TV antennas. Yet within their mirth I detect not only something malicious but also a trace of sadness, as if, like me, they're tired of being wild, and all they really want is a nice cage.

Despite this laughter, and despite the fact that the parrots seem to think we're a bit of a joke, we've gotten quite used to them. My boyfriend says that if they went away he'd miss them and wouldn't know what to do without them.

There doesn't seem to be any risk of that happening, as lately the parrots seem to be visiting us with greater frequency, on the hour. And there's a new urgency to the noise they make, which is causing me to think that I've gotten it all wrong.

Maybe they haven't been laughing at us at all; maybe parrots never laugh and are profoundly sober, humorless creatures.

All this time they've been speaking—not just mimicking our language—but in their own tongue, in complete sentences. All this time they've been trying to tell us something, an announcement, like *It's going to rain,* or perhaps it's something slightly more important, such as, *The end of the world is coming. The end of the world . . .*

PARTIES

As children we must have attended at least five hundred birthday parties held for other children. And that figure is a conservative estimate. Although we try very hard to recall the details of these parties, we remember virtually nothing of them. (Though we do recall a certain feeling that came with the arrival of an invitation.)

In fact, as I reflect upon the parties I attended, all I can see is party hats, the ones we were required to wear at those parties, with the tight elastic bands that kept the hat on your head and bit into your chin; these hats were, in fact, a condition of remaining at any party. Yes, all I can see is endless rows of gold and silver conical party hats. And, though I could be imagining it, just a hazy outline of a cut-glass bowl of fruit punch, and little glass cups next to the bowl.

PEACHES

Of all the fruit trees in our yard, the peach tree in the front is easily the most abundant. One summer, the tree was laden with peaches. At first my boyfriend and I were delighted with this abundance. So were the tiny, glossy, blue-black birds that occupied our garden, pecking with their bright yellow beaks at the peaches' red-yellow skins.

But then peaches began to fall faster than we could cup our hands to catch them. Tim laid out a checked blanket on the ground to stop the peaches from bruising, as they bruise easily. At night, it looked a bit scary, like someone was sleeping beneath the tree.

We began to feel overwhelmed by the peaches. The birds seemed to agree; from their tiny throats they issued calls like miniature screams. We hoped that there would be a late frost, or that perhaps one of the many enemies of peaches, such as brown rot, peach leaf curl, the Oriental fruit moth, Western X, or the peach mosaic disease, would come and infect our tree so it would need to be uprooted. We wished that something, anything, would come and utterly destroy our tree.

PERSONAL TRAINERS

Someone must have been telling lies about me, because somehow I have found myself with a personal trainer. When I turned up at the gym yesterday, I was met by this trainer wielding his clipboard at the entrance to the gym.

As is common with personal trainers, he had a thickset body, a large behind, and no neck. He was masculine, but catty. He was extremely positive, to the point of being destructive. I tried to explain to him that I did not require a personal trainer, that I had not asked for a personal trainer, and that, in fact, the last thing on earth I wanted was a personal trainer; but he did not hear me, or he pretended not to hear.

Instead, he walked me through my regimen and explained very calmly that I must see him three times a week, and I must do everything he says, and I must pay him. *If you wish to see results,* he said.

PERVERTS

Up until the 1950s, perverts wore felt porkpie hats, and stitched (by hand) boys' white jockey underwear into the silk lining of their hats. The pervert's hat could be considered a reliquary, a receptacle for storing something sacred, like those ornate reliquaries in churches that contain relics of medieval saints, such as the thread of a saint's shirt, although this would fall into the category of second-class relic. A first-class relic would be a splinter of a martyr's bone. Perverts were very important to the hat industry, and, recognizing this, the industry marketed hats directly to perverts. Apart from porkpie hats, bowlers, southwesters, and fedoras were also popular with perverts. However, the hat industry fell into decline, and many hat factories that used to turn out thousands of hats a week were shut down. Perverts had to move their secrets elsewhere, for example, sewing them into the lining of their skulls. Hats used to be quite common; now they are rare. No one mourns this fact more than a pervert.

PEWS

At our church the pews were as smooth as skinheads. As the priest gave his homily, I would sit there, trying to induce the pew to give me splinters, trying to seduce the pew.

PHILOSOPHY, WESTERN

The beginning of Western philosophy in 600 BC coincided with the invention of mirrors, just as all thinking implies reflection, a collision; at the academy, philosophers argued over the question *Is there anything in the world that is not a cage?* while cholos lay around wearing nothing but long white socks, listening intently. Hence philosophy can be perceived as something edged with longing, and every philosophical text is an attempt to not be distracted, to refuse tears. I'm wondering what the implications for this discipline might be if we were to shave off Socrates' beard or heighten the length of his robe by, let's say, three inches, and how philosophy is unable to cope with this ragged thing we call the self: something composed of longing. *How to allow red leakage into your answers, how to keep one's vision from turning into a system?* the pre-Socratics asked. The philosopher's thought caves in when faced with a boy as open as a doll's house, in a radical state of unblushing.

PHOTOCOPIES

Although there are simply so many terrific things about living at this particular moment in time in post-industrial capitalism, and although I would be hard pressed to single out any one of them as my absolute favorite thing, if I had to, under threat of torture and enforced isolation and extensive interrogation, I would say the thing I most like about living right now would be photocopy stores. I just love them, especially the twenty-four-hour Kinko's photocopy stores we have scattered all over Los Angeles.

It is hard to put my finger on exactly what it is I like about them, apart from the sheer romance of copies. I enjoy the sound all the machines make as they happily copy away; somehow I find it very soothing. I like the fact that they're often breaking down, just like us, and I take pleasure in the deep inky smell that wafts out of the machines when the assistants open them up to replace a cartridge.

And speaking of the assistants, there are always really cute young men working at the stores, who wear shapeless uniforms and nametags, and who lean over the machines in a suggestive fashion, at times in a state of absolute abandon. The light coming from the top of the machines is bright, like on a porno film set. The photocopies themselves can be perceived as more promiscuous originals. At this point in time, here in the West, the only erotic spaces left are Kinko's photocopy stores.

Finally, I am moved by the intimations of these stores, the implication that if we can photocopy a paper by Heidegger, perhaps, eventually, we'll be able to photocopy anything and everything: Brazil, my mother, roses, electricity, your moans. In a world without originals we'd never lose anything, a world without loss, what a weird, sweet thing!

PHOTOGRAPHY

I'm not that interested in photography, but I am interested in its origins, with man's discovery that exposure to sunlight turns some things dark. Way back in the Middle Ages, an alchemist, while working on one of his mysterious experiments, trying to find a way to live forever, accidentally splashed silver nitrate onto the smooth inner thigh of his (male) peasant assistant. Ouch! He rushed his assistant outside and noticed that the silver splash had turned black in the sunlight.

After centuries of trying to control this phenomenon, photography was the end result, indicating that most things become less interesting when controlled.

However, I do like the fact that photography finally confirmed the category of the negative, the inescapable, and quite lovely, reality of the negative.

And I am drawn toward those old cameras that required the sitter to be very still for a long time if they wanted their picture to be taken. Imagine if this were still the way! No one would have the patience to be stationary for so long, and there would be no photos! I would like to invent a camera that obliges the sitter to be still for even longer, that requires a father and son to remain motionless until the end of time.

PLAGUES

Daniel Defoe's *A Journal of the Plague Year* gives a fictional account of London's Great Plague of 1665, in which approximately 100,000 people died, and during which 40,000 dogs and 200,000 cats were destroyed, as it was believed these animals spread the plague.

At first the narrator, H. F., constantly oscillates between hope that it was just a scare and despondency over the rising death toll. He keeps careful tally of the dead, and draws up little weekly mortality charts.

As the number of deaths continues to mount, there is no more oscillation: the fear in his heart is as still as a frozen lake. Defoe's narrator takes long walks through the ever-dwindling city and imagines that soon there will be nothing left but numbers: black, abstract, glittering.

PLAGUES, THE AESTHETICS OF

Apparently, during the early days of the great plague, men wore these beaklike masks over their faces, hoping that it would protect them. Some men who participated in the practice of sodomy took off all their clothes but kept their plague masks on, and this was considered to be not only sensible but also sexy, just as men kept their white socks on during sex when that other plague began in the early 1980s.

PLANE CRASHES

Although we are terrified of plane crashes, specifically being in a plane crash, which would of course end our being, we get on planes of our own free will, so we can fly to dusty corners of the world, and so we can have a break from our identities. Yet some aviation experts speculate that not so long from now, there will be major plane crashes every day. Then there will be plane crashes on the hour. Plane crashes will increase in frequency until, eventually, every plane that takes off will crash. Despite this, people will continue to buy tickets, not to arrive at a particular destination, but to crash over a specific place. Finally coming to our senses, we will cease flying altogether. Like spiders, we will stick to our own dusty corners of the world. There will be no respite from identity.

PLANE CRASHES, THE HISTORY OF

In the history of plane crashes, the only plane crash I would recommend is the one in that dream I had, shortly after the death of my sister Jeannine's first child, Cooper, who died when he was only seven days old. In the dream, Jeannine was a passenger on a plane that crashed into the sea. She was wearing a light cotton nightgown with a lacy scalloped hem and collar, just like the one my mother used to wear. But my sister emerged from the wreckage, safe and sound, as they say, in fact, much safer than she was before the plane crash. She slowly waded back to shore in her nightie, embodying the purest form of safety.

PLASTIC

I like plastic. Currently my favorite object in the world is this nice plastic *spooky skull goblet* I bought from the Halloween section in a Rite-Aid drugstore. It sits on my writing desk, and it provides all sorts of inspiration—it's a muse of sorts—especially regarding the plasticity of death. The word *plastic* comes from the Greek and means *fit for molding*. Whenever I look at my goblet, which is increasingly often, it reminds me that death, just like life, is not only spooky but also pliable, capable of being shaped, formed, reimagined, reinvented. And that death is in some sense artificial, synthetic. Death *is* plastic. All of this makes death—and life—a little bit less spooky.

PLATO'S CAVE

In Plato's "Allegory of the Cave," everyone goes to have sex in this particular cave, because the light is very flattering, dark, and grainy. Though often people go there, and although that night they might think they look really good, they don't meet anyone. They stand with their backs against the craggy rock of the cave, feeling the moss and the water drip down the napes of their necks, and feeling lonelier and lonelier as the evening wears on. But sometimes they leave the cave for a bit and go out into the sunlight, where everyone looks haggard. Then they go back into the cave and see a couple of cute men, but they don't hook up with them. Their eyes have adjusted to the dark, and they can tell these men are not that cute.

Apparently Plato got the whole idea for the cave whilst contemplating the asshole of one of the broad-shouldered boys who was always hanging about in the corridors of the Academy, waiting for his autograph. The asshole, which according to Plato was similarly a place of shadows, a place of learning. The asshole, which could not be written down. The asshole, which was itself an allegory. Plato believed that just as with a cave, when you finally crawled out from a young man's asshole, into the sunlight, you found yourself blinking, unable to see anything.

PLINY THE ELDER

As Vesuvius erupted, Pliny the Elder put an ear to the world and listened to the lava. He recalled his own definition of a volcano: *a hot opening in the earth's surface, like a boy's mouth that is impossibly red.* The thought of red openings made him think of his nephew; he hoped he was safe.

Mentally, Pliny the Elder began to take notes for the first essay he would write in the afterlife: "On the Benefits of Volcanoes." He sat very still and took in the glow.

All of a sudden the Elder hated the Younger, hated time, hated nature. *Yet one must embrace volcanoes*—that's how the essay would close. He looked up, and as the lava swept over him, he could not help but marvel at how rigorously the gods erase and erase, until there are no more traces.

PLINY THE YOUNGER

Pliny the Younger sat in the small boat and watched as Pompeii disappeared beneath a sheet of red and black lava.

Ashes and hot cinders rained down on him, along with lapilli, or little stones, but luckily he had remembered to bring his umbrella. Somewhere in the city his uncle was suffering terribly, or perhaps had suffered terribly, and was now participating in whatever follows great suffering.

Pliny noticed a bit of lava on the hem of his robe and wondered if it would wash off. The small boat bobbed on the sea's surface, as boats will do.

POPE, ALEXANDER

At the age of twelve, the Augustan poet Alexander Pope began to develop a hunchback. The hump in his back crept up on him slowly, over a period of months; he remained a hunchback for the rest of his life. His "Essay on My Hunchback," written in heroic couplets, is considered to be his most important work. He attempted to forge a form of verse that mirrored his hunchback perfectly, one whose rhymes had their own little hunches and their own abnormal curves, but, after years of trying, he failed.

If one peers beneath the satire and the wit, one finds great sadness in Pope's work, whirlpools of it. One can see that all Pope really wanted was for some young man, reeking of the pastoral, to come over to his little cottage in Twickenham and spend a small portion of each day with him. All Pope truly yearned for was a boy with bits of straw in his hair, who smelled of warm milk. A lad who would place his rough hand beneath the poet's shirt and proceed to stroke and caress the contours of his hunchback.

POPE JOHN PAUL II

During the last months of Pope John Paul II's gradual yet irreversible decline, I could not help but notice that the hemline of his robe was often falling. Apparently, the Vatican's seamstress did not see fit to mend it—perhaps thinking that there was no point—he was on his last legs anyway.

What with the stream of drool that was a constant presence at either corner of the pope's mouth, and what with the slurring of his words, to the point that everything he said was incomprehensible—a level of the unintelligible that began to take on an air of the mystical—the falling hemline only added to his generally disheveled, slatternly appearance.

I preferred to think of him in his better days, particularly in the mid-'80s, after he recovered from the assassination attempt on his life, which occurred in 1981, the same year that we first began to hear about that *rare homosexual cancer*.

Back then, the pope was the image of glowing health, defiantly vigorous, racing around town in his bulletproof popemobile, making regular public appearances to read from his book of nature poetry, of course whilst wearing his bulletproof vestments.

At first the idea of this strapping pope dying was inconceivable. He had entered his holy office in 1978, when I was six years old. I had therefore always associated him with childhood and had at some point formulated a theory in my head, a superstitious theory, as all theories are, that the day this pope died, childhood would end; he would no longer be the Pope and I would no longer be a child.

And the very thought of the Vatican without him was also unimaginable. Surely the other people who lived there would not know what to do with themselves; for them it would be like one of those long, terrible nights at a nightclub, when there's no one even vaguely cute, no one you'd ever dream of seducing, or even rejecting.

But gradually I became not only used to the fact that Pope John Paul II was ailing but also somehow pleased with it, taking my mind as it did off the fact of my own slow and similarly irreversible decline.

POPES, ANTI-

All too often when one is getting ready to go out on a Saturday night and trying on an assortment of different outfits, one feels exactly how the pope must feel, before he has an audience, trying on all his vestments and looking at himself in the mirror and thinking he looks fat in all of them, not even like a pope, more like a bishop. Even though he reminds himself that he has far more jewels than a bishop, nothing seems to go with anything: his low, open, red shoes with the embroidered crosses clash horribly with his low, broad-brimmed hat. He would prefer to stay in his bedroom in the Vatican all night, but he forces himself to go out.

And after returning from a night out, when one is standing in front of the bathroom mirror and cleaning one's teeth, to forestall decay, one feels profoundly weary, just like the pope must feel after he returns from a trip around the world to spread the Word, and although he is so powerful, all powerful, and can make saints or break saints, for a moment or two it seems to him as if he has no power, temporal or spiritual. One feels the same, like a worn-out, completely powerless pope. Not merely power-less, but false. One sees one's own face, yet sees not the self, which has been displaced, but a self that has been improperly elected, a self that is in direct opposition to the self. In effect, one feels just like the real pope must feel when he is confronted by a good-for-nothing anti-pope.

PORN, PRE-CONDOM

Just like you, I love watching pre-condom porn. My favorite film is probably *He Seems to be Reaching for Something,* directed by Praxiteles, the greatest Greek gay porn director of the 300s BC. In this film, some of the Gods (today we call them cholos,) wan-der around, cruising through the maze of antiquity, while others just stand about, waiting to be picked up, with one hip thrust out into space in the pose that was dubbed the S-curve of Praxiteles, the *S* standing for sex. All of them have a look of dreamy, ice-creamy contemplation on their faces; life's good in the sex-curve. They all appear very relaxed, probably because they are Gods, not to mention the fact that AIDS is such an impossibly long way away.

PORN STARS, DEAD

At night, all the ghosts of dead gay porn stars swoop down from *Porno*—which is where gay porn stars go when they die, just like anyone who isn't baptized goes to *Limbo*—to visit boys and men who are dreaming that there is no plague. The porn ghosts know better than anyone that to haunt someone and to love someone amounts to the same thing. The ghosts pry open the sleeping men, who creak like haunted houses, specifically the floorboards and the doors.

POSTCARDS

My father is, as they say, a man of remarkably few words. In this sense, the postcard is the ideal medium for him, in that it is a limited space in which to say something.

Every two years my father goes back home to Scotland and always sends me a postcard written in his spidery handwriting. Although his mother passed away in 1985, in his most recent postcard he wrote that he was taking long walks with his mother, looking at the heather, and was always sure to bring his umbrella.

Although the postmark said Motherwell, Scotland, it is still in question as to where exactly this postcard was sent from, what region?

PROGENY

My paternal impulse is not what you would call strong. I'm not planning on having a child any time soon. I am the youngest of seven children; by the time I came around, my parents had tired of documenting their offspring. The novelty of photography and of progeny had worn off. This is understandable.

As a result, there are very few photos of all my siblings and I together, when we were children. There is one, however; it was taken on the occasion of my sister Julianne's First Communion, immediately after the family had returned from church. Everyone appears in the snapshot, except for my father, who was, as it were, the photographer. As I scrutinize our strange faces, all pale and washed out and squinting, starting off with my eldest brother Rory, and examining each face in descending order, ending with my own face, which is surely the strangest, I can't help but feel that I am looking at photocopies of successively inferior quality.

But who knows? There is a chance that this impulse for a descendant will kick in, and I will father a son. If so, he will be a violent, sullen son, beautiful, yet profoundly withdrawn. And I will build my son a tree house, which is the best thing a father can do for a son. I won't build it around an actual tree, but a telephone pole, right at the top. I will use very pale wood, blonde wood. It will be solidly constructed. I won't build a roof, so it will provide little, if any, shade.

This way, whenever my son needs to get away from me, and from the world, he will be able to run away to his tree house, and close his eyes, and listen to the wires stutter and hiss, just above his head, all day long.

PROUST, MARCEL

We can see *In Search of Lost Time* as a kind of anticipation of the Holocaust. Proust senses the Holocaust everywhere. In the puffy sleeves of women's ball gowns, in the lining of men's opera capes. He is in a frenzy of memory, in a hurry to get everything down, to indulge in the practice of remembering, a practice that will soon become a luxury. He is fully aware that they would have taken one look at him and shipped him off immediately, in a first-class cattle car, lined with velvet, to a place with a strange name like Dachau or Auschwitz—the very syllables cutting into one's tongue like hatchets—a place where the sun would have slanted over the roofs of the barracks, glinting the gray slates gold, and the sunset, meeting the smoke rising from the crematoriums' chimneys, would have tinged the smoke pink, and he would have felt compelled to describe everything. We sense that Proust, an anticipatory creature, is profoundly relieved to be homosexual, Jewish, and sickly in the first decades of the century.

PROXIMITY

My godmother told me that there is such a thing as getting too close to God. She said it's like when you light the stovetop, and you stand too close to the cooker, and the flame, up high, leaps up, singeing your eyebrows and a little bit of your fringe. *There is no pain,* she said, *just an odor that escapes from God, sweet and terrible, unmistakable.* We're young again. We're burning again. We are not yet ready for this proximity.

PSYCHOANALYSIS

Psychoanalysis is a science of boys, originated by Sigmund Freud, a man with a beard. Freud visited dormitories of sleeping Viennese cholos and went from bed to bed, waking them up one at a time, taking down their dreams, and then letting them go back to sleep. He taught us to pay close attention to the drool collecting at the corners of a dreaming boy's mouth. After careful consideration, Freud came to the conclusion that the boys who don't exist are more important than the boys who do, and that it is not the violent little cholo cruising down the Ringstrasse whom you love, but the painfully shy cholo who waits patiently for you in the burnt-sugar depths of your heart.

PSYCHOANALYSIS, THE END OF

It is said that at the very moment Freud formulated his conception of the ego, which in lay terms is sort of like a black patent-leather handbag, along with its dark and shiny accessories, namely the id, which is more like a big glossy pterodactyl with a very sharp beak and big pointy wings floating above the handbag, and the super-ego, which is exactly like a nice Colt .45 hidden inside the handbag, pointed directly at the pterodactyl, his mind leapt forward to a future not that far away, when all dreamers would curse him, would stop dreaming and spit on him, into his open mouth. He envisioned a time when his science would no longer be capable of explaining anything, let alone the hearts of humans, when it would make more sense to say things like the heart contains gleaming razors, the heart is made up of night and the night contains pearls.

PUB, THE

My father tells me that even when he is not physically at the pub he is still at the pub, in a metaphysical sense, because in his heart there's a tiny pub, frequented by extremely small, violently drunk, but very happy, bleary-eyed locals.

2

QUEENSLAND

Between the years 1946 and 1952, my mother lived in Brisbane, the capital of the Australian state of Queensland, where, she told me, all the houses were on stilts, so all the furniture in the houses—sofas, curtains, etc.—wouldn't get ruined when there were floods, which there often were, floods of a tropical nature, as well as big flying cockroaches, big as angels, angels that make you shiver and must be exterminated.

During her stay in Queensland, on Saturday nights my mother frequently went out dancing to a place called Cloudland, and like all the other girls she would adjust her skirt, so the lacy edge of her petticoat would show, just slightly. And, she told me, she was constantly adjusting her hair, because the humidity virtually destroyed her curls, both in the southern part of the state, which was semitropical, but even more in the northern part, which was tropical, meaning there were mangrove thickets, and where my mother once rode on a glass-bottom boat, over and along the coral ridge that is known as the Great Barrier Reef, and she looked down at all the different colors, and she became overwhelmed by all the colors, and, glad to be back on land, she wrote postcards.

QUESTION

Throughout the history of philosophy, every philosopher has sat down to work in the morning in relatively good spirits. Lurking in each philosopher's mind is the thought that perhaps this will be the book he has dreamt of all his life, the book that will destroy all questions and explain everything so thoroughly that there'll no longer be any need for the world.

By the evening, in whatever century, the philosopher is always stiff: philosophy has had a profound effect upon the spine. Even more so, he is depressed. The questions follow him everywhere, panting, snapping at his heels, questions such as what is the relationship between philosophy and bad breath, philosophy and lost love, philosophy and crow's feet, philosophy and erections, philosophy and yawning, and one question in particular: why does all thought end in failure?

QUESTION MARKS

I like question marks. I think it was sexier, though, when we called them interrogation marks. It's always quite touching when you look up someone in the encyclopedia, someone who lived a long time ago and has since dripped into obscurity, and their dates of birth and death are each followed by a question mark, as if there's a question as to whether they were ever really born at all, or ever truly died. Every direct question should end with a question mark, for example, *Do you fully understand that one day you are going to die?* But life and even more so death are more like indirect questions, which do not require question marks, for example, *I asked you whether you really understood that eventually you are going to die.*

QUINTILIAN

Quintilian was a Roman rhetorician who wrote a twelve-volume work called the *Institutio Oratoria,* which examined the training of the would-be orator from infancy to death. Beneath all of Quintilian's highly elaborate rhetorical systems one senses the presence of things decidedly non-rhetorical: things like babble, prattle, puke, baby rattles, death rattles, last gasps, and spittle.

Throughout the book he gives some strange and contradictory advice. For example, commenting on the fire that swept through Rome in AD 64, the one during which Nero was said to have played the lyre, and afterwards blamed the Christians for, putting many to death, Quintilian blames rhetoric, and advises the reader to burn it.

Another practical piece of advice the Roman instructor offers involves keeping a suitcase under one's bed, in preparation for death, a suitcase packed with the subtlest rhetoric, which, he assures us, will be of the utmost necessity when dealing with the nuances of the afterlife.

QUOITS

We didn't have a family photo album per se. Our photographs were scattered all over the house, as if our house itself were a kind of photo album. I would come across old snapshots slipped inside books, in envelopes, in shoeboxes and drawers. One afternoon I found a black-and-white photograph of two teenage boys, by the sea, playing a game of quoits. The boys were wearing strange ruched black underwear that looked very glossy against their white skin.

I took the photo to my mother; she tried to remember who the boys were but eventually admitted that she didn't recognize them. When I looked up *quoits* I discovered that this game, which involved throwing iron rings at a peg stuck in the ground, had originated in ancient Rome, and, back then when young men played quoits, they didn't wear anything. Over 2,000 years it seemed nothing had really changed, except, at some point, young men put on strange underwear.

QUOTATION MARKS

Wittgenstein later rejected his *Sad Investigations,* claiming *they just weren't sad enough: to write such a book one would require sentences composed of black tears.* Yet the book contains lasting insights, for example: *the* o *of the glory hole and the* o *of my mouth mirror the two* o*'s in philosophy. During such extra-philosophical activities one's mouth begins to taste like a goldmine. One's knees begin to ache terribly, waiting for the boys to arrive, waiting for quotation marks to flee the scene.*

QUO WARRANTO

Quo warranto is a Latin phrase that means *by what authority do I describe the world?* Today the term is used in courts of law to determine whether an individual has the authority to describe anyone or talk about anything. Inevitably, the courts decide that the individual has no authority. So what to do with the tongue? In the early days of the twenty-first century the tongue poses a problem; the individual as we formerly understood it is dead, but still describing, and still warm, like a brand new corpse.

R

RABIES

As a boy I thought about rabies quite a lot. I was convinced that any day a rabid dog who had wandered a great distance just to find me would come up and bite me on the inside of my left thigh, giving me rabies. I would run home and go into the kitchen, where my mum would be peeling potatoes, and there would be a little bit of foam at the corner of my mouth, delicate as Bruges lace, and she would know.

I knew that I didn't have to worry about contracting rabies from other boys who had already been bitten by rabid dogs. I could even French kiss a boy with rabies, because, as I learned from the *World Book,* although the virus resides happily in the saliva, it cannot enter skin that is unbroken.

Whenever I walked around our neighborhood and came across one of the local stray dogs, I'd look carefully at the fleshy folds at the corners of its mouth to see if there was any froth there. Every day I expected to meet a rabid dog, or a rabid boy, but I never did meet one or the other, and I never had rabies, and I continue to have some regrets about this.

RATS

My boyfriend and I have rats! Tiny, nervous rats, with extremely high levels of anxiety. They make themselves known only at night, by scurrying in the roof above our heads. Although the soft scampering sound keeps Tim up, I actually enjoy the noise of their little feet; I imagine it's what dreams must sound like, hastening their way through the brain.

Our rats also like the garden, especially the ivy. Sometimes I see their rat shadows in the moonlight, the outlines of their noses as pointy as party hats. This is the last straw for Tim, the gardener: he's built a small wooden house, like a birdhouse, and filled it with poison.

There is a scientific theory that one out of every ten rats is descended from the same rats who in Sicily in 1346 scuttled along the ropes that led from the ships to the docks, bringing to Europe the bubonic plague, the so-called Great Mortality, which would kill approximately twenty-five million Europeans within the space of five years—one third of the population.

This means there is a very real possibility that our rats are distant relatives of those more notable rodents. Although this sounds farfetched, just recently a boy in Los Angeles County was treated for bubonic plague, the first case here in twenty years. He came down with the usual symptoms, including the characteristic black lumps under the skin, as if the body is trying to photograph itself for posterity. And the last urban epidemic of the plague occurred in L.A. in 1924.

It seems that plagues, like love, never really disappear. They almost vanish, only to reappear. Perhaps soon in Los Angeles we'll see a new outbreak of a new plague, and just like in London when the plague arrived there in the seventeenth century, there'll be demented prophets wearing animal skins, telling everyone they're doomed. Whereas the doomsayers in London stood outside churches, ours will lurk outside mini-malls. To be honest, I think these men are already here.

However, I find it hard to imagine that our rats are carrying within them the promise of such destruction. Still, though perhaps not quite as auspicious, I am certain that our rats are trying to express something; they have something important they wish to convey.

RAZORS

In the 1970s and 1980s it was common to find razors in places children frequented. In the summer of 1981 in Perth, Western Australia, a group of juvenile delinquents somehow managed to insert a series of razor blades into the curving, labyrinthine slides of the most popular water parks. Boys innocently enjoying these slides were consequently being cut to ribbons, and, staggering out of the highly chlorinated water, which had turned a bit pink with their blood, would collapse onto the bright green Astroturf of these institutions. In fact, I met one of these boy-victims; his skin was covered in faint scars like the thin red ribbons one finds in prayer missals, and just as a ribbon in a missal is there to keep one's place, likewise this boy's scars allowed one to keep one's place on his body. At the time of all these razor incidents, water parks were at their height of popularity, and we lived for them; compared to their structural elegance and aesthetic complexity, the sea was a disorderly mess, full of weird creatures that did not care for us. The appearance of these razor blades did not stop us from attending the water parks. In fact, we attended them more frequently, and with greater anticipation. So rose the stakes of our joy, and the intensity.

RAZORS, OCCUPATIONS IN

There are boys who take razors to themselves five days a week, nine to five; it is a full-time occupation. All their polyester suits are shredded. These boys are mere civil servants in the bureaucracy of razors. When they turn sixty, they will retire and receive a big gold razor. They will live quietly on a pension of razors. They will take up gardening and use razors to trim the roses.

REASON, THE SLEEP OF

I don't know about you, but sometimes, when I think about the world too much, it makes me just want to flop over on my desk and cross my ankles and go right to sleep, but the tips of the wings of all my little beasts who are hovering gently above me, watching kindly over me, keep tickling the back of my neck, and I can smell their warm stinky breath, so I don't fall completely asleep, unlike the man in Goya's famous etching of 1798.

REFLECTION

Whenever I approach a mirror, I cannot help but feel that my reflection has arrived there hours before me. If my reflection were waiting there to welcome me and to embrace me, that would be one thing. But I am becoming increasingly certain that my reflection gets to the mirror bright and early and lurks there, like a rapist or a murderer, in wait for me.

RESURRECTION, THE

In Rubens's miraculous tapestry from the seventeenth century, which depicts Christ emerging from his tomb three days after being crucified, the fact of the Resurrection pales before the fact of the legs of the Roman guards keeping watch, who are all wearing these short tunics, which reveal their muscular calf muscles and powerful thighs. One forgets all about the Resurrection. One has to be reminded to pay attention to the Resurrection. The guards are cowering before the unbelievable terror and beauty of what is happening—just like me, they are frightened by beauty. My eyes linger on one soldier in particular, the hem of whose tunic is flying up, ever so slightly, and who is attempting to flee, just as I find myself doing when confronted with unbearable beauty.

RHINOCEROS, SUMATRAN

Recently, a Sumatran rhinoceros gave birth to a calf in the Los Angeles Zoo. Although this creature is said to endure captivity well, it was the first rhinoceros of its kind to be born in captivity in 112 years. Naturally this was a cause for celebration, although of a mournful kind, especially considering that of the five distinct species of rhinoceroses, most have found themselves in that terrible state of being almost extinct, nearly extinct, that is, rare.

By nature a profoundly solitary creature, the Sumatran rhinoceros is smaller than any other, standing at a height of around four feet, and weighing no more than a ton. It has two horns, the front one being more conspicuous. Two thick folds of skin encircle its bluish gray body.

In the wild, avoiding the day and those hunters permitted to hunt it with a special license, it takes long night-walks, inexhaustibly; it eats mangoes and twists saplings to mark its territory. In a zoo, I suppose it just thinks about these things, daydreams.

I am interested in this creature, as I am interested in all beauty that is born into captivity, all species that hover on the brink of extinction but somehow find their way back.

RICKETS

When we were children our mothers went to great lengths to protect us from the disease of the bones known as rickets. So that we did not develop the conditions that result from rickets, conditions with nice names such as rosary ribs, funnel chests, knock-knees, bow legs, and chicken breasts, our mothers made sure we received plenty of calcium and direct sunlight. They tied us upside down, by our ankles, to the sun, so that we swung back and forth like pendulums. They sewed us milk dressing gowns and coats from scraps of the sun, in a concerted effort to stop our bones from becoming soft and twisting into shapes that simply were not normal.

RIMBAUD, ARTHUR

In my boyfriend Tim's copy of Rimbaud's *Illuminations, and Other Prose Poems,* which he's had forever, there's a little poem he wrote in it, in Manhattan, around 1980, when he was barely twenty-two, and when the plague was just getting up and running:

> *everybody likes rimbaud*
> *everybody looks like rimbaud*
> *everybody wants to fuck rimbaud*

This is my favorite poem in the world (sorry, Rimbaud!). I don't think I've ever read anything wiser, or truer.

RIOTS

On the tenth day of the riots in Paris in 2005, during which young men of Arab and North African descent rebelled against the hopelessness of their situation, a McDonald's restaurant in the working-class suburb of Corbeil-Essonnes was burnt to the ground. Nothing remained except for the statue of Ronald McDonald himself, who continued to sit near the skeleton of the counter, looking over his ruined kingdom, unscathed, calm, shiny, almost jubilant.

Indeed, it is said that those statues of Ronald McDonald are formed from such sturdy material that 2,000 years from now, when every trace of you and me is long gone, when our bones have been ground down to something finer than cinnamon, Ronald McDonald statues will still be around; in fact, they may be the only enduring statuary from this century.

People will gaze in perplexed awe upon that placidly smiling form with the curly red hair, with the round, white face and the luscious, red lips, with the red nose and the curious black triangles under each twinkling eye. They will gape in wonder at the ripe, Rubenesque curves of his pear-shaped figure, draped in the yellow one-piece jumpsuit with the white and red striped legs and arms; they will gawk at the sheer abundance of his big red boots. Future generations will assume that this was our God, or that this was our ideal of beauty.

The very thought makes one collapse, makes one want to rewind the riots and lick up the ash and rubble—this being the semen of rioters.

ROMANTICISM, GERMAN

Sometimes when you gaze upon and down into the awe-inspiring ass of a man, you feel like you're the guy in that painting by the nineteenth-century German Romantic painter Caspar David Friedrich— *Wanderer Above The Sea of Fog,* I think it is—a painting in which we see the back of a man who is wearing a black coat, and who is standing by himself at the edge of a rocky gorge or precipice, filled with rolling, soft, gray mist.

Just like this lone individual, we are similarly poised at the edge of something. The sight before us, of a man's ass, is equally overwhelming. We feel very alone, isolated even, but oddly connected to it all. (Who knew we were German Romantics?) And like the little guy in the black coat we could go on looking all day, although just like him we can't see a lot, every man's ass hidden as it is in mist and fog.

ROSES

The strangest, most memorable odors rise out of boys! At first we can't place the odor, but then we realize it smells like two-week-old rose water; we are reminded of our mother's habit of never changing the water in a vase of roses, and, as the odor continues to emanate from the boy, we recall our mother and feel pleasantly reassured. The asshole is the repository of memory and of nostalgia. All boys take us directly back to childhood; all rank odors remind us of rank odors from very long ago.

ROYALTY

The only member of royalty who interests me is the cholo who rode his bicycle up and down our street that day, all day. He was wearing khakis and a white wifebeater and long white socks. I believe it was Johann Winckelmann who described *the classic simplicity and quiet grandeur of the cholo*. And on this particular cholo's perfectly shaved head there sat a bright Burger King crown.

S

SAHARA, THE

As a kid, I loved those old black-and-white movies set in the Sahara. I don't remember much about their storylines except that in every one of them there was a mute character, whose tongue had been cut out of his head. This character always knew everything that was going on but was unable to tell anyone. I daydreamed a lot about going to live in the Sahara with one of these men. I even had a scheme to get there. In the morning when I waited for the bus on Leach Highway at the end of our street, sheep trucks would come by full of bleating sheep, which, my mother informed me, were being sent to Arabia to be slaughtered in a special way. I planned to hide amongst those sheep.

It's been years now since I have seen one of these films, but every now and then I get this feeling that I actually fulfilled my dream, and that I am living in the Sahara. I sense that my life is an old black-and-white movie unfolding in the Sahara, and the narrative conditions of my life require a mute character, but that mute character has turned out to be me, and the sand is blowing into my gaping mouth, ceaselessly, ceaselessly.

SAILORS

Although there are so many appealing things about sailors—the fact that they brought the plague to Europe in the fourteenth century, and the disease known as scurvy, which was common on long voyages, as well as the disease known as gangrene, which required amputation of limbs, and of course their complex relationship to sodomy, which was common on long voyages, as well as the drowned sailors who sleep at the bottom of the sea, and the dead sailors who dream at the bottom of me—historically we have invested far too much in sailors. Viewed objectively, sailors are nothing but navy blue cloth and white stripes or white cloth and blue stripes and gold buttons.

SAINTS

There are currently more than 10,000 saints in the Roman Catholic Church. In the Roman Catholic Church only I have the power to confer sainthood. In the chapel at my school there was a wooden statue of a saint, I forget which one; at some point, saints, like boys, begin to blur into one another. Somehow over the years a hole had formed right where the saint's asshole would have been, and, over the years, boys stuck their fingers in the hole, fingerfucking the saint as it were, making the hole smoother and smoother, so you didn't have to worry about splinters. Even today, I'm at my best when I have my finger in a saint.

SALOME

They say that when Salome kissed the decapitated head of John the Baptist, she could still taste honey and locusts on the prophet's breath. However, in requesting the head of the prophet on a platter, she didn't go far enough. In my opinion, her request was far too modest. She didn't ask for enough. She should have taken her desires one step further and demanded that her stepfather Herod bring her not only the head but also the unconscious of John the Baptist, on another silver engraved platter.

That said, ever since the giving of this gift, in AD 28, no gift has quite matched up. All gifts are not entirely what we wished for. The exchange of gifts takes place in the shadow of Herod's gift, and within this shadow, we all shiver and smile and say thank you, but the look on our face gives away that fact that we are severely disappointed.

SANTA BARBARA

Located on the Pacific Ocean, Santa Barbara, population 92,325, may at first appear to be a paradise of sorts. But, as they say, appearances can be deceptive, and if we have learned anything by now, it is that there is no such thing as paradise. Santa Barbara, whose economy relies on the plastics and tourist industries, is actually filled with death, crawling with ex-hippies who have been transformed into yuppies, what are otherwise known as the living dead. It is really just a big cemetery, population 92,325 skeletons. It is a very sunny, very brightly lit cemetery.

From a class perspective, it is also a mangled capitalist dystopia. Class distinctions there are so extreme that if Karl Marx, exiled from Germany, instead of fleeing to London, had fled to Santa Barbara, he surely would have changed the first sentence of the *Communist Manifesto* to say something like *The specter of Marie Antoinette and her wig and her powder is haunting Santa Barbara.*

Actually, I think he would have taken one look at Santa Barbara and stopped writing the *Communist Manifesto* altogether. He would have lost all hope in any possibility that his theory might succeed. Though maybe, if, like me, Marx had found himself there on the weekend of the so-called Fiesta, which celebrates and fetishizes Spanish Colonialism, in particular the mission that was built at the cost of thousands of lives of Chumash Indians, if he had been out and about on the Saturday night of the Fiesta, when all the cholos come in from outlying areas, and the streets are covered with pink and blue and green confetti, he would have written another kind of manifesto, a much better manifesto, and called it the *Cholo Manifesto,* or the *Confetti Manifesto;* he would have come up with a whole other theory whose impact would have been far more enduring.

SATIRE

Whether I like it or not, I am in large part a satirist. I might as well enjoy it: having been born into an age that is unavoidably satiric—satire being a natural response to overwhelming foolishness and horror, the two qualities that perhaps most characterize the present day—I have no choice in the matter. (Though even with satire, one can still be tender.) Still, I cannot ignore the fact that there are spaces that satire cannot reach, and instances in which satire turns against us. The main instance being death. Let us call these *self-exposed* spaces.

SCABS

Approximately one third of childhood was spent picking at the scabs on our elbows and knees. For this task we required our hands, which we otherwise kept in our pockets like daggers placed in scabbards. Ah, bright red scabs, which were the jewels of childhood.

SCALPING

I was a great admirer of Laura Ingalls Wilder and her *Little House on the Prairie* books, which were such authentic portraits of frontier life. I especially enjoyed the parts about getting maple syrup directly from trees, and the scenes where white people were scalped. Somehow in my imagination the two acts would mingle: after getting scalped, maple syrup would be poured into the victim's brain. But, eventually, reading about making maple syrup and being scalped wasn't enough. I wanted firsthand experience of producing maple syrup. I needed to know what it felt like to be scalped.

SCISSORS

Just as a pair of scissors is basically two knives joined together, a boy is essentially two boys joined together. *Je est un autre,* said Rimbaud, before knifing off to Abyssinia. A naked boy is a pair of your mother's pinking scissors. We wish the boy could be more like those safety scissors they handed out to us when we were children, but, realistically, nothing can keep the boy safe.

Scott, Bon

Willagee's most famous son is surely Bon Scott, former lead singer of the heavy metal band AC/DC. Scott grew up in Willagee after his family emigrated from Kirremuir, Scotland. His turning to heavy metal seems a natural choice, given that the Scottish accent, with its harsh vowels and turgid tones—particularly in the region where he is from—is the linguistic equivalent of heavy metal.

In 1980, just a few days after Scott died of a drug overdose, some graffiti appeared on the wall of our local chemist: *BON SCOTT, FORGOTTEN NOT.* I was lucky enough to perceive this slogan, this inscription, the very first day it cropped up, as that morning I happened to have gone on an outing with my mother to the local chemist to purchase cough syrup and jelly beans (for the glucose). The local authorities quickly erased the graffiti, but overnight it resurfaced. After several efforts, the authorities gave up.

To this day, if you go to Willagee you will see this graffiti. Just a short drive away, in the local cemetery where my grandmother and my aunt Joan are buried, the cemetery in which I wish to reside one day, you can find the tombstone of Bon Scott.

Like him, I grew up in Willagee and am of Scottish descent. Unlike Bon Scott, I am destined to be forgotten.

SEDUCTION

We can pinpoint the exact moment the seduction began: July 22, 1994, in a drab little hotel room in South Kensington (one day, a museum will build an accurate reconstruction of this room). It was the night before the bombs exploded, just down the street at the Israeli Embassy. The time of the seduction was around 11:33 p.m. (see, we are already getting approximate).

First, you took off your spectacles, the frames of which were very thin and gold. I've never seen nerves, but I imagine that is what they might look like—fine and twisted and gold. I didn't take off my glasses, because I wasn't wearing them yet. I'm older and blinder now, not as nearsighted as you, my dear—I can see a bit farther—and today I require glasses to correct this defect.

So you placed your glasses on the bedside table and leaned into me.

Since then, you must have removed your glasses ten thousand times, a conservative estimate. But the seduction has not ceased. It has been continuous, at times relentless, working quietly, day and night, like a big gold machine that leaves little scraps, the scraps of seduction, which we later put to good use.

Not even the end of the world could put an end to this seduction.

SELF-AWARENESS

I can think of nothing worse than sitting with someone in silence, watching as they reflect upon themselves. It's like watching a face catch fire, watching a face do its detective work, watching a face inform on itself.

SELF-DESTRUCTION

Apparently, the most densely populated section in eternity, and the hardest one to get into, is the *Section of Self-Destruction*. Above the entrance there is a sign: *Every Boy Is a Device Designed to Destroy Himself under a Predefined Set of Circumstances.* Its residents live in dormitories, in bunk beds. At night after lights out, you can hear them whispering to one another, reminiscing about razors, how they gleamed in the moonlight.

So as to keep the inhabitants busy, they are all assigned to work on an *Encyclopedia of Self-Destruction.* The goal of the encyclopedia is to document all knowledge of self-destruction. The encyclopedia's aim is to reach both readers who are self-destructive and those readers who are not.

The categories are exactly the same as in the *World Book Encyclopedia,* but the entries must all relate the category to the topic of interest, namely self-destruction. At times, this can be a stretch—for example, identifying precisely how sewing machines or sugar beets pertain to the act of destroying oneself—but sooner or later, the writers find the connection; everything, it seems, goes back to self-destruction.

SELF-HATRED

Despite the innumerable experiments we have conducted on the self, experiments whose conditions were all carefully controlled, despite the very pretty colors that were produced during the course of these experiments, mainly within the confines of test tubes, despite the initial excitement we experienced over the loud fizzing noises emanating from the test tubes, despite the endless data we have gathered on the self, despite all the pocket calculators we have gone through—not to mention all the Bunsen burners—despite all those lab coats we have placed in black and yellow plastic trash bins clearly marked *Hazardous Waste Material* and then subsequently destroyed, after splashing a bit of the self all over ourselves, and despite all the burns we simultaneously experienced, burns of varying degrees of severity, I need not remind you that all these experiments have essentially been failures, though nowhere near as big a failure as the failure of the self. Today, the only thing we can still say for certain about the self is that it would prefer to be someone else.

SELF-REFLECTION

When we are born, we come complete with little mirrors lodged in our skulls in which we can see ourselves and everyone else 24/7. These mirrors are similar to rearview mirrors found in cars except, with our mirrors, thoughts often appear to be closer than they actually are, hence paranoia.

It seems we spend most of our lives trying to dislodge these mirrors. We seek out sex, we seek out dreams. But even within their haze and gauze, we find that we are blessed—that is to say, cursed—with the habit of self-reflection.

For example, the other night I dreamt I was on an endless escalator, but in the dream I found myself thinking, *In other dreams I've been on much longer, far grander, more infinitely unfolding escalators.*

Or you might be having the best sex, where everything is being destroyed and dissolving, but still you find yourself thinking ahead to the next time you have sex, hoping that you'll be destroyed even more.

In this sense, dreams and sex just don't work like they used to. Traditionally, there was always the last resort, this being death, but today, in the twenty-first century, not even death can supply us with what we crave: absolute oblivion. Nowadays, apparently, in death you spend even more time thinking about yourself, moping about. To find the self-forgetfulness we really crave, it seems we will have to go further than dreams, further than sex, further than death.

SEX ADDICTION IN ANTIQUITY

In antiquity everyone was a sex addict. This was 2,000 years prior to anything even remotely clinical. Amidst all the *shimmeringness,* sex addiction made perfect sense. To be a sex addict was logical, a good thing.

SHADOWS

It seems that death will be remarkably similar to life, a thought that should fill anyone with horror. Yet there will be one major difference: whereas in life it is our bodies that are first and foremost, in death it will be our shadows; our bodies will appear only at certain times of day, under certain conditions of the light. The same will go for objects. In the afterlife, the shadow of your little school desk, the one into which you carved your initials, will be a constant presence; in fact, you'll see the shadow of your initials, which were already like a shadow, and therefore can be construed as the shadow of a shadow; the school desk itself will become visible only in the late afternoon, in the movement toward dusk. Your shadow, but not you, will sit and write at the shadow of this desk. (As this is already pretty much the case, it will not require too great of an adjustment.) And it confirms something we have always suspected: that our bodies are insubstantial, secondary; it is the outline our body casts in the shade that is of far greater importance.

SHOES

In 1942, at the age of fifteen, Otto Rosenberg was sent to Auschwitz for being a gypsy. He found himself assigned to polish the shoes of Dr. Josef Mengele, until, in the doctor's words, *I can see my face in them.* While Mengele was busy injecting Gypsy children with petrol, or cutting apart and then stitching Siamese twins back together, Otto worked diligently, with a soft rag and a tin of black polish. Resting between experiments, Mengele would come around, and together they would gaze into the shoes, in which Otto saw not only the doctor's reflection but also his own, held in the shoes, trapped in those glossy black walking mirrors.

SHOES, NIGHT

When you dream, you put on your *nightshoes.*

SILENCE, MY FATHER'S

Although throughout his life my father has worked in a number of occupations, first as a sailor, then as a fitter and turner, and finally as a gardener, all along his real occupation has been silence.

He has worked for silence for close to eighty years. He has never missed a day. When it comes time for him to retire from silence they will give him a big gold watch. Silence was the trade of my grandfather, whom my father took after, just as I now follow in my father's footsteps.

I come from a long line of silence. I suppose I will need to have a son, so he can carry on this work of silence when I am gone.

SKATER BOYS

Los Angeles is virtually infested with skater boys. From time to time, when things get really bad, and it approaches epidemic proportions, the health authorities here have used the phrase *A Plague of Skater Boys,* just to scare us! In the summer, these boys cast their shadows, which are spindly, like the shadow cast by a lead pencil. These shadows announce and anticipate the imminence of the skater boys' disappearance, just as all shadows do, and the skateboards even cast their own shadows, somewhat like the shape of a stingray—stingrays are like skateboards, if the latter had souls. Oh, to see inside the soul of a skater boy! I like the clunking, whirring sound the wheels of their skateboards make on the hard concrete, and I like how focused skater boys are: all they care about is skating; everything else is dead by comparison. If only I could have some of that focus! Yet, just like us, they live for those brief, bright moments when their skateboards leave the ground and it seems—just for an instant—that they might never come back down, but simply ascend, ascend.

SKELETON

This is a nice word for cage. This is a kinder word.

SKULLS

The old skull was no good, too light, too bony. It seemed completely incapable of doing what a skull is supposed to do. But this new skull is gorgeous and brutal. It wishes you well.

SLUTS

I have extremely positive associations with the word *slut,* and, in general, I feel very warmly toward sluts, who are like wands, or a combination of a wand and a wound. Gazing down into the fleshy red hole of a volcano, listening to the bubbly lava whilst hooking one's toes to the rim of the volcano so as not to fall in, one can only conclude that nature is a slut.

When I was a child, I used to think the whole world was a slut that would freely offer itself up to me. Now that I am no longer a child, I know that the world is not a slut. It is actually quite chaste and does not yield up its bliss so easily.

SNAILS

There are 7 razors in a week, which makes 365 razors in a year. There are more than 80,000 species of snails. We could learn a thing or two from the snail, like how to live anywhere: in Arctic wastelands, in tropical jungles, or at the bottom of the sea. And if we invested in some of its lovely, slimy properties, we could have that nice, sticky, silver solution that they leave wherever they go. Just like a snail, we could crawl across the edge of a razor, taking our time, without coming to any harm.

SNAKES

A snake is lucky! It has that delightful backbone made up of three hundred small bones, whereas we—man—have a lousy thirty-three bones in our backbone. A snake can sunbathe, just like us, but can also withstand temperatures way below freezing, unlike man, who gets a cold and has to drink cherry-flavored cough syrup out of a plastic cup. Because of their astonishing back-bones, snakes are highly articulate. The reticulate python is the longest snake in the world—its length is that of six brand-new bicycles strung together, ridden by six violent boys! And, of course, what makes us envy the snake the most is that when it's tired of itself, it just sheds the old skin, turning it inside out and leaving the hollow tube before slithering off in search of new colors, whereas we cannot leave our hollowness.

SNEAKERS

Whenever I'm walking around my neighborhood of Venice and encounter a pair of sneakers dangling from a telephone wire, my thoughts inevitably turn to the boy who tossed those sneakers up there. Although most gestures are terrible, in that they imply a repetition unto death, and perhaps even beyond death, I don't mind this gesture, just as I didn't mind the gesture that cholo enacted for me, lifting up his white tank top, placing the hem in his mouth, so he could show me the name of the gang that had been recently tattooed onto his stomach. In fact, I consider throwing sneakers up on a wire to be quite a hopeful gesture. As I look up at the sneakers, I find myself wondering how many attempts it took until the sneakers stayed put.

And although I know that the sneakers are meant to serve as a gentle yet firm reminder that we have entered a particular gang's territory, alerting us to the splendid and quiet dangers that await us, and therefore urging us to enter with care, the end result is not only threatening but also full of melancholy. The sneakers indicate not only the gang's presence but also a boy's absence, for the boy who got the sneakers up there is nowhere to be seen. And whenever there is a breeze, which there generally is in Venice, the laces of the sneakers kind of flutter, recalling the ribbons on an Amish girl's bonnet.

SOCRATES, THE CLOTHES OF

I read somewhere once that Socrates loved the sun, and, when he wasn't trying to convince his fellow Athenians of their own ignorance, he liked to sunbathe. Contemporary accounts say that the philosopher's face was perpetually sunburnt. He worshipped not only the actual sun but also those miniature suns, whose rays peeped out from beneath the hems of his students' robes. Before drinking the hemlock, Socrates had requested that after his death all his belongings be evenly distributed. The women who came to clean up his house found that the collars and necklines and sleeves of all his robes were sun soiled, singed. They threw them out in a heap on the side of the road. No one respectable would wear such garments; not even the slaves would touch them.

SOCRATES, THE DEATH OF

Upon observing David's painting of the death of Socrates, specifically the young man passing the cup of hemlock to the philosopher, the first thought that occurs to us is, *well, we wouldn't mind having a boy like that pass us some hemlock; we wouldn't mind a bit of hemlock ourselves.*

The young man's strong back is turned toward us. He's wearing a rust-red robe—one sleeve falls off a creamy, muscular shoulder; the robe's hem finishes just below the knee, displaying his muscular calves, just as through the cloth of the robe the outline of his sensual behind is highly apparent. His face is hidden in his hand; he's overwhelmed with sorrow, just as we are overwhelmed with a different sensation, though perhaps sorrow and the sensual are not as far away from one another as we might think.

Upon tasting the hemlock—but before saying the bit about Asclepius and the rooster—Socrates is said to have licked his lips and commented that he knew the taste already, that it tasted like something else. Having kissed the lips of more boys than he cared to remember, having been betrayed by more boys than he cared to recall, having been deeply acquainted with the gold leaf bitterness of boys, he was already familiar with the taste. *I hope,* he said, taking another sip, *that there will not be boys in the next world.*

SODOM AND GOMORRAH

After the Flood, my favorite bit in the Bible is Sodom and Gomorrah. I think I like it because I can relate to it. I particularly like the part when the angels come to Sodom, and all the men hear about this and go to Lot's house, where the angels are staying. Naturally, the men all want to know the angels, and they're at Lot's door, and they're just about to open the door when the angels blind them, so they're left blindly groping around the frame of the door. I know just how they feel. But I also like to think about Sodom and Gomorrah prior to all the destruction. More often than not I feel like those men must have felt just a little bit earlier, when they were still very excited about the possibility of knowing the angels.

SODOMY

For the Augustan poets, sodomy was primarily a technical concern, best expressed in couplets; the act itself was full of barbs and jabs, innately satirical, incessantly verging on the mock-heroic. Yet the necessity of a top and bottom invoked harmony, balance.

For the Romantics, however, sodomy was an altogether different matter. Primarily a movement of irrational bottoms, they perceived sodomy as an act overflowing with feeling, always on the brink of becoming sentimental. Sodomy evoked ruins and fog-filled gorges and was best when conducted in deserted, moonlit graveyards, without restraint. Accordingly, language was to be barebacked!

Despite their enthusiasm, the Romantics were acutely aware of the fact that every act of sodomy was tinged with melancholy.

SODOMY, PHILOSOPHY OF

Aristotle, an obscure Greek philosopher who hardly wrote anything, has some interesting things to say on this subject: *Whereas as a philosopher I am horrified of holes, and I use thought to patch up holes, in sex they are my goal. During the day, think of one's student as an attic; at night, he becomes a crawl space. Sodomy is a spatial event. And by God, didn't Alexander look fine today in that skintight tunic, the one with the gold trim.*

SOUL, THE

The Romantics likened the body to a kind of prison in which the soul was incarcerated. If this is so, my body is the Philadelphia Federal Detention Center, and my soul is the rapper Lil' Kim, who spent just under a year there. Just like her, my soul is glamorous and busty and petite, and it can be accused of perjury at times, which is why the diminutive rapper was there in the first place.

The Romantics also compared the body to a cage in which the soul was similarly imprisoned. In this case, my body is a small rusty cage measuring three feet by three feet, the exact proportions of the cage in which my family housed our budgies. It logically follows that my soul is a little budgie, with bright feathers, yellow, green, and blue ones. Within the confines of my body, my soul seems to be able to amuse itself endlessly, doing quick jigs and deft acrobatic leaps, chirping and squawking, making light of the monotony. But at times, my soul also looks slightly bedraggled and somewhat forlorn, as our budgies often did; my soul can be seen pacing madly, and just like a budgie, it makes a real mess inside my body.

SPEARS, BRITNEY

Although I have no waking interest whatsoever in pop singer Britney Spears, I occasionally dream about her, because you can't control your dreams, which sounds a bit like a Britney Spears lyric: *You can't control your dreams / so you might as well submit to your dreams.* And in my dreams I meet her at a party, and she's very down to earth, and very friendly, and we get on really well (I think she sits on my lap), and as she prepares to leave the party I don't ask for her phone number (because after all, although we got on well, she is Britney Spears), and after she's left I kick myself, and keep kicking myself so hard I start to bleed and am filled with something far worse than regret, which would be a good name for Britney's next album: *Something Far Worse than Regret.* But I remind myself that she has my e-mail and she'll e-mail me, surely. So basically, some deeply submerged part of me that I would prefer not to have to confront really does care about Britney Spears, and what she thinks of me. At this point, the dream ends and I wake up, reentering a world in which everything is much more complex: the conditions of myself, the conditions of pop music, the conditions of Britney Spears.

SPINOZA, BARUCH

It is well known that seventeenth-century philosopher Baruch Spinoza, isolated from the intellectual community of Amsterdam and rejected by the city's Jewish community (of which he had once been a part), moonlighted as a lens grinder. After all, a philosopher needs to make a living.

When he thought about it, the two lines of work were not so different from one another, their goal the same: to make people see. But, whereas his customers, picking up the lenses for their spectacles, never failed to thank him, individuals who found themselves exposed to his dazzling ideas, Christians and Jews alike, denounced him for his terrible, future-bringing clarity.

Secretly, he often wondered if this business of lens grinding was perhaps his real work, his true calling; it was conceivable that the other thing he did, philosophy, was nothing but a frivolous pastime, a futile, rewardless hobby.

And sometimes Spinoza's thinking took him to places even he did not care to see. He was subject to visions, which he normally stitched into his philosophical system, though there was one vision that refused to be integrated. It usually came to him while he was at work on a pair of lenses. Looking up for a moment, he would, in a distance that was beyond distance, perceive workers building a strange, gray structure comprised of rows and rows of prison houses, and brick buildings with chimneys, a place called Auschwitz, thousands of miles and 250-odd years away. Disconcerted, Spinoza would look back down and try to concentrate on the task in front of him, but even over the interminable sound of the lens grinding—like God grinding his teeth while he dreams—he could hear the workers busily hammering away.

STALACTITES AND STALAGMITES

As a child I was very interested in stalactites and stalagmites. In our *Childcraft* encyclopedia there was a whole section on these formations, complete with pictures of boys in caves. (If I remember correctly, the *World Book* entry on the same phenomena was not nearly as comprehensive.) It seemed that whereas stalactites drip on you and can gouge out one or both of your eyes, one trips over a stalagmite, which then rips through the flesh and muscle and tissue of your leg, grazing the bone.

Even with this clearly defined distinction, for the life of me, no matter how hard I tried, I could never remember which was which, just as when you become an adult, it can be difficult to distinguish states of joy from states of despair; I find myself unable to appreciate the difference to this day. But sometimes I feel that I am in a dark cave, treacherous with both stalactites and stalagmites.

STALIN, JOSEPH

Stalin's dad was a cobbler. It is said that young Joseph liked nothing better than to watch his father hammer new heels into old shoes. It was expected the boy would follow in his father's footsteps; apparently, Stalin Sr. was disappointed when Joseph did not adopt the family trade, and didn't think much of his son's eventual career choice.

Still, the transition from cobbler to dictator is a surprisingly small one. Stalin himself claimed that he approached his job employing exactly the same skill and application that his father had brought to the job of shoemaking and shoe mending.

In his later years, whilst touring the Soviet Union, Stalin would often pop into the local cobbler's, to share a few words with the man; he'd listen to the sweet sound of the hammering and inhale the warm smell of the leather.

Yet whenever Stalin reflected upon the millions of Soviet citizens who were dying from the purges and the famines and the deportations, he could not bear to think of their shoes. He preferred to ponder the loss in strictly human terms—for what is a human if not an abstraction? But a pair of shoes is a fact. One can control a human; it is far more difficult to order about a pair of shoes, to ask some shoes to dig a ditch for you.

Faced with the problem of what to do with all those millions of pairs of empty shoes, Stalin saw them in his imagination lined up very neatly, stretching farther than Siberia, and it overwhelmed him.

STARFISH

I like starfish. They truly know how to handle loss. If a starfish, which is like a star that lives in the sea, needs to escape quickly from an enemy, it breaks off whichever of its five arms is in the enemy's clutches. It then has the ability to grow a new arm to replace the arm it has lost. Even if something so violent happens that the starfish is literally broken off in the middle, whatever remains grows back to form a new, and much stronger, much stranger, starrier individual.

When faced with unbearable loss, we should go down to the sea at night and wade amongst the rocks. Completely ignoring the stars—which in their distance are genuinely lost to us— we should look toward the starfish.

STARS

When you stick your fingers in a man, you can feel stars swirling rapidly inside. You pull your hand out and notice that your fingers are all bloodied. You must have cut yourself on the cold, sharp tips of the stars. Your fingers are stained with stars. You peer inside him and it's like *2001: A Space Odyssey. My God,* you gasp, *it's full of stars.*

STARS, DREAMS OF

I dreamt my all-time favorite dream in London back in 1994. In the dream there was a boy who lifted up his T-shirt and revealed a crude backyard tattoo of a constellation of stars on his flat stomach. He said, *I'm the boy with the stars on his belly,* and then I woke up. That's it. I don't really know why I like this dream so much. I've had far more complex and elusive dreams. I think it's my favorite because at the time it was winter and I hated London and the boy somehow made me feel less cold and less lonely. Although it was nice and mysterious, he also stated the obvious, and besides, he had a really great stomach.

STARS, YELLOW

There is an anecdote about the first time Walter Benjamin saw someone he knew wearing a yellow star: it seems Benjamin went up to his friend on the street and ran his fingers over the star, going from tip to tip, and he couldn't think of anything to say except how soft the felt was.

STINGRAYS

If the unconscious were to finally escape the body—an act it attempts at least once a day—it would look very similar to that flat sea fish known as a stingray. My unconscious would look not like the gigantic fourteen-foot stingrays found floating off the coast of Australia, which I sighted occasionally as a boy, but more like the small stingrays skimming through the shallows of California's Pacific Ocean that I encounter today as an adult. These stingrays move slowly, at the speed of dream; they arouse in one a sensation of the uncanny, similar to the sinister feeling one experiences in a bad dream. They like nothing better than to lash with their spiny, whiplike tails the Achilles' heels of boys who are foolish enough to tread on them, causing a painful wound.

Yes, my unconscious is a baby stingray. And, if it ever manages to get out of my body, it will do just as the stingrays do, loitering where it is warm, in the sun-basked shallows, waiting patiently to sting me or those who come anywhere near me.

STORIES

My mother's stories of her childhood were always very short and broke off abruptly and jaggedly, like, *When I was a little girl, I came down with scarlet fever and almost died; I thought there were ants marching across my pillow, I thought I saw the face of the devil in my bedside lamp;* or, *When your Auntie Helen was little she went down to the big castor oil bush near our house, picked off a bunch of the thorny berries, and ate the seeds inside, which are poisonous, and almost died.* They're barely stories, just shards really. They ended not in death but in a brush with death.

My father constantly smoked a pipe and was therefore unable to tell any stories.

STORIES, ABSENCE OF

Take me seriously when I say *I have no stories.* I couldn't tell a story to save my life, though perhaps I could tell a story to endure this life. And probably, under certain circumstances, say, for example, if I were kidnapped by terrorists and placed in a cage measuring four feet by four feet, and informed that unless I came up with a story, I would be beheaded and it would be videotaped, then, I suppose, under such circumstances, I might be able to come up with a pretty good story.

STORIES, HATRED OF

I don't hate them anymore, but I used to hate them so much that I made quite a name for myself. As I walked down the cobblestone streets of Santa Monica's Third Street Promenade, little kids would run behind me throwing stones at my coattails, squeaking in their high-pitched voices, *Look, look, there goes the story-hater!*

STRIPES

In Luchino Visconti's film *Death in Venice,* the stripes on Tadzio's sweater are black and white and horizontal and thick; the sweater buttons up: four buttons extend down from the polo collar along the shoulder. The stripes on this sweater are similar to the black-and-white horizontal stripes on the sweaters of the gondoliers, whereas the stripes on the collars of Tadzio's sailor suits are diagonal—one suit has a blue collar with thin white stripes, while another suit has a white collar with blue stripes, also quite thin. It is these stripes that cause Gustav von Aschenbach to feel as if nine pit bull puppies are barking in his heart and to subsequently die whilst lounging on a deck chair on the seashore, a chair whose fabric is likewise striped, blue and white, with the horizon. All these stripes are relatively different from the stripes on the collars of the sailor suits worn by the Vienna Boys' Choir, the choir of boy sopranos founded in 1924, shortly after Adolf Hitler's failed putsch of 1923, which resulted in him being imprisoned and writing *Mein Kampf* from behind bars, which are like stripes. The Vienna Boys' Choir wore navy blue sailor suits, with pale blue collars, and with white diagonal stripes, as distinct from the stripes on the uniforms worn by inmates at Auschwitz, which were thick and vertical, either dark gray and light gray, or dark gray and white, though the stripes on the collars of these uniforms were also on a diagonal. Today, these uniforms are disintegrating at an alarming rate. To slow down the rate of disintegration, and to keep the stripes from falling apart and altogether disappearing, attendants fill the uniforms with bodies made out of foam, like large, human-sized rag dolls.

SUBLIME, THE

According to eighteenth-century philosopher Edmund Burke, when we watch the porn movie *Hot Rods 2: Young and Hung,* in particular the scene in which the movie's star, Kevin Williams, is sodomized by one man, we find this beautiful—it is well formed and aesthetically pleasing, and all elements are in proportion to one another. However, later on in the movie, as we watch Kevin get sodomized by two men simultaneously in the so-called act of double penetration and observe the astonishment and terror and pain wash over his face in a pleasurable wave of grimaces, this scene shocks and overpowers us; in this sense it is not merely beautiful, but sublime.

SUICIDAL TEENAGE BOYS

Recent reports have linked the suicides of several teenage boys to the drug Prozac. I guess the theory is that although the drug lifts these boys out of their depression, it also gives them the motivation to kill themselves, a motivation they did not have when they were depressed. The term is *involuntary intoxication.* It has something to do with the gloomy specificity of teenage male hormones. I've also read that whereas with male adults, Prozac is meant to diminish the libido, to the point that it seems such a thing as the libido was never invented and never existed, with teenage boys, the effect is contrary. For them, it's like taking ecstasy. Again, something to do with the blissful specificity of teenage hormones, like finding oneself in an avalanche of bliss. Recently in Riverside, California, the parents of one suicidal teenage boy on Prozac found him in his bedroom doing inappropriate things to his friend, another suicidal teenage boy subscribing to Prozac. The boys defended themselves by saying that they were fucking to distract themselves from thoughts of death. Both of them were wearing nothing but salmon-pink bandages on their wrists, covering up their most recent attempts.

SUICIDE BOMBERS

Today, terrorists are very active and very popular, just like they were in the 1970s. The most common form of terrorist is what is known as a suicide bomber. Unlike the terrorists in the 1970s, who almost always wore ski masks—sometimes made of pure, 100 percent wool, and sometimes acrylic—to hide their identities, suicide bombers usually don't wear masks, because, paradoxically, these masks would attract too much attention and reveal their identities.

As a result, whereas in the 1970s people had no idea what the terrorists' faces looked like, whether or not they were handsome, whether or not they were blushing like brides, embarrassed and overwhelmed by the magnitude of what they were doing, today we can see the suicide bombers' faces.

(Suicide bombers are not to be confused with insurgents who kidnap Western boys and then behead these boys on videos that other Westerners eagerly watch via the Internet. Insurgents wear masks.)

Instead of ski masks, suicide bombers working on the ground like to wear dynamite vests. Before they go out on their missions, they will often stand in front of their bedroom mirrors, wearing nothing but these dynamite vests, seeing how they look, examining themselves from every angle, wondering what it will feel like to explode. Suicide bombers traveling by air prefer to wear Nikes, because they can hide wires in the thick soles, and there is talk that one day corporations will sponsor suicide bombers, just like they sponsor sports stars, and some say that terrorism is going to replace rock and roll, which has lost its edge.

Most suicide bombers fall between the ages of seventeen and thirty-five, which means that I am right at the cut-off point. After my next birthday, I will be too old to be a suicide bomber; I am already over the hill, just as, objectively speaking, I am over the hill in the gay community, which worships youth, and I suppose suicide bombers also worship youth—or its potential for destruction—in their own way. In fact, the average age of suicide bombers is eighteen. Most of them are still boys, exploding boys, putting their hormones to other uses. The difference between a normal teenage boy with regular suicidal tendencies and a teenage boy with aspirations to become a suicide-bomber, is, at times, marginal.

Being so young, a lot of these suicide bombers are naturally smooth. But even so, and especially if they're hairy, before setting off to explode themselves and the people around them, they shave their entire bodies, except for their eyebrows and the hair on their heads, in preparation for destruction and for paradise.

Ever since 9/11, shaving one's body hair has been complicated, as it were, by suicide bombers; it used to seem a rather gay thing to do; now it seems a sort of suicide bomberish thing to do. Somehow, whenever one picks up one's disposable blue razor, one immediately thinks of Mohammed Atta, the deeply unattractive ringleader of the attack on the World Trade Center. It has become impossible to dissociate the idea of a smooth body from the idea of destruction, the body as impending doom. Statistics indicate that there has been a significant decrease in gay men's shaving of their bodies since 9/11.

Many efforts have been undertaken to make it more difficult for suicide bombers to explode planes. People are no longer allowed to carry on any knives or knifelike instruments, such as box cutters or scalpels. There is also a device known as the body scanner that has been introduced at some airports. This X-ray security device makes it possible to see through a suicide bomber's clothing and to perceive immediately if there is a ceramic knife strapped to his calf muscle, a detonating device stuck to his left buttock, a plastic gun plastered at the base of his spine, just above his ass crack, a plastic explosive taped to his dick, or if there are wires attached to the inside of his left thigh. Now that we can see every curve of a suicide bomber's body, we feel infinitely safer. The images the scanner reveals are confined to the skin; they do not allow us to see what a suicide bomber has hidden inside his cavities, and in this sense, the technology needs to be further refined.

SUICIDE BOMBERS, THOSE OF US WHO ARE NOT

If you ask me who I am, although it's a treacherous question, one impossible to answer, a question I could die in the process of attempting to answer, I think I can safely say, in all certainty, well, I am not a suicide bomber. And I have no plans to become a suicide bomber. The closest I'll ever get would perhaps involve putting on a ski mask, and, metaphorically speaking, blowing up some of my favorite nineteenth-century novels, then reassembling the fragments. Although in one of his presidential addresses George Bush stated that the biggest threats to the stability of this country were terrorists and gay marriage, I don't pose much of a threat to you, except in the realm of your psyche. Perhaps if someone, or some system, were able to convince me, with a money-back guarantee, that if I blew myself up in the midst of a designated enemy, upon exploding, I would, like a rocket, be launched directly into paradise, where 100 of the most beautiful virgin cholos or Italian soccer players would be waiting to greet me, I too might get motivated enough to become a suicide bomber.

But, we can only speculate, for no system could ever offer such a wondrous vision.

SUN, THE

There is only one sun in our solar system, so its self-esteem must be high, and its identity, clear. It must be easy to be the sun.

SUNSET

Every day the sun sets on us, all drippy and pink and contemptuous.

SUPERGLUE

Superglue was an integral part of the 1970s. Certain tasks demanded not just regular glue, but superglue. Boys in my neighborhood breathed in the fumes, then went wandering around, damaging and defacing. One heard stories of boys who had sat down on toilets in public restrooms only to find that the seats had been smeared with superglue. Stuck to the seats, firemen had to come and peel the boys off, in the process ripping up skin. To this day we continue to turn to superglue to repair things that have been broken. We remain beholden to and haunted by superglue.

SWANS, BLACK

The bird known as the black swan is found only in Australia and is the symbol of Western Australia, the state I am from. Up until the Dutch explorer Willem de Vlamingh first sighted this species in 1697, Europeans used the term *black swan* as a metaphor for something that could never exist. I have no memories of these birds, with their dark, glossy black feathers, their strangely distorted necks that curve like question marks, their scarlet bills banded with a strip of white, and their elegant, ceaseless gliding. But their hissing haunts my dreams; the mere thought of them floods me with a blank nostalgia that is deeper and more substantial than memory.

SYCHOV, ANDREI

Currently, at the time of writing, there is only one angel, twenty-one-year-old Russian Andrei Sychov. On New Year's Eve 2005, Sychov, who two days earlier had joined the Logistics Battalion of the Chelyabinsk Tank Military College, found himself the subject of a brutal hazing—the practice known as *dedovshchina,* which translates roughly as the rule of grandfathers. He was forced to crouch in the snow for hours on end with his arms outstretched, tied to a stool, and, it seems, brutally raped. What ensued was the severe swelling of Sychov's legs, the death of muscle, and gangrene. To save his life, doctors had to amputate both legs, his genitals and one finger.

Angels as we formerly knew them were erased sometime in the second half of the twentieth century. Sychov is the first example of a new species of angels: these angels won't have wings but will be missing limbs, like in those old pictures of angels where they are just heads and wings. Angels have always been amputated. Historically, we have reached the end of the wing.

SYNTHPOP

In 1981, at approximately the same time the plague that would come to be known as AIDS appeared as if out of nowhere, the phenomenon that would come to be known as synthpop also appeared seemingly out of nowhere, though, like AIDS, it had been percolating quietly for a number of years. Whereas AIDS was characterized by diseases with names like toxoplasmosis and Kaposi's sarcoma and pneumocystis and cytomegalovirus, odd words that could have been easily mistaken for names of synth-pop bands, synthpop itself was characterized by boys singing about love over simple and quick, tinny melodies played on an instrument called a synthesizer. Other typical instruments included drum machines and tape loops. The music had a sort of nice robotic quality to it, lovely and inhuman, that almost made it sound like it was played by robots, but it wasn't.

Boys in synthpop bands were often very pretty and wore their hair in a spiky style, fueled by plenty of blue and pink hair gel, and, in the earliest days of AIDS, some boys took to using hair gel as lubricant because a rumor circulated that hair gel would protect you from the plague (it didn't).

In 1981 a number of landmark albums were released in this genre, including Depeche Mode's *Speak and Spell* and the Human League's *Dare*. Later on, when people listened to these albums, the music reminded them of the plague, as if synthpop were the plague's soundtrack.

Today, some historians claim that the period known as the early 1980s, a period that we have come to associate exclusively with the plague, was probably very much like the period known as the Dark Ages except that during the Dark Ages there was no such thing as synthpop.

In recent years there has been a resurgence of interest in synthpop, just as in recent years there has been a resurgence in the plague. Scientists even refer to *the new wave of the plague.* Still, after vast amounts of research into the relation between AIDS and synthpop, we have concluded that there is no relation whatsoever between these two phenomena.

$\mathscr{T}$

TEARS, TATTOOED

I like those small teardrops gang members sometimes have tattooed beneath the corners of their eyes. Some say it's meant to indicate that the individual has killed someone and represents tears he is unable to cry, while others say that it means someone the gang member loved has died. I knew a boy once who had such a tear. It had faded, but you could still see it, in sea-green ink, hovering at the corner of his right eye. He never told me why he got it, but he did tell me his theory of tears, which was that by the end of this century humans would have run out of actual tears— a side effect of global warming—and, as a result, everyone would eventually get one of these tattooed tears. Everyone would be in a state of permanent grief. Everyone's relationship to the world would be clear.

TECHNOLOGY

Although every form of technology is essentially a failure, the camera, in its inability to tell us what the boy was thinking and imagining and dreaming of and wishing for and most of all, fearing, is surely one of the greatest technological failures. In fact, the camera is considered the second-most failed technology. It has failed to penetrate the boy's interior and that is precisely why we came here in the first place. It gives us no sense of the stench of the boy. In this respect, its failure is quite spectacular.

If the camera only knew how much it had failed, it would kill itself, probably very violently, shoot itself in the lens, slit its shutters, and take a roll of pictures of its own death.

But it can take comfort, for its ill success is nothing when compared to the technology of boys, which is the technology that has failed us most spectacularly.

TELEVISION

Large-scale network television broadcasting began in the United States in 1946, shortly after the Holocaust, which began in 1938 and can be perceived as the first act of technologically aided large-scale mass murder, though television was around before the Holocaust. In fact, during the 1933 Berlin Olympics, the Nazis transmitted the first public TV broadcasts in the world, showing images of athletes in their whites. The first person my mother saw on TV was Liberace, in 1956. The TV set was in a storefront window. My mother stood in the street in her coat and watched Liberace sparkle and play piano. Whereas the plague was televised live, during the Holocaust people preferred the radio, which they also called the wireless. They were not able to see the Holocaust; at home they gathered around the radio and listened to the Holocaust.

TERROR, THE WAR ON GLOBAL

The leaked report concerning the war on global terror clarified for me not only the fact that we can expect more (global terror) and that the war (on global terror) is, how to put it—failing—it also clarified some things that I had been wondering about in regards to myself, namely that the status of the war in Iraq is exactly the same as my own status; both of us are *progressing toward a result that is unspecified and uncertain.*

THINKING

I'm not sure where we pick up this bad habit, but we acquire it very early on, like one acquires a sexually transmitted disease that is extremely difficult to shake. It's as if we go through our lives wearing weird *thoughthats* that are very unflattering and secured to our skulls in such a way—perhaps with superglue or a staple gun—that they are almost impossible to take off.

Each day becomes a concerted effort to not-think. We go to great lengths, we do everything we can, to avoid thought. Either way, we are utterly absorbed.

THOUGHT, MY

If one is to think with any sense of originality, one must think sodomitically, that is to say, one must go through thought's back door . . .

TIMBERLAKE, JUSTIN

Just as pop singer Justin Timberlake recently claimed that he is bringing sexy back, I intend to bring melancholy back, depression back, pessimism back: I'm interested in reviving a form of futility you can dance to. But as my boyfriend, Tim, pointed out, the notion of sexiness has never left culture, so the idea of bringing it back doesn't make any sense whatsoever. There is nothing to be brought back. In this light, Justin Timberlake and I are one and the same. I am Justin Timberlake. Our claims are equally sexy, yet equally futile.

TIME CAPSULES

When we were children, time capsules were all the rage. I wonder whether kids still do time capsules, or perhaps we've just given up on time. The capsules were shaped like giant pills. We placed useless yet precious objects inside of them and buried the capsules on the school grounds. It was always exciting, the idea of communicating with people in the future, and we'd get very giddy, though this giddiness was due to something else, something unacknowledged: the fact that by the time people cracked open the capsule, we'd be long gone. In a way, it was a bit like attending your own burial. In this sense, the real purpose of the time capsule was an attempt to hide ourselves from the deep and devouring monotony of time.

TIME, IN SEARCH OF LOST

In *Swann's Way,* the first volume of Proust's six-volume masterpiece, my favorite part is when young Marcel checks out Monsieur Legrandin's behind. Up until then we believe that Proust's primary fetish is memory—it's the fetish that gets him the wettest, the one that he submits to, nightly—naturally memory is a 100 percent top—and it's the fetish that most blissfully erases the inevitability of decay.

But in this moment we come to realize that, actually, it's the ass that is the main fetish here: young Marcel is a budding butt man, with a thing for big, bourgeois rumps. As Legrandin bends over—I forget what he is doing, I think he might be getting into a carriage, or just fiddling with something—Marcel's eyes go all googly; he's veritably hypnotized by what he sees. The power of Legrandin's ass, like the power of all asses, almost (but not quite) puts a stop to all the remembering. Yet memory, and more importantly, time, marches on; time somehow gets around (or over) the ass.

TOLSTOY, LEO

Although we go on and on about the end of the world, and although at times it seems that we are secretly looking forward to it, when it actually happens, we will be taken aback and extremely annoyed. In our defense, we will say that everything we did, and everything we said, was meant to be taken rhetorically. Of course this won't make much sense, because we will have found ourselves in a space beyond rhetoric.

As a result, we will have no idea what to do with ourselves. I suppose we can expect a lot of fidgeting and pacing. Surely the only thing more boring than the world is the end of it. Let's hope we have a book with us. Let's hope we have a choice, because then we will bring *Anna Karenina*, which we love, and which will certainly take our mind off things. Though maybe it would be better to bring *War and Peace*, which we have been meaning to read forever. No, best to stick with something we know, something safer.

Though inevitably, at some point we'll get tired of reading and realize that we are terribly hungry. To keep our place, we'll fold the page of *Anna Karenina*, just like we did before the world ended. Let's hope we also happen to have a stick of lipstick with us. That way, we can bury the novel beneath some rubble and write a big red *T* on the rubble, so when we come back from scavenging for food, if we come back, we will know where to find it and can resume our reading.

TOMATOES

After leaving one gigantic bruise upon the entire surface of the so-called New World, Hernán Cortés sailed back to Europe. His cargo included seven tomatls or tomatoes.

The Europeans did not know what to make of these voluptuous red things, like blood bruises that had escaped their surface to become three-dimensional. They did not trust these bruises you could hold in your hand. Tomatoes made the old world nervous. What to do with them?

Some believed tomatoes glowed in the dark and could therefore be used as lanterns. Botanists thought they were poisonous, naming them *solanum lycopersicum: solanum* for nightshade, *lycopersicum* meaning wolf's peach. For two centuries botanists planted tomatoes and crouched behind bushes, waiting for the wolves to come and eat the sinister red things. The wolves always came. The botanists then had to explain the dirt stains on their breeches to their wives and boy-lovers.

Eventually, science became tired of crouching and grew jealous of the wolves: by the eighteenth century humans were eating tomatoes, now named *lycopersicum esculentum:* edible wolf's peach. We cannot blame humans for their envy. After all, who would not want to eat what the wolves eat? Who doesn't want their mouth stained red? Who doesn't crave a little bit of nightshade?

TONGUE

I'm attached to the world, but tentatively, like a tongue is attached at its root to the hyoid bone. This leaves me free to move, but only in so many possible ways.

TONGUE, MY

When my father received the good news of my homosexuality, he cut off my tongue. He did it in the kitchen, with the carving knife normally reserved for Sunday roasts. It didn't hurt as much as you would expect, and it hardly bled at all, just dripped a trail of little red spots all over the linoleum.

My mother went to the laundry where she washed my tongue (by hand) and then used two pale blue plastic pegs to attach it to the clothesline outside. She was humming a tune, which was distorted by the pegs that she held in her mouth. My tongue dripped gently and steadily, along with the bedsheets and all my mother's under-things: her off-white slips, her peach-colored girdles, her flesh-tone stockings. A strong wind came up, and the clothesline began to creak. My mother assured me that everything would be dry in no time.

TOTALITARIANISM

Up until the year 2000, or thereabouts, the imagination was a space of freedom—in fact, it was the last space of freedom available to what used to be known as human beings.

Today, the imagination is not only no longer free, but it is actually less free than anywhere else; it resembles a totalitarian police state and is organized around a principle of pervasive paranoia.

TOYS

God made sure that even the toys would have actual souls and real intestines. He did everything within his powers to guarantee that the toys would shit at the twist of a key and have nightmares and get headaches. The toys would develop all sorts of cancers and be very neurotic and take all sorts of pills that would work, temporarily. God invented psychoanalysis so the toys could talk through their woes, which would help, temporarily. God was so thorough he created a world where even the toys would suffer terribly.

TRAILER TRASH

In my white abjectness, I am not so much trailer trash; I am more like the actual decrepit space of the trailer.

TRANSCENDENCE

There have been long stretches of my life where all I can think about is transcendence. During these periods, all my worldly efforts have been directed toward surpassing and exceeding; I've had no time or energy for anything but transcending.

Like most things, transcendence used to be much easier when I was younger. As I get older, it's gotten a little more difficult. With this in mind, I went onto eBay and bought myself a transcendence machine, circa 1945. It resembles a butter churner and whips you into a state not unlike that of butter.

There are drawbacks: the individual transcending is attached to plenty of wires; not only can everyone see the wires and therefore know that you are using a machine to transcend, but these wires also cut deeply into your skin. Furthermore, someone must be churning, stuck in material existence, while you are busy transcending. This can create some tension. At first, my boyfriend worked the machine, but now I hire male whores who wear little white hats and aprons.

However, these drawbacks are minor. Since I purchased the machine I have been transcending everything I don't like about the twenty-first century, regularly.

TRANSCENDENCE, THE OPPOSITE OF

What is the opposite of transcendence? The commonplace, the ordinary?

Wouldn't you know it, but I seem to have lost all interest in transcendence. I've stopped using my machine. It's just sitting there, rusting. Going beyond is boring. This century makes me so tired that all I really want to do at the end of the day is not transcend it but just sit on the couch with my boyfriend and my dog, beneath a blanket, and watch the world destroy itself on TV, while receiving updates on global terror. This is an experience.

Instead of desiring to rise above, or exist above the world, we need a horizontal form of transcendence.

Or we need to go beneath transcendence.

TRANSLATION

The history of translation has always been a history of violence, centuries of forcing that which is foreign and inexplicable to become familiar, comprehensible. But it seems that in the twenty-first century this violence has reached new heights.

It is said that recently in Iraq, a translator for the occupying forces was struggling with translating a particularly difficult document and decided to take a break. While on his break, he allegedly raped a teenage Iraqi boy. Afterwards, the translator, his mind cleared, immediately went back to finish his task. (Another account states that the translator brought his work with him and continued to work on the translation during the act of rape.)

In the near future a symposium is to be held where the suggestion will be raised that, as a human race, we should cease translating altogether. *Let the strange be strange,* is the symposium's motto. *Let the strange be made stranger.*

TSUNAMIS

For a number of weeks after the tsunami of 2005, the human corpses kept appearing; the death toll mounted rapidly, reaching a grand total that was unimaginable. Yet I am told that the aid workers came across remarkably few corpses of other species. Sensing what was approaching, it seems all the other animals moved to higher ground

Just days after the event, elephants, deer, boars, and leopards could be seen roaming around in the same numbers as prior to the tsunami. In fact, while some counted and calculated the number of humans who had died, others took to counting the animals who had survived; they speculated that this latter figure was somehow higher than it was prior to the wave, though they admitted this abundance could easily be a case of mere appearance, an illusion, or a simple matter of miscounting.

All in all, this information merely confirms for me what I have long suspected: that in these early days of the twenty-first century, it is safer to be an animal than it is to be human. When faced with the infinite array of horrors the world has in store for us, to be without rational consciousness would be not only acceptable but also preferable.

TWENTY-FIRST CENTURY, THE

At some point during the twentieth century, while no one was looking—sometime between the end of the Holocaust and the invention of the VCR—the opposition between life and death was reversed. Now it is dying that precedes living; we do everything we can to forget the fact that one day we all must live. In these first breaths of the twenty-first century, what we inaccurately call humans are actually ghosts, who know their way around death.

TWINS

We can all agree that the gruesome entity we so mildly call *the self*—personally I like to refer to it as *the grimace*—is terrible, horrible, hideous. And undoubtedly there is nothing more gruesome than the self—except perhaps for twins. (I am of course speaking of identical twins here; non-identical twins are of no interest to us.)

Surely the only thing worse than having one self would be having two selves. The belief that having an identical twin might somehow lessen the burden of the self is a myth; studies show that it only makes things much worse, doubling every heartache, every headache, every failure, every loss.

Having an identical twin must be like having a photocopy of one's self—admittedly a very high-quality photocopy, like a color laser photocopy, though which is the original and which is the duplicate? In Disney comedies starring identical twins and in those gay porn movies featuring identical twins, no one can ever tell who is who. In the former, this is always meant to be the source of humor, and in the latter, the source of titillation, but this inability to distinguish one twin from the other is really the source of a barely concealed horror.

By the very fact of their existence, twins taunt us. Like specters, they serve as a constant reminder of our own death, our own proximity to non-identity; for despite all the drawbacks of being a twin, at least when an identical twin dies, he dies secure in the knowledge that there is another version of him left; when it is our time to leave this earth, there will be nothing left of us.

Conversely, the existence of twins raises the horrifying possibility that there *is* another one of us, hiding away in the back of a cupboard like a birthday gift bought far too early, another self full of even more self-hatred, and that just when we think this sorrowful business of living is finally over and done with, and we can welcome the sweet relief of death, this other self will emerge slowly from its hiding place.

TWINS, THE BARTOK

Although our feelings about identical twins are well known, as with almost everything, there are exceptions. In this case, it is the Czech gay porn stars and identical twins Jirka and Karel Bartok, whom we found charming in the movie *Double Czech*. Admittedly, their charm lies mainly in the fact that in this feature film the twins are repeatedly tied up and sexually ravaged by non-twins.

The plot involves the Bartoks stumbling into a semi-enchanted forest—as if the enchanted nature of their replicated identity weren't enough! On entering the enigmatic forest, the brothers are forced repeatedly (by feudal lords and elegantly regaled militia) into wonderfully submissive and degrading sexual acts.

Surely even Franz Kafka would have approved of this film, though he probably would have thought that the movie had not gone far enough: under his shrewd directorial eye, the twins, after being tied to the tree and violently seduced, would have been summarily executed, most likely beheaded, a scimitar cleanly lopping off both heads simultaneously.

In fact, I don't think anyone could refuse the identical charms of Jirka and Karel, not even President Bush, not even his daughters, the so-called Bush twins, who are non-identical, not only to one another but also to themselves, in the depths of themselves; for the Bartoks invite destruction so joyfully, hold hands so tenderly throughout every violation, and, inviting us to do our worst, wait patiently side by side for all of us, naked, in a forest, kneeling in the dark mulch.

TWINS, THE KACZYŃSKI

Although there is something eerie and evil about all identical twins, and all identical twins have a touch of the Twin Towers about them, the eeriest and most evil identical twins in the world are easily Lech and Jarosław Kaczyński, leaders of Poland's far-right parliamentary ruling party, the deeply conservative so-called Law and Justice party, which is itself like the identical twin of the equally conservative party it co-leads with, the ridiculously named League of Polish Families Party.

We had always suspected that there was something intrinsically fascistic about identical twins, and the Kaczyńskis, who banned gay-pride parades in Poland and in their place promoted oppositional *Parades of Normality,* who do not wish for homosexuals to be teachers, and who have likened gay men to weeds infesting their lovely country, have only confirmed our deepest suspicions.

Of all the Kaczyńskis' retrograde platforms, one of the strangest is the slogan that brought them to power: *One Day We Will All Have an Identical Twin.*

Interestingly enough, there is much gossip suggesting that Jarosław (pronounced like *coleslaw*) Kaczyński is a deeply closeted gay man, or *pedal* (meaning *fag* in popular Polish lingo). This is the same man who has stated in print that he cannot accept homosexuality, as he believes it will lead to the destruction of civilization.

Men claiming to be lovers of Jarosław are constantly popping up. Many of them swear that he can only attain orgasm if you whisper to him in his ear about shipbuilding, which has become a leading industry in Poland since WWII, and which employs many Polish (non-Jewish) workers. These men say that at the moment of orgasm, Jarosław always sees ships being built in the dark of his mind, large ocean-going vessels, and always in the shipyards of Gdańsk (formerly Danzig).

There was even widespread speculation when the Law and Justice Party won Poland's parliamentary elections in 2005 that the brothers—both 100 percent bottoms, naturally—celebrated privately by having an all-night session on a double-headed dildo, pink like marzipan, whilst discussing the beauty of their conservative ideologies.

Perhaps dear Jarosław is right, and homosexuals are bringing about the downfall of civilization. For whenever I close my eyes, all I see is him and his brother, pleasuring themselves on their double-headed dildo, which is as identical and pink and blank as they are, self-pleasuring themselves in these last days, amidst the ruins and the rubble.

$\mathcal{U}$

UMBRELLA, MY AUNT JOAN'S

My Aunt Joan's decline was gradual and took place over a period of fifty years, but after the death of her daughter, Robin, my Aunt broke her hip and became utterly housebound. She spent the rest of her days in bed, beneath her mauve polyester eiderdown, watching daytime soap operas and reading women's magazines. When she had visitors she put on her housecoat.

She confided in me that the thing she missed most in the world was walking in the rain beneath an umbrella. *How good and sweet the world seems when it rains,* she often said. Even more, she missed getting to collapse her umbrella when the rain had ended; she missed walking in a world that was green and still dripping, filled with a feeling that she and the world could start all over again.

Although she no longer required its use, she kept her old umbrella in sight, at the foot of her bed. Her umbrella was red, with a pattern of oranges on it.

Sometimes when I visited, it would begin to rain, and my Aunt would ask me to bring her the umbrella. I'd open the windows. Sitting up in her bed, she'd open the umbrella and from beneath its canopy try to approximate the feeling.

UMBRELLAS

I like all umbrellas. I'm partial to those white frilly parasols skater boys carry around here in Los Angeles in the summer, holding them above their buzzed heads as they whiz past me on their skateboards, in an effort to protect their complexions. And although I don't condone the use of them, I appreciate poisonous umbrellas, like the kind a KGB agent jabbed into the thigh of the Bulgarian writer Georgi Markov in London in 1978 while the Bulgarian was waiting for one of those red Routemaster double-decker buses that are now extinct. The tip of this umbrella happened to be filled with the poison known as ricin, and Markov would die four days later. It is said that the offending umbrella had a black background with a pattern of red and white bicycles. It would be safe to say that life has been a passion of umbrellas. The word *umbrella* comes from a Latin word meaning *little shadow.* Some Roman theologians speculated that the underworld was just one big endless umbrella, beneath which all of its inhabitants cowered. I tend to forget I am mortal, but then I find myself out walking on a rainy, blustery day: the force of the wind inverts my plain and sober black umbrella, the fabric lifts up like the skirt of a can-can dancer, revealing its silver underlying structure, soaking me through to the bone, gently reminding me that everything has a skeleton.

UNCONSCIOUS, THE

Prior to Freud's invention of the unconscious, where did people put things?

The ancients thought in terms of caves. Each person had his own cave, lined with moss and lichen. I have to say I like the idea of these caves, and if Freud were around, I think I'd tell him that I'd like to do an exchange, that I want to return my unconscious, and to please give me back my cave.

In *Anna Karenina,* they think they are too modern for

caves. It is the 1870s, and they are somewhere between caves and psychoanalysis. The characters are constantly digging holes in which to bury the things they'd rather keep hidden. Usually they send one of the servants in to do the digging, so the frightening thing will be concealed not only from others but, more importantly, also from themselves. This explains the dirt on Anna's long, perfumed gloves, the dark soil around the plunging neckline of her gown. Her cheeks are growing hollow, sunken from all the repression (or is that just the morphine?).

Repression also takes place on the outside, on the surface of the skin. Whenever Anna is approached by a feeling she does not wish to feel, which, as the novel goes on, is increasingly often, she drives it away with a blush, like the crack of a hot pink whip.

But it seems that in nineteenth-century Russia, wishes of every persuasion are mainly being stored inside. Everyone in the salons of Moscow and St. Petersburg is waiting impatiently for Freud to arrive. Everyone is divided. They all sense this inner division, are haunted by this division, but no one has the language to describe exactly what it is they are feeling. Until Freud comes, they must make do.

I feel like there is a red, gold, and black lacquered Chinese screen in my brain, says Anna to Vronsky, *partitioning the better part of me off from myself.*

UNCONSCIOUS, THE FUTURE OF THE

A U.S. company with factories in China is currently working on an unconscious that will be detachable. The user will be able to put the unconscious on and take it off at will, with the aid of a little strip of Velcro. It's unclear what effect this will have on the conscious mind, but it will make repression so much more user friendly and bodes well for repression's future.

UNCONSCIOUS, MY

The thing I most enjoy about being alive is the fact that you get to have an unconscious. Without it, living would be unacceptable.

Just between you and me, I spend far too much time there, browsing all the glittery information. But judgment aside, it's so nice having an unconscious. It's like having an abyss in my head, just behind my face, and God must have invented the face to hide this abyss. On waking, if you wish to remember your dreams, you have to be very quick, because you can already hear your dreams going back to where they came from, hurling themselves into the abyss.

UNDERWEAR

There is nothing more sexy to me than a man who has barely any conscious mind and whose unconscious is dangerously close to the surface; it's as if he is walking around wearing nothing but a pair of white jockey underwear.

UNDERWORLD, THE

As soon as Rimbaud arrived in the underworld, he sent Verlaine a postcard:

I can't wait until you get here. Can you come a few days earlier? Be sure to bring a few cardigans: at night the temperature drops quite rapidly. I didn't think I would miss living and all its complex arrangements, its days like little accordions, but I do.

Speaking of which, I've taken up the accordion. It is a demanding instrument.

I've also started writing again, but they refuse to provide me with a desk, claiming there's a shortage of them, so as soon as you arrive, I'm going to need your corpse.

UNIFORMS, SCHOOL

I expect that just before we die, it will be like when we were children, on that evening prior to the start of the new school year, when we were filled with dread. Before carefully packing our schoolbags, we'd sit on the bedroom floor and line up all our new books and pens and pencils and pencil cases and erasers. We'd gaze at them with a feeling approaching, yet beyond, apprehension.

With this is mind, perhaps like Quintilian we need to start making some preparations for death and acquire some things that will be not only useful but also necessary in death; perhaps there is a list somewhere of items that are required in death.

At the Catholic Boys School I attended, the uniform consisted of a light gray shirt, a green and gold striped tie, a green blazer with the school's insignia stitched in gold, long gray socks with one green and one gold stripe running horizontally at the top, shiny black shoes, dark gray trousers during the winter, and tight gray shorts for the summer.

Each night my mother would iron my uniform and lay each item on the back of a chair in the kitchen.

Perhaps death will smell just like those freshly ironed articles of clothing. And maybe there is a uniform I will be similarly obliged to wear when I am finally accepted into that institution we call death. Each year, I will outgrow death's uniform, out-glow it, and will have to make a special visit to a store where I will be fitted with a new uniform.

Surely in death we will learn many things, many essential things and many useless things. Everything we learn we will do so by memorizing.

At the start of each school year, nothing inspired more dread than those black school shoes. Inside their cardboard box, which was like a cheap coffin, they nested in pale gray tissue paper. When we opened the box we were greeted by a rustle and the deep odor of brand-new leather. Everything was brand new, terribly new.

UNION STATION

Whenever I find myself downtown at Los Angeles' Union Station, waiting to take a train ride, I'm reminded of a game I used to play: I'd look up cities in the pages of the *World Book Encyclopedia* and pretend that instead of living in Perth, Western Australia, I was living somewhere else.

I generally picked places in the United States; at one time or another I must have imagined that I was residing in every one of the then fifty-biggest cities in America. I lived in them all: not only the obvious choices, like New York or Chicago, but also less obvious ones, like St. Louis, Cincinnati, Baltimore, Detroit, Indianapolis, Milwaukee. At the time, any of these seemed preferable to the city in which I had been born.

However, when playing this game, the cities I returned to were those major urban centers where it would be easiest for me to get lost, cities such as Los Angeles, for instance.

I must have spent countless hours poring over photographs of noteworthy places to visit in Los Angeles. I would picture myself superimposed in front of some of these structures, like the 32-story Civic Hall, which, at 464 feet, was the tallest building in Southern California (remember, although I was absorbed in this activity during the 1970s and early '80s, my family's edition of the *World Book* was published in the early 1960s). I often envisioned riding the elevator in this building straight to the top (usually accompanied by a chiseled, handsome man wearing a porkpie hat). We'd stand on the roof, holding hands, looking out over the sprawl of Los Angeles, at *all the low white and pastel buildings, with their red tiled roofs,* our eyes temporarily blinded by the light's *brilliant glow.*

Once in a while I envisaged that together this strange man and I would leap off the roof, still holding hands, preceded by his porkpie hat. We'd flutter down swiftly after it, where it would be waiting for us, upturned on the pavement. The police would paint outlines of both our bodies and the hat.

My other visions of life in L.A. weren't quite as dramatic. And in them I was always alone. I'd be eating a cheeseburger and a thick shake at one of the city's many *strange-shaped restaurants, in the form of hats, rabbits, or shoes.* I'd find myself standing in the ragged shadows provided by the fronds of the palm trees lining one of the city's many boulevards, the trees that, according to *World Book, remind travelers of the trees in tropical Africa.*

Or, like today, I'd simply be waiting to take a train at *the beautiful and unusual* Los Angeles Union Station, *which follows the Spanish Mission Style of architecture so popular in California.*

Of course it's only in retrospect that I realize I played this game with the sole intention of forgetting myself and imagining another, brighter version of myself.

As adults, we learn all too quickly that such forgetting is impossible for any sustained period of time. However, standing in the white sun outside Union Station, whose stucco exterior looks exactly as it appeared in those photographs from fifty years ago, or, standing inside the station's dim, tiled halls, which, apart from the electronic schedule—whose digits announce whether my train is on time or if it has been endlessly delayed—also look identical to those black-and-white images, I do feel like someone else, at least temporarily, a superimposed version of myself.

Often slightly overheated, the station has a musty, stale smell, which recalls not only the claustrophobia of childhood, with its dense, close odors, but also the claustrophobia of an old encyclopedia, with its moldy pages. Either way, I feel remarkably at home and unusually peaceful, for it is as if I am literally wait-ing inside *The World Book,* volume *L* for *Los Angeles,* and this is exactly where I have always wanted to be.

UNIQUE, THE

Profoundly embarrassed by their uniqueness, my fingertips are constantly blushing, not only when strangers enter the room but even in my own presence. Deeply private, they have taken to wearing miniature masks to cover up their dizzying, singular little patterns (this has helped with my vertigo!). My index fingers now wear the tiniest executioner's masks, sewn out of thick black cloth, with three minute slits where the eyes and mouth would be, if they had them. My thumbs prefer to conceal their identity behind diminutive black-wool ski masks, just like Lilliputian terrorists might don if they wanted to commit miniature atrocities in a miniature model of the world. And my so-called pinkies, in the manner of rapists, wear teeny bits of pantyhose, which distort and give a scary appearance to their whorls.

UNWINDING

Everybody should have some way in which they can unwind, forget themselves, negate themselves and, more importantly, the century. I myself enjoy jumping repeatedly through a hoop that has been set on fire. There's something about it that is very relaxing. Plus, if people want to watch, you can charge ten cents apiece and the applause at the end is deeply satisfying. I used to be so good at it, leaping effortlessly out of my century. But lately I have been finding this task increasingly difficult, one that requires a good deal of forethought. Perhaps it is just me, but it seems to be harder to escape this century; I think it was much easier to escape the last century. The fires these days are growing warmer and warmer, while the hoops themselves are becoming tinier and tinier.

$\mathcal{V}$

VACATIONS

Every now and then I feel a pressing need to flee the alphabet. So I put on a jacket, pack a suitcase full of razors, and stow away on a silver rocket. It's a long journey to the moon, but I clench my teeth and try to be patient. When I finally arrive, it's always cold, and I'm glad my jacket has a zipper. I take out the first razor. Crouching down, I slice off a little of the moon's gray rind to send to the folks back home.

VALENTINE'S DAY

My father was born on Valentine's Day 1930. The fact that he was born on this day interests me, as he has always struck me as a man with a most austere heart.

In 2001 he experienced a series of minor heart attacks, like those mild earthquakes that don't do much damage, just cause the teacups to tremble, but scare you into humanness nonetheless.

What is the word for these reminders of mortality? How often do you get them? Let us call them *heartmassacres*. There are those among us who experience them daily.

Most days I can feel my heart itching to get out of me. It is brown and grainy, the same color and texture as dog food.

VAMPIRE BATS

I like to think of my heart as a sort of vampire bat, with nice, pointy, razor-sharp teeth, a wingspan of approximately one foot, and a face that is ugly, yet cute. Though I wish my heart were the *true vampire bat,* more than likely it is merely the *common vampire bat.* Still, most people are pretty scared of my heart. When it is daytime in my body, my heart sleeps; just like a bat, it hangs upside down from the ceiling of my body, its silky wings wrapped around it like an opera cape. But most of the time my hearts flies aimlessly around inside me, where it is almost always night.

VAMPIRE BATS, RABID

My heart is probably (no, definitely) rabid, just like the rabid bat that here in Los Angeles flew through the open window of an eighteen-year-old boy's room and bit the boy, who has subsequently become the first boy to contract rabies in L.A. since 1991. The boy woke up from his dream not because of the bite on the inside of his left leg but because he felt something dripping onto him, which, health authorities claimed, must have been rainwater falling from the bat's wings. The bat was captured, but then, after questioning, released out the window. The boy's prognosis looks grim. The bat flew directly to my house here in Venice, where I keep it in a cage. I've named my bat Memory.

VANDALS

I like all vandals and find all acts of vandalism interesting, but the most interesting vandals of late are the three sixteen-year-old Boy Scouts, who, whilst on a scouting expedition in Red Fleet State Park in eastern Utah, dug up a 190-million-year-old set of dinosaur footprints and promptly proceeded to rigorously and systematically destroy the ancient artifact.

(The identities of the boys were never disclosed; this is fine by us, for it is not their identities we are interested in; we have no interest whatsoever in anything remotely to do with their identity or, for that matter, anyone else's identity.)

It seems one of the boys put his fingers in the cracks in the dinosaur footprints, trying to pry them apart, fingerfucking the ancient as it were. When this failed to work, he proceeded to throw the tracks against the ground, thus shattering them. The two other lads gathered up the chunks and proceeded to throw them into the reservoir, slowly and silently and rather solemnly. The splashes made were impressive.

Although a sign clearly identified the dinosaur tracks, the ringleader of the group, who, like the others, wore his uniform to the hearing, claimed that he had not seen the sign, and that although he knew they were destroying something, he was not exactly sure what they were destroying. *In all honesty,* he said, *it was an innocent act of destruction.*

Later on he admitted he knew that, whatever it was, it was *very old;* he further admitted that he hated the idea of anything being older than him.

A park ranger observed the entire incident from nearby, crouched behind a bush. When asked as to why he did not stop the proceedings, he claimed that he was unable to move, pondering the strange combination and philosophical implications of the adolescent and the prehistoric. He was fixed to the ground, mesmerized, as it were, by the destruction.

VANISHING
Vanishing is just as important.

VARICOSE VEINS
As a kid I was fascinated by the dark purple, knotted, so-called varicose veins that snaked beneath the pale skin on my mother's legs. When I asked her about these swollen veins, she said she believed she acquired them after bearing seven children, and from carrying so many shopping bags full of groceries over the

years. I was always listening in on conversations where women discussed their veins and hearing about women who'd had their veins removed in the hospital and then had to wear special elastic stockings.

Just before she leapt off the rocks, Sappho, in an interview conducted right at the edge of the cliff, claimed she did not fear death. *Never,* she said, *will I get varicose veins. My thighs will forever be those of an altar boy's.*

VAUDEVILLE

Sometimes I feel like I'm a ventriloquist's dummy, like little Charlie McCarthy, the dummy that belonged to 1930s vaudeville artist Edgar Bergen.

In his act, Bergen wore a black top hat, a black silk cape, and a monocle, and Charlie wore a matching hat, cape, and monocle. At one time the most popular ventriloquist in the world, with the decline in interest in ventriloquism, Bergen lost favor. He subsequently fell into a deep depression and would apparently just sit inside his house for days on end, saying absolutely nothing, with his fist inside little Charlie.

I don't really know who my ventriloquist is. I suppose it must be God, whose fist is buried so deep inside me I cannot get away, whose lips are held as motionless as possible, and who's been practicing steadily to develop this ability.

VCRs

Although the video cassette recorder, otherwise known as the VCR, was invented in 1971, it was not until 1981 that an affordable version became available to the general public. At approximately the same time, AIDS appeared on the horizon, similarly becoming available to the general public.

In retrospect, one cannot help but notice that the VCR,

with its unnerving ability to fast-forward and to speed up time and in its power to erase—that is, to effectively annul time—bore a remarkable resemblance to the workings of the AIDS virus, which seemingly overnight turned twenty-year-old men into doddering eighty-year-old ladies.

Furthermore, it now seems suspiciously convenient that in the same year gaggles of gay men began to die so suddenly, the accompanying technology of the video camera also appeared on the market, allowing these young men to document themselves for posterity and to somehow freeze, as it were, the all-too-rapid flow of time.

Perhaps this was mere coincidence, and the two events were utterly unrelated; remember, unlike VCRs, these young men were ultimately unable to store time or to replay or rewind it. Yet one cannot deny that in 1981 something very odd was happening to time.

VERTIGO

Whereas in everyday life, young men do everything they can to conceal the fact that they have an abyss, in gay pornography there is no such concealment.

In so-called centerfolds, boys and men spread their abysses wide open. Some particularly virtuosic boys pry their abysses apart with their thumbs. Often these abysses are shaved, so as to display their depths to better advantage. The models smile broadly, as if to say, *Look how happy I am to have my very own abyss!*

In gazing at these centerfolds, we find ourselves standing at the edge of an abyss; we peer into its pale and dark pink depths. In doing so we become giddy, faint.

VICTORIAN ERA, THE

In my Victorian era, life is even more repressive than in the *real* Victorian era. There are corsets, just like there were in the Victorian era, but only boys wear them, and just like the women

who wore corsets in the other Victorian era—the one that
ended, unlike my Victorian era, which is just getting up and
running—these boys are continually fainting because the strings
on their corsets have been pulled far too tight. Furthermore,
these corsets have even more strings and require even more time
to put on and take off. In my Victorian era, which you are all invited to, there are also opiates and smelling salts and crinolines,
the constant swishing sound of crinolines. There are two Jack
the Rippers. There is a writer by the name of Charles Dickens,
but he does not work in the genre of realism. And there are no
bustles. Though there are some boys who appear to be wearing
bustles, when you get near to them, on closer inspection, beneath
the gas lamps, you realize they are not.

VIEWMASTERS

I'd really like to see the Grand Canyon, both for intellectual
reasons—you just have to love a nation that turns an abyss into a
national monument—and for aesthetic ones, because I hear it is
actually very beautiful; some abysses disappoint deeply, but this
abyss, I hear, is a genuinely majestic, awe-inspiring abyss. However, if I am truthful, I have to say that I would much rather go
back to the house I grew up in, probably around 9 a.m. on a Sunday while everyone is at church, break in through a window,
sneak into my brother Andrew's bedroom, pull the old fruitcake
tins out from under his bed, specifically the scratched gold one
that contains the boxes of slides, and perceive that slide we had of
the Grand Canyon: I think there was a little burro in the image if
I remember correctly, and a cute boy on the burro, and maybe
someone wearing a poncho, and behind all of them the Grand
Canyon's orangey emptiness. Yes, I would like to lie on the carpet
and perceive this three-dimensional image through the magical
technology known as the Viewmaster, perhaps the only technology that has served humanity well, the only technology that will
ultimately survive.

VIOLINS

There is no evidence that the nerves of boys were ever used to string violins.

VOICE

Surely there is nothing more natural or more normal than to hate one's own voice. Every red-blooded American boy despises his voice. All my life I have been profoundly disconcerted by my own voice, not to mention repulsed by it, ever since that day in first grade, when, for the first time, my voice was recorded and then played back to me on a tape deck, sounding high and uncanny, like the Swiss Alps!

Leave it to me then to become a writer, that pitiable profession that involves staring all day at a page, an act that is in essence no different from gazing all day down one's own throat, examining all the little nicks and scratches on the lid of one's voice box and peering at those bands of tissue that stretch across it, the so-called vocal cords.

The very thought of one's voice is enough to make one want to reach into the throat, cut out the vocal cords with a pair of sewing scissors, and put the cords to better use, perhaps tie them, like a bow, around a birthday gift.

Giraffes, which seldom use their voices, have the right idea! We could learn from giraffes. They say this exotic animal's reticence is due to its underdeveloped voice box, but, in fact, its voice is highly sophisticated, sort of like Katherine Hepburn's—a giraffe's silence is simply due to its detesting the sound of its own voice.

The only respite I ever get from my voice is when I come down with a lovely case of laryngitis. My voice unwraps itself from the rest of my body like a skinny red scarf, as if it wants nothing whatsoever to do with me. For as long as I am unable to speak, I feel so much happier, and lighter; there is no greater pleasure.

However, even I must admit that, now and then, there are those rare occasions when something enchanting appears out of my voice and I am delighted, just as I was delighted when I'd open my sister's jewelry box and the tiny plastic ballerina with her scrap of net lace for a tutu would pirouette awkwardly and obsessively to the hurdy-gurdy music.

But, all in all, my attitude toward my voice is, to put it mildly, not good. More than anything, I would like my voice to somehow find its way to the bottom of an ocean floor, sort of like when there is a terrible plane crash and all the necessary information lies on the bed of an ocean that is so deep no diver could ever possibly access it; what is essential is irretrievable, contained in the so-called black box.

VOICE, MY

Whether I like it or not, my voice is a product of the grammar of this century and the last century. As it says in the Bible, Proverbs 71:2–7, *We are born amidst bloody bits of grammar, and we die in jet-black streams of grammar.* Yet my voice also comes from very far away, *dreamgrammar,* from so far away you can barely hear it. My voice is the linguistic equivalent of the moon. To fully appreciate it, you'll need a big, old-fashioned ear trumpet.

VOICE, THE NEXT

It is said that the concept of the voice as we understand it today begins about 439 BC with Socrates, who is said to have had a husky voice, not unlike the voice of Burt Reynolds. When the philosopher spoke, the boys would sit beneath him with their faces upturned, letting the irony drip like honey into their open mouths.

This playful philosopher was deeply troubled by the thought of what happened to the voice while the tongue was engaged in other, more pressing matters, for example, while French-kissing his male groupies in-between lessons, in the cool passageways of the Academy. Where did the voice go? And what became of the voice after we died, how long did it echo?

With this in mind, seeing that the voice was in fact invented, it seems that it could be similarly dis-invented, or replaced by a better invention. Historically, we are approaching the end of the voice.

von Gloeden, Wilhelm

In his photographs, von Gloeden came up with a mathematical formula for beauty: boys and rocks with a bit of sea. When the fascists came to his house, he was out watering the geraniums, enjoying their odor. The musty smell of the leaves reminded him of something else he liked, something even mustier, but he couldn't think what. The first thing he noticed about the soldiers was their boots: the leather was supple and as shiny as licorice. While they smashed the glass plates of his photos, he wept openly, unable to take his eyes off their splendid boots.

Look closely: you can see evidence of his tears all over the ruined negatives.

VOWELS

Whereas Rimbaud gave each vowel its own color and texture, I see vowels as plain, uniform things. Despite their different sounds, when I shut my eyes all vowels look alike, and they come on a string, like those strings of balls daddies inserted into their boys' assholes (the asshole being the sixth vowel) in all those Falcon porn movies from the late eighties, when we were already deep in the plague. What new plagues await us? AIDS has two vowels.

VOYAGES

The four weeks it took my parents to get to Australia by boat is nothing compared to the length of time it will take me to return to childhood, where everyone lives in corduroy slums and shabby tents of blue and orange cellophane. All my loved ones have come to wave me off at the dock. There will be absolutely nothing to do on this voyage but sit and remember and throw memories—which are not in themselves interesting—off the deck and watch them splash and sink. This voyage will be endless, interminable.

WALKS

No doubt when the world ends—and it is not a question of *if*
but *when*—we'll take a lot of walks, in an attempt to walk off the
discomfort that will surely arise in us with the end of the world.
We'll probably go for walks in the morning and the evening—that
is, if we'll still call these times of day *morning* and *evening*. Just
as before the world ended, we'll bring the dog, but most likely,
based on a *what's the point* argument, we won't bother with the
leash. Our walks will be meandering, and the conversations we
have along the way will be even more meandering, and I bet that
on our walks we'll find strange things, things we've never seen
before. For example, we'll find an apple crate on the side of the
road, and at first we'll be very excited at the thought of all those
apples, which we probably won't have seen for a long time—no
doubt we'll have been dreaming of apples—assuming that at this
stage of the game we'll still call it dreaming. But then we'll open
the crate up, only to discover that it's full not of apples but of
boys' heads, teenage boys with buzz cuts—around sixteen by the
look of it. Their heads will be packed very neatly, stacked carefully one on top of another, in pale yellow straw.

WAVES

I think about my mother's bathing suit all the time, at least once a day. After she stopped going swimming, it hung in my parent's closet, in the dark, on a wooden coat hanger, and I suppose you could say it similarly hangs on a coat hanger in my brain, in the dark.

It was, if memory serves me correctly, a one-piece suit, navy blue, with big white polka dots, a little frill around the waist, and padded breast cups. Of course, there is no such thing as correct memory, and perhaps that is why I think about my mother's bathing suit constantly, in an attempt to remember and reconstruct it.

I happened to be there the day my mother stopped going into the sea. It was a Sunday afternoon sometime in the late '70s. I sat on the beach and watched as a wave advanced and as my mother ran in an attempt to avoid it. Her dyed red hair looked very bright against the wave, which looked very green. Although the wave would eventually, inevitably, catch up with my mother and dunk her, and she would pull her ankle and this would be the last time she would ever immerse herself in the sea—a historic occasion—for a while it seemed somewhat possible that she might outrun the wave and return safely back to shore.

But how could my mother, or anyone, for that matter, outrun something that is not in forward motion?

A wave is simply a rising and falling. The wind, which messes up my mother's hair, is lifting particles of salt water, and gravity is pulling the water down again. The wave is not moving forward at all. This can be proved.

WEIGHT, THE GREATEST

Just when I was finally getting used to no longer being a child, it seems that now I have been ordered to repeat childhood, from the beginning, word for word, as it were.

Whereas Friedrich Nietzsche's concept of the eternal return states that everything we go through in our lifetime we will be forced to repeat again and again, an infinite number of times, and that everything will be exactly the same, from the biggest thing to the smallest thing, the contract I just signed states that this time around there will be *small but significant differences.* For instance, the toffee my mother made, the burnt sugar smell of which always drew me into the kitchen, will be slightly more brittle, and life will be even more gold, in a gold, dark way. And apparently whenever I open my little school desk to reach in for some pencils, they will be sticking out of something gooey, which, according to the contract, will be an old boy's brain.

I start first thing tomorrow! They'll wake me up just before dawn.

WEST, THE DECLINE OF THE

Back in antiquity, when ruins were brand new, men were the hottest. Since then, historically, beauty has been on a slow and irreversible decline.

WHITE ALBUM, THE

When the world ends there will be a little scratchy noise, like when you lower the stylus on an old LP. Something will be lowered.

After the world ends, when it is the end of time, perhaps it will finally be time for me to listen to a Beatles record. Perhaps it will finally be safe for me. I think I'll start off with *The Beatles,* also known as *The White Album.* My boyfriend's copy has four photographs inside, each bearing the image of one of the band's members. Once I was cleaning and I picked the album up off the floor and the photos fell out of the inner sleeve and fluttered down onto the ground. They looked like four retro, hippiefied versions of me.

The end of the world will not annul the self; it will lead to the terrible multiplication of the self.

Maybe I will enjoy the record. But maybe, just as I thought, I will hate it, and take it off immediately.

WHITENESS

When will all the other white people catch up and see that there is nothing more hideous than being white? As the century gets underway one feels increasingly sinister, nauseating, and somehow kitsch, like a miniature white chocolate sculpture of Count Dracula. Yes, one feels like a vampire: something without a reflection.

WIDOWS

In these late days of the plague, young men strip off their white jockey underwear solemnly and deliberately, like a dense, black lace veil being lifted slowly off the face of a widow.

WILDY, BOB

In 1990 my Uncle Bob died of cancer of the throat. The fact that the cancer struck his throat was particularly cruel; according to my mother, her brother was a beautiful singer, with a pure, deep voice.

My mother often spoke of one time when she and her brother were just teenagers. They were sitting on the verandah of their house in Adelaide. It was a warm summer evening, just getting dark. The slats on the windows were casting shadows as precise as the pleats in a skirt. As the shadows lengthened, Bob sang to her. According to my mother, a hummingbird appeared and hovered there, very close to Bob's mouth, for what seemed like forever. *It was,* she said, *as if the bird were also entranced by his singing, so entranced that it wished to dive into Bob's mouth and disappear.*

Bob went off to fight in WWII and spent some time in a Japanese prison on Borneo. My mother said that while he was away, although of course she missed her brother, she missed his singing even more. Sometimes she dreamt of a gramophone and that she had a record with Bob singing on it. She'd wake up, and although she knew it was impossible, she'd search through their collection just to make sure. Apparently when he came back his skeleton showed through and most of his teeth had fallen out. He didn't talk much about his time in the camp, but he continued to sing.

After my uncle died, I dreamt of a map of his throat. Lodged in the blue-gray space between the larynx and the pharynx was a hummingbird with bright patches of violet and red on its breast. The tiny bird was building a nest out of brown bark and green lichen in the relative safety of my Uncle Bob's throat.

From my own memories, I recall that my uncle was tall and very thin and very devout. There was something faintly metallic about him, as if his limbs were made out of rain gutters.

Four years before he died, he and approximately three thousand other believers gathered at Adelaide's Encounter Bay, at the edge of the Indian Ocean, to await the end of the world. His wife, my Aunt Alison, accompanied him. They brought a blanket to sit on, along with some sandwiches, a thermos of hot cocoa, and a transistor radio. Like everyone else, they sat and waited, watched and listened for signs—little rents in the sky, or perhaps the sound of hooves. Everyone had their radios tuned in to the same station.

The moment the world was supposed to end came and went. It seemed the world was not going away—at least for the time being. Most people waited around for a few more minutes but then left, disillusioned, heartbroken. My uncle and my aunt were also disappointed but decided that while they were at the beach, they might as well take advantage of it, for they did not get to the sea often. They ate their packed lunch and drank their cocoa. A kiosk was open, so they bought ice cream and took a long walk along the beach, wading through the shallows. Bob rolled up his navy blue trousers, to stop them from getting wet, but, without his noticing it, the legs of his trousers unrolled into the waves, with their restless sense of order. The dark blue cloth became even darker.

WILDY, HILDA

My grandmother on my mother's side was born in 1898 and died in 1975 when I was three. From the few photographs I have seen of her, I know she was thin and strung as tightly as a tennis racket. She often wore her hair in twists and wore violently and exuberantly patterned dresses from another era, the Victorian equivalent of the psychedelic. There's even a photo of her holding me in her arms, taken not long before she died, but of course I have no memory of this.

Once I went to the cemetery where she is buried, and, after much wandering around, I finally found her grave. I heard something coming from the grave, a kind of mumbling, and I knelt in the dirt so as to hear better, putting my ear to the ground, just like I used to put a glass to the door of my sisters' room so I could listen in on them gossiping. I remained in that position for a long time and sure enough, it was my grandmother talking to me, but, alas, everything she said was unintelligible.

WILDY, MILLICENT

My Aunt Millie had curly gray hair. She was a big woman and always wore bright polyester dresses with matching belts made from the fabric. She brought a platter of sandwiches to every family gathering: cheese and pickle, cheese and chutney, ham and pickle, ham and chutney, plain cheese, or plain ham. Her platters were highly anticipated. She always brought the sandwiches on a big china plate patterned with roses. She always remembered to take the plate home with her. Once, she failed to bring the sandwiches, and everyone was disappointed. My mother couldn't believe that Millie had not brought her sandwiches. That night the party fell apart early.

At these family gatherings, which I generally found unbearable, Aunt Millie was always kind to me. She would kiss me with the distance of an aunt. She would ask me questions, gently. Somehow her questions made these functions slightly more bearable.

My aunt and her husband, Colin, liked to *get away.* They'd head down south in their caravan and park it near the shoreline, as close as they could get to the hem of the sea. They liked to wade in the shallows and catch crabs in wicker traps and boil them in silver pots. Crabs would run sideways all around their caravan, but my aunt and uncle never ate these crabs; they only ate the ones they found in the sea. This is morality. Aunt Millie would wade in her dress. She'd hold up the skirt of her dress, but sometimes she'd be enjoying herself so much, she wouldn't notice that she had let her skirt drop and it had gotten a little wet, indicated by a darkening along the hem.

In 1998 my Aunt Millie died of cancer of the pancreas; there were too many cells clustered in her body, their points cutting into her, as sharp as stars. My mother referred to it as a mercifully quick cancer. We're forced to go looking for mercy in the most hidden places, just as a hermit crab finds an empty seashell, and, using its claw as a door, closes the shell tightly.

Aware that their mother was going to die swiftly, her daughters rented a ferry and invited all the family to take a slow boat ride up and down the Swan River. By then I had already moved away, but my mother told me all about it on the phone. The boat ride began at three o'clock in the afternoon and went on well into the night. *It was very nice,* she said. Everyone got too much sun and had a bit too much to drink. My aunt spent most of the time sitting on a big plush chair. According to my mother she looked so small in the chair and so frail. Her face looked thin, and her dress just hung on her. *That's not how I want to remember her,* my mother said. *You remember she was a big woman.*

According to my mother, as soon as it got dark, fairy lights came on. Yellow and pink and green. There was a hired DJ, and the young ones even did a little dancing.

WILDY, WILLIAM

My mother's father died a good ten years before I was born. In photographs he looks extremely distinguished with his slicked-back white hair and in his three-piece suits—always with a fob watch peeking out from the waistcoat pocket. I believe he worked in insurance, which saw the family moving about quite a lot. For a time, when my mother was a young girl, they lived in Perth in the suburb of Claremont, in a big old rambling house with rooms that used to be servants' quarters and even a stable. Apparently my grandfather used to go out to the stables at odd hours and talk to the ghosts of the horses that were once kept there. According to him, the horses were all albinos with pink and pale-blue eyes. He would go out with a brush and comb to groom these horse ghosts until their coats glowed.

WISH, BIRTHDAY

During childhood, the best part of a birthday occurred at night, when one was sitting at the kitchen table, holding the knife above the birthday cake, about to make a wish. One sat hunched over the cake like a miniature old man. The candles on the cake were lit and were in fact the room's only source of light.

At this moment, no one is more alone or enigmatic than the birthday boy. Although surrounded by his family, as he silently makes his wish it is as if he has plunged into a deep crevasse, or gone away on a slow voyage to the Arctic. There is always the possibility that he could turn his knife on all his family, or on himself. As he pushes the knife down into the cake's frosted depths, everyone searches his face, trying to penetrate his wish, but without success.

WISH, DEATH

I used to think I had a death wish. On clear days, I could see it shining there, caught in the folds running across my brain. It must have gotten stuck on its way down.

Small and bright, it looked like something a jackdaw might want to steal or a cheap gewgaw one finds in a Cracker Jack box. At other times it looked more like a scalpel someone had placed carefully on a little shelf in my soul. It seemed to be lodged there, indefinitely. But it turned out to be another kind of wish.

I must admit I feel a little lost without my death wish. Life can be boring without its shine. As we speak, nothing has replaced it. Where my death wish used to be, there's just an empty, scooped-out space.

WITCHES

Throughout history, people have liked burning witches. In the sixteenth century, hems on witches' dresses rose four inches, so you could see the witches' knees as they burned. The utmost tip of the witch's hat was always the last thing to burn. Although some people made the effort to go to the actual burning, most people stayed home to watch it on TV.

Prior to the Enlightenment, people thought a witch burned due to the escape of an imaginary substance called phlogiston, but then science proved that a substance (for example, a witch) needed oxygen if she wished to burn. This laid the groundwork for the future of the discipline known as chemistry and clarified things for the witches.

WITCHES' HATS

When the Enlightenment began and the witch-burnings stopped, people had no idea what to do with themselves. They began to watch a lot more TV. And then there was the problem of all the leftover witches' hats. Some people threw them in the trash.

Everywhere you went, you saw black, pointy hats poking through the holes in wire trashcans. Others left them out on the curb in the sun to fade and rot and get peed on by dogs. Those with a tendency to hoard put all their witches' hats in the closet, just in case.

WITTGENSTEIN, LUDWIG

Wittgenstein claimed that from the age of twelve he ceased dreaming almost entirely. *Thought,* he said, *erases dream, and naturally, for someone whose business it is to think, there can be no such thing as dreaming. The entire history and structure of philosophy,* he said, *could be destroyed by one single dream.*

He became resigned to a life without dream, though occasionally, perhaps once every ten years, Wittgenstein dreamt that he was touching the hem of Socrates' robe, and the hem was unraveling. Believing this to be the case, he would wake up and go immediately to the kitchen drawer where he would pull out his sewing kit, grab a needle and thread and a silver thimble, fully intending to mend Socrates' robe at once and to perhaps give the thimble to Socrates as a parting gift.

WONDER

We have learned that it is possible to die from too much wonder.

WONDERS, THE SEVEN

I've always been enamored of, and far too interested in, things that inspire wonder. Inevitably, this predilection of mine goes back to childhood. (Though I dream of an age where nothing will go back to childhood, an epoch in which, to make sense of the self, we will look in the opposite direction.)

But, unfortunately, my taste for wonder can be traced directly back to childhood, to that *Book of Wonders* I spent so much time with as a kid. I remember the book had a red spine and gold lettering. What I wouldn't give to be back home, sitting in front of our bookcase, reading all the names on the books' spines like one reads the names engraved on headstones—a bookshelf is a kind of cemetery—and, upon finding that *Book of Wonders,* to leaf through its pages, while coughing from all the dust. Whereas in my memory the book is a hefty tome, I bet if I held it in my hands today it would seem quite modest, maybe even tiny— when we encounter objects from our childhood they appear drastically reduced in size and sinister, like a skull shrunk by a headhunter.

The section of the book I spent most of my time looking at, or loitering in, was the chapter on the Seven Wonders of the Ancient World. Although I liked them all—the Hanging Gardens of Babylon, built by the mad King Nebuchadrezzar II, so his wife would feel more at home, and of which there is no record that they ever actually existed; the forty-foot-high Statue of Zeus at Olympia, destroyed by fire in 426 AD; the Lighthouse of Alexandria, as tall as a thirty-six-story skyscraper, which was toppled by an earthquake in 1375; the Mausoleum of Halicarnassus, which was gradually destroyed by a series of earthquakes over a period of time; the Temple of Artemis with its 100 columns, razed and burned so thoroughly by the Goths in 262 AD that no stone remained, destroyed so completely that when the Crusaders came in the 1100s and inquired about the temple, people looked at them weirdly and asked, *What temple?*; and, of course, the Pyramids of Egypt, the only structure on the list still standing—the wonder I spent the most time salivating over was the Colossus of Rhodes, the 160-foot-high bronze statue of the sun god that stood over the harbor of Rhodes in the 200s BC. Apparently ships had to pass beneath his legs to get into the harbor. The thing that most intrigued me about this statue, apart from the fact that it was this giant naked man, was how short-lived it was. Whereas the Temple at Halicarnassus stood for 1,000 years, and the Lighthouse for 1,600 years, the Colossus only stood for 56 years. In 224 BC an earthquake caused Colossus to break off at the knees. His ruins, however, lay on the ground for the next 800 years; apparently the bronze chunks excited more wonder than when Colossus was standing.

The Twin Towers of the World Trade Center opened in 1973 and were of course destroyed in 2001, giving them a lifespan of less than thirty years. As, like you, I watched the destruction on TV, again and again, rewinding the destruction, fast-forwarding the destruction, pausing the destruction, I found myself thinking about the Seven Ancient Wonders and feeling that at this point in time antiquity and modernity were somehow touching. Some-one called Antipater first compiled the list of wonders in the 100s BC. Surely, I thought, if he were around, he would have gone immediately to his list, crossed off the pyramids, and added in their place the Twin Towers. Perhaps it had been obvious to everyone else all along, but he would have finally realized some-thing: now, for a structure to make the list, it must no longer exist. This is the condition of wonder.

WORDS

Give me a word that doesn't fold back on the world.

WORDS, FAVORITE

In my mother's vocabulary, the most commonly used word was *garish*. She organized her world around the concept of garishness. We all need an organizing principle to make life livable and to make sense of a world, which, on closer inspection, makes no sense. My creed is lust: what is yours?

When I was a boy, mum taught me to see the world ac-cording to this principle. Whereas our next-door neighbor Mrs. Ibensen's purple bougainvillea was far too gaudy, our pink and orange bougainvilleas were pleasing to the eye. And whenever my Aunt Helen dyed her hair a shrieking red, although mum would assure her sister that the color was fine, she would later confide in me that, in her opinion, the shade was a tad too red.

Together my mother and I wandered the neighborhood, separating the garish from the somber, gently policing the border of that which is bright.

WORDS, LAST

Except for my mother, no one uses the word *garish* anymore. Perhaps she is the last person on earth to use this word, and when she dies, the word will die with her. They will bury her with that word, and we will all be overtaken by unprecedented levels of brightness. We will die from too much brightness.

WORDS, MY LAST

I already know what my last words will be. Someone sent them to me in the mail, in an envelope marked *Urgent,* with a note in the upper-right corner saying, *If this is not the address of Alistair McCartney, return in five days.* As you can imagine, I was excited to receive them. I tore open the envelope at the dotted line, like some animal, and read the words. As per the instructions, I memorized the words and then destroyed the document. Not only did the letter disclose my last words, but it also revealed the dimensions of my deathbed (though not, interestingly enough, the date or method of my death). And, as per the instructions, every afternoon at four, I think of my last words; I recall them, as if I've already died, and then I rehearse them.

WORKS, ABANDONED

I am less interested in the works philosophers bring to light than in those they abandon, abolish, and destroy, such as René Descartes's book *The World,* which he planned to publish in 1633. However, upon hearing of Galileo's fate, Descartes, whose own book also advocated the heliocentric Copernican model — positing that the earth moves around the sun and that therefore we are less important than we thought—put his book aside and started on something else.

It seems *The World* was comprised of treatises on things like machines and animals and man. Only small fragments of it have survived. Within these fragments, however, several themes emerge, one in particular: *Rationality is to humans as a studded dog collar is to a dog,* states one aphorism; another, *Something hot and red constantly laps at me from within. The being who I casually refer to as "I" is merely a dog kennel;* and, perhaps most suggestively, *Although I have consciousness of the inevitability of my own death—which means I must be human, but barely—in every other respect I am profoundly doglike: the fear that grips me in the knowledge of my own death is nice and tight like a dog collar. In fact, I'm more of a dog than most dogs, just a canine with a scrap of consciousness. Let us bark in the face of death! I have nothing to offer but my saliva when faced with the world's calm indifference.*

WORLD, THE

Perhaps, in the way I sometimes write about the world, you might suspect that I would prefer it to end, and in a sense you are right.

For the longest time I was profoundly indifferent to the world. In fact, it would be fair to say that I didn't really like the world; I despised every single object contained within it. I was only interested in those things the world couldn't hold, slippery, eel-like, electric things.

But lately, without my noticing it, a change seems to have taken place. I find that I have become increasingly interested in the world; some accuse me of being besotted with it. I admit it. I love every object and every hairline crack in every object.

WORLD, THE BEGINNING OF THE

They say that smack in the heart of eternity there sits a voluptuous cholo who is slowly and methodically knitting the world and everything held within it. For example, he knits woolen king crabs, which, due to their intricate anatomy, are extremely difficult to knit: he starts with the crab's shell and the long, sharp spine, then moves on to the tricky parts, such as the egg ducts and gill books. He knits woolen pairs of lovers, which are also difficult—he begins with the hands and feet, and keeps the lips and hearts till last. He knits woolen grand canyons, which are much simpler, and woolen lies, which are surprisingly easy.

From far away, the constant sound of the needles clicking is merely irritating, but up close, if you are in eternity and standing beneath the giant thigh of the cholo, the noise of the needles is said to be deafening. So much so that you want to leave eternity, which of course cannot be left.

WORLD, THE END OF THE

When the world ends, and it is time for God to announce who the winners are and who the losers are, I just know I will be so nervous that I will not listen very carefully, like when I am meeting people for the first time and their names go in one ear and out the other.

I had better be listening, because imagine how embarrassing it will be if, when God reads my name off the list, I am so distracted that I don't hear it. Or, even more embarrassing, imagine if I hear my name, but I can't be 100 percent certain if he told me to go on the right side with all the people going to heaven, the people who are condemned to eternal bliss, or to go stand on the left side, with all the dogs and sorcerers and fornicators condemned to eternal damnation.

If my eternal fate goes in one ear and out the other, this will make for an extremely awkward situation. I will have to put up my hand, like in primary school, and ask God if he could please repeat where it is he wants me to go. Most likely, he will get so annoyed with me, he will tell me that although he initially wanted me to go with him and the angels, just to teach me a lesson, a very harsh lesson, now I need to go stand on the left side with the dogs and the sorcerers.

But probably I will be too shy to even raise my hand, and I will just sort of loiter around the middle, in between the wet snouts of the dogs and the quivering wings of the angels, trying to make myself appear inconspicuous.

WORLD, GLOBES OF THE

It is said that somewhere in Los Angeles there is a boy locked in a room. The room is in one of the thousands of mini-malls that can be found on street corners here, those small, seemingly identical complexes of shops that give the city a sweet monotony, preparing us for the even deeper monotony of eternity, and behind whose blank facades are housed restaurants, nail salons, liquor stores, Laundromats, and money-exchange centers.

The only things in this room are the boy, a desk, a chair, and a globe of the world. The boy sits at the desk. His leg is manacled to the metal leg of the chair. The globe is on top of the desk and is a little tattered. Here and there, the paper has ripped, and the plastic of the globe shows through.

The boy has been given a task and the task is this: with his small, delicate hand, he must keep spinning the globe. He must make sure that the globe never stops spinning, even if his hand gets tired, as boys' hands tend to do. Even if his wrist gets broken from all the spinning, he must continue.

If he stops to take a rest, the world won't end. Nothing on that scale will happen. But it will be made abundantly clear that the boy has failed his task and measures will be taken accordingly. The boy has been cleared of all his other duties. He now has no other responsibility but to keep the globe of the world spinning. This has made his life simpler, but at the same time infinitely more difficult.

WORLD, MY MOTHER AT THE END OF THE

After the world and everything in it is gone, nothing will remain but my mother's red hair. The atmosphere will be sort of suffused with the exact shade of red she used to dye her hair.

WORLD, THE OTHER

In preparation for the end of the world, God has already created another world, the sequel to this world, if you will; he has it all ready to go. As soon as this world ends, the other world (as opposed to the next world) will take effect immediately, and it will be twice as difficult to live in, and twice as beautiful, and twice as difficult to get out of.

WORLD, PHILOSOPHY AT THE END OF THE

After the world ends, there will be a lot to think about; you will have plenty of thoughts. But, actually, from here on in, there will be no such thing as thoughts per se; all of the things that fill your head will be afterthoughts, explanations and ideas that occur after an event, for example, the end of the world.

WORLD BOOK ENCYCLOPEDIA

They say that when the world ends, the *World Book Encyclopedia* will remain intact, and that, in fact, its twenty-two gold-edged volumes will replace the world.

WRESTLING

Currently, the most promising epidemic here in Los Angeles is one that primarily affects college wrestlers. It is a staph infection that is resistant to everything and spreading quickly. Before wrestling, the boys lather themselves in a special wrestling foam that prevents skin infections and then mop the purple wrestling mats with a special mop and disinfectant while the coach looks on. Despite their best efforts, many young men have been exposed, their smooth skin covered in dark, oozing sores like blueberry jam stains and red flush scabs like Chinese wax seals. What would the Scottish surgeon Alexander Ogston, who in the late nineteenth century discovered this bacterium, make of these wrestlers? Perhaps he already had them in mind when he named his infection Staphylococcus aureus, the latter of which is Latin for *golden*.

WRISTS

There should be a sign on the wrists flashing *EXIT* in red neon letters. Anyone who has slit his wrists knows that these joints between the hand and the forearm are the most private part of the body and somehow obscene, like genitals. In a wrist-slitter's universe, the wrists would only be displayed to one's lover or in centerfolds in hard-core pornography. Otherwise, one would always wear long sleeves to conceal one's wrists, out of modesty, or maybe a wristwatch on either wrist. However, some argue that wrists are not so much the nearest emergency exit when the world is on fire, but an entry into eternity. The wrist is a way out. The wrist is important.

WRITING

Although sometimes I feel a bit sad for Proust, and wish that, while out walking in the vicinity of Roussainville, instead of longing for the forests of that region to send him a peasant girl, he was honest with himself, and admitted, in writing, that what he really desired was one of the region's sturdy peasant boys, I'm actually glad that he wasn't honest, because he might have been virtually inundated with offers; not only would his longing have been met, but it also would have been destroyed, and writing, above all, needs longing. He would have been so preoccupied with peasant boys, peasant-boy crazy, as it were, he wouldn't have had the time or the inclination to write anything at all.

Even worse, what if when Proust was still a small boy he had met some sinister aristocratic sadist in a sweeping, black crepe cloak, who had promised to take him to the opera but instead had taken Proust to his mansion where he proceeded to do unspeakable things to him, things equally refined yet debased, and then did away with him, leaving his remains in a forest on the outskirts of Paris?

Then there would have been no way that *In Search of Lost Time* could have ever been written, because, having suffered at the hands of the creep, Proust would have been spared all the adult suffering that fed his writing, and writing, above all, needs suffering; instead of the six volumes there'd just be this hole in the world of exactly the same dimensions as the six volumes combined, and through this hole a steady draft would be coming through, and we'd have to plug up the draft with that octopus blue crushed velvet suit Proust wears in a famous childhood photo, the one with the big lace collar.

But who knows. Maybe Proust not only got the work done but was also sexually active—Proust as slut—as promiscuous with men as he was with memory, and whenever he got sick of remembering, he'd go out cruising, pick up sailors, and take them back to his rooms, up to three at a time, where two of them would double-dick him, and another would fuck his mouth— altogether an unusual sensation—and he'd feel all glowing, like a pomegranate splitting, and he'd try to relax, and as he did, he would be taken back to that day in the carriage when he glimpsed the twin steeples of Martinville and the steeple of Vieuxvicq, the latter spire somehow seeming very close to the former pair, though in reality, it was considerably far away, and then he'd send the sailors off, clean up, and get back to writing.

X

X

If, after countless painful and unnecessarily invasive procedures, on doctor's orders I was told to evacuate language, I suppose I would do so, though I think I would still take one letter with me (assuming that there would be room in my luggage), even if the doctors warned me that just one letter could kill me.

As to which letter I would take, I am still undecided. I know for certain I would not take the *I*—such a brutal letter.

At the moment I am strongly leaning toward the letter *X*. I like that *X* is used in science to indicate an unknown quantity, and I like many of the words *X* appears in, words such as *anxious* and *luxurious;* finding myself deprived of the alphabet's other letters, *X* would surely invoke these words. Besides, it seems the most practical choice. With *X*, I would never lose you again. Whenever I misplaced you, I'd know where to find you. Standing in for a kiss, it is surely the most romantic letter, and despite everything, I am still first and foremost a romantic.

X-RAYS

Although I dislike and want to destroy most inventions, I do make some exceptions, and not only for the Viewmaster! I also make an exception for the X-ray machine, which is my favorite invention. I love X-rays as much as I love sunrays and stingrays!

The highpoint of my childhood was when I broke my left arm and was taken directly to the Fremantle hospital to be x-rayed. The X-ray operator, with his receding hairline and his thick, horn-rimmed spectacles, was so nice. His hands were big and warm, in stark contrast to the cold metal plate I was pressed up against. I had to remain very still so they could locate the exact nature of the fracture. I liked how solemn it all felt, and I appreciated the green, papery gown he made me put on and take off and put back on.

The X-ray operator made me feel so special, like I was the only one, like he was interested in my bones and no one else's bones. He looked right through me, as if my body were an article of scanty, sexy, see-through lingerie. The resulting picture of my shattered bones was clear and sharp. If only the rest of childhood were so vivid!

It was so much fun, like having one's picture taken, but deeper. In fact, I had never liked being photographed, but that afternoon I discovered that I felt extremely comfortable being x-rayed. I still think I look better in X-rays than in photographs, and I wish X-rays would replace photographs as the dominant medium of human representation. To this day, I can't think of anything that is more enjoyable; there is no better way I like to spend my free time than being x-rayed, to see if I am diseased.

Speaking of discoveries, X-rays were discovered in 1895 by Wilhelm Conrad Röntgen, a man with a bushy beard. Apparently, Röntgen was very unlucky in love, always chasing after boys whose hearts were like lead-lined rooms. He tried to come up with an X-ray method that could penetrate beyond the soft parts of boys, past the tissue and muscles and fat that wrapped and draped around their bones like fox furs or mink stoles, an X-ray that could penetrate beyond bones and peer directly into the heart of a boy, taking inventory of the contents of the boy's heart, but he did not come up with this method and had to make do with taking snapshots of boys' skeletons.

When the world ends, while we are all waiting to be judged by God, who will see right through us like an X-ray machine, in fact, much better than an X-ray machine, Röntgen will be the first person I will look for. I will go to the line of people who died in 1923, the year he died, and walk along that line until I find him. It will be a long line I'm sure, but not the longest. Perhaps I will cut out the little picture I have of him from the *World Book Encyclopedia* and will carry it with me, to make sure I remember how he looks. As soon as I find him, I will shake his hand—or, who knows, what with all the emotion accompanying Judgment Day, maybe I will even hug him—before thanking him personally for his invention.

X-RAY OPERATORS

I'm not an X-ray operator working at the Walter Reed Army Hospital, but I might as well be an X-ray operator; I should have listened to my mother and become an X-ray operator.

On second thought, I am an X-ray operator, ruled by rays of an unknown nature. I must somehow make peace with these rays that cannot be seen.

XANTHIPPE

Poor Xanthippe! History has not been kind to the wife of Socrates. In an encyclopedia's entry on the philosopher, she is usually compressed into one or two sentences. Within those sentences, she is invariably described in less-than-flattering terms, as a nag, a harridan, a hag, *of bitter tongue and poor disposition,* and, perhaps most famously, *the unbearable shrew that made philosophy a necessity.* It is said that the philosopher married her merely as an act of self-discipline and self-measure.

Sick to death of his wife's poor temper, it was in fact Socrates who invented both the concept of evidence and the accompanying concept of posterity. The only way in which married life was tolerable was the thought that future generations would talk ill of her, the certainty that a long streak of poor opinion would follow her. He began to leave clues about her ill will around the house; in his talks he provided sound proof of her bitterness. Alert to this, Xanthippe would feed the clues to the local dogs, but, constant thinker that he was, her husband always provided more.

Perhaps Xanthippe simply had one bad mood, one sour turn, which now stretches on into eternity. I hope posterity will be kinder to me. Yet surely the very concept of posterity is caustic and unkind in that it not only implies but also requires our absence. One considers Xanthippe's fate and sees that perhaps it would be better to be erased, joyfully and thoroughly.

𝒴

YACHTS

I have never been interested in yachts; in fact, I have always felt a certain hostility—at times a hatred—toward those relatively small vessels used mainly for pleasure, along with a hatred for the men who sail them, and a deep dislike for anything even vaguely associated with yachting, for example, navy blue double-breasted blazers with gold buttons. Most likely, this phobia can be traced back to the yachts on my childhood pajamas.

But recently I happened to be passing on my bicycle through the Marina del Rey district of Los Angeles, that bland nightmare of anonymous high-rise apartment buildings, sort of like communism, but luxurious, all of the apartments housing horny heterosexual singles and sexless heterosexual seniors nostalgic for lost horniness. It was an extremely windy day and I happened to be very sleepy, a state that is surely the best way to be in the twenty-first century.

In the wind, the rigging of the yachts was making a clanking sound, like a milk bottle symphony; it was as if all the milk bottles from my childhood had been stored somewhere by the conductor of an orchestra especially for that purpose, and the conductor was finally ready. I stopped my bicycle, right in the middle of the bike path, and was so taken by the sound I was oblivious to the fact that I was endangering not only my own life but also that of the cyclists behind me in their hideous, skintight Lycra cycling gear. *Perhaps*, I thought, waking up a little, continuing to listen, *I need to reconsider my hatred of yachts.*

YARD WORK

Any time my dad asked me to do yard work, I wanted to murder him; my small hand would grip the handle of the rake; as I raked up the red leaves they crunched beneath my feet like my father's bones.

Today, I continue to be disinclined toward yard work, except for sweeping up the tree fungus water that pools at the base of our driveway every morning like poisonous soul slime. This work requires a sturdy broom. As I sweep up the last stagnant drops, I am already anticipating and looking forward to the water's inevitable return.

YAWNING

Whenever I am around, the abyss yawns. Although I try not to take it personally—after all, surely this is what abysses do: they open wide, they gape—I still end up feeling hurt. It is horrible to realize that the abyss is growing bored with you.

YEARNING

Humans yearn: the object they yearn for is of no importance; what matters is the act of yearning. Sometimes when I am falling asleep or still waking up, I mean to say *yearning* but instead say *destruction*. There is a form of yearning—or so I have heard—the intensity of which buries alive the yearner in a kind of lava. What do volcanoes yearn for? What role did yearning play in the eruption of Krakatao? Yearning often causes humans to suddenly appear and disappear. When one yearns over an extended period of time, the yearning ties itself around one's neck like a noose, the feeling turns into something else, something wholly unrelated to yearning, something harsher and deeper.

YEARS

Dear clinically depressed reader, sexually addicted reader, desperately lonely (albeit hot) reader, politically-despondent-with-the-potential-to-be-violent reader, low, low and beyond low self-esteemed reader, occasionally suicidal reader, and ultimately, far-too-gentle-for-this-world reader, I hear you asking, well, when is the world going to end? And how?

So immersed were you in your own troubles, and so anxiously were you awaiting the end, biting your fingernails until the polished wooden floors of your house were covered in the little torn-off bits, like the torn-off stubs of movie tickets, you failed to notice that the world had already ended.

I tell you, there's no longer any need to worry. These things we call days are just shards; the years, rubble. That weird, dappled light you are reading this book by comes from the embers, the soft and steady afterglow.

$\mathcal{Z}$

ZERO, PATIENT

When I think of Gaëtan Dugas, the French-Canadian flight attendant who paid his first known visit to a New York City bathhouse on October 31, 1980, the man to whom all the city's initial cases of AIDS would be traced back—hence the moniker he was given: *patient zero*—I start off thinking about big things, like fate, the fate that is assigned to us, and the fate of the time and place in which we are born, for surely there are good times to be born, and there are not-so-good times, and just before things got really bad, those men in the bathhouses must have believed they were living in the most wondrous of times; they must have felt sublime, like bodies that had escaped the clutches of history.

But, inevitably, my mind caves in beneath these thoughts and I ponder small things, like Dugas's mustache, which was wild and Nietzschean. Finally, I return to the question of towels. I think about the white towel Dugas would have worn at the bathhouse and about the style in which he wore it (specifically the knot). I wonder how many towels he used. Did he go back more than once to the counter to get fresh towels? Is there a museum where one can view, behind a glass case, one of these towels?

ZERO, YEAR

I am interested in the idea of erasing time and returning to the beginning. Throughout history there have been several variations on this concept. In 1795, during the French Revolution, the revolutionary committee, having already abolished the monarchy, saw fit to abolish time, resulting in my favorite revolutionary act: the removal of the hands off town-hall clocks. The clock hands were subsequently melted down to make blades for guillotines and a new calendar was created, beginning with *Year One*.

Close to two hundred years later, Pol Pot, who was, of course, educated at the Sorbonne, took his Parisian education back to Cambodia and developed this idea further, turning history back to a year zero; this involved sending the intelligentsia off into the fields and murdering two million people, whose skulls were set one on top of the other, like timelines constructed from bones.

And then there is my mother, who at the time of writing is almost eighty years old, and her concept of year zero. She believes it is when we are younger that we are in fact closer to death. Just as we are capable of living backwards through the compulsive activity known as remembering, she likes to think that perhaps, as we get older, and wearier, we are somehow miraculously moving further and further away from death, slowly as a snail. Just like a snail we leave a strange, silver substance that protects us from our main enemy, this being time, and that ultimately erases the years.

ZEUS

I've always liked the story of Zeus and Ganymede, ever since I was a kid. I recall first reading about it in a book of mythology I took out of the library. The story was simple and extreme. Zeus, bored with being a god, eyed Ganymede, who was bored with being a boy. Overcome by Ganymede's beauty, Zeus transformed himself into an eagle, swooped down, and seized the boy, taking him away to Mount Olympus where he became cupbearer for the gods, which basically involved standing around all day and pouring out nectar. Feeling guilty, Zeus offered Ganymede's father two immortal horses to make up for the loss of his son.

It would be years before I understood all the implications of this relationship, but even then it stirred me, deeply. After reading the story, I remember lying on my bed and thinking about the bird's sharp talons and how they must have left bloody scratch marks in Ganymede's alabaster skin.

Unlike Ganymede, I never learned the name of the god who one afternoon in the guise of a magpie flew down and uprooted me from the world, tearing me out of childhood, taking me to Los Angeles to pour Coronas for the gods. It seems this god, whoever he was, did offer my father a little something in return, something immortal, but my father declined the god's kind offer, telling him that he did not require anything for his loss. And, unlike the boy, who became ageless, I did not stay young. I slowly grew older and then I got old.

ZIPLOCK BAGS

In every couple there is always someone who is more practical; in the couple of which I am a component, that is most definitely not me. That summer when we were virtually being inundated with peaches, harassed by peaches, my boyfriend carefully analyzed the situation.

Following his brilliant and groundbreaking analysis of the peaches, Tim jumped on his bicycle and rode to the corner shop, where he purchased a large quantity of ziplock sandwich bags. On his return, he gathered every single peach: both those that were still attached to the tree, and those lying beneath it.

In the kitchen, in a systematic fashion, he cut the peaches into quarters. Then, after some further calculations, he carefully placed the segments of the peaches into the ziplock bags; in each bag there was exactly the amount of peaches required for our morning oatmeal. He proceeded to stack the bags in the freezer, on the same shelf as the paintbrushes, which are in there so we don't forget the color we used to paint the house.

While doing this he took no calls; it was imperative that he not be disturbed. Now we have enough peaches to last us a lifetime. Actually, we have more peaches than we could ever possibly consume in one life. So now it is my job to figure out how we can smuggle the remainder of these peaches with us, perhaps by virtue of some kind of secret compartment, into eternity.

ZIPPERS

Zippers were invented in 1892; this means Arthur Rimbaud, who died in 1891, just missed out on zippers. While out cruising in the sex clubs of Abyssinia—a country that he moved to under the impression that it was the kingdom of abysses, which it ended up being, at least for him—no one ever unzipped the bright silver zipper on his trousers because there were no such things as zippers.

When we were boys and went camping, the sleeping bags we lay awake in, and crawled out of, had zippers running down the length of them. I think they were gold. Sleeping bags were sexy, but there was something sinister about them, like soft coffins.

My mother wore these red and navy blue crew neck sweaters that had zippers at the back. Apart from my mother, I've never seen anyone else wear these sweaters. Perhaps they have become extinct, like musical doorbells, but this is no reason for concern, as surely they will return and come back in style, one hundred years from now, when all of us are gone.

Often I wish there were a little zipper in the back of me, so I could climb into and out of myself whenever I pleased. I have looked around for someone capable of such an alteration, but inserting a zipper is one of the more advanced tasks in sewing, requiring a skilled seamstress. We must wear these selves out, until they are threadbare.

I haven't been to a zoo for over twenty years, but I always enjoyed going to the zoo. What child doesn't? It was like a kind of encyclopedia, each category housed in its cage, but this was even better than the actual encyclopedia, because these categories could salivate all over you before they devoured you.

At the Perth Zoo, I had my favorite animals. I liked the polar bears, who in 1980 devoured a teenage boy with a death wish and long stringy brown hair who had leapt into their sunken enclosure. I remember visiting the zoo shortly after this incident. In fact, I think the front-page article that appeared in the local newspaper, complete with photographs of the boy and the polar bear in question—though photographed separately—led to me asking or even begging my mother to please take me to the zoo.

That day, we went to look at the polar bears, who were separated from us by a kind of moat-like structure, and I remember mum telling me that the moat was there to make it perfectly clear who was the visitor and who was the animal, who was rational and who was wild; however, given the boy's leap into the welcoming arms of the bears, it seemed there was still some confusion regarding this matter.

I also appreciated the Tasmanian devil that lived in the nocturnal house in a kind of glowing glass case. When he wasn't hiding, he would race around and around in frenzied circles, as if he were going insane or already insane, just trying to take the edge off his insanity. Even then, I felt an odd affinity with this creature, perhaps because of its painfully shy and violent nature, or perhaps because of its frantic, restless sensibility.

Though if I am to speak truthfully, I recall very little of the animals. I mean, I know there must have been lions there, but I have no recollection of them. When I think back, I just see the word *lion*, written in orange crayon, or an image of a lion from the TV.

I do recall the cages quite vividly. Sometimes, when I was standing at a certain distance from a cage and the light was at a certain angle, the shadows of the bars would fall across my skin, as if I were my own cage or in the process of becoming a cage.

And, if we are to speak truthfully, the animals were just an excuse for us to visit the zoo—we were really there for the cages.

Although I haven't been to the zoo in a long time, I don't really need to go, because occasionally I dream I'm once again at the zoo.

At this zoo, there are zookeepers who look very handsome in their drab and tight, dark blue uniforms. The zookeepers are emotionally distant. They pay no attention to me. They're preoccupied with cleaning out the boys' cages, which they do on a daily basis, on their hands and knees, scrubbing the wooden floors of the cages with hot water and disinfectant.

The boys attract many visitors. They claw their trainers, leaving terrible sex marks.

And there are lions at this zoo. I can say this for certain. Their fur is red, the same shade my mother dyes her hair. The pads of their paws are as soft as blackboard erasers, in contrast to their sharp claws.

But the lions are not in their cages. Their cages are nowhere to be seen. Instead, these lions leap over a wall in an orderly fashion, while I balance upon the wall, wearing nothing but a pair of new school shoes. Every time a lion leaps, a mechanism descends. It's like a giant version of a mechanical claw you find in one of those arcade games, where you're pushing a button, trying to pick up a stuffed toy with the claw, but invariably you never win, and you've wasted all your money.

Whenever the mechanism descends, I grab hold; it lifts me up, just out of the lion's reach. The mechanism seems to be in relatively good working order. The zoo hopes to purchase a newer model in the near future.

As soon as the lion lands on the other side of the wall, the mechanism places me back down, very gently. The mechanism folds up and ascends. Then another lion leaps, and once again the claw comes down, lifting me up, ever so slightly, to a place of relative safety.

Acknowledgments

Excerpts from this work were published in *Bloom, The James White Review, Suspect Thoughts, Queer and Catholic, Two Crows, Paws and Reflect,* and *Mirage #4 Periodical.*

Many thanks to the following people for their aesthetic guidance and for reading the manuscript throughout its various stages: Jim Krusoe, Dennis Cooper, James McCourt, Richard Canning, Susana Chávez-Silverman, Teresa Carmody, Anne Hawthorne, Sakada, and Amanda Walzer-Prieto.

I'm indebted to all my writing teachers, particularly Kate Haake, Rod Val Moore, Jill Ciment, and Brenda Walker. I'm equally and blissfully indebted to anyone who's published my work, especially Patrick Merla, Don Weise, Charles Flowers, Richard LaBonte, Lawrence Schimel, and Karen Finley. I receive constant inspiration and support of all kinds from all my friends and fellow-writers, all my creative writing students, Antioch University L.A. and Santa Barbara, Frida, and my family, especially my parents.

The *World Book Encyclopedia* was an invaluable store of knowledge and wonder, specifically the 1957 and 1960 editions.

I'm deeply grateful to everyone at the University of Wisconsin Press who worked so hard on the book, particularly Raphael Kadushin, Sheila Moermond, Andrea Christofferson, Carla Aspelmeier, Chris Caldwell, Adam Mehring, Amy Johnson, Nadine Zimmerli, and Amy Caes. Thanks to Vivian van Blerk for the beautiful image on the cover.

And of course, eternal thanks to Tim Miller, who's my guiding light in writing and in life.